All About The Benjamins

(a novel)
by Zev Good

Also by Zev Good

A Map of the World (Stories)   2017

.About This Book.

© 2019 by Zev Good. All rights reserved. No part of this publication may be reproduced, distributed, or transmitted in any form or by any means, including photocopying, recording, or other electronic or mechanical methods, without the prior written permission of the publisher, except in the case of brief quotations embodied in critical reviews and certain other noncommercial uses permitted by copyright law.

This is a work of fiction. Names, characters, businesses, places, events, locales, and incidents are either the products of the author's imagination or used in a fictitious manner. Any resemblance to actual persons, living or dead, or actual events is purely coincidental.

Cover photo by John Granen. Used with permission.
johngranen.com

Cover design by Jay Marsh

Author photo by Matt Lane

Text design by Renee Butler

For Darin and Bill, again.

.one.

The first time Joel Benjamin had sex with a man, he expected it to leave a permanent mark, something he could point to years later—like a scar, or a tattoo—and recount how he'd gotten it and who'd given it to him. He was twenty-five years old when it happened in the fall of 1985 at the NCTE Convention in Philadelphia. In the middle of it that first time, he'd thought he would never forget even the tiniest detail: not the stiffness of the hotel sheets or the woodsy smell of the other man's skin and hair, the way his mouth tasted like the beer he'd drunk, mixed with something sweet, or how he wanted to trace designs and connect the moles across the other man's chest and shoulders.

His memory of that man, Dwight, remained untarnished by time: Marlboro Man good looks, tall and well-built, almost athletically so, which struck Joel as odd for an English professor. Dwight spoke first, to ask if Joel followed the Mets, and Joel stammered a polite response that wouldn't insult the guy asking, but that made it clear he knew nothing about baseball. To his relief, Dwight confessed he didn't really follow baseball either, he was just trying to strike up a conversation. Then they laughed and glanced from one another to their beers and back again. "I'm in town for the English teachers' convention," Joel confessed.

"Same here," Dwight said.

They sat at the bar and talked until it was obvious the bartender wanted them to pay and leave so she could close down. They argued over who would pay. Joel insisted, and Dwight relented, then suggested they go to a place he knew. Something about those words, the way Dwight said them, touched something in Joel and for the briefest of instants he was afraid. Not for his life, but the way Dwight whispered it—*"this place I know"*—sent a signal to his brain that felt like premonition. He searched his mind for a reason he couldn't go—he was tired, he needed to call his wife, anything. Dwight insisted, and he wasn't rude about it, so in the end they went. It was close enough that they walked, and when they arrived, Joel would have been unaware of its existence had there not been a drag queen standing at the door checking IDs.

A curious lump of dread settled in Joel's belly as she gave their IDs a cursory glance and waved them through. A gay bar. Dwight had brought him to a gay bar, and as he stood so his eyes could get accustomed to the dimness, he tried to decide how offended he was. Who the hell was this guy? What the hell was he trying to say, bringing Joel to a place like this? Hadn't they just spent over two hours talking about their wives, their kids, and all the other stuff married men talk about when they get together in hotel bars away from home? Then Dwight handed him a beer, smiled and winked, and Joel relaxed. They were in this together, that wink said: two men trapped in unsatisfying marriages who had traveled—Joel from Atlanta, Dwight from Iowa—to this place at this time, found one another, and though Joel's heart beat so hard he imagined it could be heard over the pounding of the music in that place he would never remember the name of, he vowed to make his first time in a gay bar something he would never forget. So, when Dwight took his hand and led him into a corner and kissed him, clumsy and wet, he assured himself that it was the most natural thing in the world.

They kissed more than they spoke, and held hands like they were longtime lovers. Dwight asked Joel if he wanted to dance and of all the things he did that night, the concept of dancing in front of this strange man terrified Joel the most. Later they went to Dwight's hotel room and Joel stood, transfixed, as Dwight undressed. Then he took his own clothes off and they stood there, and when Dwight touched him, Joel trembled like he had palsy.

"Are you okay?" Dwight asked him.

"I'm fine," Joel lied. He alternated between an immense desire to explore every inch of Dwight and a profound shame at what he was doing. He thought he might throw up, and when that didn't happen, he thought he might pass out from the thrill of it all.

Then Dwight kissed him again and Joel stroked the golden hair that covered Dwight's chest and somehow, he got through it unharmed. Afterward, Dwight asked him again, "Are you okay?"

"Yes," Joel said, and wondered if he would be okay later. Like, would he regret it and would that pang of conscience expose him. He bolted upright in the bed, Dwight's hotel bed, which smelled of their lovemaking, and was not sure what to do with himself.

Dwight stroked his back. "Relax," he whispered. Joel tried. "Lie back down."

In the morning, Joel dressed and they didn't speak. Dwight saw him to the door and kissed him before he left. Joel had no idea what to say. "Thanks," he said, and immediately felt like a fool. Later, though, as he flew home to Atlanta, to his wife and his children, he felt it was the most appropriate thing he could have said.

Now, thirty-four years later, Joel was ready to come out of the closet. He just wasn't sure how to go about it. There were days where he was convinced of his purpose, and he stood in front of the bathroom mirror and rehearsed the words he wanted to say and how he wanted to say them. The next day, that certainty would vanish and he would be in emotional agony. It always looked so easy in movies and on TV, or in the tabloids when actors and singers came out: for years they were straight, they married and they divorced, and then one day they were coming out and people talked only of their courage, their strength. He couldn't understand why he was having such difficulty with it. He was fifty-eight years old. He wasn't getting any younger and it was time, so on one of those days where he was sure of himself, he called his daughter.

"Dad! Hi! Is something wrong?" Since the death of his wife six months ago, Amy made a habit of asking him this any time he called.

Joel laughed and gave her the same reply he always gave. "Nothing's wrong, honey. I can call you when nothing's wrong, can't I?"

"Well... yeah, of course."

"Are you busy? I can call back later."

"No," Amy said, though Joel heard activity on her end and knew she was at work. She was a hairdresser—or, she always reminded him, that was an old-fashioned term and conjured images of beehives and bubble flips, and Amy insisted that he understand she was a *stylist*.

"I'll make it quick, then," Joel said. "I want you and Ethan to come over for dinner on Friday. I'm calling your brother, too."

Amy was silent on her end. "I thought you said everything was okay," she said at last, and her voice had already risen several octaves.

"Everything's fine," Joel said. "Really. I swear. It's just dinner." Only it wasn't, and he felt the whole thing derailing already.

"And Adam's coming?" she asked.

"Yes, I'm calling him as soon as I hang up with you."

More silence from Amy. "And you're sure everything is fine...?" She did not sound convinced, and she had every right to be doubtful. He and Susan had called them together almost four years ago to announce her cancer diagnosis and prognosis, and Joel was kicking himself for not having practiced this phone call better.

"Honey, it's just dinner," he said again. "It's just dinner. You and me and Ethan and Adam. Just the four of us. And we'll talk."

"About what?"

"Just...nothing. Everything. Anything." On his end, Joel waved his arms even though she couldn't see. "It'll be nice. We haven't seen each other in a while..."

"I saw you last weekend," Amy pointed out.

He heaved a sigh. "I meant we haven't all been together in a while."

Then silence. Joel listened to the bustle in the salon on Amy's end. Someone talked about bangs, someone else asked about a good shampoo for curly hair. "You're sure nothing's the matter?" Amy asked, finally.

"Positive," he lied.

"Okay," she said. And again: "Okay, fine. We'll be there. What time? What do I need to bring?"

"Seven o'clock," Joel said, "and you don't have to bring anything."

"I'll bring something."

He shrugged, as if she could see it. "Okay. I'll see you then. I've got to call your brother."

"What's the matter?" Adam asked when Joel called him

"Everything's fine," Joel said. "We'll talk. It'll be a nice time."

Adam was still suspicious. "About what?"

"About whatever."

Like Amy, Adam recalled the last time their father called to invite them all to dinner, it was so their parents could deliver the news of his mother's life expectancy and her final wishes. Adam clearly remembered Joel saying they would talk about "whatever" then, too. "Okay," he said, reluctantly. "What should I bring?"

"Nothing," Joel told him. "Just bring yourself."

"I'll bring something," Adam said, and immediately started to worry about what it would be. Probably a loaf of supermarket challah.

"Okay. I'll see you Friday, then."

Adam called Amy after he hung up with Joel and it went to voice mail, which meant that she was probably with a client, and he understood that, but it did nothing for his anxiety. He left her a voice mail: "Dad just called and I assume he called you, too, and he's inviting us to dinner on Friday, and I'm sure you already know that, and he says it's just to talk, but that's what he told us when he invited us to dinner to tell us Mom was dying, and I think he probably has cancer, too, and he just isn't telling us, so I need you to fucking call me back as soon as you get this. Bye."

Then he paced, made an effort to straighten up his apartment, started a load of laundry, and stepped out onto his balcony to smoke. He took one drag, then texted her.

Call me. Then, *I left you a VM message.* Then, *I think Dad has cancer. Or something.* Then, *Call me. Fuck!!!*

He'd finished the cigarette, scrubbed his toilet, transferred the laundry to the dryer, and was lighting another cigarette while he typed out another text message when Amy finally returned his call.

"What the fuck, Amy?" he barked.

"Damn, Adam, I was with a client. It was a triple process."

"Whatever," he said.

"And Dad is *not* dying."

Adam rolled his eyes as he lit the cigarette.

"Are you smoking again?" Amy asked.

"How do you know?" he asked.

"I heard the lighter."

"Not that," he said, and waved a dismissive hand. "Yeah, I'm smoking again. So what? How do you know Dad's not dying?"

She sighed. "Because he didn't sound like he was dying." That won a laugh from Adam. "What's so funny?"

"What does cancer sound like, Amy?"

"Oh, for shit's sake, Adam. I've got to go, I've got another client waiting, just… it's been a while since Mom died, and Dad's getting older and he's probably feeling lonely, so he's inviting us all over for Shabbat dinner. That's all. He's not dying."

Adam grunted.

"And I thought you said the Chantix was working."

"It did, but I started having nightmares where everything was nuclear war, and I'd wake up all freaked out, so I'd smoke." He exhaled. "I'll quit again, I'm sure. This makes my fifth time quitting so far. I'm getting good at it."

Adam knew his sister was probably right. Joel wasn't dying. They'd gone to lunch a month ago, and Joel was fine. Sad, yes, and like Amy said probably lonely, but not dying. They went for Thai food and talked about nothing important, except Joel seemed more interested in Adam's love life than before. "Are you seeing anyone?" Joel had asked, and Adam peered at him across their bowls of pad thai, wary.

"No." He said it slowly. "Why?" They'd never had the kind of relationship where Adam could discuss his love life with his father. With his mother, yes, and he had done so regularly, but Joel had always kept that part of his son's life at arm's length.

Joel shrugged. "Just wondering."

Adam stirred the noodles in his bowl because he needed to focus on something that wasn't his confusion about his father suddenly asking about something he'd never cared about before. He supposed, now that his mother was gone, his father felt he needed to step in and monitor his children's love lives, so he softened some. "I mean, there was this guy, but he's not interested."

"What do you mean he's not interested?" His father's reaction was so overwrought that Adam had to catch himself before he laughed. It was like his father's interpretation of the way his mother would have responded learning someone wasn't interested in one of her children.

"Just that. He wasn't interested." Adam shrugged.

Joel was aghast. Then he was furious. "Well," he huffed. "His loss. I mean… I don't know this guy, and maybe I don't want to know him, but if he can't see what a catch you are, then…" He trailed off, waved a hand, dismissed any further thought or discussion of this unnamed cretin who would so roundly reject Adam.

"It's really no big deal, Dad."

"You're right." And Joel gave a firm nod. "Forget him."

Afterward, they strolled next door to a store called Midcentury. Adam was further confused. Joel had never seemed interested in the design of the house or the furniture that went into it; those were his mother's core competencies.

"I'm looking for a lamp," Joel explained. "I've never really liked that lamp in the foyer. You know… the big green one? Looks like someone made a genie's lamp out of an avocado? Thought I might replace it with something less… heavy."

"Oh." Adam had no interest in antiques and couldn't understand anyone else's interest in them either. He shoved his hands into his pockets and stood, awkward, pretended to study a console table against one wall. "This stuff's pretty expensive." He shopped at thrift stores and tended to furnish his apartment from yard sales and the Salvation Army store.

"Well, they're midcentury originals," Joel pointed out.

"Yeah." Adam had only the vaguest idea what made that a good thing. He heard people talk a lot—old ladies and fussy gay men, for the most part—and knew that midcentury was really trendy, but other than that, he didn't get it. He didn't really understand the whole attraction to antiques at all. To him, they smelled like old people, and the thought of paying such ridiculous prices for something that wouldn't even be on the market if someone hadn't died and had their entire life sold away by their children in an estate sale seemed morbid.

"I'm thinking about updating the whole house, actually," Joel said, more to himself than to Adam. He picked up lamps, studied their bases, their cords, the price tags.

For some reason he couldn't articulate, the remark angered Adam. He opened his mouth to question his father, maybe demand why the house needed to be redecorated now, maybe suggest waiting so it didn't seem so insensitive to his mother's memory, but he caught himself and bit back whatever might have come out. "Are you really gonna buy one of these?" he asked, and nodded to the selection of lamps. He found them all hideous for one reason or another.

"I don't know…"

A man stepped up, smiling, his hands clasped in front of him like he might recite Shakespeare. He was dressed like a lumberjack, Adam thought, and was roughly the size of one. "Do you gentlemen need help today?" Adam would have found the man attractive if they were in a bar and not an antiques store.

"I was looking for a lamp," Joel said, smiling a little too broadly.

"Well, you found them!" the guy said, then he and Joel laughed like neither had ever heard anything so funny. Adam wished he were anywhere else in the world.

Several weeks after the lunch with Adam, Joel had gone onto Grindr.

It was late, he'd had a few glasses of wine, and he thought why the hell not? He'd used it before with varying degrees of success and always some measure of shame, but he tried to stay off it during the worst of Susan's struggle with cancer. It had been close to a year, and it took several tries to recall his password.

His forays into the world of dating apps were always a mixture of optimism and hopelessness. At any given time, night or day, there were more men online than seemed reasonable, but he learned long ago to ignore the profiles that revealed nothing about the person on the other side of them. Names that suggested sex or penis size, too. Joel himself got the cold shoulder a lot because his own profile did not reveal his face, so finding anyone interested took longer than it should have, since everyone assumed he couldn't be trusted. It was frustrating, and he often gave up. People were assholes and he just didn't have the energy to deal with it.

Still, sometimes he got lucky, and this was one of those nights.

A guy whose photo showed only his chest hair and a glimpse of a ruddy beard messaged him almost immediately. A general issue screenname, KentATL, like Joel's, with no hint of anything brazen.

—Hi.

—Hi.

Then a lengthy silence, which Joel hated more than being told outright that he wasn't what the other person was looking for.

—*You looking?*

That thrill of possibility made his pulse quicken. He felt his stomach flutter.

—*Yeah. U?*

He immediately regretted shortening *you* to just a letter, like a teenager.

—*Yeah. What U looking for?*

Joel relaxed and the conversation progressed quickly to the decision of where to meet. Joel offered to host—he had been drinking and did not need to get behind the wheel of a car—and Kent (he assumed that was the guy's name) agreed immediately.

—*Great. I'm in Midtown. Where R U?*

This was the other part that Joel dreaded. So often he would tell guys he was in Dunwoody and they would immediately lose interest because it was too far to drive. Or they would just stop responding at all. But he told the guy and waited.

—*Great. I can B there in 15 mins.*

—*Perfect.*

They exchanged numbers, then texts and face pics. Joel thought he looked familiar but couldn't place him. For all he knew, they'd already had sex, back when Susan was alive and the contact that Joel had with men was furtive and so fraught with peril that he could rarely recall their faces or names the next day.

When he arrived, Kent looked around in awe at the house and furniture, like he was there as a potential buyer and not as a trick. "Your place is amazing," he told Joel, who mumbled a polite thanks. "I own an antiques store, so…" Then it clicked where Joel had seen him before: the day he'd been looking for lamps. Kent admired the original knotty pine paneling, the vaulted ceilings, and the original bar separating the kitchen from the dining area.

Joel led him downstairs to the spare bedroom in the basement—it was Adam's when he lived at home—where he'd been sleeping for the last three years of the marriage. Kent inspected the paneling closer as he unbuttoned his shirt. Joel stared at him, then at the bed, then at the floor. On Grindr, he was intrigued by that peek at Kent's auburn chest hair and when they chatted, the prospect of a quick romp with such a burly specimen had certainly aroused him.

"My wife just died," he heard himself say.

Kent stopped scrutinizing the paneling, turned slowly. "Okay," he said, not looking at Joel where he stood across the room. He looked everywhere but at Joel, like he suspected Joel might have Susan's body lying in state somewhere in the house.

"Recently, I mean," Joel added, to clarify. "In February."

"Oh."

Then silence.

Kent finally said, "We don't have to do this if you don't want to…"

So they ended up at Waffle House drinking bad coffee and commiserating. Kent had been married before, in his twenties, and was just out of a ten-year relationship with a man. "He developed a thing for twinks," he said, and blinked his astonishment. "I guess that's a thing now: older, bigger, hairy guys who are into young, skinny guys who shave their entire bodies and vice versa, the whole dichotomy of it, I guess…"

Joel guessed it was a lot like men who marry women even though they're attracted to men. He knew better than to marry Susan, but he did it anyway, then sought sex elsewhere. To be honest, he understood it perfectly. "Tastes change," he suggested, to make Kent feel better.

Kent shrugged. "I guess…"

"I should apologize about tonight," Joel offered. "For wasting your time." He paused. "I don't know what I was even thinking, really…"

"To be honest, neither do I," Kent said, with a laugh. "I mean—and please don't take this personally—you're not exactly the type of guy I'm attracted to. I tend to go for bigger guys with beards and hair."

"You're not mine, either," Joel confessed. "I usually like guys more like myself. Or younger," he added, sheepishly.

But they both knew why they went onto the app and what they were looking for: a connection with someone, anyone. Kent knew, and Joel suspected, that the majority of the men on those apps and websites were doing the same, though none would ever admit it. And when you got lonely enough, or desperate enough, even sex with a stranger you weren't attracted to was better than being alone.

"I'm still new to this."

Kent was confused. "New to what?"

Joel waved a hand. "*This.* Being out. I mean… I don't even know if I *am* out. I'm just… doing some things more openly than before." He stared hard at his coffee cup, his hands wrapped around it, thought how pink they were and wondered if they had always been so pink and dry. "Like inviting someone over for sex."

"Ah," Kent said. "Well, we've all been there."

They ended the night with a handshake, but a couple weeks later, Kent called.

"I'm sorry," Joel said. "Who?"

"Kent… we were supposed to have sex, then we didn't. We had coffee instead."

"Oh. Hi."

They met again for drinks and Joel was still confused until Kent explained himself: he figured Joel could use a friend who had been through something similar, who was gay, and who could be there to lend moral support and answer questions.

Joel met Kent's friends and heard their stories—of coming out young, of marrying young and then divorcing and coming out, of staying married and having sex with men—and Joel, at last, did not feel like he was the only gay man in the world going through what he was going through. One of the men—a flamboyant man named Gregory (*not* Greg)—had grown children, too. "Honey," he told Joel as they sipped mimosas on Kent's deck one Sunday afternoon, "you will be amazed at just how little your kids care about you being gay. I certainly was."

Joel tried to imagine a scenario where Gregory was married and people had no idea he was gay. It seemed so obvious to him, and then he felt a tiny flare of panic as he wondered if maybe Amy and Adam already knew and he was making a problem out of something that was a nonissue for them. He wondered if the same could be said of himself—was he as flamboyant as Gregory? Was his homosexuality as obvious? But what he said made Joel feel less like a heel and helped make his decision to tell Amy and Adam easier.

"You're sure you want to do this?" Kent asked him. Joel had asked him to lunch, just the two of them, to lay out his plan.

"You think I shouldn't?" Joel asked, and for the first time doubted himself.

"I didn't say that. I just asked if you were sure you wanted to do it."

"Well... I think it's time," Joel said, more to convince himself than Kent. "It's been time, really. For a while." He paused. "So, yes... I'm sure."

"That's good," Kent said. "And you think they're ready? Because, really... that's the important part." And he went on to explain that Joel had known about, and had been acting on, his sexuality for years, even though he'd told no one. So, while he might think the admission was overdue, for Amy and Adam, it was going to come out of the blue. To them, Joel was their father, their mother's husband, not the man who met other men on the internet and in out-of-the-way hotels to have sex. "So, it seems very cut and dried, but it isn't. And that's what I meant when I asked if you were sure."

And Joel wasn't sure all of a sudden. "Well..."

Six months had passed since that conversation and he still hadn't told them. Now, almost a year since Susan's death, he had decided it was time. He wanted it over with. He wanted to stop worrying how they were going to respond and let them react however they were going to so that he could get on with his life. They could take as much time as they needed to come around—or not—but he was not getting any younger.

.two.

Two months before she died, Susan sat Joel down in the den and muted the sound on the television. "I don't think I have much more time," she told him, very coolly he thought, "and we need to make sure we're on the same page." She had lost all her hair and wore scarves—stylish things, silk mostly, with vivid prints and colors—but she came to him then bareheaded and something in that moment, either the sight of her scalp or the gravity of her tone, made Joel burst into tears.

"Oh, for God's sake, Joel," she said, with a roll of her eyes.

"I'm sorry," he said, blubbering, sobs wracking his chest. He looked around for a tissue, anything. Susan heaved a sigh, stood, and disappeared into the kitchen. Joel took the opportunity to compose himself. She returned with a roll of paper towels, handed them to him.

"Get it together," she grumbled.

"I'm sorry," he said again, and wiped his eyes, blew his nose.

"It's not like we didn't know it was coming," she pointed out, and took her seat again on the ottoman facing him. "I was given three years at the max."

Joel wiped his eyes again. "But what makes you think this is the end?"

Susan shrugged. "It just feels like it."

Joel started crying again.

"For the love of God, Joel..."

He pulled himself together as quickly as he could, took a breath, tore another towel off the roll. "I'm sorry. Go ahead. I just—it's so sudden." He considered how that sounded, then said, "Not like *sudden*, but just... you seem fine."

Susan waved a hand. "I haven't been fine for years." Joel felt a pang of guilt and wondered if she meant her health or their marriage. He did not ask for clarification. "Anyway," she said with a deep breath, and leaned forward with her hands on her knees. "You need to be prepared for this when it happens. Adam is going to take it hardest, and that's probably my fault, and I'm telling you I'm sorry for that now." She shrugged. "I spoiled him, and I knew I was doing it, and I shouldn't have, but I did it anyway... I'm a mother. We spoil our sons. It's what we do."

"Adam isn't spoiled," Joel said, certain he had been a great success at making sure all the doting Susan had done on Adam when he was a child had done no lasting damage.

"Trust me, he's spoiled."

"But—"

"We're not going to debate whether or not I spoiled my son, Joel! And you know why I did it, so let's not argue over it. I did it because you were so hard on him, and I'll be gone, and he's going to feel lost." She stared away at some point beyond Joel, beyond both of them where they sat in the den.

He fell silent. She was right, he had been very tough on Adam and Susan had been the balm to ease the friction between them. "Okay, fine."

Susan heaved a sigh, picked up her line of thought. "Adam will take it hard, so you'll have to be patient with him. Amy will help, you know she's always looked out for him, but he's going to need time and space. Just be nice to him, Joel. Don't be an asshole. You know you can really be an asshole sometimes, and especially with Adam."

Joel recoiled as if she'd slapped him.

"And don't act so surprised," she said. "Everyone knows it."

He started to speak, to defend himself, but she cut him off.

"Amy will be fine. She hates me, so it won't phase her in the least."

Joel was aghast. "Amy doesn't hate you! That's crazy talk!"

Susan fixed him with a look. "Are you fucking kidding me, Joel? You think I misheard her every time she told me she wished

I wasn't her mother? You think I made that up?" She made a sound of disgust and leaned back on the ottoman. "She hates me. She tolerates me, but she doesn't like me."

"She doesn't hate you!" How many times did he have to say it? Maybe it was the medication talking. Maybe she'd remembered some horrible argument she had with Amy twenty years ago and it stuck in her head. Maybe it seemed so fresh she couldn't place it in the past where it happened.

Susan held up a hand to silence him. "Anyway... they're both taken care of. You're all taken care of with the insurance and my IRA. It's in the will. The attorney will take care of everything." She seemed to stare at the coffee table as she spoke, her words practiced and her tone measured. "I don't want any bickering between them, though. Make sure they don't bicker."

"I will," he promised, though he couldn't actually recall an instance of Amy and Adam arguing over anything that really mattered. They'd argued over time in the bathroom as teenagers, over what to watch on TV as children, but never anything significant. Or was she saying she'd left more to Adam than to Amy and she anticipated a blowup? He wondered if he should ask, and if it would change anything if he did.

Three weeks after their conversation, Susan fell into a coma.

"I'm definitely telling them on Friday," Joel told Kent over dinner the day after he called Adam and Amy. He was on an upswing again and again was certain it was the right time.

Kent glanced up from his hot and sour soup, one brow arched. They'd had this conversation several times before, then when he asked how it went, Joel would confess that he hadn't been able to go through with it.

"And I'm a nervous wreck." Joel stared down at his own soup, decided he wasn't as hungry as he thought, then ate a spoonful of it anyway. It tasted like nothing.

"Are you sure Adam doesn't already know," Kent said through a mouthful of soup and fried noodles. "He's gay, right?"

"Adam doesn't pay a whole lot of attention to me," Joel told him. His son had always gravitated more toward Susan, and Joel had been glad for it and disappointed at the same time.

Kent scowled. "Well... still. Gaydar and all."

"Well, don't you think he would have asked if he suspected something?" Joel tried to imagine how that would have played out, his grown son broaching the subject of whether or not his father was gay.

"Like, you think there are that many gay men who think because they're gay that they got it from their father?" Kent shook his head. "Doesn't work that way. My dad wasn't exactly butch, but it never occurred to me to consider he might be gay."

"And was he?" Joel pushed his uneaten soup away.

"Of course not," Kent said, and the look on his face suggested mild offense.

"Then how is that relevant to Adam suspecting that I am?"

"Because you are!" Kent nodded to Joel's soup. "You gonna eat that?"

Joel waved a dismissive hand at the soup, at the possibility of Adam already knowing he was gay, at this harebrained idea to come out at the age of fifty-eight to his children less than a year after their mother's death. There was no way it could end well for him, and that was what he kept coming back to when he played the scene out in his mind: everyone assembled around the dining room table (maybe he would do a brisket), the meal consumed, everyone in a good mood because their bellies were full, then himself standing to deliver the news. He had written it out, memorized it the way a child would remember the lines in a school play, but really the only part of it that mattered was the last line: *I'm gay and I always have been, and I am finally at a place where I can live my life honestly.*

That was where the scene jumped the tracks. He imagined them gaping at him at first, stunned into silence. Like in the movies when a character delivered a truly monumental speech and there was that extended moment of silence at its conclusion before the assembled crowd roared into life, only this would not be applause or praise for his courage. This would be screaming and cursing and insults. How could he have lied to them their entire lives? How could he have lied to Susan? And now, this? This is how he chose to mark the anniversary of her death—by coming out and basically admitting that he had cheated on her the entire time they were married?

He pictured chairs overturned, if not thrown. He imagined Amy, in a rage, swiping everything on the dining room table onto the floor, then stepping through it to come at him, her arms outstretched and her fingers like claws. He imagined Adam sitting, seething, fists clenching and unclenching before him on the table, the muscles in his jaw working as he ground his teeth, biting back the rage that boiled inside him. And Ethan... how would his grandson react? Joel hadn't considered that.

Kent snapped his fingers in front of Joel's face. "Hel-*LO*! Earth to Joel."

"Oh." Joel shook his head to clear it. "Sorry..."

"You really zoned out there for a minute," Kent said. "What the hell were you thinking about?"

"Friday night," Joel replied, "and what's going to happen when I tell them." He gripped his stomach as a flare of panic bloomed there. "Maybe it's not a good idea..." He could easily talk himself out of doing it if he gave himself enough time. They would find out when they found out, why turn it into a big production? He would live his life, and somewhere down the road, he would meet someone and want to spend the rest of his life with that person, so he would introduce this man to them and it would be the right time, and *then* he would come out and they wouldn't overreact and flip the dining room table and throw empty wine bottles at him. They would be pleasantly surprised, but they would see that he was happy with this man, and they would be happy for him, and that would be it.

"You want me there, too?" Kent asked, again breaking into Joel's reverie.

Joel shook his head. "I don't know how that would look to them," he said. "I told them it was just going to be the four of us…"

Kent shrugged. "Suit yourself, but maybe if someone who isn't family were there, no one would overreact, which is what I'm sure you're worried about."

Their server appeared bearing their entrées and Joel's stomach lurched. "I don't even think I can eat now."

Kent dug into his kung pao chicken with glee. "Take it home, then. You'll be starved later."

"Maybe…" Joel spooned a child's portion of rice and mu shu pork onto his plate, then stared at it like he wasn't sure how it got there.

"Anyway, you're overthinking it," Kent told him. "I did the exact same thing when I came out to my family. I made myself sick worrying about how they were going to react when I told them. Like, I broke out in a rash… I couldn't eat… I couldn't sleep… Then I told them and they were like, 'Yeah, Kent, we know,' and that was pretty much it."

Joel fixed him with a look. "You weren't coming out to your kids, Kent."

"No, but I was coming out after being married—to a woman, mind you—to people I thought had no idea." He refilled his plate. "I'm telling you, Joel. They're your kids. They've known you as long as they've been alive, and you're telling me you've been gay as long as they've been alive, and I'm telling you that they probably aren't going to be as shocked and appalled as you think." He aimed his chopsticks at Joel. "Now, relax, for fuck's sake. You're going to give yourself a heart attack or something."

On Wednesday, Joel called his sister Rhoda and invited her to lunch the next afternoon. She, like the kids, was immediately suspicious. "What's wrong?" she asked.

Joel laughed. "Everyone always thinks there's something wrong!"

"Is there?" Rhoda asked.

"No! Nothing's wrong. Can't I call up my sister and invite her for lunch without there being a problem?" Joel was the same way, though. If someone told him they needed to talk to him, he imagined the worst and agonized over what the reason might be, and why not just say it up front, why schedule a date and time in the future to discuss it? If it were really as important as all that—important enough to set aside time on a specific day, away from others where it could be discussed without interruption—then surely it need not wait. He wondered if it weren't something genetic, handed down through the generations, Benjamin after Benjamin. Or were other families like this? Susan hadn't been. She added appointments to her day planner and only worried about them when their time came. Joel was amazed at her composure.

"Aren't you just the least bit worried it might be something *bad?*" he asked her once, when she happened to mention that she had a meeting with their rabbi's wife coming up, so she might not be home when Joel got in.

Susan had shrugged. "I'll worry about that if it is. I've got other shit to worry about until then." And she listed them for him: Amy's braces, Adam wasn't eating at school and she thought he was being bullied, the Japanese maple in the back yard wasn't looking so good. "And anyway, how horrible can a meeting with the *rebbetzin* be? She probably wants me to head some committee, or donate money."

Rhoda said, "Just tell me now."

Joel considered just blurting it out, "Rho, I'm gay! Surprise!"—and letting her deal with it on the other side of town. He would hang up and then wait for her to call him back. It would take some time to process, and she would go through all the emotions: shock, denial, anger, hurt, then she would want to discuss it so she would call him back and they would talk. "What the hell was that all about?" she would say. "You're *gay?* Since when?" And he would be able to start at the beginning and there would be a phone between them so it would be easier for him to tell and for her to hear, and when he was finished she would have some smart-ass remark to make about it and they would laugh.

That's how he wished he could do it. Or maybe a letter. That thought hadn't occurred to him until that minute. Why not a letter? No one wrote letters anymore, sure, but what better way was there to deliver what could turn out to be bad news than a handwritten missive that could be mulled over on both ends, the writer over the right words to use to build to the revelation, the reader picking up on all the cues and deciding whether or not he was ready to hear?

Instead, he said, "It would be better in person."

Rhoda huffed. "Sounds pretty bad."

Joel laughed, and even to his own ears it sounded fake, forced. "I guess that depends on how you look at it," he said, and tried to laugh some more but it sounded even worse than the first time.

"Well, what the hell does *that* mean?" Rhoda wanted to know.

She was still suspicious when they met for lunch. Joel got there first, and practiced what he would say as he drove from Dunwoody to Toco Hills, then sat in his car in the parking lot and practiced it again and again until he saw Rhoda's car slide by in the rearview mirror. Rhoda would prowl the lot until she found the parking space closest to the door, so he knew he had more time and used it to calm himself.

He got a table, asked for a diet Coke, and waited. Fifteen minutes later, Rhoda swept into the café out of breath, like she'd sprinted across the parking lot and not walked a mere twenty feet. "You know," she said, "the employees get here early and grab all the good spots."

"I don't think that's the case, Rho," he said, and pretended to study the menu.

"Bullshit," she said, and pushed her enormous sunglasses back onto the top of her head. "How are you? Have you lost weight? You look like you've got some nice color. Did you go to the beach?"

"I'm good," he said, and chose to ignore the remark about his weight. In Rhodaspeak, "You look like you've lost weight" really translated to "You should lose some weight," never mind that she outweighed him by twenty pounds. "And it's a self-tanner."

"Oh," she said. "Well, be careful you don't overdo it. You remember Sharon Feuer? She went and got a spray tan and it turned her hair orange, too. Horrible. Eyebrows, eyelashes, lips. Everything." She made a sweeping motion to demonstrate exactly how bad Sharon Feuer had it after her experience.

"I have it professionally done," he told her.

"At one of those tanning places, you mean?" Rhoda motioned frantically for the server, her arms moving like she was on the deck of an aircraft carrier.

"At a spa."

"Well... that sounds rich." The server came and Rhoda ordered a small prune juice, a coffee, and a glass of water, no ice, room temperature, please. "So, what was such a big secret you couldn't tell me over the phone?" she asked. She studied the menu, though both of them knew she would order the same thing she always ordered: a pumpernickel bagel, lightly toasted, with lox, one *thin* slice of the ripest tomato they had, with capers and very thinly shaved red onion, both on the side.

"I didn't say it was a secret," Joel said. "I said it would be better if I told you in person."

Rhoda huffed. "Well, are you going to tell me or not?"

"Let's order first," he said, buying time. He needed time. Even now, he still needed time. Maybe he shouldn't have brought Rhoda here where there were other people to witness her reaction; maybe he should have gone to her house for coffee and told her there. Or—and this idea suddenly appealed to him—he should have invited her to his house for coffee and told her. From his house she could escape if she decided she didn't want to hear any more of what he had to tell her. She could slam the door on him and be gone. At her own house, she could order him out and slam the door on him. Here, though, there were people who would see, maybe they would overhear and know and pity her. Maybe this wasn't such a great idea, bringing her where her reaction would have to be subdued. She might never forgive him for shaming her like this.

"Joel?"

He snapped back. The server was waiting to take his order and Rhoda was scowling at him. "I'll have the tuna fish on rye," he said. "Side of potato salad." He doubted he would be able to swallow a single bite of it with the lumps in both his throat and his belly, but it would look bad if he didn't order something. And Rhoda was already suspicious; he didn't need to exacerbate that.

Once the server was gone, Rhoda asked him, "So, how are the kids?"

"They're both good," he said. "They're doing really well. You know, the unveiling is coming up…" Maybe he should wait and tell everyone until after Susan's headstone was unveiled.

"I did," Rhoda said, and gave a firm nod, so he knew she was lying. She'd forgotten it, just as he had almost forgotten it himself until he checked his planner at work and saw the date circled in red. He thought he had another month.

"Will you be there?"

"Of course," she said, and feigned surprise that he felt it necessary to ask her.

"Good, good. Yes… Amy and Adam are both doing very well. Adam got a new job—well, it's kind of a new job; he's been there for about five or six months now. And Amy's still at the salon."

"I need to go see her," Rhoda said, and absently gave her hair a fluff. "I need something new." She'd had the same hairstyle for thirty years.

"And how is Sheila?" Joel asked.

Rhoda waved a hand, like she was shooing away the mention of her daughter. "Sheila's fine." She sipped her coffee, eyed Joel expectantly.

Their food came and he was relieved, even if he wasn't hungry. Rhoda examined her bagel and lox with the precision of a coroner. Joel knew what was coming next. He'd known Rhoda his entire life and he couldn't recall a single instance where she had accepted the first plate of food delivered to her in a restaurant. She gestured for their server, again with the air traffic controller signals. The young lady was gracious as she took it back and assured Rhoda that the next one would be perfect.

"It looked fine to me," Joel said.

Rhoda sniffed. "Nobody knows how to toast a fucking bagel."

The knot of dread settled once more in his belly. Joel tried to ignore it, took a bite of his tuna salad sandwich, and had to fight the urge to spit it right back out.

"So, why are we here, Joel?" Rhoda asked, at last dispensing with the pleasantries. "Just say it, whatever the hell it is. I'm tired of worrying about it." She aimed a finger at him. "And it was shitty of you to not even give me a hint of whatever it is. You know how I worry. You could have given me a fucking clue, Joel. Now. Tell me what the hell I'm doing here."

Joel chewed the mouthful of tuna and bread and somehow choked it down. He followed it with diet Coke, buying himself as much time as possible, going over in his head how he had planned to deliver the news.

"Okay," he said, slowly.

Rhoda waited, her gaze fixed on him. When the server returned with her replacement bagel and lox, she gave it the most cursory of glances and returned her attention to Joel.

"So, it's been almost a year since Susan passed. It's been… there's been a lot to deal with, even before she passed away, you know: getting everything in order for the funeral, for the burial, for the *shivah*… And we were married for thirty-six years, you know."

"It was a long time," Rhoda remarked, and Joel wasn't certain if she was extending sympathy or making some other commentary about his marriage to Susan.

"I was twenty-two when I married her," Joel said, and his eyes fixed on the table between them, on Rhoda's untouched bagel and lox and his own tuna sandwich where he had taken the bite. His mind was thirty-six years in the past. He was able to recall everything about that day. He had wondered then what the hell he was doing, marrying Susan—marrying *any* woman, for that matter— and what the hell did he think was going to happen after he went through with it? Did he think he'd smash the glass and it would somehow shatter the person he'd been before, the one who knew he was attracted to men but who struggled with it every day of his life since coming to the realization? Did he really believe that he could marry the gay away? "I was just a kid. We were both so young. We had no idea what we were doing…"

At that, Rhoda arched one brow but said nothing.

"Then we found out Susan was pregnant and Amy was born, and I was so busy trying to get tenure… and next thing we knew, she was pregnant again and Adam was born… and everything seemed to be fine. I mean, it looked fine." He paused for thought. "I mean, it *was* fine. She was a good mother and I love my kids…"

Rhoda's eyes narrowed. "Where is this going, Joel?"

He sighed. "I'm getting there."

"No, you aren't. You're just telling me everything I already know. You met Susan in college, you barely dated and the next thing we all knew you were getting married. You were young and stupid and you started making babies, and she was a good mother and you love your kids." Rhoda stopped, shrugged, spread her hands. "These are things we know."

"If you'd just listen…"

"Well, if you'd just get to the point…"

Joel sighed again. This was not how he imagined it going. He'd pictured himself delivering his spiel and Rhoda sitting politely and listening, nodding here and there at a point she agreed with but otherwise just letting him say what he had to say at his own pace. He should have known Rhoda was impatient and would have preferred that he just get to the fucking point already, for shit's sake. And now here they were and he felt like the entire thing was going off the rails. Maybe it wasn't, but that's not how it felt. "Fine," he heard himself say. "I'll just skip to the fun part."

"Good," Rhoda said, ignoring the sarcasm and shifting in her seat, like they were about to take a rollercoaster ride and she needed to be as comfortable as possible during the ascent before they plummeted down the other side.

Joel threw her a look. He did not get more comfortable. He sat rigid and clasped his hands together on the table in front of him and squeezed his eyes shut and said, "Rho, I'm gay and I've always been gay and I never should have married Susan because I knew it before I married her. I knew it growing up and I was always terrified of anyone finding out so I didn't dare do anything about it, and I knew I was attracted to men, but I dated girls so no one would ever suspect. And then I met Susan in college and we started dating and I knew I was still attracted to men, but I dated her anyway, and the next thing I knew I'd asked her to marry me and she'd said yes, and we got married and we started having kids and I just couldn't see a way out at that point, but I'm gay and that's why I asked you here today, so I could tell you, because it seemed like it would—it *should*—be easier after Susan's death, but it's still just as hard, but I wanted you to know because I'm tired of living like this. I want to be myself, finally, for the first time in my life, I want to be who I really am, and stop pretending." There he stopped, unclasped his hands, and opened his eyes to register Rhoda's reaction. "I'm gay. That's what I brought you here to tell you, Rho."

Silence. Even the chatter from the other patrons, the tinkling of silverware and coffee cups, had stopped it seemed. Rhoda sat blinking at him for a long moment, then she glanced away to a point somewhere just to his left, then to his right, then she glanced down at her plate, then back at Joel. Her mouth moved, but nothing came out.

Joel felt his hands starting to shake and he clasped them together in his lap. He opened his own mouth to speak, to ask if she was mad at him, if she hated him, anything to break that discomfiting silence, but like Rhoda, nothing came out. He actually felt his voice catch in the back of his throat.

She spoke then, at last. "Well," she said. All the sounds of the restaurant rushed back then, too, and Joel was glad to know he hadn't been suffering a stroke. That was all Rhoda said, though, and they lapsed back into another long silence.

"Are you mad?" he asked her, and picked at the crust of his sandwich.

She regarded him as if he'd called her a name. "Mad? Why would I be mad?"

He shrugged.

She rejected the idea with a wave of her hand, slumped a bit in her chair. Like she simply had no more anticipation left for anything after waiting all that time to find out her brother was gay. "I'm not mad," she told him again.

"Okay," he said, and tried to smile.

"At least not about you being gay," she added, and pointed a finger at him. "But I am mad that you felt like you couldn't tell me before this. Hell, Joel, you could have told me forty years ago and saved yourself all this!"

"I know," he said. But did he really?

Rhoda had appointed herself Joel's protector at some point prior to his earliest memory of them, so he imagined she had done so when he was born. As children they went everywhere together, and if Rhoda received an invitation to some place that Joel was not welcome, she simply did not go. If the other children refused—as children were wont to do—to allow Joel to join them in whatever game they were playing, Rhoda excused herself with a few choice words for whichever child had handed down the decree. It was the 1960s, before the advent of playdates supervised by helicopter parents, and children were meaner. Joel tended to accept whatever the older kids said, but Rhoda would have none of it. "Come on, Joel," she would say and take him by the hand to lead him away. "Nobody with any sense would wanna play with this bunch of *nishtikeits*, anyway." Joel allowed himself to be led, unsure of the exact meaning of the word she'd used, but assuming it—like all the Yiddish their mother blurted when she was upset—was not nice.

Middle school was more difficult, as adolescent hormones got added to the stew of ordinary childish behavior and imagined privilege. Joel was smaller than the other boys and preferred reading over playing sports, so of course he was the target of bullies. Rhoda, older and larger, assigned herself his defender. She landed in the principal's office on many occasions, but she didn't mind, and she let them all know it. When they threatened her and the boy whose nose she'd busted with suspension, she merely dug her heels in and lifted her chin (and rubbed her sore knuckles; she'd had no idea hitting someone in the face like that would hurt so much). Their father vowed unspeakable punishments if she didn't start acting, as he put it, "like a lady," and she pointed out that the only reason she was acting so unladylike was because all the bigger kids kept picking on Joel. "They call him names," she cried across the dinner table. "They call him a sissy!"

Joel did not participate in the conversation, though it had become about him suddenly. He looked down at his plate, pretended to concentrate only on cutting his Salisbury steak into bite sized pieces.

"They call you that?" their father asked.

"I guess," Joel said, though he didn't want to say anything at all. "They call me a lot of names." He shrugged. *What could he do?* that shrug said. *Kids are kids, and they're always going to be kids.*

"They do!" Rhoda declared. "They're mean and I'm the only one who'll do anything about it. They're mean to all the smaller kids."

She did not get suspended or otherwise reprimanded, and eventually the other kids grew tired of bullying Joel, who never gave them the response they craved, and left him alone. The experience inspired their father, though, and he picked up where the kids at school left off, suggesting to Joel that he put the Hemingway and the F. Scott Fitzgerald away and go out and find some boys his age. "Throw around a football or something," he suggested. "Play baseball."

"I don't want to," Joel responded.

"Well, it's no wonder those kids call you a queer."

It infuriated Rhoda, but she couldn't deal with their father the way she'd dealt with the boys at school. "Just ignore him," she advised Joel.

"I do," he said, "but it doesn't seem to work!" They laughed.

The truth was that their father didn't really have any room to talk. He worked in a bank, which was no more athletic than staying inside and reading books all the time, and his waistline proved it. Still, he stayed after Joel to join the Boy Scouts or the YMCA and get with other boys his age and do the things that boys were supposed to do. Joel said he'd consider it, but he never did. He already knew, even at eleven years old, that he wanted to be an English professor at a prestigious university somewhere (in his mind, he pictured Oxford, but he had a feeling that might be out of his league) and be able to quote the classics from memory. Rhoda stood firmly by Joel as their father hounded him to do more masculine things, and then one day it just stopped, and dinners were presided over by their mother for a few weeks, which Rhoda took to mean their mother had put her foot down about their father's incessant harrying of Joel. She asked Joel what book he was reading, she asked Rhoda if she was finally starting to enjoy home economics (she wasn't), but it was a welcome change from all the thinly disguised bullying their father was doing.

They would speak about it years later, both of them married then and both of their parents deceased. "I think Dad really thought you might be gay," Rhoda said, and laughed. Joel laughed, too, but said nothing. He had been having sex with men for years by then.

And now they sat over their half-eaten lunch, both of them silent. They stared anywhere but at one another, and finally Joel asked, "You're mad, aren't you, Rho?"

"No," she said, and she wasn't. "I'm not exactly sure what I am. Surprised?" She shrugged. "Confused?" Another shrug. "I mean, yes, I guess I'm surprised because of the way you told me, but am I surprised you're gay?" And she shrugged again. "I guess I just need some time, Joel."

"It's a lot, I know," he said. "I'm sorry."

She signaled to the server to bring their check. Joel told her that he'd planned to pay and she didn't argue. The server brought boxes, but they left the uneaten food on the table. Rhoda turned to him in the parking lot and swept him into an embrace so fierce and unexpected that he felt a sob well up inside him. Then it was over and she stepped back, put her hand on his cheek and stared hard into his face. Her mouth opened and Joel imagined a million things that might come out of it, but in the end she just said, "I'll call you." Then she was gone, her bracelets rattling, and Joel wanted desperately to go with her and keep her by his side the way she'd always been when they were children.

"That's great, though," Kent declared when Joel called him.

Joel just groaned, neither agreeing nor disagreeing.

"You don't think it's great?"

"I guess... but she was definitely upset. I'm sure after she processes it all, she'll realize she's mad."

"Stop being such a pessimist, Joel, geez. When someone tells you something, just try believing they're actually telling you the truth."

Later, Joel gathered together boxes from the attic and the basement: all the evidence of the lives lived in that house, his and Susan's as young newlyweds, then the additions of Amy and Adam, and even Ethan. He passed by a photograph of Ethan as a baby, maybe a year old, chubby and laughing, with the first sign of a tooth coming in. His hair was a riot of black curls and one strap of his overalls had fallen off one shoulder. Joel took it down off the wall and stared hard at it, astonished at how much he favored Adam at the same age, and wondered if he just hadn't noticed it at the time. He went into the living room where he'd gathered all the memorabilia and found the photo album Susan had created when Adam was born. Amy had her own, too. Susan had insisted that each child have their own record of their life and Joel had acquiesced, though he didn't really understand the need for chronicling so much back then. Now it made sense. Susan always understood better than he the way families worked. Babies were born, children became adolescents, then went away to become adults and the parents stayed there, beacons, so there was always a place to return to. And when they returned, they would consult the chronicle of their existence and laugh or cringe, whichever was appropriate. Then parents died, and these collections of artifacts carried more weight.

"I've labeled the boxes for them," Susan told Joel when it was confirmed that she was dying. She pointed to each box. AMY, then ADAM, written in her precise script with a Sharpie. She still had hair at that point and it fell in her face. She absentmindedly tucked it behind one ear. "They may not want any of this, but you'll want to give them the option of what they want to do with it."

"Okay," Joel said, because he wasn't sure what else he could say.

"And I know you never really understood my mania for recording everything like this, so if they don't want it, just throw it out, I guess."

Joel was appalled. "I would never just throw all this away!"

Susan shrugged. "Well, keep it then. I'm certainly not going to take it with me."

Now, Joel sat surrounded by it all, overwhelmed by emotions he never knew he had. He did a side-by-side comparison of Adam's and Ethan's baby pictures and marveled at them. He was certain Susan had noted the resemblance, had probably even pointed it out to him then, but if he had registered it, he'd just as quickly forgotten. Fourteen years ago, he left Georgia State and went to Emory to teach, and he was busy trying to keep his secret life a secret, though he was having regular sexual encounters with two other faculty members—one also married, one not. He'd never had time to spot how alike Ethan was to Adam at that age.

How much else had he willingly missed out on? It was all there in those boxes and albums, in scrapbooks and shoeboxes: Amy at one year old, nothing whatsoever like her own son; Amy in kindergarten; Amy at her bat mitzvah; Amy at her high school graduation. He found the corresponding photos in Adam's album. His children only vaguely resembled one another and they shared none of the same interests. Amy favored Susan's side of the family: fair-skinned, straight hair that teetered on the edge between brown and red but never went one way or the other, blue-eyed. She was tall, too, like Susan had been tall. Well, taller than Joel and the Benjamin side of the family, which Adam resembled: short and stocky with thick, curly black hair, dark eyes, and a certain duskiness to his complexion that hinted at a blending of races. Ethan was a hybrid, with the addition of his father's facial features. Tall like the Schechters and the Cohens, with the coloring of the Benjamins. Like his father's face on Adam's head on Amy's body.

He searched for Ethan's bar mitzvah portrait and had gone through every single shoebox before he remembered that Ethan chose not to have a bar mitzvah. Susan was aghast but Amy shrugged it off. "He's just not all that into the whole Jewish thing, Mom," she'd told Susan, whose confusion had been so complete she couldn't even form one of the many questions Joel was certain were careening about in her brain at the news.

When she found her voice, she simply asked, "How the hell is a Jew not that into the whole Jewish thing?"

Joel could only shrug. "Kids these days are… different that way," he said.

"Bah!" from Susan, but she would pursue it until she got to the root of it: money. Ethan couldn't justify the expense, even when Amy and his dad assured him they'd been saving his entire life to be able to afford anything he wanted. When he suggested they donate the money they would have spent on his bar mitzvah to breast cancer research, it shut everyone up and he turned thirteen with no fanfare other than a chocolate chip cookie cake from the mall and a set of Bluetooth headphones. Twenty thousand dollars was quietly donated in his name to The Breast Cancer Research Foundation, in honor of Susan.

Joel was in tears by then, surrounded by all that evidence of so much of his life and the way it connected and intertwined with everyone around him. He gathered it all back together, stacked it neatly, and arranged it back in the boxes. Then he sat and stared at all the boxes and wondered how in the hell he was going to get through dinner tomorrow night.

.three.

Adam unofficially came out to his family when he was in eighth grade, at the table over dinner. Susan had made spaghetti. Amy was going through a vegetarian phase inspired by a friend from school and was having only buttered noodles and salad. It began with Joel asking about an upcoming dance. "So, at work today, Carol Bauman was talking about shopping for her daughter's dress for some dance that's coming up soon," Joel said, swirling noodles with his fork. "You're in the same grade as Julie Bauman, right, Adam?"

Adam nodded. "Yeah," was all he said.

Susan asked, "Is there a dance at school?" She glanced at Amy, a sophomore in high school and received a shrug.

"Yeah, but it's dumb and I'm not going," Adam said, and forked salad into his mouth. Ranch dressing dripped down his chin. He wiped it away.

Joel and Susan exchanged a look across the table. "Why not?" Joel asked his son.

Adam fixed his father with one of those classic teenager looks that could be interpreted any number of ways: disbelief, outright shock, apathy, disinterest. "Because I don't want to," he replied, and did not feel an explanation was called for.

"Well, dances can be *fun*, though," Susan pointed out. "You get to dress nice and fix your hair. What's the dance for? Valentine's Day?" It was the closest holiday.

"It's the Sweetheart Dance, and it's stupid," Adam said, and rolled his eyes. "And just calling it that is misleading, because there are people going together who aren't sweethearts. And if I go just because everyone else is going, and I asked some random girl to go with me, she might get it in her head that she's my sweetheart, or that I want her to be my sweetheart, and I don't want any of that."

Amy was snickering at her end of the table, but she held her tongue. Adam told her to shut up anyway.

Susan and Joel laughed. "You're in the eighth grade, Adam. Asking a girl to a Valentine's dance isn't going to have her expecting you to propose marriage," Joel said.

"Well, you and Mom can go, since it's so much fun," Adam suggested.

That got an outright guffaw from Amy.

Adam added, "Anyway, I don't even like girls." Then there was silence, the kind that follows a statement no one is quite certain what to do with.

Joel laughed and said, "We were all like that at thirteen, Adam." Only he was still like that, and he had a feeling Adam would always be like that, too. He hated himself for doing that—saying the kind of shit his own father had said to him, the same tired platitudes. Adam didn't want to go to the dance because it was stupid and he didn't like girls. Joel could totally relate. Yet here he was, passive-aggressively pressuring his son into conformity—boys asked girls to dances at school, it was what they did—and he hated himself for it, even though he knew he was only doing it so that his own manliness, his own sexuality and his abilities as a father, were not called into question. This, as Joel understood it, was what fathers did with their sons. He laughed again, so that no one thought he was being mean.

Adam was not laughing. He stared at his plate of spaghetti for a long moment, then set his fork and spoon down and clasped his hands together. He glanced at Susan, then at Amy, then settled his eyes on Joel and repeated, "I don't like girls. And it has nothing to do with being thirteen."

Joel and Susan stared at their son, who sat still and silent, daring either or both of them to comment any further—to question whether or not he was sure, or remark that he would certainly change his mind as he matured—and then at each other, and finally at Amy who sat grinning ear to ear. Nothing more was said about the Sweetheart Dance or about Adam's interest in girls, and though it had not been a proper coming out, it would have to do for one until the official one later, after high school.

Amy was the first to broach the subject with him about it. "So you like boys, huh?" she asked him as she leaned in the door to his bedroom, which was in the basement. This was several days later, when Amy figured everyone had chilled out about it. He was cross-legged on his bed, alternately reading *To Kill A Mockingbird* for a book report and watching *Fresh Prince of Bel-Air*.

"I guess...," he said, and marked his page. "Are Mom and Dad freaking out about it?"

She entered his room and closed the door behind her. "No, they just sit and whisper back and forth at each other." She sat next to him on the bed, nudged him with her shoulder. "That was pretty bad ass, though. I'm proud of you."

Adam made a face. "Are you gonna get all emotional about it?" he asked.

She laughed. "No. I just wanted to let you know how cool it was."

Susan sought out their rabbi, who gave her names and addresses of counselors, and pamphlets, and lists of reading material. She scoured bookstores and libraries and came home with stacks of books and magazines. "You should look at this, too," she told Joel. He graded essays while she pored over the literature.

"I'll be fine," he said, and scowled at the piles of books spread across the foot of the bed. "And don't you think you might be overdoing it just a bit?"

Susan shook her head. "I want to make sure I say and do the right things," she said. "If we handle this wrong, it could affect him for the rest of his life, and I don't want him to be ashamed of who he is."

A pang of guilt shot through Joel. He felt a desperate longing to not be ashamed of himself for who he was, too. He envied

Adam for knowing who he was at such a young age and standing up for himself under the timeworn parental guidance Joel and Susan would have surely continued giving had Adam not spoken up. He wished he, too, had been in a position all those years ago to tell his parents that he didn't want to go to the dance and he didn't want to hold a girl's hand because he didn't like girls. Adam was lucky to have such liberal parents as Joel and Susan, and his own father was jealous of him for it.

Susan bolted upright. "Do you think he has a boyfriend?"

Joel laughed. "At thirteen? I doubt it." He longed for a boyfriend of his own, had often at different times throughout his adult life.

She swatted at him with a hand. "You know what I mean, Joel. Not a boyfriend, per se, but maybe there's some boy at his school that he has a crush on…" She seemed to be scheming something and it made Joel nervous. "I wonder how we could find out…"

He put down the essay he was grading. "He could tell us," he said.

"Exactly!" Susan's eyes glowed with the need to know.

"And when he's ready, he will," Joel added, and went back to his essays.

Susan huffed and threw him a look, more crestfallen than angry. "I just want him to know that he can tell us," she said. She went back to the article she was reading and no more was said. If Adam had a boyfriend, or if he was just enamored of some boy at school, they never found out.

Now Joel wished his own coming out could go as smoothly as Adam's, and that the kids would throw themselves into accepting him the way Susan had accepted Adam.

The thought of the talk he was planning so terrified him that he took a swig of scotch straight from the bottle to settle himself, then poured a glass. He was cooking and the house was filled with the aromas of comfort food, though he did not feel comforted. He felt as if he might vomit, but he had to mind the sauce, so he popped a Xanax and followed it with more scotch. He stared out the window over the sink and into the rain. *Of course it would rain,* he thought, and then remembered reading or hearing somewhere that rain on a wedding day was supposed to be a good omen, signaling happiness in the marriage, and good luck. He wondered what it symbolized for an occasion like this and guessed that whatever it portended couldn't be favorable. He sighed, added more chianti to the sauce, and stirred.

"Ethan, we're going to be late!" Amy called up the stairs as she stuffed her foot into her boot.

"I'm ready," came his muffled response. "I'm coming." Then his footfalls from upstairs, then descending the stairs, then he presented himself to her. "It's just Grandpa," he pointed out.

"I know that," she said as she fought with the boot, "but he's had a rough year with your grandma dying, and it would be rude for us to be late to dinner." She got the boot on and started with the other, giving her son the once over. "Is that shirt clean?"

Ethan glanced down at it. "Um... yeah."

"It's just wrinkled," she said, and waved a hand at it, illustrated its wrinkledness with her fingers, gave him a look of mild disgust.

He cocked his head to one side and gave her a look that was unadulterated teen condescension. "Seriously, Mom?"

"What?" Her boot on at last, she stood triumphantly.

"You're doing that whole passive-aggressive thing again, where instead of just saying you don't like my shirt, you make up a list of excuses why I shouldn't wear it, then you spend thirty minutes trying to get me to agree with you."

Amy managed to fake a laugh. "I don't do that," she said, and wondered silently: *Do I?* God, she hoped not because her mother used to do it to her and it was infuriating.

"I like this shirt," Ethan went on. "Dad got it for me."

Amy stood before the mirror in the foyer and swept her hair back and into a messy bun. "It's a nice shirt," she said. "It just looks a little shlubby."

He stepped alongside her and inspected his own hair in the mirror. "You're just saying that because Dad bought it," he told her, and that stunned her into silence.

She stared at their reflections. Ethan was a full head taller than she was already, and he would only grow more. He got that from his father's side of the family. Mike Cohen was well over six feet tall and Amy could see Ethan matching him by the time he stopped growing. He was slighter built than his father, more like her family, but he got his coloring from her father's side of the family: thick, dark hair that tended toward curls and a dusky complexion. She had given him eyes like her own—people called it blue, but it was really closer to gray—otherwise, he might not have come from her body at all.

Even after fifteen years, it took her by surprise that she had a son. That she had a child at all, really, and especially a son who was almost six feet tall and fast becoming a man. And she still had no real idea what she was doing. Those first few years had been hellish—a baby, always needing something, always needing *her*, and she unsure of how to go about giving it what it needed. Ethan had cried a lot and Amy hadn't known how to make it stop, so she'd let him. Susan, who she'd expected to be appalled at her failings, had been the most patient with her and with Ethan in those early days of her motherhood. "I can't get him to stop crying," Amy sobbed to her mother, and Susan laughed.

"He's a baby," she said. "Babies cry!" This from the same woman who had exasperated—and been exasperated by—Amy for as long as Amy could remember.

Then she showed Amy how to hold him just right when she fed him his bottle, how to hold him when she rocked him, how to bathe him, how to change his diaper. Amy felt like a colossal failure. Weren't mothers supposed to know all that instinctively? Isn't that what made women mothers and not just vessels? Any woman could, technically, give birth to a child but it took a special kind of woman to actually *mother* a child. The sentiment was shared countless times daily across all social media platforms by women so unlike Amy that she took it as an affront every time she encountered it. In other words, these special women who didn't work, who spent their days running from yoga class to Pilates to barre, who diagnosed themselves lactose-intolerant one week, then gluten-free the next, then allergic to cologne, to sulfites, to chlorinated water; they sat in Amy's chair and spent their husbands' money on expensive treatments to straighten their natural curls or elaborate chemical processes that wove three colors together for the most natural look, and they waxed rhapsodic about their abilities as a mother, how their children had breast fed because it was better for the baby, or how their technique to trick their recalcitrant three-year-old into eating her vegetables was better than her friends', and Amy smiled and nodded and feigned genuine interest, though she was really thinking how she was not one of those mothers, because the things she had done when Ethan was a baby would have her arrested today.

"He hates me," she sobbed to Adam on more than one occasion, when Susan wasn't around and Ethan would not respond to her the way he did to his grandmother.

Adam made a sound in the back of his throat to register his disagreement. "How can he hate you? He doesn't even know you yet."

Amy cried harder.

He held out his hands for the baby. "Here. Let me take him. You go put yourself back together." He made a sweeping gesture with one hand that took in her hair, her face, her clothes.

She gladly handed Ethan over and he stopped bawling the second he was settled in Adam's arms. "What the *fuck?*" she cried.

"Just go," Adam said and shooed her away.

The shower was nice, and she fixed her hair for the first time since Ethan's birth, and when she returned to the living room, Adam wasn't there with Ethan. She found them upstairs in the nursery. Ethan was asleep in his crib and Adam was standing over him, staring intently at him. Amy stepped up beside him and regarded her sleeping infant with something like disbelief. "What did you do, slip him some bourbon?" she whispered.

"I think he was just exhausted from crying all day," Adam whispered back. "He fell asleep the minute you left the room."

Amy huffed.

"Well, I'm not the fucking baby whisperer, if that's what you're thinking. Maybe he can sense how stressed out you are when you hold him, and maybe that stresses him out and he cries about it."

"No, I think he just hates me," Amy said.

"That's dumb," Adam said.

They stood over Ethan and watched as he made those inexplicable faces babies made while they slept: like he was suckling one minute, then the next on the verge of tears only no sound came out, then peaceful again, almost smiling.

Adam said, "Babies are ugly."

"Yeah, you should've seen him when he first came out if you think this is ugly," Amy said, and Adam made a face. "I seriously thought Mike was going to hurl."

"I would have," Adam said, and reached out one finger to feel Ethan's curls.

"He looks like you when you were a baby," Amy said.

"Like you remember," Adam shot back. "You were only two yourself."

"I mean the pictures. And don't say he doesn't." Amy sighed. "It's almost like he isn't even my baby." She had a feeling that was post-natal hormone imbalance talking, so she didn't pursue it.

Downstairs, they drank cheap wine and ate Doritos. Amy explained how Susan came and worked wonders with Ethan, and how she made it look so effortless. "And it makes me feel like a bad mother," Amy said. "Like, I feel like I need to get the baby part right so he won't hate me when he's a teenager, but I suck at this and he'll probably kill me in my sleep when he's older." She'd read news stories and watched afternoon talk shows about teens who tried to murder their parents.

Adam swirled the wine in his glass. On the baby monitor between them, Ethan made a noise in his sleep and Amy was upright in half a second. "Relax, mama. He's just sleeping."

"That noise, though..." Amy bent close to the monitor, strained to hear more like it, or some new noise, more dire.

Adam pushed her back against the cushions, refilled her glass, and handed it to her. "Sit the fuck down, drink your wine, and eat your Doritos. Your baby's not going to die." He sounded quite certain of that.

Amy sat and sipped her wine, but she worried. "I haven't had a decent night's sleep in weeks," she said. "I hear every little sound he makes and I jump out of bed and run down the hall. I think he's choking to death, or if he doesn't make enough noise, I think it's SIDS. Or I'm afraid gypsies are going to steal him. Then I run down the hall and there aren't any gypsies, and he's still breathing, and he's alive. When does this shit end?" She raked her fingers through her hair.

Adam regarded her over the rim of his wine glass. "Gypsies?" he asked. "Seriously?" Then he grinned, and that turned into an all-out laugh. Amy slapped him on the leg and told him to stop laughing at her, but in the next instant, she was laughing along with him.

Ethan hadn't tried to kill her in her sleep yet, but she still wasn't convinced he didn't hate her. The divorce hadn't really helped, either. Now his response to every question she had, or every suggestion she made, was a grunt of disgust or a roll of the eyes, if not an outright refusal. He caught her studying him in the mirror. "What?" he asked.

"Nothing," she said, and shook her head, and then, for some reason she wasn't sure of, she added, "You look like your dad."

Ethan rolled his eyes. "No, I don't. I look like you."

It was unexpected and just hearing it spoken, Ethan acknowledging that he looked like her, seemed like some sort of acceptance she had never gotten from him before. She felt emotion well up inside her, it was in her throat, choking her, and she knew she was going to cry. Then her phone rang, and it was Adam. She took the opportunity to turn away from Ethan to answer it.

"You may get there before us," she said by way of a greeting.

"I know," Adam told her. "I'm already here."

That sent Amy into a low-grade panic. "Shit! Okay... we're on our way. We're leaving now." She hung up, grabbed her keys and her purse and started out the door. Ethan could only run after her.

"Can I drive?" he asked.

"No," she said, and it came out abrupt, like a bark. Ethan heaved a huge sigh of disappointment and it made her feel bad. She slipped into the driver's seat and gave him a smile. "Maybe on the way back," she suggested, thinking she would have wine in her by then and would be better able to handle it.

Ethan did not smile. "Whatever."

Adam stood in the gathering dusk on the back patio and stared at the rain-soaked ruin his mother's garden had become. Weeds and brambles had taken over, and what wasn't suffocated by dandelions or Johnson grass was brown and withering. It infuriated him at first and he blamed his father. How could Joel have let it get this bad? Then he considered maybe Joel had tried, but grief had made it impossible. Maybe. In the end he just stood and felt his disappointment deepen. He could have done it himself, but since Susan's death he honestly hadn't thought about the garden for even a second, so he couldn't be frustrated with Joel without being displeased with himself. He drank his beer and stared at it, because he could think of nothing else to do, and lighting it on fire was out of the question since there was more than likely some local code that prohibited the burning of things within the city limits of Dunwoody.

Joel found him out there. "What are you hiding from?" he asked with a laugh.

"I'm just checking out Mom's garden," Adam said, and pointed his beer bottle at it.

They stood together and gazed at it. Joel could sense the emotion emanating from his son, but he couldn't be certain which one: anger? sadness? hopelessness? Had he come out here thinking he would find it lush and verdant, a reminder of his mother and her devotion to it, which would remind him how devoted she had been to her children, to them all really? Was finding it in this state of decline like losing her again in some small way? He opened his mouth to apologize, to make up excuses why he hadn't maintained it over the past year, but Adam spoke first.

"This sucks," he said, and took another drink of his Corona.

Joel almost laughed. It was an understatement if ever there was one. "Well... yeah," he said. "It does, indeed."

"Mom would be pissed."

Joel considered that. Were she still alive, the garden never would have slipped into such a state of disrepair, but he couldn't ignore that there were definitely things he could have done that he simply didn't. He hadn't intentionally let the garden go—or had he? Was it subconscious, just letting the one thing that would always stand as a testament to Susan go to ruin? He felt bad about it for the first time. "Maybe I should call some landscapers over and see what can be saved…"

"I could probably come over and salvage it," Adam heard himself say. He turned to Joel to see if he'd heard it, too.

Joel's eyes were wide with surprise. "Well… sure," he said. "I guess…" He tried to remember if Adam had ever displayed an interest in gardening or landscaping before and couldn't.

"I mean I could clean it up," Adam said, because he didn't want to commit to something he couldn't follow through with. "The Japanese maple seems to be doing okay." He nodded to where it stood among the weeds.

A car horn sounded, signaling the arrival of Amy and Ethan. "There's your sister."

Amy entered out of breath, like she'd jogged all the way from Decatur. "I brought wine," she announced, and held up two bottles. Ethan sulked behind her.

"What's wrong with you?" Adam asked him.

"Nothing."

"Doesn't look like nothing."

They all headed inside, to the kitchen. Amy rummaged through the drawers for the corkscrew she knew was there.

Joel handed it to her. "I keep it on the counter these days," he said with a wry grin.

Amy laughed. "Within reach. Good idea." She attacked the cork on the bottle of cabernet franc she'd brought.

"This is the first time we've all been in the same room together since your mother's *shivah*." Joel shook his head, made a tsk-ing noise. "We haven't even hugged each other, or asked how we're doing." And with that, he swept Amy into a hug. "How are you?"

"I'm good," she said. "How are you?"

Joel shrugged. "You know..." he said. "I'm getting better, though." She would interpret it as him getting over Susan's passing, and that was part of it, but really he was terrified of what he had to tell them. Honestly, he had pretty much talked himself out of it. Did he really need to tell them? He wasn't so sure anymore. Maybe he should just go on with his life—he was entitled to do that, he had convinced himself. When they found out, there could be a discussion. He just wasn't certain there needed to be an announcement.

Adam whispered to Ethan: "Seriously, what's wrong with you?"

The boy sighed. "Dad's teaching me how to drive and I think it's pissing Mom off some, but I asked if I could drive over and she got snippy."

He whispered it, but Amy overheard. "I didn't get snippy."

Joel said, "I thought this generation wasn't interested in driving and owning a car and all that. You guys have Uber and tiny houses and things we old farts never imagined!"

"Who taught you guys how to drive?" Ethan asked. Amy and Adam shared a look across the island and burst out laughing. Ethan turned to Joel. "Was it you, Grandpa?"

"It was their mother," Joel said.

"And she was a total basket case the entire time!" Amy declared. "Adam, remember, she'd take us to the mall parking lot and let us go on our own, pulling forward and backing up and using the signal, and she'd stand there with her hands cupped around her mouth the entire time, yelling 'Stop! Now turn right!' or 'Now back up!'"

Adam stood and demonstrated Susan's technique, his fingers flared around his mouth and his eyes comically wide. When he spoke, it was Susan's voice coming from his mouth, shrill and strident. "Stop slamming the brakes, Adam, you're gonna give yourself whiplash! Do it again! No, not like that! *Slower*, honey! Yes, now stop… that's right… that's good. Now act like you're gonna turn." He paused there for dramatic effect. "You forgot your signal! Oh my God, you're gonna get yourself *killed!*"

Everyone was laughing, Amy so hard that she could hardly breathe. "And she looked so Boca out there in the Perimeter Mall parking lot, too. Those sunglasses. Remember, Adam?"

"They were *huge*," he said.

"So Boca" was their favorite descriptive for their mother. Susan had grown up there and despite having lived longer in Atlanta, she never really left Boca Raton that far behind. It was both a source of shame and pride for her children. At first, Susan was appalled to know her children described her that way. "They say *what* about me?" she'd gasped, and clutched at her chest.

Joel was laughing. "Well, they don't mean it disparagingly," he explained. "I think they kind of like it."

Susan scowled at him, unconvinced.

"You're not like the other moms at school. Look at it that way."

When she tried to dial it back, not wanting to be a source of shame for her kids, Amy called her out on it immediately. "What's with all the black and gray all of a sudden?" she asked when Susan appeared at her school to attend a choral concert.

"What do you mean?" Susan asked. "I'm stylish." She inspected herself, turned this way and that so that her skirt flared, wrapped her wooden beads around a finger.

"Yeah, but it's boring. You look just like all the other moms here." And Amy made a sweeping gesture that took in all the mothers in varying shades and different textures of gray and black. There were at least four other variations of her mother's outfit in the sea of women and Susan looked more ashamed than if she had shown up naked. Her mother was not one of these women and Amy and Adam knew it, and had given her personal style a name: *So Boca*. Like it was Susan's own label. Joel was right.

He didn't gloat, though. "I told you," he said later that night as she rubbed Oil of Olay around her eyes and lips. "They don't want a mother like that. They want *So Boca*."

And from that moment on, Susan dialed up her flamboyant style to the point that it verged on caricature, but her kids just laughed and threw one another knowing glances as she peered at them through her enormous Chanel sunglasses, attached to a rhinestone-encrusted chain around her neck. "Does this make me look hippy?" she asked them as she modeled a new sundress in a pattern of flamingo pink and orange flowers.

"Like a hippy...from the Sixties?" Adam asked from where he lay on the floor reading from his history textbook.

"I think she means does it make her hips look big," Amy explained.

"Oh."

"Well, does it?" Susan asked, and spun around so they could see it from all angles.

"You look fine," Amy said.

"Good," Susan said, and started back upstairs. "It was half price."

Now they reminisced about her most outlandish outfits—"costumes," Amy called them, because that was basically what they were. Susan was putting on a show when she wore them, an act: the perfectly coiffured, manicured, lipsticked, and mascaraed Boca Raton mother with her oversized accessories and opinions.

"Which reminds me," Joel said, holding up a finger. "We all need to go into the den."

Amy and Adam looked both perplexed and anxious, certain that he would take them there and disclose his reason for asking them over. They grabbed their wine and beer and followed him, Ethan bringing up the rear.

"Your mother kept everything, as you know," Joel said, and motioned to the neat piles of boxes throughout the room. "And she spent several months toward the end just gathering everything together and separating it all into these boxes for each of you." He nodded to his grandson. "Even you, Ethan."

"Wow," said Adam and Amy, in unison.

Amy sat cross-legged on the floor in front of the boxes with her name on them and opened the topmost one slowly, as if something might spring out at her. "What in the world…" She found only a neat stack of dusty photo albums, took the top one and opened it. There, on the first page, was the first photo ever taken of her, just moments after her birth, red, angry, almost inhuman. She'd thought the same thing about Ethan when they'd handed him to her in the hospital and she'd cried because he was so ugly. She wondered if Susan had cried to find her so unpleasant looking after all those hours of labor.

"That's you?" Ethan asked, leaning in over her shoulder.

"That's me," she said.

Joel was smiling. "About thirty minutes after she was born," he explained. "That was back when the hospitals took pictures of newborn babies. I don't think they do that anymore. Do they still do that?" He asked it of no one in particular, didn't really expect an answer, but he wondered.

Adam held up his own photo and laughed. "I look like a frog," he declared.

Ethan searched his own box, frowned. "I don't have one."

"Well, that's what you looked like" Amy told him, and pointed to Adam's.

"I'm going to check the lasagna," Joel announced, but they didn't hear him, so wrapped up were they in the contents of their boxes.

They made a game of lining up photos of Adam and Ethan at the same age, from birth on, to prove to Ethan that he, too, had looked like a frog when he was first born. "You guys could have been twins," Amy said. "Seriously."

Adam inspected each photo of himself next to each photo of

Ethan. He remembered being four, and five, and six, and he remembered Ethan at those ages, but he did not remember ever thinking Ethan resembled him. Maybe because he had other priorities then—boyfriends, rent, alcohol to consume, a job. He didn't recall Amy mentioning it, either, so maybe no one had noticed. Had Susan? If so, she never spoke of it. And anyway, they were as unalike now as it was possible to be—Ethan had shed the pudginess and become tall and lean like the Cohens, whereas Adam lost it briefly through adolescence, only to settle back into it as he got older and less active.

Amy looked at them now and saw only the slightest of resemblances between them, and that around the eyes. "Well, I looked like a lizard," she remarked, and turned the page, saw herself evolve into something more human as the months and years progressed. The photo albums, she noticed, had been meticulously curated by Susan. There were no candid shots; every photograph was either professionally done or it was posed. She craned her neck to see Adam's and noticed that his was the same.

They'd seen them all before, of course, when they were younger and lived at home, but they'd forgotten these photographs and the albums that they filled existed. Susan had even saved their artwork from elementary school—construction paper Valentine's Day cards and turkeys for Thanksgiving made from poster paint handprints and brightly colored feathers. There was a baby book for both Amy and Adam, chronicling the first three years of their lives and carefully filled in by their mother: their first words, their first steps, their first teeth, and the dates for every milestone. Adam was transfixed by his. Amy flipped through the pages of hers, silent, amazed that Susan had taken so much time and effort to log every tiny detail about both of her children, and relieved that such things no longer existed when Ethan was born.

In the kitchen, Joel texted Kent. *I don't think I can tell them.*

And Kent's response after a minute: *Ok. Don't.*

It gave Joel the resolve he needed. He would tell them, but not tonight, not after presenting them with those boxes of memories and many of those of Susan or connected to her in some way. He checked the lasagna, pulled ingredients for the salad from the refrigerator, then had more doubts. He texted Kent again: *Unless you think I should…*

Kent's response was almost instantaneous: *What do U think U should do?*

I don't know, Joel texted back without giving it any thought. He held the phone and stared hard at the screen, watched as Kent started and stopped several times. It was agonizing. What was so bad that he couldn't just say it? He convinced himself, in mere seconds, that whatever Kent was typing on his end would be bad, some chastisement for backing out at the last minute. Joel was sure it was something he needed to hear; Kent was very good at knowing what to say when Joel needed to hear it. That, of course, didn't mean Joel wanted to hear it. He had been so ready to do it: everyone would arrive, they'd have a couple drinks, then they would dig through all the memorabilia Susan had collected; they would have dinner, and after everyone was finished eating but before the table was cleared, Joel would tell them why he had asked them to come. Once he had, he would stand and gather the dirty dishes while they digested what he had told them. He would spray the dishes off in the sink, load the dishwasher, and it would give him something to do instead of sit and wait for their reactions to the news.

Kent replied at last: *Ur decision.*

Joel laughed, part with surprise and part with relief. It wasn't as bad as he anticipated, but he certainly expected more than those two simple words. And what exactly did Kent mean by advising Joel all that time, helping him to plan and giving him feedback, only to now step back and throw his hands in the air and leave it all up to Joel like that? For a second, he was pissed, then he realized Kent was right. It was his decision, and his alone, and ultimately whatever he decided would be the right decision because he wouldn't make it lightly, and he would choose the right time, and this was not it.

I know, he texted back.

Adam bounded into the kitchen then, grinning from all the reminiscing in the den. He yanked open the refrigerator and grabbed another beer. "Who are you texting?" he asked, and the look on his face hinted to Joel that he found it suspect.

"A friend," Joel said, simply.

Adam gave him a grunt, a nod, and twisted the cap off his beer.

"You think I don't have friends?" Joel asked.

"I didn't say that," Adam replied, and grinned.

Joel was confused. "What, then?"

Adam just grinned and went with his beer back to the den. "I think Dad may be seeing someone," he whispered to Amy, and Ethan narrowed his eyes at them.

"No whispering," he said.

Amy's mouth was agape. "*What?*" Then she grinned. "Who?"

Adam shrugged. "He was texting someone when I went to get my beer and when I asked him who it was, all he said was 'a friend.'"

She was suspicious immediately, and wondered if she should be upset that her father was already carrying on with someone less than a year after her mother's death. Then she told herself she was being silly and old-fashioned. He was a grown man and Susan was gone; he could do as he pleased with whomever he pleased, and they could stay out of his business. Still, though, she would like to know *something* about the woman. "Has he started going to temple again?" she asked, thinking aloud.

Adam shrugged.

"It has to be someone he met there," Amy continued, and stroked her chin like she had a beard. "Or maybe at the JCC?" She thought some more. "Or work, too, I guess, but is he the kind of person to date someone he works with?"

From the dining room, Joel called to them. Dinner was ready.

Now that he wasn't going to tell them, Joel was able to relax and enjoy the food and their company. He brought out more wine, filled their glasses, made like he would pour some into Ethan's glass but Amy stopped him. "Don't give him any ideas," she said and put her hand over the glass.

Ethan rolled his eyes. "It's not like I've never had wine," he said, like every other teenager in the history of adolescence. "Beer, too. Even the hard stuff."

"So, you're a dumb teenager," Amy said with a dramatic shrug. "We were all dumb teenagers once, and we know what dumb teenagers do. You aren't reinventing the wheel here, mister." *God, I sound like Mom*, she realized, but didn't mind so much. She certainly minded much less than she thought she would.

"I'm pretty sure, if we're handing out the Dumbest Teenager Award, I would beat everyone at this table," Adam informed them all, and drained his beer.

Amy threw up her hands in defeat. "And you will get absolutely no argument from me," she said. She'd witnessed the majority of it, had even covered for him on several occasions. "You were a hellion."

Joel seemed genuinely surprised. "Were you?" he asked Adam. "I don't remember you ever getting into any trouble..." Adam and Amy burst into laughter. Ethan laughed, too, though he didn't know why. Joel was at a loss. "I'm serious," he said.

"That's because he was crafty, Dad," Amy explained. "He just never got caught."

Adam pointed at his sister. "Because *she* covered for me all the time." And they laughed again.

"Well... did your mother know?" Joel asked.

They stopped laughing, their lips clamped shut, and stared at one another across the table, each one waiting for the other to speak first. Joel and Ethan waited, too. Then Amy and Adam burst out laughing again.

"Oh, for the love of God," Joel groaned. He looked at Ethan. "Let's just ignore them, since we can't get a straight answer."

"Maybe it's time to cut them off," Ethan suggested.

Amy held her hand up. "Wait! That will not be necessary," she said, although Ethan suspected otherwise. "Yes. Mom did know, because—"

Adam finished for her: "—She came to pick me up at the police station a couple times." He shrugged; at this point, nothing could be done.

Joel was aghast. "The *police* station?" If he was wearing pearls, he would have clutched them the way his hand went to his throat and grabbed at nothing. He searched his brain for any memory of Susan telling him she'd had to go pick their son up from the police station and couldn't recall a single instance. Maybe they were making it up to upset him, now that Susan was gone and couldn't corroborate their story. Not that it really mattered at this point, anyway; Adam was grown and whatever had happened—if anything had happened at all—had no lasting effects: he had no criminal record to Joel's knowledge and he had no trouble passing background checks at potential employers.

"Twice," Adam said, and held up two fingers.

"You were arrested *twice*?" Joel actually pushed himself back from the table, though he wasn't sure why. It just felt good to grip the edge of the table like that, and the sound of the chair scraping the floor cut through the blood pounding in his ears. "Why can't I remember this? Are you two jerking me around?"

They laughed. "No," Amy said.

"I wasn't arrested," Adam said. "I was *taken in*, and they called Mom, and she came and got me. You were out of town both times, I guess." He thought back, decided that must have been the case, nodded. "I know they called and Mom answered and she demanded to talk to me and I don't think she was ever so pissed at me about something in my entire life." Even now, he could hear Susan's voice through the cold, black phone at the police station. He had been riding with friends and they got pulled over for speeding and weaving. Adam had been in the back seat, so he got off easily with an embarrassing phone call to his mother. The first time, she'd come immediately, disheveled and irate, and they hadn't spoken on the ride home. The second time—and it was the same offense, the same friends—she had not even asked to speak to him, and she had not come immediately. They put Adam into a room by himself, telling him only that his mother said she was on her way. He fell asleep waiting, and Susan arrived the next morning. Adam was grounded for a month, and Susan never said a thing to Joel.

"I guess she never told me," Joel said. He felt cheated and disappointed.

"It was nothing, really," Adam insisted.

Amy stood to clear the dishes.

"I'll help," Joel said and stood so fast it nearly tipped his chair over.

"I've got it, Dad," Amy said. "You and Adam go into the den. Ethan will help me and we'll come join you."

He went reluctantly, took his wine, and sat while Adam rummaged through the shoebox of photos Susan had gathered for him. "I can't believe she kept all this," he said, between exclamations of surprise or disbelief.

Joel moved forward in his chair to see better what Adam was pulling from the box.

"I had such a crush on this guy," Adam said, more to himself than to Joel.

"Who's that?"

Adam showed him the photograph: two boys, shirtless and dripping wet, a swimming pool and the blurred figures of other kids behind them. Joel recognized Adam instantly: pudgy and dimpled and pink cheeked. Their arms were around one another, Adam and this other boy, who was lean and athletic and fair. "Jeremy Silverman," Adam told him, and sighed just a little. It made Joel's heart ache.

"Where was this?" he asked. They didn't have a pool.

"The JCC, I think," he said. "It was Jeremy's bar mitzvah."

Joel studied the photo more than he should have, he supposed. He had known boys like Jeremy Silverman when he was that age—boys who reeked of masculinity and athletic prowess when they got close, and who became the subject of his fantasies at night; he was friends with those boys, too, the way Adam was with this boy, but Joel had taken all the necessary steps to make sure none of them ever suspected a thing. He wondered now, gazing down at his son and this other boy by a pool twenty years ago, where those boys were now, and if any of them were like himself, then and now. "You still in contact?" he asked.

Adam shook his head. "His dad got transferred with Boeing and they moved out to California when we were sophomores." He gave a wistful smile. "I remember thinking my entire life was over. There would never be another boy like Jeremy Silverman."

Joel smiled, too, but there was a tightness in his chest, and his heart was thumping, and he realized he was feeling Adam's loss like it was his own. That pain of something you called love even when you knew it wasn't, then it went away and you weren't sure what to do next. He had felt it—or something like it—once or twice. "Did your mother know?" he heard himself ask, and it surprised him, but he couldn't take it back now. After hearing about the secrets Susan kept from him about Adam's behavior, Joel suspected she knew about everything.

"About Jeremy?" Adam laughed. "God, no. I think Amy did."

"What did I know?" she asked as she came in from the kitchen, drying her hands.

"That I wanted Jeremy Silverman to be my boyfriend," Adam said, and that made his sister laugh. Joel blinked at her.

"Yeah, you were pretty messed up when the Silvermans moved away," she said, and sat next to him on the floor. She opened her shoebox and searched for her own embarrassing memories.

Joel had never felt so disconnected from Adam as he felt then, knowing he should be taking the necessary steps that would bring them closer. He needed Adam to help him navigate the world as an out gay man. He had Kent, true, but he had always imagined, when he finally did announce himself to his son, that it would form the bond they had never had before, throughout Adam's childhood and beyond. In just one night, he had learned of two very significant moments in his son's life he missed out on, and Joel could only guess he'd been traveling, like always. When he was away, he was another person, and he liked that person, preferred it over the dour, crabbed person he was when he was at home, always concerned with how he came across, always on his guard so that no one would ever suspect he had sex with men.

Susan never filled him in on anything he missed, either, whether for good or for bad. And he never missed the important things: he was present when Amy became bat mitzvah and when Adam became bar mitzvah, he watched them both graduate high school, he saw them both off on their trips—Amy to Israel and Adam to Europe—and was there to receive them when they returned. When they left for college, he helped them load the car and he drove them. So perhaps he hadn't missed as much as he thought, but somehow, with these boxes opened and these photographs handed around, it seemed he had missed the things that carried all the weight. It felt like Susan was pointing at him from beyond the grave and laughing, telling him that this was how she got him back for the secrets and the infidelity—this: showing him all the things he had chosen to miss and making it clear that he could never have them back again.

"Dad?" Amy leaned in. "You okay?"

He turned to her and she was blurred, out of focus. He was crying, and he laughed. "I'm fine," he said, and wiped his eyes.

Amy was not convinced. Adam looked back and forth between them.

"Really," Joel said. "I'm fine. It's just—this is a lot." He waved his hands at all the boxes, the photographs, the memories that weren't his own. At everything. He wanted to cry again, harder. He wanted them to leave so he could sit in the dark and wail, but he didn't know how to ask them to go without seeming rude. So he smiled. "I'm fine, though."

"Don't you have a box of your own, Grandpa?" Ethan asked, innocently.

"I do," Joel said, and welcomed the change of subject. And he did, but he'd left his where it was, at the back on the top self in the closet he'd shared with Susan. "But there's nothing in it I haven't already seen." That may have been the case, but the truth was Joel was afraid to open his box, for fear of what he might find: receipts from adult bookstores, slips of paper with the phone numbers of the men he'd met and had sex with, unused condoms she might have found in his jacket pockets. He'd always taken time and extra steps to be as careful as possible, but what if he'd missed something and she'd found it? And what if she'd collected it all in that box for him to find now? "Remember, I was right alongside your grandmother for everything." He dabbed at his eyes again as fresh tears flowed.

"Maybe we should head out," Amy suggested to Adam, and Joel pretended to talk them out of going—he was fine... it was still early... didn't they want to finish going through their boxes? But he wanted them to go. He was exhausted from all the mental preparation he'd done in advance of coming out, then changing course at the last minute had left him feeling like he'd trained years for a marathon only to quit before the starter gun. He wanted to sit in the dark and drink wine, he wanted to cry and feel inadequate where no one would see him.

"Yeah," Adam agreed.

They gathered their photos and albums into the respective boxes and carried them outside to their cars. Joel protested, but half-heartedly. Ethan asked if he could drive home, and Joel was grateful for the subject change. "Let him drive, Amy," Joel said, though it was really none of his business.

"I'll go slow," Ethan promised, his hand held out, his tone entreating.

Amy took a moment to consider it as moths swooped in the air around them all, attacking the lights inside the carport. Her buzz was intact, so she relented. "What the fuck," she said, and dropped the keys into her son's hand.

"Yes!" Ethan pumped his fist.

Amy asked Joel, "Do you need anything before we go?"

He shook his head as he regarded them, his grown children. They were both out of place here in the house where they'd been children, and perfectly at place, like it had grown to accommodate them, or they'd not grown so much that they no longer fit. "I have wine," he said, and held up his glass as proof.

She frowned, but moved in to hug him. "I feel bad leaving you alone."

"It's been a long day," Joel said as they pulled apart. It was a shitty, generic explanation for pretty much anything when someone didn't want to say what was really wrong. And what could he say? *Yeah, kids, before you go, I wanted to tell you that I'm gay and that I knew I was gay before you guys were born, then I had sex with men whose names and faces I can't even remember for the entire time I was married to your mother. But, I'm fine, I promise...*

"Well, call if you need anything," she said, and climbed into the passenger seat of her own car. "Do *not* give me a heart attack," she said just before the door closed and Ethan backed out of the driveway.

"Hey, I think I'll come by tomorrow and take a look at the garden in the daylight," Adam said when he and Joel were alone. "The more I think about it, the more I think all it needs is some attention and it'll be back in shape before fall."

"I think your mother would like that," Joel said.

Then Adam left and he was alone. He went inside, poured himself another glass of wine, and sat in the dark, staring out at Susan's decaying garden. The next thing he knew, he was crying, and his phone rang. Kent. He composed himself as quickly as he could and answered. "Hello. I was just wondering if I should call you." He tried to laugh, but it sounded like a croak.

"I was getting ready for bed, and I found myself wondering—okay, *hoping*—that you had changed your mind again and told them." Kent paused, and even Joel could hear that he was holding his breath. "So, did you?"

Fresh tears flowed. "No," Joel said, and sighed. He wiped his eyes, sniffed. "The first chance I get, and I can't go through with it. And who even knows if there'll be another opportunity." He heard himself and thought he sounded a little overdramatic, so he could only imagine how he must sound to Kent. But he felt like a complete failure: as a husband, as a father, as a man.

Kent chuckled. "There'll be other chances," he said.

Joel sniffed.

"Are you okay?" Kent asked, and his tone changed from mildly chiding to concern.

"I'm fine," Joel told him, but he sniffed again and gave himself away.

"Are you *crying*?" Kent sounded genuinely distressed. "Do you want me to come over?"

"No," Joel said, and began crying in earnest.

"My God... what happened?"

"Nothing. That's just it. *Nothing happened.* They came over, I showed them all the boxes Susan had organized for them and they looked through everything—that's when I was texting you that I might have changed my mind—then we had dinner, then they left." He punctuated his sentence with a sob. "If this is what living openly is like, I'm already failing." He went in search of a tissue, found only a slightly damp dish towel in the kitchen, so he used that to wipe his eyes and nose.

"I'm coming over," Kent announced, and Joel heard the faint jingle of keys.

"It's the middle of the night!" But according to the clock on the stove, it wasn't even ten o'clock.

"I'm on my way." Kent hung up and Joel leaned against the counter. He wondered if he should make coffee.

Kent lived in Virginia-Highland, less than twenty minutes away, so Joel pulled another bottle of wine out, took down a second glass, and switched the front porch light on. He met Kent at the front door. "You didn't have to come," he said.

Kent dismissed the statement with a flick of his wrist. It was almost comical, a man his size making such a girlish gesture. "You're going through a lot right now," he told Joel, "and you need someone around." He aimed a finger at Joel. "That doesn't mean I'm not disappointed in you, because I am. You were set up perfectly to tell your kids and you chickened out, so... yes. I'm disappointed. But you still need someone around. Coming out isn't a walk in the park."

They went inside, to the kitchen. Joel poured wine for them both, then leaned against the counter and stared down at the floor. He saw Kent was wearing slippers and he wanted to laugh, but ended up crying again.

Kent stood next to him and they leaned together. "I'm sorry," Joel said, and wiped at his eyes between sips of his cabernet.

"What for?" Kent asked.

"I don't know." And Joel shrugged. "For being a lousy gay man, I guess."

Kent laughed, threw his head back and truly guffawed. He slipped his arm around Joel's slight shoulders and gave them a squeeze. "That's a good one," he said, and tried to drink his wine, but more laughter shook him.

"I'm being serious," Joel said, and that made Kent laugh more.

"I know you are, and that's what's so funny..."

Joel scowled up at him.

Kent's laughter settled down. He took a sip of his wine and gave Joel's shoulders another squeeze. "Look, no one has it perfected, God knows." He thought about that for a second, then rephrased it. "Well, you'll meet some guys who *think* they have being gay down to an art, and they'll act like it, but trust me—the more you get out there doing it, and the more gay people you meet, you'll realize that we're *all* trying not to be lousy at being gay."

Joel frowned. "I don't know. It's almost like it was easier when I was sneaking around, meeting men in hotels when I was traveling. Being out is... something else entirely. It's a *commitment*. Like, once you say it, that's it. You're stuck and you can't take it back." He shook his head.

It was Kent's turn to frown. "Maybe," he said. "I know it got easier," he finally told Joel. "It was definitely hard, saying the words to the people who needed to hear them, but goddamn, life got so much simpler after I said them."

Joel heaved a huge sigh and leaned into Kent's chest. He tried to remember if they had ever been so close, even that first night they'd tried to hook up; he decided they must not have, or he would remember it. But Kent smelled nice, and that was probably all the wine he'd consumed telling him that, but he didn't care. He felt Kent's lips kiss the top of his head and he froze, but only for half a second before he pressed his face harder into that big, fragrant chest.

And then their hands were everywhere—Joel's and Kent's: in hair, snaking inside shirts, fumbling with buttons and snaps, steadying them both against the counter. Then Kent's on Joel's shoulders, pushing him away and holding him at arm's length. "Are we really doing this?" he asked. Breathless, his cheeks flushed like a virgin's.

"Yes," Joel answered, and his voice was barely audible.

"This is what you want?" Kent asked. He needed to be clear.

Joel nodded.

Kent smiled, drained his wine glass and grabbed Joel's hand, led him out of the kitchen toward the bedroom.

.four.

JOEL WOKE FIRST THE next morning, sat up in bed and groaned at the sight of Kent, asleep on his side, one freckled shoulder exposed. Of course he remembered everything; he hadn't been *that* drunk. He recalled Kent asking if they wanted to go through with it, if it was actually what Joel wanted, and he recalled answering in the affirmative to both. He also remembered thinking he was an idiot, too, and while he was saying yes, he should have been saying no, but he'd been drunk enough that reasoning with his own desire was impossible. And throughout, he'd told himself he should say no, but even then, he didn't make Kent stop, and he didn't stop himself, and now he regretted it. Because now things would get awkward between him and Kent, and knowing how awkward things were going to get with the kids, he'd hoped—planned, even—to keep Kent as a sounding board, a touchstone. Now, that seemed unlikely.

He couldn't get the song "The Morning After" by Maureen McGovern out of his head, either. He stood as carefully as he could and tiptoed to the bathroom where he glared at his reflection in the mirror. "Idiot," he muttered.

Kent was awake when he eased the door open to sneak back into the bedroom. He made a quick move to hide his nakedness and Kent laughed. "So, we're being modest now?" he asked, then stood and turned to face Joel directly.

Joel blushed. "Well, I'm sober now…"

Kent pulled his boxers on, then his shorts. "I see," he said, his tone curt.

If it was said to make Joel feel bad, it worked. "That's not what

I meant," he said, but it was, really. He had been fully prepared to use drunkenness as an excuse, and now here was Kent calling him on it, and he felt exactly the way he should feel: like a heel.

"It's okay," Kent said, and pulled his t-shirt on.

Joel reached back around the bathroom door and grabbed his bathrobe off the hook there. When he was covered, he felt better, more capable of having a discussion about what they had done. "Look... I'm sorry. You asked if it was what I wanted to do and I told you that it was, and we did it. I even thought that we should stop doing it *while we were doing it*, but I didn't say anything, so we kept doing it." He shrugged and stared at the rumpled bed between them.

Kent held up a hand to silence him. "Joel. Relax. It's okay."

"But it's *not*," Joel said, and his voice annoyed him. "It's going to get weird between us and I don't want it to." He moved to run his fingers through his hair, felt that it was sticking up, and instead smoothed it. "You're my friend," he said, and still could not meet Kent's eye. "You're pretty much the only friend I've got, and I need you to stay my friend, because I need you to help me through all this." He waved his arm in an enormous circle, signifying everything about being gay in the entire world, he supposed. "I should have said no, and I know that now—hell, I knew it *then*—but I didn't, and I can't lose the most important friend I've ever had just because I was drunk and emotional and horny. I just can't."

"I said it was okay," Kent said again. He made it sound so simple.

Joel could finally look directly at him across the bed. "But, see, you say that so flippantly. Like, you say it's okay, and it sounds good, but I'm not sure if you mean it's okay or if you're just saying it to shut me up." He realized he was very close to tears, just like last night, and he stopped.

Kent stood where he was, his hands stuffed into the pockets of his cutoffs, rocking back and forth on the balls of his feet. He chuckled, not because he found Joel's hysteria amusing—although it was, he would be able to admit later—but because he felt he needed to make some kind of noise to fill the silence as Joel waited for his response. "I don't know what else to say, Joel," he said. "I said it's okay, and it's okay." He shrugged. "I can't think of any other way to say it."

Joel sighed, and it was like all the air being let out of a balloon. "Okay," he said. Then again: "Okay. Fine."

He would have said more, given some sort of outline of their friendship going forward and suggest ways they could both keep things from becoming strained and awkward between them. It was all on the tip of his tongue, and his mouth was open to speak, when Adam's voice drifted up from downstairs.

"Dad...?"

They froze, eyes wide with shock as they regarded one another across the bed.

Adam! Joel mouthed it to Kent.

Kent was confused. *Who?*

My son!

Why is he here? Kent mouthed back.

I don't know! Then Joel recalled their discussion about Susan's garden the night before, and Adam's suggestion that he come by and see it in daylight to assess its condition and what would be needed to restore it.

Again from downstairs: "Dad...?"

Joel found his voice at last. "Yeah, Adam, hey! I'll be right down!"

"Okay...," from Adam, and there was a certain tone to his voice that neither Joel nor Kent could quite identify. "Say, Dad, is somebody here? There's a van parked in the driveway..."

Kent hid his face in his hands and Joel felt his knees buckle. His insides fluttered and he thought he might vomit. "Fuck," was all Kent said, a whisper really, but Joel had a feeling Adam heard it all the way downstairs in the kitchen.

"Um... I'll be right down, Adam," Joel called again, and though he tried to sound sunny, it sounded anything but.

"What the hell...?" Kent hissed at him from across the room.

"He said he was coming by today to see the garden," Joel said with a shrug. "I didn't think he'd be here first thing in the morning like this…"

Kent ran his fingers through his hair, chewed his lip as he considered their options.

Joel sat on the edge of the bed and held his head in his hands. So much for waiting for a better time to come out to his kids, he supposed. This way was messy and seemed to strip it of any dignity it might have had. Now he was caught red-handed so it seemed more like he'd been actively lying, instead of just willfully omitting.

"What are we going to do?" Kent asked him in that same panicked whisper, never mind that he had considerably less to lose than Joel.

"I don't know…"

"What are we going to say?"

"I don't know…"

"Fuck." And Kent started to pace.

Joel stood and stepped toward the door, pausing so Kent could pace out of his way. He wasn't entirely certain he could feel his legs, but he sensed they were shaking, so he must have felt something. His hands were ice cold and he could actually hear his heart beating.

"Well, what am I supposed to do?"

"I don't know," Joel said, and looked at him finally. Kent was attractive, definitely, and had it been thirty years ago—or twenty, even—he would have been the exact physical type that Joel found himself attracted to: tall, burly, the right personality and just fun to be around. He regretted last night, but he suspected he would do it again if given the chance. Or maybe it was a good thing the way it had lined up—his decision not to come out to the kids and drowning his sorrow afterwards, then Kent coming over to give him a shoulder to cry on, and one thing leading to another until here they were, caught. There was no way out of this, and maybe that was a good thing.

"Fuck," Kent said again.

Joel went downstairs. He found Adam in the kitchen, leaning against the island with his arms crossed. "I didn't think you'd be here so early," he said, and his voice sounded small to him, far away. He went to the cabinet and pulled down the things to make coffee. He needed something to do so he wouldn't have to face Adam and see that look of mistrust he'd caught a glimpse of as he entered the kitchen.

"I said I'd be here today," Adam said. "To look at the garden."

"I know. I remember. I just didn't think it would be so early."

"It's ten o'clock," Adam pointed out.

"Oh."

"I didn't expect you to have company." And Joel thought he detected the briefest hint of a grin when Adam said it.

A number of lies flashed through Joel's brain as he fumbled with the coffeemaker: Kent was here to appraise some furniture Joel was thinking of selling on consignment; he was taking a look at the house because Joel was considering selling; he was giving Joel his price on the set of Barcelona chairs in the study. Any one of them sounded plausible and could have been argued if Adam scoffed at them, and Joel had pretty much decided on the furniture appraisal scenario when Kent stepped into the kitchen, the rattle of his keys signaling his appearance, and eliminated that option.

"Joel, I'm headed out."

"But I was just making coffee," Joel said, and turned from doing so.

Had their lives been a sitcom—one about roommates, perhaps, one gay and the other straight—it would have been that scene where the straight roommate (who, because it was television and nothing whatsoever like actual life, had no earthly idea that his best friend was gay) realizes that his bro has spent the night with someone and that someone is in the bedroom, and the two roommates have met in the kitchen and things are awkward because the straight guy assumes it's a woman in the bedroom but the audience knows better, so the trick steps into the kitchen to say he is on his way out and the audience has burst into raucous laughter and the roommates are just standing there, wide eyed, each waiting for the other to speak first. On television, though, it would cut to a commercial about cleaning products or pregnancy tests or frozen waffles, giving everyone a break from the shock. When the show returned, they would speak and they would talk through their surprise and their confusion and the trick would interject from time to time—he was just trying to go home, after all—and the audience would find the whole thing supremely hilarious.

Joel wished in that long, awkward moment where they all stood there, glancing back and forth from one to the other, that his life was scripted and neat like a sitcom. He would have even taken a soap opera at that point. Adam didn't move from where he stood in front of the island, he just turned a perplexed look to Joel, then turned and threw it at Kent.

He was thinking hard. Then he got it, and the realization seeped through him slowly, the way honey would pour from an upturned jar, and he felt the blood rise into his face. He was embarrassed, yes; he'd caught his father in an awkward situation. He was also pissed, because he'd caught his father with a man, and that meant two things: that his father had spent the night with a man, and that his father was gay.

Adam laughed because he couldn't think of anything to say. He couldn't decide on any one emotion, either. He was furious at them both, he was embarrassed for himself, he was ashamed for Joel, he wondered why he wasn't happy for his father. He felt betrayed and made a fool of at the same time, and he couldn't find the appropriate words to articulate everything he was feeling in those seconds that he stood there, gripping the cold marble top of the island for support, incapable of looking at either of them so he just stared at a spot on the wall to the left of the refrigerator.

"Adam..." Joel's voice came to him as if through a tunnel.

Adam held up a finger, for silence maybe, or for more time to process everything. He wasn't sure. Joel and Kent exchanged a look. No one moved. Nobody said a word. Behind Joel, the coffee maker gurgled and the coffee streamed into the carafe and the kitchen filled with the aroma, but still, no one moved or said a word.

Adam straightened up, took a step back from the island, said, "I can't do this right now." He fished his keys out of his shorts and walked out, left the door open behind him.

Joel and Kent blinked at one another. Kent was the first to speak. "Are you going to go after him?"

"Should I?" Joel asked. He had a feeling he knew the answer, but that didn't help him make up his mind. He could run after Adam, but he doubted it would help.

"I would," Kent said.

So Joel went. "Adam!" he called from the carport. "Wait…"

Adam was in his car. He did not wait. He turned the key and started the engine. Joel moved to stand by the driver's side, his hands in the pockets of his bathrobe. For the briefest instant, he worried that the neighbors might see him in his robe with no slippers, but that concern vanished once Adam spoke to him.

"I said I can't do this right now." He didn't bother to roll the window down, so his voice was muffled.

"Well, you can't just run away, either," Joel pointed out.

Adam laughed again. "You mean I should stay and we should talk about it?"

"That would be a start," Joel said.

Adam thought about that for a second, then he shrugged, rolled the window down, and killed the engine. "Okay, Dad, let's talk about it. I've been gay my entire life. How long have you been gay?"

Joel wasn't prepared for that question. He'd expected something else, he wasn't exactly sure what, but he knew it wasn't that question. "Well… I don't… I mean… I guess my entire life, like you."

Adam nodded, an exaggerated pantomime of processing this new information. "So, what you're saying is, you were gay but you married Mom anyway, and you were gay the entire time you were married to her, and what that means is that you fucked around on her. Got it." He turned the key again, put the car into reverse, and spoke out the window to his father. "See, that's what I thought when I saw a man come downstairs. I thought *Oh my God, Dad's gay and he's fucking this guy.* And then I thought, *Hey, if Dad's gay, that probably means he always knew he was gay, so he probably fucked around with men while he was married to Mom.* And then I thought, *Man, that fucking sucks... so, while my mother was dying, my dad was fucking guys. Because he's gay.*" Adam paused for breath, then added, "And *that* is what I meant when I said I couldn't do this right now. So I'm leaving, Dad. Move."

"I just... I don't want you to be mad at me," Joel said, feebly.

"Really?" Adam rolled his eyes. "Maybe you should have thought about that... oh, I don't know... thirty years ago? Move."

Joel stepped away from the car and Adam backed down the driveway and into the street. He disappeared with a squeal of tires as Kent joined Joel in the carport. "Well?" Kent asked.

"He's pissed," Joel said, and choked back fresh tears.

Kent put a reassuring hand on his shoulder. "It'll be okay."

But would it? Joel wondered. And when?

.five.

"So... Dad's gay," Adam told Amy when he called her. It had been three days since he found out, and he'd spent the entire time wondering how he was going to tell her. He considered an email because he would be able to take his time composing it, choose his words carefully and not have to factor in his emotions. He talked himself out of that in the end because it would just be too detached, and news like that needed to be more personal. So he didn't send a text, either. And he didn't want to deliver it face to face because he was never really good in situations where people reacted in ways he wasn't prepared for, and what if Amy burst into hysterical tears or something? So, he called her.

Amy laughed. "What did he do?" she asked, and it was immediately clear to Adam that she thought he was making a joke. Like the way Ethan and other kids his age called anything they didn't like or agree with "gay." Even the gay kids, it seemed, though she might be wrong. She was pretty out of touch with anyone under the age of thirty these days.

"Well, he fucked some guy," Adam said.

There was noise on Amy's end, a rustle of something. She was distracted, so she wasn't fully absorbing what he was saying.

"I need you to listen to me," he said, and there was more rustling.

"I am listening," she lied.

"I hear noise. You're distracted."

"I'm putting away the groceries," she said, "but I'm listening. You said Dad was gay and I asked what did he do, and you said—" She stopped and so did the rustling. "I'm confused."

It was Adam's turn to laugh. "So am I." He related the entire experience to her, throwing in all his reasons for not telling her until then.

"Bullshit," she said.

"I am not lying," Adam told her. "Call him yourself."

On her end, Amy stood in the middle of the kitchen with a can of black beans in her hand, empty plastic grocery bags littering the counters and the floor. There were steaks and chicken and vegetables to be put away, but groceries were no longer important. She chewed her lip and thought about what she should do next.

"Amy?"

"I'm here," she said, then, "But I have to go."

"Okay, but—"

"I'll call you later." She ended the call, gathered up all the remaining groceries, and threw them into the refrigerator. They would be fine there until she could get to them. All the empty bags she gathered together and stuffed into the garbage can, then she scrawled a quick note to Ethan and stuck it to the refrigerator door with a magnet shaped like a bagel. Susan had given her a whole set—bagel, rugelach, challah, hamantaschen, black and white cookie—but somehow only the bagel had survived.

Then she stood, suddenly unsure of her own intent. Was she going to confront Joel? And how? Her thoughts spun. Her father had sex with a man and Adam had seen them. No, he hadn't *seen* them, but he'd caught them together afterward and that was proof enough. Wasn't it? What if Adam had misunderstood what he saw? She dug her phone out of her pocket, stood for a long moment with her thumb poised over the button that would call her father. What would she say? And what was she hoping to accomplish?

She called Adam back instead. "What?" he asked.

"Meet me at Dad's," she said.

"Yeah... no," he told her.

"Why not?"

"Because I'm not ready yet."

She held the phone away from her ear and scowled hard at it, like he might feel her derision since he couldn't see it. "What does that even mean?" she wanted to know. "Don't you have anything you want to ask him? Or tell him?"

Adam laughed at that. "Oh, there are lots of things I want to tell him, but it would probably be best if no one else was around when I did it."

"I'm just so confused," Amy said, more to herself than to Adam. She leaned against the refrigerator and slid down into a crouch. "Well, how is he doing? Like, I mean, how did he seem the other day? Was he mad at you? Was he freaked out that you knew? What?" Joel hadn't called or texted her, and while she normally wouldn't think anything of it if she didn't hear from him for several days, knowing now what had happened, it was of great concern to her, and she again felt that same sudden need to go to him.

Adam related the entire story to her again, word for word, from the moment he arrived and saw the unfamiliar van sitting in the driveway, to the moment he realized what finding his father in a bathrobe with a disheveled man he'd never met indicated, to the words he and Joel had exchanged in the driveway. "So, that's how he was, Amy," Adam said, and his tone was curt. "He was gay. After thirty-eight years of marriage and two children and years of telling me that I should play football instead of doing theater because the boys might make fun of me… or why not tennis or something like that? Remember how he used to fucking do that? Because I do. And now he's gay and I want to punch him, so maybe it's not such a good idea that I go over there with you."

Amy sighed. "No, I guess not. I'll go by myself."

"Okay…"

"I'll call you after."

"Okay…"

Joel was not surprised to find Amy's car parked on the street when he pulled into the driveway or to find her sitting on the front stoop, her chin resting on her knees. "This is unexpected," he said. He decided against using *surprise*, because that had a nice, delightful sound to it. Seeing her sitting there might be good or it might be bad, and this word conveyed his uncertainty better.

She looked up at him and smiled. She hadn't practiced what she would say to him on the drive over, so she didn't have some witty preamble that would lead them both into the discussion they needed to have. "Yeah," she said.

"I'm guessing you talked to Adam."

Oh, thank God he mentioned it first, she thought. "Yeah."

He nodded and cast his eyes down at the ground between them. There were dandelions growing between the stones in the walk. He would need to take care of those. "Are you mad at me?"

"No," Amy said. She knew that much, at least.

Joel heaved a sigh of relief. "You have no idea how happy that makes me," he said, and his voice cracked with emotion.

Amy stood up, and for a minute they just faced one another. She stared hard at his face, like she expected it might have changed with the revelation that he was gay, that the confession might have cracked some façade and she would see, more or less, a complete stranger in front of her, but Joel was still the same as he'd always been: small, almost waifish, his features elfin. His hair looked grayer, and he needed a trim, and he looked exhausted, but there was nothing monumentally changed about him.

"Let's go in," she said.

Joel poured them wine and they sat in the living room and stared out at the ruins of Susan's garden. "I'm sure you have a million questions…," he said, to prompt her.

She shook her head. "I don't, actually," she told him. "And that's surprising, because I feel like I should, but seriously—what is there to ask? I know what 'gay' means and I can imagine what it must have been like to be gay your entire life and not be able to say or do anything about it." She shrugged, sipped her wine, glanced over at him.

"Well, you can ask me anything."

"I know that. And maybe I will later, but right now I really don't have any questions." She could tell, though, that he was desperate to talk about it. Living with a secret that long and finally having it revealed, by accident or otherwise, had to feel like the weight of the world lifted off his shoulders. "Is there anything you want to tell me?" she asked, and braced herself for a deluge.

Joel took a deep breath and said, without even having to think about it: "I'm sorry." Amy opened her mouth to tell him that an apology wasn't necessary, but he raised a hand to silence her. "Hear me out."

"Okay…"

"Right now you don't have any questions, and that's probably because of the suddenness of this. I mean, it came out of the blue, and I've meant to tell you since your mother got diagnosed, but caring for her took so much time and energy that I just kept putting it off and putting it off, and then she passed, and there was all that to take care of, and I put it off again and again, but all that time I was practicing what I would say to you kids, and how I would say it, and… it was easier said than done." He sat now with his elbows on his knees, perched on the edge of his chair, his wine glass in both hands.

"Did Mom know?" Amy asked. Apparently, she had questions after all.

Joel almost nodded, then caught himself. "I… think so…?" He paused. "I mean, she never said she did, but…" He shrugged. "How could she not have?"

Amy could have spent hours telling him exactly how a woman, married to a man, raising his children, could have no idea what kind of man she had married. Instead, she said, "So, you didn't tell her. Did she ever suspect it? Did she ask?" Okay, so she had more questions. She perched on the edge of her own chair and leaned into the conversation.

Joel shook his head. "She never asked, and I certainly didn't volunteer the information." He seemed to notice the glass of wine in his hands, so he drank deeply of it and smacked his lips and sighed. "I was just always so scared of what might happen if anyone knew. I was afraid of losing my job... I was afraid my parents would disown me... I was afraid of losing you and Adam..." He paused, took a breath, and went on. "It was different back then. I mean, I always knew I was attracted to men, and I fought it because I was always taught that it was wrong."

"But surely you knew gay men, Dad," Amy said. "You worked in academia, for God's sake! Half the professors I had were gay or lesbian."

Joel grinned in spite of himself. Oh, he had known plenty of gay professors throughout his career, and he had slept with most of them. He'd even slept with a few of the ones who claimed they weren't gay, like himself, but he wasn't sure it was the right time to let Amy in on everything. Not yet. "I did, sweetie, but I was just too terrified to come out. Not to mention that I really didn't even know *how* to come out. There wasn't as much information on it back then as there is now. I didn't have any gay friends who could help me through it." He shrugged.

Amy sipped her wine. She felt horrible for him, and she felt bad because she wasn't even sure she was saying the things he needed to hear. Maybe instead of expressing her own confusion, she should just start over and let him tell his story his way, without her interjecting. After all, coming out was a marathon, not a sprint. They wouldn't accomplish everything in one sitting.

"And I hope you understand that I didn't hate your mother," he said, suddenly.

She felt immediately uncomfortable. She'd hoped to avoid bringing his feelings for Susan into the discussion until much, much later. There would be a point, she knew, when it would be impossible not to include them, but she had hoped to cover everything else first. "I never assumed that," she said, just as quickly as he'd blurted it.

"I just want to be clear on that."

"Okay..."

"I may not have felt any physical attraction to her, but I loved and respected her very much. She was a beautiful woman. I want you to know that." He fixed her with one of his sternest looks, the ones he reserved for lectures in her youth, where his eyebrows were both raised and knit at the same time, his eyes so wide she could see the whites around the irises, the corners of his mouth turned down.

Amy nodded. "Yes. I get it."

Joel's face softened then. "I wish your brother was here."

"Yes." She sat straighter in her chair as she thought through what she might say. "I called him before I came over."

"And...?" Joel leaned toward her across the space between them.

"He needs more time," she said, which was true without going into details that might upset Joel or compel him to call Adam. "He'll come around. Just let him work through it on his own, and when he's ready, he'll get in touch." This was all conjecture, but it sounded good and plausible.

Joel did not press her for more details, and she was glad for that. "Yes," he said with a nod. "I'm sure it was upsetting the way he found out."

And there they were again, at the beginning of their conversation. Amy took the opportunity to take their glasses into the kitchen and refill them. While she was there, she collected her thoughts. She realized she had more questions, and she wanted answers to them all. So she asked herself which answers to which questions were most important to her, and she kept coming back to the simplest, most logical one of all of them: if Joel knew he was attracted to men, why had he ever gotten married in the first place?

She also knew that had he not, neither she nor Adam would have been conceived and so simply asking that question seemed pointless. No matter his reasoning, sound or otherwise, he had ignored his basic urges and married a woman and they had conceived children and now here they all were in the wake of that woman's death and their father's coming out, and asking questions that had no answers was a waste of time and energy. She wouldn't do it.

"You okay in there?" Joel called.

"Yes," she called back. "Sorry... Just thinking." She took their wine back into the living room.

"You look upset," he remarked, regarding her over the rim of his wine glass.

"I'm just thinking," she said.

"About...?"

"Mom," she said.

"Oh."

"This is a lot," she said to him, and made a sweeping gesture with one arm to signify the size of his revelation. It encompassed years, that gesture—it went back before she was even born, before Joel and Susan even met, back to whatever forces might have conspired in those days to lead a man to live a life that he knew would leave him unfulfilled. And Amy wasn't an idiot; she just couldn't imagine her father in the arms of a man, kissing him, and when the pictures formed in her mind, she squeezed her eyes shut against them the way she had squeezed her eyes shut against nightmares when she was a girl.

Joel mistook it for something else. Disgust, maybe; he wasn't sure. He exhaled and blinked back tears. "I'm sorry," he said again, and felt like he'd said nothing else to her the entire time they'd been talking.

"You don't have to keep saying that," she said, and smiled a little, so he wouldn't think she was angry.

He just shrugged in response.

"You don't have anything to be sorry about," she said. "It's... it's just one of those things. Like when Adam came out. You and Mom were great about that, and he didn't apologize."

Joel felt the color rise into his face at the mention of Adam's coming out. He remembered it very well, and he remembered it much differently than Amy because there were things that he and Susan had not shared with either of their children.

"Yes...," he said, slowly.

That seemed sufficient to her, since she didn't pursue it and his reticence didn't throw up a red flag. "So... are you seeing anyone?" She asked it in a way that he imagined women asked private things of their girlfriends, almost playfully, like she didn't actually think he would answer her, but hoped he would.

He chuckled. "No. I'm not seeing anyone."

"But, Adam said—" And she caught herself, clamped a hand over her mouth. "Or maybe I misunderstood him..."

"No, no," Joel said. "It's fine. Adam did come over and there was someone here, but... we're not seeing one another. Kent is just a friend." He made a pained face, just for half a second. "He's been helping me through all this, and... well, last night was just... It was a mistake."

Amy nodded. He would open up more as he moved through the process. This was as new to him as it was to her, and though she realized with every second that she had more questions, she kept them all to herself. "I hope I get to meet him soon."

"Oh, you will," Joel said.

They lapsed into silence, sipped their wine, stared out at the ruins of the garden. When her glass was empty, Amy stood. "I guess that's my cue to leave," she said, and Joel went through all the regular requests that she stay a bit longer, or for dinner, or they could go out, but Amy refused. "I need to feed Ethan or he'll have ice cream for dinner and someone will call child services on me." She laughed as she said it, but knowing some of the women she knew, it wasn't entirely out of the question.

"Let's all get together again soon," he suggested, and they hugged, and he held her just a bit tighter and longer than usual. "Thank you," he said. The whole conversation could have been a lot worse.

She pulled out of the hug and saw the dejected look on his face and her heart broke. "Dad... c'mon, don't look so down. This is a whole new chapter for you! It's like starting over as the person you were always supposed to be!"

He considered that and smiled, shrugged. "Maybe…"

"Maybe nothing. Call your friend—what did you say his name was? Call him and you guys go out and have fun." Amy knew she sounded silly, but she pictured him sitting alone in his Barcelona chair, drinking wine and staring out at what was left of his dead wife's garden and wishing he'd done everything in his life differently, and that made her sad. He was gay now—*officially* gay; he should be out having cocktails and laughing and ogling guys young enough to be his son. She worked with several gay men who were close to Joel's age, and knew that was what they did when they went out.

"I'll do that," he said, but he didn't sound encouraged

"Just don't sit here alone," she said. "Call Adam. Go see Aunt Rhoda. Do something."

"I will."

But once Amy was gone, he sat in his chair and did exactly what she'd imagined he would do: he drank wine and he stared out at Susan's garden, and he remembered back to all the times he'd failed Adam as a father, all because he was secretly gay and Adam had come out and Joel had been afraid of something he couldn't quite name, though Susan really stepped up. She joined PFLAG and met other parents of recently out young men and women. She went to hear people speak, she went to seminars, she bought books and subscribed to magazines. She suggested Joel read them, marked their pages with brightly colored Post-It notes, but he avoided them. He saw them on the coffee table in the den, those Post-Its beckoning, and he skirted them, would not look at them. Then they appeared on his bedside table and he hid them under his own books about Faulkner and Shakespeare and James Joyce.

"Have you read that article I marked for you?" Susan would finally ask him, though she knew the answer.

"Not yet," he said, "but I will."

"Just read it now," she said, and stretched across him to pull the *The Advocate* or *Out* from under the pile of books he had placed atop it and open it to the designated article. "It's not going to kill you."

So he pretended to read, skimmed it enough to get the gist of what was being said, then handed the magazine back to her. "There."

"Now was that so goddamned hard, Joel?" she asked, truly upset. "Our son just came out to us. He trusted us enough that he came out to us, the least you can do is read a goddamned article about how to parent a gay child."

The truth was that he *was* extremely proud of Adam. Knowing yourself that well at eighteen—and, what's more, being true to who you were—was commendable. He'd been wracked with doubt and swung between a resigned acceptance and shame that he'd allowed himself to be tempted away from what he was meant to be: a husband to a good woman and a father to children. Choosing homosexuality (because at that age, he had heard it was a choice and since he knew no gays or lesbians and therefore had no one to bounce it off of, he believed it) would not allow him to do that, and so he dated girls and played baseball and golf and tennis, because that was what boys his age did. When he got to college, he saw the boys he might have been and he was both ashamed of them and for them, but even then, he secretly longed to be like them, majoring in theater or music. The girls he dated seemed always to be friends with those boys, so Joel wasn't able to avoid them, and his discomfort around them was interpreted as dislike. Even when he explained himself to those girls and their friends, he made sure to do it in a way that would never lead them to suspect that he was just like the guys he seemed to detest so much.

Adam had wanted to take dance lessons. He'd caught a broadcast of Mikhail Baryshnikov in *The Nutcracker* and begged Joel and Susan to let him enroll. Susan, who had taken ballet herself as a child, was neither for nor against it. When they discussed it, she shrugged. "I ended up not liking it as much as I thought I would," she told Joel. "It looked and sounded a lot better than it really was."

"What was it really, then?" he asked.

"A fat, old witch banging a stick on the floor yelling at everyone because she couldn't do it herself anymore," Susan said. "Maybe Adam will get in and find it's not as cool as Baryshnikov made it look."

Joel suspected it was more than Baryshnikov and some vague coolness factor, so he decided to talk Adam out of it. "How about baseball?" he suggested. "Or tennis?" They were at dinner and Adam refused to look at him from the moment he'd suggested anything other than signing Adam up for ballet classes as soon as possible. Joel could barely breathe around the weight of the shame in his chest. He sounded like his own father.

"Because I don't want to play baseball or tennis," Adam said simply and ate another forkful of meatloaf. "I want to take ballet."

"You're not worried the other boys will make fun of you, though?" Joel asked. To him, it was a legitimate concern. Even at his age, he was terrified of what people would think of him if they learned of the things he did when his wife was out of town.

"I don't worry what other kids think of me," Adam said. "That's what you and Mom always told me to do."

Joel and Susan exchanged a look across the table, but neither of them could dispute what their son was saying. They'd always told both their children to ignore what others said about them and just be themselves. Now Adam wanted to be a ballet dancer, and Joel was saying he couldn't.

Adam didn't speak to him for six months.

When he mentioned an interest in theater in his early teens, and hinted that he wanted to enroll in some classes taught by a local theater group, it was much the same conversation. Joel suggested painting or sculpture—again, something that he wouldn't be mercilessly teased about. Just something, anything else. Adam put up less of a fight that time, but it was the last time he expressed an interest in anything to his parents.

"You're too hard on him," Susan told Joel.

"I don't want him to be made fun of," Joel pointed out. "That's being hard on him?"

She changed the subject. "We let Amy take dance lessons."

"That was four years ago. And Amy's a girl."

That won a laugh from Susan. "God, that's the oldest and cheapest excuse in the book. Is Baryshnikov a girl? And there are plenty of very successful men on Broadway. You think their parents were worried what other kids would say about them?"

Joel had no response. He wasn't refusing to allow Adam to take dance or acting lessons to protect Adam's feelings and he knew that very well. He was protecting himself from the way he would react watching his son experience things in life that he never would. And later, when Adam came out to them at seventeen, the week after he'd graduated high school, Joel realized it was his own shame, and on top of that, a jealousy so acute it rendered him speechless. So, instead of working through why he felt that way about that, he pushed it aside and did everything his own father had done short of calling Adam a sissy. If Adam expressed an interest in anything artistic, Joel suggested sports, or, at the least, academia or science or medicine. "He could go to law school," Joel told Susan.

"He doesn't want to go to law school," Susan reminded him.

"I just don't want him to be made fun of."

Susan fixed him with a stern look. "You don't want kids to make fun of Adam, or you don't want people to make fun of you because your son is gay?"

Joel did not reply.

Now he sat alone and drank his wine and understood why Adam had responded the way he had. Not because Joel was gay, or because he'd found Joel with Kent; he was pretty sure neither of those things really mattered that much to Adam. No, what had upset Adam so much was that Joel never allowed him to express himself the way he wanted, but now expected to be afforded that same respect, and Adam was having none of it.

He thought of calling Adam, decided against it. Whatever discussion they had needed to be face to face, not over a phone. He called Rhoda and got her voice mail, but didn't feel like leaving her a message about it. He would call her back some other time.

"You mean to tell me," Rhoda asked through the phone when he finally did reach her, and her voice was so strident that Joel had to hold it away from his ear, "that he's mad at you because you're gay?" It had been three days since Adam found Joel and Kent together.

"Basically," Joel replied.

"Well, that's ridiculous." Rhoda spat it. "He's gay himself!"

Joel could understand her reasoning, but he knew there was more to this, he just didn't want to go into it, not over the phone, so he made a sound that could have been interpreted as agreement or uncertainty.

"Well, what then?" Rhoda asked.

So, Joel told her. In one rush of breath, he explained what it meant when he said he had always been gay, even before he met and married Susan and had children. "It means I was having sex with men," he said. "Outside of my marriage, for the entire time that I was married, and even when I was engaged to Susan. And that means I was unfaithful. And that's a large part of why Adam is so upset with me. Because I cheated on his mother, and *now*, not even a year after her death, I'm out of the closet and he thinks it's deliberately disrespectful to Susan's memory." He paused for breath, thought *And I'm not entirely sure I don't agree with him...*

Rhoda was silent for a long moment.

"You still there?" Joel asked into the silence. "Rho?"

"I'm here," she said.

"Okay, good." Then he felt a quick stab of panic. "Are you mad?"

"No," she said. Then again: "No." More silence, and then she said, "I'm just thinking."

"I understand that," he said, and gave a nervous titter of a laugh. "It's a lot to take in all at once, and unexpected like that." He was rambling and he knew it, just throwing words at the silence between them. It was just over two weeks since he'd come out to her, and he still wasn't certain where she stood, other than she wasn't mad at him and she didn't hate him and she'd told him to go make himself happy. "I'll let you go, then."

"Okay, yes," Rhoda said. "I'll call you back later."

When she said "later," Joel figured a couple of hours. Maybe she had an errand to run, groceries or banking, and she would call him back when it was finished. And when she didn't call him back, he got worried, and he started imagining the worse—she never wanted to speak to him again, or she'd called Adam and given him hell about the way he was treating Joel—and eventually, he was consumed with anxiety. He considered calling her, but decided against it. If she was upset, he didn't want to upset her any more.

Kent had stopped answering his calls, and when Joel left a message, he didn't get a call back. He'd never felt so alone in his adult life as he did waiting for Rhoda to call him "later," as she had said.

She called him back three days later, and Joel couldn't recall the last time he'd felt such relief. "I was starting to think you'd forgotten me," he said, and laughed.

Rhoda did not laugh. "I've been thinking," she said, simply.

Joel felt his stomach lurch.

"I've been thinking," she said again, "and you need to know this." Then she proceeded to tell him that he didn't need to waste his time and energy castigating himself over his infidelity because she knew for a fact that Susan had not sat around the house bemoaning her situation.

Joel listened, even though what he was hearing made little sense to him. When Rhoda had finished, he asked, "So... what are you saying?"

"What do you mean what am I saying?" Rhoda snapped. "I'm telling you not to beat yourself up because you think you did Susan wrong all those years, Joel. I'm telling you that it doesn't matter that you had sex with men outside of your marriage, because Susan was doing it, too."

Joel almost dropped his phone.

"She wasn't an idiot, Joel," Rhoda told him.

"There was no way she could have known I was gay," he said, more to himself than to Rhoda. Hadn't he been careful and covered his tracks and double checked that he left no trail? His mind raced as he tried to remember where he slipped up or what he had done wrong or said that might have clued her in.

"I'm not saying she knew," Rhoda pointed out. "I'm just saying that whether she suspected it or not, she was not as affected by what you were doing as you may think."

"I can't believe this," Joel said, and felt a sharp flare of anger at his sister.

"Fine," Rhoda said. "Don't believe me. I'll talk to you later, then." Joel knew how she was about getting involved in situations that didn't really affect her one way or the other. She was nosy, but kept drama at arm's length. He also knew how she had always looked out for him, so it made sense that she would give him this information if it would alleviate some of his own anxiety about coming out.

Still, the mere thought that Susan might have gone outside their marriage was like a kick in the head. He tried to imagine it in order to process it, but he couldn't. When would she have had the time, and with whom would she have done it? He wracked his brain for the answers, but ended up standing in the den and staring out at the remains of her garden, confused but relieved in some small way, too.

He called Kent again, ignored the knot of dread in his stomach as it rang and rang. He had just convinced himself that Kent wasn't going to answer, didn't want to talk to him either, and he was about to end the call when Kent finally picked up.

"Hey," he said.

"Hey."

Then silence.

Joel took a deep breath and said, "I'm sitting alone in the dark, drinking wine, and I'm miserable, and my daughter suggested I should call you to go out and meet people and have fun." He chuckled. "So... here I am." There was a long silence from Kent's end, and

Joel panicked. "Are you there? Hello?" He pulled the phone away from his ear, checked that the call hadn't disconnected.

"I'm here," Kent said at last. Joel waited for more, but nothing came.

"Okay, good. Look, Kent... I know I'm probably the last person in the world you want to hear from right now, but I don't have anyone else to call. I don't know any other gay people, and if I'm going to do this right, I need someone who can help me through it. I need to meet people and go do things, but I don't know where to go to do either, and I'm lonely and miserable right now, and my daughter doesn't know how to deal with me now that I'm gay, and Adam doesn't want to have anything to do with me, so please... help me do this the right way. Please..."

More silence from Kent, but Joel could hear him breathing.

"What time is it?" Kent finally asked.

Joel consulted his watch. "It's almost eight o'clock." He realized he hadn't eaten. "Maybe we can have dinner and go for drinks after...?"

Kent heaved an enormous sigh of resignation, but he said, "Okay. Give me thirty minutes to get ready and get dressed, then... I guess I'll come pick you up, since you've already started drinking."

"Great idea!" Joel declared, and he was so relieved he thought he might cry. "I'll be ready."

They hung up and he went to take a shower. Then he worried over what he should wear, and if he should wear cologne, and if he did were the colognes he had to choose from outdated? He had so much to learn, and he found himself thinking back to Adam at eighteen, cheeks flushed with the risk he was taking as he announced himself to his parents. Joel wondered if, later that night when he went out with friends, Adam had worried over which shirt to wear, or whether he should wear shorts or jeans, cologne or not.

In the end he settled for no cologne, and when Kent arrived, he was still checking his appearance in the mirror in the foyer.

"You look fine," Kent told him, and rolled his eyes.

"Okay," Joel said, but he didn't feel okay.

"We're going to eat, then we're going to a gay bar," Kent explained. "We're not going to have an audience with the Queen. Relax."

Joel tried to relax, but it was difficult.

.six.

AMY WAS WORRIED ABOUT Joel.

It had been a month since he'd come out—or, rather, since what would have to pass for coming out—and she didn't hear from him as often as she had. Before, he would call or text regularly, just to check in. Now, she was the one who had to reach out first, and if he answered, he seemed rushed. "I'm fine, I'm fine," he said. "How are you? Good?" If she called at night, she often got his answering machine (he still had a land line and an answering machine), and if she texted, she might not get a response until the next morning.

At work, she told her coworker about it. They were both between clients and had rushed down the street from the salon for a quick bowl of ramen. "Wait," Finn said, and held up a hand to silence her halfway through her explanation of her concerns. "Your dad is gay?"

Amy nodded.

"Like... *gay* gay?"

"Is there some other kind of gay I don't know about?" she asked, and scowled. "Yes, that kind of gay. The same kind of gay as you." She said it and immediately wished she could take it back. "Only a lot less thirsty, I hope," she added. Finn was unabashedly promiscuous, so she hoped her father wasn't the same kind of gay. He had moved to Atlanta from a small town in east Tennessee and changed his name from Delbert (he was a Junior, he'd explained once after shots of tequila) or something. He loved to share ribald stories of his nights out and he was the closest thing to a friend Amy had at work, since their stations were next to one another.

He threw her a look through his sunglasses, which were pink and encrusted with rhinestones, and twice the size of his face. "Bitch."

"Just forget it," she said and returned her attention to her ramen.

Finn ignored that. "But why are you worried about him?"

Amy sighed. "Because he's new to it all," she said, "and I want him to be happy, but he doesn't seem very happy when I see him, and I'm afraid he's depressed." She paused to fish a shrimp out of her bowl. "Or I'm afraid he's not going to know how to protect himself, and there are lots of dishonest people out there, and I've heard of guys who tell people they're undetectable and on PrEP, but they aren't, and it scares me."

"Girl, you sound like his mother instead of his daughter," Finn pointed out.

She considered it and realized he was right. "Well, what should I do?" she wanted to know.

"Nothing," Finn said. "It's his life."

Amy gave a derisive bark of laughter. "Yeah, no. He's my dad. I can't just do nothing."

"Okay," he said. He was nodding and swirling his chopsticks in his bowl. Amy knew what he meant with that *okay*: he was checking out of the conversation, which was probably the exact same thing she would do if someone brought up a subject and asked for advice, then not liked the advice she gave them. Actually, Adam did that a lot, and this was her response every single time.

"Fine," she said, and threw her hands out in a gesture of surrender. "Fine. I'll do nothing. But it will drive me crazy and you'll just have to listen to me more. Is that what you want?"

He slid his sunglasses down the bridge of his nose and regarded her over the rhinestones. "Just so I understand everything you're telling me here," he said, and fluttered the fingers on one hand as he said it. "Your dad knew he was gay from, like, birth… but it was the good ol' days, so he couldn't live his truth, and he dated girls anyway… and he met your mother and they got married, and according to you he had sex with other men throughout the marriage—like, throughout the 1980s and 1990s—and your mother passed away and now he's out and proud and living his best life, and *now* you're afraid he's going to make a poor choice, or catch something, or get his heart broken, or whatever…" Again with the fluttering of the fingers. "Is that what I'm hearing? Because that's what I'm getting, and I just have to ask—girl, did you not think he was at risk of catching all that shit for thirty years? Through the AIDS crisis and everything? And getting his heart broken?"

Hearing it stated that way, Amy felt like she might be overreacting. Joel was probably fine, happy for once in his life, and doing all the things that happy people did. Maybe he'd met someone and just wasn't sure how to introduce him to the family. Maybe he was out for cocktails with the boys every night after work, ogling younger men, or enjoying a drag show. She needed to stop worrying.

That night, though, she called Adam. "Have you heard from Dad?"

"No," he said, simply.

"Are you guys still not talking, then?"

"Nope. I gotta go, you can fuss at me later. I got a new job and I have to be up at the crack of dawn."

"A *job*? That's great!" And she started firing questions at him. Where was he working? What was he doing? Did he like it? What did it pay?

Adam answered them all, then heaved a huge sigh and said, "Really, Amy. I need to go to bed."

"Okay, fine. Bye." She sat stunned for a moment after the call ended. So, apparently everyone had something going on in their lives but her. Even Ethan had slipped up and mentioned the name of a girl at school to her the other day. Amy's ears perked up immediately. "Who's Leah?"

A noncommittal shrug from her son. "She's just a girl."

"Well, you brought her up, so…"

"We were talking. She's my lab partner for biology." Another shrug, a swipe of his hand across his bangs.

"She sounds nice."

Ethan looked at her, his eyes narrowed with confusion. "I said her name, Mom. How does that make her sound 'nice?'"

It was Amy's turn to shrug. "I like the name Leah," she said. "It's a nice name. She sounds nice. What? You're telling me she's not nice? Fine. Don't hang out with her." She stepped away before she said something else he could dissect and declare idiotic, yanked open a cabinet and pretended to search for something.

"She's my lab partner," he reminded her. "We don't hang out." He punctuated the statement with air quotes. "I hang out with Isaac and you never took this kind of interest when I said his name."

"Fine," she said, and took down a jar of peanut butter, which she opened and ate with a spoon. Ethan pored over his literature textbook.

"Stop staring," he said to her, over his shoulder.

"I'm not staring."

"I can feel your eyes on my back," he said, and turned. "What?"

"You need a haircut." It was her go-to statement any time she didn't have anything else to say, but what she'd been wondering was whether he was right, and he had zero interest in this Leah who was his biology lab partner, and did that mean her son was gay, because that meant all the men in her family were gay, and she was wondering what the odds were of something like that happening. Then she wondered whether he was just saying he had no interest in this girl to put her off the scent. But what if she should have taken more of an interest in Isaac when they were growing up and having sleep overs?

"No, I don't," he said, and immediately changed the subject. "How's Grandpa?"

Amy put the peanut butter away and shrugged. "I haven't heard from him."

Ethan frowned. "Should we go check on him?"

Honestly, Amy had considered that, but talked herself out of it. She didn't want to interrupt anything the way Adam had. Not because she feared knowing her father was a sexual creature, or seeing the evidence of his homosexuality like that, but because she didn't trust how she would react if confronted with it.

Instead, she called Rhoda, who flew into a panic when she asked if her aunt had heard from Joel. "Oh, my God, something's wrong!"

"No, no... Aunt Rhoda—"

"I'm hanging up so I can call your father," Rhoda said. "Something's wrong. Oh, my God." Then she was gone and Amy was left mildly bewildered and wondered if the penchant for overreacting was a trait all the Benjamins shared.

Rhoda didn't call her back that night and Amy lay awake worried that something was, in fact, the matter and berating herself for not being proactive in the situation and going to see how Joel was. Scenarios played behind her eyes when she closed them and tried to sleep—Joel so depressed that he turned to drinking, lost his job, the house and everything else; Joel lonely, scouring the dating and hookup apps Adam and Finn often mentioned, in search of any form of human contact; Joel putting the house on the market, quitting his job, and moving to Palm Springs. By the time she decided to take something to help her sleep, it was already too late, so she got up and cleaned house. She was folding laundry and watching an infomercial when Ethan shuffled in, rumpled from sleep, squinting at her as if trying to determine whether she was or wasn't his mother.

"Have you been up all night?" he wanted to know.

"What time is it?" she asked.

"It's almost seven o'clock..."

"Then, yes." She pointed to a pile of folded laundry. "Take that upstairs with you when you go."

At work, she was exhausted and coffee didn't help. Finn wanted to share all the details about the leather daddy he'd hooked up with the night before, but she only half listened. She was still imagining catastrophe and despair, all of it heightened by her lack of sleep and the caffeine she'd ingested to counteract it. Then she heard Finn say, "Isn't that your husband?" She looked at him, confused. She didn't have a husband, she was about to tell him, but his eyes were on the door and he was smiling, and she turned and there was Mike Cohen, grinning sheepishly and running his fingers through his hair.

My God... Ethan looks just like him, she thought, but she said, "What are you doing here?" and even though she didn't mean it rudely, it came out that way, because Finn gave her a playful slap on the arm.

"Well... I was thinking I'd get a haircut," Mike said, still grinning, and his dimples showed.

"I have an opening," Finn said, which was a lie, but Amy decided to let him run with it.

"Finn can take you," she told Mike.

He pretended to consider it, rocked back and forth on the balls of his feet and chewed his lip. "I appreciate it, but is there any way you could do it?" he asked Amy. "I don't mind waiting. I've been going to this guy—it's supposed to be one of those upscale barber shops that harken back to the good ol' days of men's grooming, but he can't ever seem to get it right..." And to prove it, he ran his fingers through his hair again.

The truth was Amy's client had canceled, so she did have time. "Sure, whatever. Let's get you shampooed."

He wanted to chat as she settled him over the shampoo bowl and wet his hair. "So, how've you been?"

Amy shrugged. "A lot's going on."

"I heard that."

Hearing that triggered something inside her and she was instantly mad at him, like she'd been mad at him during and after the divorce when she'd vowed to herself to never have any contact with him outside of meetings to drop off or pick up Ethan, or the telephone conversations necessary to plan and coordinate those. Now here she was, washing his hair and he was smiling and chatting her up like he was just another one of her clients. And the worst part of it was she wasn't exactly certain who she was mad at—Mike or herself.

"How's... what's her name? Tiffany?"

"Stephanie," he corrected her.

"Oh." She knew the correct name but pretended to always get it wrong. She felt it conveyed her contempt for the woman who had slept with her husband knowing he was married and irritated Mike just enough so that he never fully forgot his role in it. Amy assigned a new name—"cheerleader names" she called them to Adam; names like Tiffany or Courtney or Amber—any time she spoke of the woman, and Mike patiently corrected her each time. Adam always rolled his eyes and reminded her that cheerleaders named Amy weren't unheard of, and she ignored him and his logic.

"She moved out," he said, and Amy had to will herself not to betray her surprise. "About a month ago."

"Oh." She wondered if she should add something, some condolence. *I'm sorry for your loss* was on the tip of her tongue, because she was still bitter about it and she had made her peace with that long ago, but Mike spoke first.

"How's your dad?"

Amy turned scarlet, grateful that she was behind him and his eyes were closed. She knew immediately that Ethan had told him; they had a great relationship, so Ethan told Mike everything. And she also understood that Mike had asked only because she had accidentally-on-purpose forgotten his girlfriend's (his *ex*-girlfriend now, she reminded herself) name and he wanted her to be clear that he could be just as petty as she could.

"He's... fine," she said, and rinsed him.

"You hesitated," Mike pointed out.

"Yeah, well..."

Back at her station, she draped him with a cape and tried to organize her thoughts about Joel. Rhoda still hadn't called back, so she was still imagining the worst, and now here was Mike asking, not that he really cared—or maybe he did, and Amy was just being an asshole because it was her ex-husband—and he was the last person she wanted to discuss it with.

"Ethan told me," he said, and he lowered his voice, so she was thankful for that at least.

"I figured," she said and she ran a comb through his wet hair.

"And I'm serious—how's he doing?"

Amy considered that while she combed his hair into the previous cut. Sometimes it was easy to believe Mike Cohen was a nice guy and he really cared—and maybe he did actually want to know how Joel was doing; they'd always gotten along when she and Mike were married. So she could tell him the truth: that Joel seemed depressed last time she'd seen him and she hadn't heard from him in a while and she was worried. She was also worried about a man who repressed his sexuality for his entire life suddenly being unleashed into a world where he could, at long last, do everything he'd had to sneak around to do before. She was worried that while that sounded great, and she should support her father one hundred percent—and she did, really; she wanted him to be fulfilled and happy—that he wouldn't be careful, that he might not even know how to be careful. She could have told him all of that, and he would have listened and cared, but she remembered that he'd fucked around on her with one of his hygienists, a vapid girl with a cheerleader name who had only just achieved the legal drinking age, so she just said, "He's doing great. You know Dad."

Mike grunted. Maybe it meant he accepted her response, maybe it didn't.

"You want to keep the same cut?" she asked.

"I just want it short," he replied. "I don't have a lot of time to style it in the morning, and it's just longer than I like it. It was St—" He caught himself and Amy saw his cheeks flush. "I tried something new and it's just not for me."

It was her turn to grunt. "How short?"

"As short as you can make it."

"Well, I can shave it…"

Mike laughed. "Just use scissors."

She set to work, hoping to finish quickly and get him out of her chair before her mood worsened. Exhaustion had been enough, and now here she was, cutting her ex-husband's hair, chatting like they were old pals.

"How's Adam?" he asked, after a few minutes.

Amy shrugged. "He's good, I guess. He never really changes." Except now he was probably never going to speak to their father again, but she left that part out. She really didn't want to get into a question and answer period with Mike. Why had she even agreed to cut his fucking hair? Why didn't she just walk away, the way she always imagined herself doing in all her fantasies of him returning to her with his tail between his legs after his fling with Millennial Barbie went up in smoke. And suddenly she burned to know why Tiffany/Chelsea/Kelsey/Kayla had left. Had he kicked her out, exhausted finally by her youth and immaturity, or had she decided an older man—and her boss, nonetheless—just wasn't all it was cracked up to be. Mike was forty now, and she remembered herself in her early twenties—she never would have considered a man almost twice her age.

They'd met during Amy's sophomore year at the University of Michigan.

Amy's roommate her freshman year was a lesbian who called herself Mish because she found the name Michelle unsuitable. Mish had a nose ring and tattoos and she wore combat boots and shopped for clothes at The Salvation Army. Amy was mystified and mistakenly interpreted that as attraction. Certain that she, too, was a lesbian, Amy embarked on what she was certain was the briefest phase in the life of any post-adolescent unsure of what to do with so much freedom. She didn't chart her course, and it was clumsy, but she managed to convince Mish that she was a lesbian and Mish believed her until they started kissing. "I thought you said you've done this before," she grumbled to Amy, who insisted that she had. Mish was skeptical, and by the time they were undressing, Amy was close to tears and apologizing.

"I thought I could do this," she sobbed. "But I can't. I thought I was…but I'm not."

Mish stormed out and filed a request for another roommate the next day. Amy never saw her again, but she stayed friends with Cary ("Like Grant," he told people, "only not in the closet."), who she met through Mish and never believed for a second that Amy was a lesbian. It was through Cary that she met Mike Cohen.

Mike's roommate was gay and dating Cary and the two of them had ended up ersatz chaperones to a gay bar one evening.

"Come here often?" Mike asked her as they stood together and watched the boys gyrating on the dance floor to a Britney Spears song Amy hated but somehow knew all the words to.

"Unfortunately, I'm not even remotely this cool," Amy confessed. "You?" She knew he wasn't gay. How she knew, she couldn't say, she just knew. She only suspected that he might be Jewish, but she was certain he was straight.

"Every weekend, pretty much."

They laughed. Later, they escaped the gay bar and went for coffee. When he didn't come on to her, she decided he was the man she would marry and asked for his phone number. They started dating with no fanfare. She called home and Susan wanted to know if she'd met anyone. "Yeah, I'm seeing this guy," she said.

"And?" Susan asked.

"And what?"

"And everything else, what the hell do you think I mean?"

Amy had hoped to avoid this, because she knew if she spoke his name to Susan—to either parent, really; Joel was just as bad— her mother would want to meet Mike, and that would mean arranging a trip home to Georgia, and Amy had chosen the University of Michigan for two reasons: one, to avoid having to introduce every boy she dated to her parents and have them start planning a wedding, and two, because she wanted to live somewhere, even for a brief time, that had actual seasons. So she told Susan about Mike: he was from Miami, he was the youngest of four boys, he was studying to be a dentist.

"A dentist!" Susan crowed with delight, and Amy was grateful for the hundreds of miles of telephone wire separating them.

"We're just dating, Mom," she said.

"Well, everyone has to start somewhere," Susan replied.

She finished with Mike as fast as she could and still give him a decent cut, and he seemed pleased as he inspected the back and sides with a hand mirror. "Nice," he said. "Thanks, Amy. I mean that."

Hearing her name come out of his mouth like that broke something in her. She felt as if she were waking from one of those dreams where she couldn't move, and even though she knew it was a dream, she couldn't make herself wake up until it had run its course. "You're welcome," she said, curtly, and removed the cape from around his neck. "I'll take you up front to pay."

He stood where he was, though, preening and posing in the mirror. "You think I should cover my gray?" he asked her.

"Do you want to cover your gray?" She hoped he didn't mean he wanted to start right then. She wanted to get away from him. Could he not see that?

He turned his head this way and that. "I dunno. Don't you think it makes me look distinguished?"

Amy threw him a look. "You're asking me?"

Mike grinned. "You're the professional."

She rolled her eyes and turned away from him. "I think you can make that decision yourself. Or ask What's-Her-Name." She realized what she'd said the instant the words were out of her mouth and for just a second she regretted them. It was a low blow, and she didn't want to be that kind of ex-wife—the disgruntled harridan who always took cheap shots. Then again, she didn't want to be the kind of woman whose ex-husband showed up out of the blue where she worked to get his hair cut, as if his girlfriend leaving gave him permission to do so.

Amy didn't apologize, and she didn't turn to see Mike's reaction. She said, "Finn will cash you out. I need to go get ready for my next client," and disappeared into the back of the salon.

"So, why didn't you tell me your dad broke up with Brittany?" she asked Ethan later, over dinner. She hadn't felt like cooking, so she let him pick and he chose Ethiopian.

He was scooping up *kitfo* and stopped, looked at her through his bangs, which she still wanted to cut but he wouldn't let her near his head. "You mean Stephanie?"

Amy waved a hand. "Whatever, yeah."

"Who told you?"

"Your father did," she told him, and chewed her *injera*, which she always found slightly weird because it was gray, but it didn't taste gray, and for that she was glad.

Ethan arched a brow. "You guys are friends now?" Last thing he knew, his parents only spoke when they absolutely had to, usually when he made a request that required their participation in a civil discussion.

"No!" Amy actually shuddered at the suggestion. "He came by the salon. I cut his hair and he told me about—" She made a gesture that was both dismissive and suggestive of Mike's ex-girlfriend.

"Stephanie," Ethan said. He scooped his *kitfo* into his mouth and chewed. "But, yeah. She left a while ago, like..." He paused to count back. "...Six or seven months ago? Something like that."

"Oh." For some reason, Amy was surprised by that news. Mike said it had been a month and it seemed he was taking advantage of being freed from the shackles of their relationship by getting a new haircut and considering covering his gray. She chewed her food and considered the implications. No, she definitely would not allow herself to be wooed by her ex-husband into thinking he was ready to repent for what he had done. It would be a cold day in Hell before she entertained that.

"You okay?" Ethan asked. "Did we get it too spicy?" He liked to pile on the optional *awaze* they gave you, and Amy had to regularly stay his hand.

"No, no. It's not that..."

"What, then? You got a funny look on your face."

She shook her head. "It's nothing."

He shrugged, and she knew that would be the end of it, because that was how teenagers ended conversations they didn't want to have in the first place. Then he asked, "So why haven't you dated anyone since you and Dad got divorced?"

Amy jerked as if he'd slapped her. "Well, that came out of nowhere, huh?" She tried to laugh, but it sounded more like a wheeze.

"Seriously, though." Ethan was not going to let her off the hook that easily. "Dad's dated a—" He caught himself, reconsidered what he almost said, then continued. "—A few women, but you've gone celibate or something."

She arched one brow and cocked her head to one side. "My son is talking to me about celibacy? Really?" She would do anything to get out of this conversation, but seeing as that wasn't going to happen, and she would have to see her way through to the end of it, she decided she would at least try to stall it as much as she could. "Next, you'll be advising me on birth control, or Brazilian waxing."

He rolled his eyes. "It's the twenty-first century, Mom. We know what celibacy is and what it isn't." He paused, then added, "And for the record, we also know about birth control and waxing. It's not like when you were my age."

That won a real laugh from Amy. They had touched on this subject before—Ethan's complete lack of understanding about what life for teenagers was like in the nineties. "Right, right," she said, still laughing. "We were all so sheltered from everything back then. Plus it was hard to really learn anything about human sexuality because we were all so busy running from the dinosaurs."

"I just mean I'm not a kid anymore."

"You're still *my* kid, though, and I don't think I want to discuss my sex life with you."

"Oh, good grief, Mom. We were talking about *dating*, not sex." He brushed his bangs out of his eyes.

"I wish you'd let me cut—"

He aimed a finger at her. "Don't do that. Don't change the subject." Then he tapped the table with the same finger. "We're talking about why you haven't seen anyone since the divorce." He tapped his finger with each word, and it annoyed the shit out of Amy.

"I've dated," she said, and knew she sounded like a petulant little girl.

She had, but not seriously. She dated like it was a chore she needed to complete or she wouldn't be allowed to talk on the phone or go to the mall—like cleaning a litterbox or taking out the trash when she was Ethan's age.

Finn suggested she try the dating apps and she had, but it was just too much to concentrate on. She had a kid to raise and a job, and all she could think while she was swiping right or left was that she could be doing a million other things. Like cleaning a litterbox, even though they didn't have a cat, or the laundry. "It's too much," she told Finn. "I don't see how you do it. It's like sensory overload."

"Girl, please… You sound like someone's grandmother." Finn fished his own cell phone out and leaned in. "It's easy. If it weren't, do you think all these thirsty queens in Atlanta would be logging all these hours on these apps." Amy took her own phone out and they sat shoulder to shoulder. "You use Tinder, I guess?"

"Jdate," she said, and showed him the app.

Finn blinked at her.

"It's for Jewish people," she explained. "See? It's like part of a Star of David, a J, and a heart." The logo suddenly seemed ugly to her. "Anyway, I guess it's Tinder for Jews."

"You mean I could have been meeting hot Jewish guys on this app and you never told me about it?"

"I'm pretty sure you have to be Jewish to use it," Amy said.

"Psssh. As if." And Finn was already searching for it in the app store on his phone.

Amy browsed a few of the matches it had found for her: an attorney, a pediatrician, a violinist. Susan would be thrilled with such matches; Joel, too. But they bored her, and she was pretty sure she knew what Adam would say if she told him about them. It was as if, instead of an algorithm based on interests and age range, the app employed a cohort of Jewish aunts and grandmothers to match singles with other singles. She pictured them in a big room, not unlike a bingo hall at the JCC, crunching bridge mix and drinking Sanka as they peered over the rims of their glasses at all the available data for Jewish singles throughout the country. "Oh, look, she's cute!" one would proclaim, and hold Amy's photo up. "Says here she's a hairdresser, now how about that?"

"I knew a hairdresser once," said another. "Not my own hairdresser, no. She was a nice girl. This other hairdresser—I forget her name—she was what we called in those days a *fast girl*. Trouble."

"She's cute, though," insisted the first. "I see her with someone more sedate. Is that the right word? Sedate?"

"Like what?" asked another, reaching across and taking Amy's photo and profile, flipping through the pages. "Oh, she's been to Israel."

"Maybe a rabbi?" asked the first, and all the other women around her gaped at her. "What?"

"You look at her and you see a *rebbetzin*? I think you need to lay off the schnapps, Trudie."

Now Finn had the app downloaded. "It's asking me a lot of questions I don't know the answers to," he said. "What's a *kibitz*? Is that something you eat?" He squinted at his phone, like the answer might be revealed somehow. "Oh, apparently not. I guess it means talk or chat or something." He frowned at her. "You're not much help, you know."

"I thought you were helping me," she pointed out.

"Oh." He set his phone down. "Okay, so… go to your app store and download Tinder."

She sighed and put her phone away. "Never mind."

"What? I thought you wanted to meet someone."

"I do," she told him, "but I'm not used to all this. I met Mike in college and it was all old-fashioned; we had to speak to each other and stand face-to-face, and it was harder to pretend you weren't really interested in anything but a blow job or sex. And it was a hell of a lot harder to... what do they call it? *Ghost someone?*"

"Ghosting," Finn said. "Yeah." He had his phone again and was singularly bent on solving the riddle of the Jdate app.

"Maybe I should just go out, like I did in college. Before I met Mike."

"Mm hmm," Finn said.

Now Ethan was putting her on the spot about dating and she realized she should have prepared a statement for when people questioned her reticence. "I've dated," she said again. "Remember that one guy? I forget his name. He owned his own tech company and he drove a Ferrari." *And he was freakishly small for a man his age; his hands and feet were tiny, and that was really creepy,* she thought.

"Greg?" Ethan asked.

"Craig?" Amy tried to remember back. She could remember his face, but not his name.

"He looked like a worm," Ethan remarked, and Amy feigned surprise because that was what mothers did when their children said something mean about someone else, but Ethan was right: Greg or Craig had looked like a cartoon representation of a bookworm with his oversized glasses, his tiny features, and his blinking eyes.

"Well, he never called back anyway, so..."

They ate in silence for a moment, then Ethan said, "Anyway, you should go out. Don't you have girlfriends you could go out with and ogle men with? Isn't that what women your age are supposed to do?"

Now her expression of astonishment was genuine. "My age?"

"Yeah. Leah and Isaac are always talking about how their moms go out every weekend with all their girlfriends." He realized he'd said something he shouldn't have, but knew it was too late. Amy caught his mention of the girl from school who wasn't his girlfriend, but she would come back to that.

"I hate women my age," she told him.

He laughed.

"I'm serious," she said. "I cut their hair and I have to listen to all their bullshit, imaginary problems. Which, I might add, they've mostly created for themselves but are too vapid to realize. They blame their husbands, their kids, their mothers, their jobs—everyone but themselves, and it drives me fucking insane." She raised her hands, fingers like claws, to demonstrate just how harrowing it was to deal with these women on a daily basis. "I can only imagine what they're like after a couple glasses of wine. Or, worse, a couple shots of tequila."

"Well, go out alone," Ethan suggested, on the verge of exasperation. "Go *make* some friends your age who don't complain about everything. Maybe try the temple?"

That earned him a look. "Really? You think I'm going to meet someone like me at temple? A divorced, single mother who cuts hair for a living and drinks too much wine from time to time, who hasn't been on a date since that guy who looked like a worm, six months after the divorce was finalized four years ago? Maybe I'll just ask the rabbi if he knows anyone like that."

"You're making excuses," he said.

"No, I'm not." But she was, she supposed. "It's not that easy," she said after a minute. "It's not the same as when you're in high school or college and you're surrounded by people who are, literally, exactly like you five days a week, eight hours a day. You don't even have to go out of your way to meet people who are like you—all you have to do is show up and there they are."

Ethan was chuckling. "Man, high school must have changed a lot since you graduated."

"I'm being serious," Amy said.

"So am I."

"No, you aren't. You're doing that patronizing thing that kids do when they want to make their mothers feel completely out of touch with the world today. I graduated high school in 1997, Ethan. That's not exactly the Dark Ages."

"But we aren't all the same," he said, and gesticulated wildly to prove how crazy such a notion was. "God, Mom. I don't have everything in common with everyone just because we're all between the ages of fourteen and eighteen and are enrolled at the same school. That sounds like something off the Disney Channel!"

Amy took a breath, closed her eyes, gathered her thoughts. "I'm just saying—" She stopped. What was she saying? She wasn't sure. And whatever it was, she probably didn't need to be saying it to her son, who either didn't want to hear it or wouldn't even understand it if he did. "Never mind."

"What?" Ethan was smiling, but not because he was pleased.

She pushed her plate away. "We should go."

"So, you're seriously doing this?"

"I'm not doing anything," she said, and knew from the tone of her voice that she wasn't convincing. "Let's just go home. We can argue there." She wondered if they'd gotten too loud, and glanced around to see if anyone was staring. No one seemed to be, but that didn't mean they hadn't been and just averted their eyes. She wanted to go. At home, she could lock herself in the laundry room and not have to have this discussion.

But when they got home, Ethan followed her downstairs and into the laundry room and leaned against the dryer with his arms crossed. "What?" she asked him, as if she had no idea.

"Nice try, but no," he said, and she was struck by how much like his father he was as he leaned there with his arms folded across his chest and his ankles crossed. "We're going to finish our talk."

And he sounded a lot like Joel when he would not let her take the easy way out of a difficult conversation and go sulk in her room when she was younger. Like when she and Susan had argued about something—Amy's grades or that boy she was dating or how long she had been taking birth control pills and having sex. That one had been a particularly serious fight, because Susan found the pills in Amy's closet—which meant she was snooping—and Amy told Susan she hated her and wished she wasn't her mother, which made Susan cry.

"But I'm not sorry," she told Joel as they both sat on the edge of her bed.

"Maybe not now, but I'm sure—"

Amy interrupted him. "No! I'm not sorry now and I won't be sorry later."

Joel tried to smile. "Amy, she's your mother..."

"Exactly. She's my mother, which means I'm her daughter and she should respect me enough not to go snooping through my closet because she suspects I'm having sex and she wants to find proof." Saying all that renewed her anger. "God! Who does that?"

"I think you'd be surprised," Joel said.

"It's pathetic," Amy declared.

"Well, you need to talk to her," Joel said. "Her feelings are really hurt."

Amy shook her head and her hair whipped back and forth. "No. I'm never speaking to her again."

Of course they spoke again, but only after Susan came to her with an apology, and even that discussion ended in another argument after Amy revealed she had been having sex, in one form or another, for several years and with several different guys. Susan was aghast.

"I need to get this laundry done," she told Ethan, who would not budge. "Fine." She tossed the wet clothes back into the washer and slammed the lid. "Let's talk. You want me to go out? Hang out with the girls? Meet some man? Okay. What do I win?"

"This isn't talking," he said. "This is you losing your patience like you always do and getting pissy and sarcastic."

"I'm not pissy!" she said. "Why is it so important to you that I date?"

"Because I don't want my mom to be depressed and miserable," he said. "Is that not obvious?"

Amy wrenched the washing machine open again, then slammed it shut. "Well, why don't you date?"

Ethan's face betrayed his confusion. "Where did that come from?"

"I don't know. Maybe it came from the same place your concern for my well-being and state of mind did. So, why don't you date? Maybe I don't want to see my son miserable and depressed."

He rolled his eyes. "Now you're just being a bitch," he said and started out of the room. "Do whatever you want. I don't give a shit." Then he was gone.

"And don't talk to me like that!" she called after him, trying to sound both upset and authoritative, but failing at both. She wasn't mad, anyway. Instead she was remembering all the times she fought with her own mother over things that, at the time, Susan (and even Joel) assured her wouldn't matter at all later in life—which boys she chose to date, how late she chose to stay out, whether or not she went to Israel or Hawaii between high school and college. Everything, it seemed now, had been an argument, and she felt all the guilt she'd never felt then. It welled up inside her and threatened to choke her and she leaned against the washing machine, took deep breaths.

She called Adam. "So, remember all those times when Ethan was a baby and he would cry when I held him, or when I rocked him, or when I tried to feed him... but when Mom would come and take him, he'd stop crying... and when you took him from me he'd stop crying? And I told you that I thought he hated me, and you told me I was being stupid?"

Adam vaguely recalled a few of those conversations. "I guess...?"

"And you said that there was no way he could hate me, because he didn't really know me yet?" she asked. "And we laughed?"

"Where is this coming from?" Adam wanted to know. "And where is it going?"

Amy felt herself about to cry, but she swallowed the lump rising into her throat, took a deep breath, and said, "Well, he hates me now. I guess he got to know me and he hates me. All we do is argue."

There was a moment of silence so complete that Amy could hear only the hum of the connection between them and she thought for a second that either she or Adam had been dropped from the call. Then Adam laughed. "Really?" he asked her.

"Really," she said.

"Seriously?"

Amy felt her annoyance growing. "Yes, Adam, fuck! He hates me. He's spent the last fifteen years with me and he's decided that he hates me, just like you said he would."

Adam was still laughing, but he managed to disagree. "Hang on. I never said he was going to grow up to hate you. I just said he couldn't hate you when he was a baby because he didn't know you." He paused for that to sink in, then he added, "And I was joking. You should have known I was joking, too. And to be honest, Amy, I can't believe you remember shit I said fifteen years ago. What the hell, did you write it down or something? I can't even remember things I said last week sometimes and you pull out this shit from years ago."

"Well, you said it," she said.

"Okay, fine. I said it. But I'm not a prophet, Amy. I probably said it so you'd quit freaking out because your baby cried all the time." There was another silence, then he asked, "Anyway... what makes you think he hates you?"

Amy gave him all the examples of Ethan's recent behavior she could recall. She left out the talks they'd had about her going out and meeting people and having fun; she wasn't sure it fit the pattern and therefore didn't support her argument.

"Just so I'm clear," Adam said when she finished, "you're saying he's acting like a teenager?"

"Never mind," Amy said, and ended the call.

The next day they met for lunch and after they argued over

whether to have falafel or Thai, Adam reminded her that Ethan was just being a kid. "He's in that phase where he's decided he's smarter than you are and he knows what's best for you," he said as he inspected the falafel in his pita. It always seemed overcooked to him, too dark, and he was reminded that he always wished he'd not chosen falafel. "Like we were at fifteen. Like every kid in the world is at fifteen."

Amy frowned. "We didn't go through a phase like that. What is this phase?"

"We were simpler," he explained as he chewed. "This generation of kids has grown up with the answers to everything at their fingertips. We kind of had that, but it was later. After we got to high school. Ethan's had the internet and cell phones and Google his entire life, not to mention the content—all those '10 Things You Can Do Right Now To Live A Better Life' links in his social media feed. And 'How To Be Condescending Toward Your Mother.'"

"I wish he would just have all the same problems we had," she confessed. "That would be so much easier. Like, he's fifteen. He should be obsessed with sex and porn and girls." She considered that remark, then added: "Or boys, considering this family."

He threw her a look. "That's not as funny as you think it is," he told her. "But, yeah. I'll give it to you."

"Like, what fifteen-year-old is counseling his mother on dating and making friends? It's crazy. If I had a group of girlfriends who met every week after car pool on Fridays, they'd probably make fun of me for that. Why doesn't he want to play hockey or tennis? Why doesn't he pester me about a backpacking trip to the Alps?"

It occurred to Adam then that perhaps Ethan had a point. "When *was* the last time you went on a date?"

Oh, God, she thought, and wondered if they'd been talking this over between themselves and were conspiring to get her laid, whether she liked it or not.

"Well?" he asked when she didn't answer.

"Not that long ago…," she said, and tried to recall. "Right before Mom died…? I think…?" And if he gave her any shit about it, she would use that as her excuse—that for twelve months after their mother's death she felt it inappropriate to date. He would argue, because there was nothing stating that she couldn't date during that time, but she would hold firm.

"So, it's time," he said. "When was the last time you had sex?"

"I am *not* telling you that," Amy said.

"So, a long time. Whatever."

"Why is everyone so worried about my sex life all of a sudden? The only one who isn't hounding me about it is Dad, and the only reason I can come up with why *he* isn't concerned is because he's probably out having sex himself and doesn't give a shit."

Adam gaped at her, a look of mild disgust on his face. "Okay, ew. Dad having sex is *not* the picture I needed."

Amy laughed. "Yeah… sorry." She shook her head to clear the mental image she'd given herself. "Have you talked to him?" she asked.

"No," he snapped.

Amy suspected Joel had tried and been rebuffed. "I wish you would."

Adam shrugged. They finished eating in relative silence and walked back to the salon. His car was parked around back in a lot shared by several nearby businesses.

She gave him her to-go bag from the restaurant. "Take this. I'm not going to eat it." Then: "Seriously, though, are you gonna call Dad?"

They stared one another down hard for a long moment, until Adam rolled his eyes. "I'll talk to him when I'm ready," he said, and it was that simple. It sounded like a shitty excuse, but it was the truth. He wasn't ready to talk to Joel because he wasn't sure what would come out if he just called up or went over. He had a lot of things he needed to unpack first, things Amy thought she knew and understood but didn't, and he wanted to be prepared when he finally spoke to Joel. And he thought it would do his father good to worry about where he stood with his son for a change, since Adam had spent his entire childhood wondering the exact same thing.

"Well, do it soon," she said. "I think he's lonely and probably depressed."

"I doubt he's lonely and depressed because I don't want to hang out with him," Adam said.

She considered that. "No, but I can't imagine that coming out at his age, less than a year after Mom died, with no friends to support him would be easy." Hell, she didn't really have any friends herself, and she'd had to work through her divorce with support from Joel and Susan and Adam, so she felt she knew what she was talking about.

"I've gotta go," Adam said, and hoped that would end the conversation about whether or not Joel was lonely and what Adam could do about it.

"Well, call Dad," she called after him. "Or go see him."

"We'll see," he said, and what he meant was, "No."

"Why are you, of all people, acting this way about it?"

That made him stop, and he turned back to her. "Are you kidding?" he asked. "Why am I acting 'like this'—" He even did the air quotes. "—After I caught my dad fucking some guy? Gosh, Amy… I don't know. How selfish of me."

"But *you're* gay, Adam!" She shouldn't have to point that out, she thought, and yet here they were. "I'm the one who should be freaked out about it, not you. Is it because you found him like that?" She really needed to understand the whole thing. She felt if she understood everything, she could formulate a strategy and they could all move forward.

"I don't give a shit who Dad has sex with, Amy," he said. "But I do care that he probably fucked around on Mom, because being gay isn't like catching a cold. It doesn't just happen overnight. And I do care that he now wants me to be okay with him being gay when he was, literally, *never* okay with me.'"

Amy stood for a second, in the wake of Adam's theory, in a daze. Of course Joel had sex with men before, and that meant he'd been doing it while he was married. Or maybe she assumed it, but the immediate concern was not what happened ten, twenty, and thirty years ago but what was happening now, and she couldn't shake the image of her father sitting, dejected, nursing that bottle of wine in the dark the last time she saw him. "I... guess I didn't really go that deep about it," she confessed.

"Well, you're welcome," he said, and turned away again. "I've gotta go. This waking up at four a.m. fucking sucks."

"I just think," she said to his back, "that since you and I are really the only people he has to support him in this, we should do whatever we can. He looked so sad when I left him that night."

Adam wheeled on her. "And maybe he should be sad. Maybe that's part of this for him, like I was sad when he wouldn't let me do all those things I wanted to do when I was a kid because he was afraid everyone would make fun of me and call me a faggot. Maybe this is what he gets for being such a fucking dick to me, Amy. And maybe he gets to be sad and lonely because he fucked around—*with men*—on Mom *while* he was telling me, his gay son, that I couldn't take theater or ballet because people would think I was gay." He raked his fingers through his hair and turned in a complete circle. "Fuck!"

Amy thought of how she might respond to all that. People passed them on the sidewalk and cut glances in their direction and she wanted to take him by the arm and lead him away to somewhere secluded so he could yell and tear his hair as much as he needed. *This is good,* she told herself. *At least he's talking about it.*

"And how the fuck are you okay with all this?" he demanded to know, pointing at her.

"I'm—" What? Was she not okay with it? Because she felt the need to defend herself against that accusation. "I never said that," she said finally. It was the best she could do on such short notice.

"No, you just said I should be okay with it because I'm gay... and he's gay now, too." He stopped there, held up a finger. "Or, *actually*, he's always been gay... he's just been lying about it. And

I guess I should be okay with that, too. Because he might be sad and alone."

Amy felt her anger rising. He was being snide now and his priority had shifted from actually discussing Joel's plight to mocking it. "You don't have to be an asshole, Adam," she snapped, and a couple walking their black Lab moved several feet away to avoid this insane woman who would curse at another person right there on the street. She stepped closer to him so she could lower her voice and still be heard. "Okay, Dad was a dick to you when we were growing up. Fine. Be pissed about that. But—" And she had to stop and think because she needed to make sure she said the right thing, and that she said it the right way, otherwise Adam would shut down again. "—Can't you be pissed about all that *and* sympathetic to what he's going through now? You had people around you when you came out. Mom was, like, your biggest cheerleader, remember that? She bought all those books? And Dad... yeah, okay, Dad was a little quieter about it than Mom was, but he certainly didn't react the way some parents do when their child comes out."

Adam listened with a scowl, his arms folded across his chest.

"Can't you just call him—or, hell, if you don't want to hear his voice, then send him a text and just see how he is? See if he needs anything? You've been out your entire life, Adam, and Dad's been out for a month."

He rolled his eyes. "It's not that hard," he said.

"Says you," she pointed out. "Dad's not like you. He's educated and he's smart and he can carry on a discussion about anything literary, but he's never been all that outgoing. I don't even think he has any friends that he doesn't work with." She realized then how pitiable Joel sounded when she talked about him and it occurred to her that she should stop. So they stood there, silent, each sizing up the other's commitment to their argument. Neither budged.

"I've got to go," Adam said, and he turned to do that.

"Well... call Dad!" Amy called after him.

"No," he called back, and kept walking toward his car.

.seven.

AMY WAS SURPRISED TO learn, when she finally called Joel herself to see how he was doing, that he was the exact opposite of what she had imagined. He wasn't spending every night with a bottle of wine, watching the Home Shopping Network and ordering products he had no use for. Had she been asked, Amy wouldn't have been able to adequately explain why she was surprised, she just was. But Joel had made friends, he was going out, he was having fun. Had he met anyone? "A few someones," he said, and giggled. Her first response to hearing that was unmitigated affront, then she remembered. *Oh. Mom's dead. It's okay. He can see other people.* And she had to remind herself that she was being supportive; she was not going to act like Adam. Her father was gay now. This was a man Joel was referring to, not Debbie Bornstein from the anthropology department.

"He's younger than I am, though," Joel confessed. He whispered it, like it was an unspeakable taboo.

"It's not the fifties, Dad," Amy reminded him. "You can date a younger... guy."

They were shopping. Joel suggested it when she called: lunch and then the mall. He needed to update his wardrobe, he told her, and she couldn't argue that. For as long as she could recall, Joel had dressed and acted like the quintessential English lit professor. He was almost a caricature in his tweeds and corduroys year-round, with maybe a short-sleeved polo thrown in during the warmer months, and all of it shades of brown or gray or olive green. Now he inspected bold floral and paisley prints, linen pants and jackets, in shades ranging from pastels to jewel tones.

"I know *that*," he said. "I know I *can*. I just never thought I would."

"Well, I'm sure you're doing a lot of things now that you never thought you would," she said, and for a long moment they stared at one another across a rack of Lilly Pulitzer blazers, their mouths wide with astonishment. "I didn't mean that the way it sounded," she said.

Joel laughed, waved a hand to dismiss the apology. "Oh, sweetie, but it's true" he said. "No one should be fifty-eight years old and just coming out of the closet. It's exhausting. I'm so *behind*."

Amy wondered what he meant by that exactly. Behind in which aspect of homosexuality? If what Adam said was true, Joel hadn't exactly lived a monastic existence during his marriage, so he most certainly wasn't saying he needed to make up for all the sex he never had with men. So she guessed he meant the culture of being gay—the lingo, the social mores, the do's and don'ts. "You should talk to Adam," she said, and pretended to study the blazers.

"I'd love to talk to Adam," he said, selected one of them. "But he doesn't want to talk to me." He held the blazer up to himself for Amy to see. "I like the colors, but is it me?"

It most definitely was not him, but she took her time deciding how to tell him that without being too harsh. He was spreading his wings, testing the waters of his new life, and she didn't want to be that voice, the one that would tell him no, that he shouldn't explore and discover who he really was and what he really liked. But honestly, the blazer was hideous; it would have looked bad on anyone. Actually, it reminded her a lot of the things that Susan wore, so she smiled and said, "Well, it's pretty Boca."

Joel held the blazer at arm's length and smiled as he studied it. He guessed it to be a floral, although an abstract one, and it looked like a child might have created the pattern with finger paints. "So Boca," he said, half to himself and half to Amy. "I like it, but… I don't know…"

"Well, let's keep looking," Amy suggested. "That's what I do when I can't make my mind up about something—I put it back on the rack and go look at other things, and if I just can't get it out of my head or I can't find something that I like more, then I get it." She shrugged. "Usually I just forget about it, and I take that to mean I didn't really want or need it in the first place."

Joel put the blazer back and they moved toward a display of Lacoste polo shirts arranged in order by the colors of the rainbow. "Have you talked to him?" he asked over his shoulder.

"Adam?"

He nodded.

"Yeah. We had lunch a few days ago."

"Is he doing okay? Has he found a job yet?" Joel studied the polos. They were all identical in style, but he unfolded one in each color, shook it out and held it up, like he couldn't be certain of it unless he saw it spread out.

"Yes," she said.

Joel sighed. "Good. I was worried. It isn't easy to find a job when you quit one the way he did." He paused for thought. "I guess it's my fault."

"Believe me, Dad… it is *not* your fault that Adam quit his job the way he did." Adam did that a lot, and always had: he quit jobs when he got tired of them, usually without another one lined up. Amy didn't know how he did it, and she always warned him that it would catch up with him one of these days, then it never did.

"Well, I mean… you know what happened. I can't help feeling if it hadn't happened the way it did… I'm sure it shook him up so much he just stopped going to work…" Joel spread the polos out on the table now and stared at them. Amy noticed a salesperson orbiting them, suspicious and more than likely irked at Joel's treatment of the merchandise, but Amy recognized this behavior because Susan had shopped like this. Every article of clothing, every dish, every box had to be carefully considered and viewed from all angles, in light and in shadow.

"That blue is nice," Amy said, and hoped he'd pick up on the cue.

"Maybe," Joel said, and examined the yellow one instead. "Do you think he'll come to the unveiling?"

"Of course he'll be at the unveiling," Amy said, impatient.

"Well, you know how he gets," Joel said. He straightened up and selected both the blue polo and the yellow. The others he left lying where he'd spread them, much to the chagrin of the salesperson, who now scowled at them from behind a rack of bowties.

"We should straighten these up first," Amy said, and moved to do just that.

"They'll get it, sweetie," Joel said. He made a fluttering motion with his fingers to indicate the salespeople, or maybe the elves who came in the night to straighten everything with their magic. "They work here. You don't."

It was a classic Susanism and it struck Amy as both surprising and appropriate that though she was gone, her mother had left pieces of herself embedded in everyone's speech and behavior, like little time bombs that would go off when triggered: Amy in the things she said when she argued with Ethan, and Joel the way he shopped. She wondered what Adam's would be.

"I'm sorry," she whispered to the salesperson when he stepped up to refold the polos. She didn't want Joel to hear.

"It's fine, ma'am," he said with a tight smile, and she knew it wasn't. And the way he called her "ma'am," even though he clearly wasn't younger than she was. She wanted to stay and refold all the polos and dust the racks and tables and organize everything by color, from lightest to darkest, because she felt so bad, but she had to catch up with Joel who was walking to pay and still talking, assuming she was on his heels.

"I just want him to be there," Joel said. "He can be mad at me all he wants, but I want him to be there, so if you talk to him, please don't let him say he isn't going to come."

"He'll be there," Amy assured him.

"And what about Mike?" Joel asked.

Amy froze. "Mike? What about him?"

Joel blinked at her. "Well, you told him about the unveiling, didn't you? I'm sure he'd want to be there, if he can. He and Susan always got along so well. She really cared a lot about him."

Of course she hadn't told her ex-husband about the unveiling of her mother's headstone. She didn't want him there, and she almost spat that at Joel but caught herself in time, took a deep breath, and said simply, "No. I didn't tell him. I think Ethan may have." It was both the truth and a possible lie, so she didn't feel bad about it.

"Good," Joel said, and they went to pay for his shirts.

Ethan told her he hadn't mentioned the unveiling to his father. "Well, mention it next time you talk to him," Amy said, because she didn't want to be the one to do it. Mike's visit to the salon for a haircut was all the contact she cared to have with him, and she guessed if he were to come to the unveiling, she would tolerate his presence. There would be other people there, and the ritual wasn't about him or her or whatever existed—or no longer existed—between them.

Her son wasn't reliable, though. "I keep forgetting!" he told her when she asked again. "Why don't you call him?"

Amy just made a sound of disgust in the back of her throat and hoped for the best.

Susan really had loved Mike Cohen, though. Joel was right about that.

Amy was home for the first time since meeting Mike and declaring their casual relationship actual *dating*, and this was the preamble to both of them introducing the other to their parents over the holidays. "He'll be a doctor?" Susan clasped her hands and held them over her heart in a gesture reserved for silent film actresses and Christian saints in classical paintings. The look on her face was nothing short of beatific.

Amy corrected her. "Dentistry school. But yeah, he'll be a doctor."

Susan swiped at the air. "Same difference."

"Actually," Joel said, from where he sat reading and grading essays, "there's quite a bit of difference."

Susan ignored him. "What's his name?" And when Amy told her, she began to search for some connection to anyone she already knew. "I wonder if Effie Cohen knows him?"

"He's from Miami," Amy pointed out.

Susan chewed her lip and thought hard. "Or Linda Cohen…"

Amy rolled her eyes. "Whatever, Mom. You can stop swooning. I just wanted to let you and Dad know so when I mentioned Mike, you'd have at least a vague idea of who I was talking about. And he may visit over winter break." She braced herself for disapproval, a lecture on responsibility, and either a firm refusal to allow such a thing or a noncommittal "We'll see." She'd heard it throughout her teenage years, more from Susan than Joel, but her mother—for the first time that Amy could recall—was ecstatic.

"What a great idea! I'll have to start getting things ready!" And to show her commitment, Susan bent down and straightened the magazines on an end table.

"Mom, it's April," Amy said.

"It'll be here before you know it," Susan declared, and searched the room for other things she could do.

Amy almost told her that, for all any of them knew, she and Mike might have broken up by the time winter break rolled around, but she bit her tongue. She didn't want to jinx what they had by entertaining any and all unforeseen outcomes. Mike always said they should just go with it, let it happen how it would, and she was getting better at that. At least she thought she was, but she lacked his ability to just allow things to progress naturally and accept them for what they were, instead obsessed over what she might make them into, and how she would go about doing that.

But they were still together when winter break rolled around, so Mike flew into Atlanta and Susan insisted they all go welcome him at the airport. She made a sign with his name on it, surrounded by hearts which she had accented with glitter. It looked like a child's Valentine's Day art project and Amy was ashamed of it, though Susan held it aloft and beamed as they waited. Joel craned his neck as he searched the stream of arrivals, though he had no idea what Mike looked like.

"What am I looking for here, Amy?" he asked.

"He's tall," Amy said, then realized that compared to the three of them, most people were tall. "He'll probably be wearing a Michigan hat." She thought that should narrow it down a great deal, considering the geography, but the minute she said it, there seemed to be a Michigan hat on every other head.

"Is that him?" Joel and Susan asked, over and over, passing it back and forth between them, until Amy thought she was going to scream.

Mike appeared at last and she felt such relief that she ran and leaped into his arms before she could catch herself. He laughed. "It's only been a week!"

On the ride north from the airport, Joel and Susan fired questions at him. Joel drove and Mike sat with him in the front, shotgun. It was always the seat of honor, for some reason, and Amy suddenly decided it was an idiotic idea because she would much rather have Mike in the back seat with her than Susan, who kept asking Mike questions and turning to Amy, as if for approval or that she might answer for him.

"What does your father do?" she called up to him, her voice louder than necessary. "What does your mother do? Are they still married?" Mike's father was a pediatrician. "Oh, a doctor!" Susan threw her a wink. Amy wanted to hide. She considered flinging open the door and throwing herself out onto the asphalt. "What's your father's name? What's your mother's name? Oh, I've always liked the name Evelyn."

Later, as Susan scurried around to get the spare bedroom ready, Amy apologized profusely for all of Susan's questions, but Mike just laughed. "I like your mom," he told her, and Amy was incredulous.

He meant it, though, and Susan loved everything about Mike Cohen. Joel, too, approved, though not so outwardly as Susan, and Adam was suspicious. "What do you think of him?" Amy asked him. "And don't lie." Susan had taken Mike into the kitchen where she could be heard explaining to him exactly how to get the fluffiest matzoh balls.

"Schmaltz!" they heard her proclaim from the kitchen.

"He's not your type," Adam said simply, and aimed the remote at the television.

Amy opened her mouth to argue—Mike *was* her type, anyone could see that; how dare Adam say such a thing!—but she realized he was right, in a way. Throughout middle school and high school, Amy had dated two distinct types of boys: the brooding, artistic type or the angst-ridden nonconformist with no real agenda other than to disagree with everything. Mike Cohen was neither of those things. Mike was an athlete, he laughed at everything, and he was agreeable to the point that it annoyed Amy sometimes. "Well, what does that mean?" she snapped. She felt she needed to say something.

Adam blinked at her through his bangs which grew almost to his chin and were a constant source of concern for Susan. "Seriously?"

"Well, maybe my type has changed," she pointed out.

He shrugged. "Maybe." He'd found a rerun of *Seinfeld* by that time and settled back on the sofa to watch it.

Amy liked Mike, though. Maybe because he wasn't like any of those other boys she'd dated. There was only so much misdirected anger and gratuitous depression one person should have to deal with in their life, and maybe she had reached her saturation point. Mike was refreshing, and even better than not being angry or sad all the time, he had goals and he was clearly working toward them, instead of just saying he wanted to be a dentist and then delivering pizzas, smoking weed, and never finishing college. Next to Mike, Amy looked like the slacker, since she still hadn't declared her major and had no actual end in mind. She chose the University of Michigan because she wanted to see snow, so maybe she should be a climatologist. She would figure it out eventually, she supposed. Neither Susan nor Joel were pressuring her to pick anything, and all of her friends from high school, scattered across the country and several even in Europe, were facing the same dilemma: after being guided through school by a set curriculum and counseled on which courses to take to prepare for college, suddenly being the one and only person in charge of their futures left most of them adrift, hoping something would come and carry them along on a current to some lightbulb moment.

Or, she always joked with herself (she wouldn't dare mention it to her parents or Adam, especially) she could just pick some easy major, minor in nothing, graduate from college and marry a dentist. There were certainly worse fates than marriage and family after college.

Amy ended up being the one to call Mike about the unveiling. "Well, this is certainly a surprise," he said when he answered his cell phone.

"I'll make it quick," she said.

He immediately got serious. "Is Ethan okay?"

"Ethan is fine. I'm actually calling about Mom." She was uncomfortable talking to him and she wished she'd made notes. "Well, her unveiling, actually. Not Mom herself... she's dead."

"Okay..." Mike drew the word out longer than necessary and that annoyed her.

"Yeah, Dad wanted me to call and invite you to the unveiling because you and Mom got along so well. And it's on Sunday." She paused, pleased with herself for making it perfectly clear that she was calling, but she was not the one extending the invitation. "I'm actually kind of surprised Ethan didn't mention it to you."

"I'm glad you called, Amy. Thanks. I'll be there. What time is it?"

No, she screamed inside her head. *He isn't going to do this. He's not going to twist it all around like I invited him and then tell everyone he knows how his ex-wife is always calling him up and there's never a moment's peace.* She knew how men were. She listened to them as she cut their hair, the things they said about their crazy ex-wives and their crazy ex-girlfriends, like Amy wasn't a woman herself; like she was some mechanical thing programmed to cut hair and listen to bullshit. Ex-wives were always the instigator and the men were always so nonplussed by the behavior of these women. Amy was not going to be one of those women. She said, "Well, Dad asked me to call you."

"I'm glad you did," Mike said again.

"He invited you." She needed that to be clear. She would repeat it as many times as necessary.

"I'll thank him on Sunday."

The talk turned to Ethan and whether or not he would be going to summer camp this year. He hadn't mentioned it to either of them. Amy was fine accepting that if he hadn't mentioned it, he probably wasn't interested. Mike was not so sure.

"But he's always gone."

"You know how Ethan is," Amy said. "Everything's important until it isn't."

"But Ethan loves Camp Barney." Mike sounded genuinely sad at the idea of Ethan sitting it out this summer.

"He's growing up. And I think he may have a girlfriend at school."

Mike laughed. "A *girlfriend?*" Then he laughed again.

"Why is that so funny?" Amy wanted to know.

"Ethan doesn't have a girlfriend," Mike said. "What makes you think that?" He laughed again and Amy wished he would stop.

"Because he talks about her all the time," Amy said. "Her name is Leah and he brings her up every chance he gets." Okay, so maybe she was exaggerating just a bit, but she was his mother. She was allowed to overreact to everything.

Mike was silent and Amy felt an enormous sense of triumph. Finally, she knew something about Ethan that Mike didn't. "Cool," was all he said, and she caught herself about to challenge him on his typically male response. She wanted him to be concerned. She wanted him to ask questions and demand to meet this girl. She wanted him to feel the way she felt about it—their precious baby boy was growing up too fast—but all he could say was "Cool."

Ethan called Amy at work, in a rage, once Mike brought it up to him. "Why did you tell Dad I had a girlfriend?" he demanded to know. He didn't even say hello or ask if she was busy. He just ripped right into her.

"What?" She knew what he was talking about, but she felt it important to feign confusion. Ethan did not sound like himself.

"You told Dad Leah was my girlfriend," Ethan spat.

"That's not what I—"

He cut her off. "And don't lie about it. He told me what you said. He told me *exactly* what you said, and I know you said it, because it sounds like something you would say."

Amy was on a break at work and she'd walked up the street for coffee. "Hang on," she told Ethan. She paid for her coffee and went to stand with the other people waiting for the barista to mispronounce their names when he called for them.

Ethan ignored her. "No. This is important. I'm not going to wait. Why would you tell Dad that?"

"Look, Ethan, I can't really talk right now…"

"Of course!" She pictured Ethan smiting his forehead when he said that, flailing his arms. "You have all the time in the world to stick your nose in my business and tell Dad I have a girlfriend, but you don't have time to tell me why you did it. Whatever, Mom."

"I'm getting coffee right now," she explained.

"So?"

"So, we can talk about it when I get home tonight. I'm working late, my last client is at eight and it's just a cut, but we can talk when I get home."

"Annie!" the barista called.

"Maybe I won't be here," Ethan said, and he sounded exactly the way he sounded when he was little and threatened to run away from home because he couldn't have a horse for a pet.

Amy laughed. "Well, where are you going to be?"

"I dunno. Out." Ethan paused. "Maybe I'll go over to my girlfriend's house."

"Annie!" the barista called again. No one moved, but several people turned and looked at Amy.

Amy laughed. She would play along. "Fine," she said. "Go over to your girlfriend's house, just text me if you decide to stay overnight."

"Extra-large iced coffee with a shot of espresso for Annie!" called the barista. His voice was a lot like a fog horn.

Amy recognized the order as her own. "Oh! That's my order. I have to go. We'll talk later. You can scream at me then. Or not, I guess, if you're over at your girlfriend's."

Ethan made a sound like a grunt that wanted badly to turn into a scream. "Whatever, Mom," he said, and ended the call.

Amy dropped her phone into her pocket and went for her drink. "It's Amy," she told the barista. He was the size of an offensive lineman and wore thick-framed glasses.

"Excuse me?" he said. His volume level was the same as when he was calling for people to pick up their orders.

"Amy," she said, and pointed to where the cashier had written ANNIE on her cup.

"Yeah," he said. "Annie."

She gave up and left.

.eight.

"Moms are like that, though," Leah said when Ethan told her what Amy had done. "You gotta shake that shit off, otherwise it'll drive you crazy." She'd texted him and asked him to meet her after sixth period. Usually, he would have walked straight home, but since he was pissed at Amy, he said yes and met her at the park across the street from school. She smoked, and normally that would have been a turn off for him, but not with Leah. "You want one?" she asked him, and proffered the pack.

"I'm good."

"So, what are we doing?" she asked him.

He laughed. "Well, you texted me…"

"True that," she said, and smoked while she considered it. "Well, I guess since we're boyfriend and girlfriend now, we can go to my place and have sex." Ethan laughed again, but when he turned to Leah and saw that she wasn't laughing, he stopped. It was like someone just flipped a switch. "I was being serious," she said.

"Oh." A lump formed in his throat and he felt heat creep up his neck and into his cheeks. He guessed this was normal, this was what desire felt like. He'd been horny before—he was a pubescent male, of course he had—but not like this. This was different because it wasn't all playing out in his imagination. Here was a real, live, flesh and blood girl telling him that she wanted to have sex with him. And here he was, feeling like he might actually throw up, because the lump had dropped from his throat to his stomach and sat there like a hot coal.

Leah smoked her cigarette and swept her hair, which was thick and dark and curly, out of her face. "I know you're probably thinking I must be a real thot, texting you like that and telling you to meet me here after class, and when you get here, telling you that I want to have sex with you... but I didn't know how else to get it across to you, because you didn't seem very interested in me and I was wondering if you might be gay." She paused and turned her full gaze on him. "Are you gay?"

"No!" he said, the way he would have denied being a rapist or a serial killer had she asked.

"Because it's perfectly fine if you are. We'll just forget this ever happened, and when we're older and objectifying men together, we'll look back on this and laugh."

He laughed then. "No. I'm not gay. I promise." He was, however, nervous. This was not at all how he had envisioned his first time going. He'd pictured a date, at least—something tame, like a movie or prom—and hand holding, and some awkward kissing. Then they would become more sure of themselves and know where to put hands and lips, and what to do with tongues, and the suggestion that they "do it" would be whispered, either asked or demanded, but in dim lighting. Not on a park bench in broad sunlight with mothers walking by pushing babies in strollers and old women in track suits eyeing them suspiciously because Leah was smoking and would probably throw the butt into the grass.

"Then you're interested?" she asked him.

"Yes," he replied.

"In me?"

"Yes."

Leah stood and, in fact, tossed her cigarette away into the grass. "Okay, then." She sounded like she had just sold him a used Volkswagen. "Let's do this." She grabbed her backpack and started walking out of the park, back toward the high school. "I don't live far."

"Cool," he said, but he felt anything but. He wondered if he was supposed to take her hand as they walked, or if all that about them being boyfriend and girlfriend was just facetiousness after he'd shared his argument with his mom about it. Then again, he told himself, they were going to her house to have sex, so that had to mean something. And she'd said she didn't know how else to tell him that she wanted to have sex with him, so had he been missing some signals or something all along? He was nervous. His stomach hurt and his palms were sweaty, so he decided it probably wasn't a good idea to hold her hand. And the silence was only adding to his anxiety. "So, what time will your parents be home?" he asked, and it was like he'd screamed it.

"Next weekend," Leah told him. "They're in Malta. Or somewhere."

"Oh."

"So, we don't have to rush, and I've got some good weed, too." She winked at him and flashed him a smile. It was supposed to put him at ease, but it just worsened his nervousness.

Ethan took a deep breath and tried to control his breathing as they walked along. Cars and buses passed by on the street, and there was soccer practice on the field at Decatur High, but all he was aware of was the pounding of his heart and the rhythm of his and Leah's feet on the sidewalk. He shouldn't be nervous. Other guys wouldn't be nervous, not like this. Then again, other guys would never have made it to the point where the girl had to make the first move. They would have gone for it from the beginning, probably gotten it, too, and be well beyond this. He felt like a putz. And he wondered why she'd picked him out of all the other guys at school she could have sex with. He thought he might ask, but decided against it. He needed to make her think this wasn't his first time. For some reason, that seemed very important.

"Is this your first time?" she asked him, as if on cue.

Ethan jumped like he'd been shocked. "No," he lied, and laughed. "Is it yours?"

Leah rolled her eyes. "God, no. And I was actually kinda hoping it was your first time." She shrugged. "Oh, well. Nobody's perfect."

Fuck, he thought. *Fuck fuck fuck!* Why had he lied? What would have been so bad if he'd just told the truth? Apparently it wasn't a problem for her, but he'd already told the lie and there was no backing out of it. He would just have to get his shit together and not act like an idiot.

At Leah's house, they entered through a side door and she led him through the kitchen and dining room, into a cluttered den. She dropped her backpack onto the floor and kicked her shoes off. Ethan stood, unsure. "Get comfortable," she told him, and smiled as she pulled her shirt off and unbuttoned her jeans.

"Here?" Ethan asked. It was out of his mouth before he could stop it.

Leah narrowed her eyes at him. "What? You never had sex on a sofa before?"

"Well... sure." He'd certainly jacked off on a sofa quite a few times, and he guessed that counted for something. "I just figured we'd go to your room or something." He kicked his own shoes off and pulled his shirt over his head.

She fell back onto the sofa and watched him, and it made him a lot more nervous than he thought it would. Movies and porn would have you believe that there was no nervousness, that everyone's first time was carried out with aplomb, and Ethan suddenly felt cheated by every porn he'd ever watched. He dropped his pants and kicked them away. He knew what the next move was: he was supposed to lie with Leah on the sofa and they were supposed to kiss. Then he was supposed to grope her breasts and remove her bra and they would undress one another. Then it could go one of two ways—they could get right to intercourse, or they could engage in some foreplay. He glanced down at himself and wondered, fleetingly, why he wasn't getting aroused by this. The sight of a girl in her bra and panties should have had him ripping the seams on his boxers. He really wished he'd worked up the nerve to discuss sex with his dad, but he'd always talked himself out of it because he knew Mike would tell Amy, who would then freak out knowing that her precious boy was thinking about having sex.

"Come here," Leah said. She sat up and reached for him, grabbed him by the hand and pulled him down onto the couch with her. "Relax." She whispered it close to his ear and it sent goose bumps down his arms.

He recalled she'd mentioned having some good weed, so he reminded her of that. It would buy him some time and it would help him relax, so while she ran upstairs to retrieve it, he sat on the couch and willed himself not to fuck up his first time, the way an Olympian might sit and meditate his way to a gold medal.

Leah returned and lit the pipe and they passed it between them in silence. She peered at him the entire time, and finally asked, "Are you just not into me, Ethan?"

"What?" he said, and laughed. It ended in a coughing fit. "No."

"Then why the fuck are you so nervous? If you don't want to do this, we don't have to." She stopped, but it seemed like there was more she wanted to say. Ethan guessed it to be *I can find someone else to have sex with*. Honestly, if she'd said that, he wouldn't have been surprised.

"No, no. I'm good." He set the pipe aside and moved to kiss her again, to show her that he was neither nervous nor gay, and that he was definitely into her. It was clumsy, and his mouth ended up to the left of hers, so he licked her cheek more than anything. She groaned and he interpreted it as desire, encouragement. He rubbed her breasts through her bra and felt the weed start to take effect. He was transfixed by her breasts, by the fabric of her bra, by the way her nipples showed through it. In all of his years wishing he could fondle a girl's breasts, this was not how he'd imagined it. This was nothing like the movies he'd seen. Leah was small, but her breasts seemed enormous to him, like they were someone else's breasts transferred to her body, and he wondered how her tiny waist could support them. He held one in each hand, weighed them in comparison to one another.

"What are you doing?" she asked him.

"I—" What was he doing? He was weighing her boobs. That was some good weed. "Nothing." He moved in to kiss her again, but she put an arm up to stop him.

"Never mind," she said, and rolled off the sofa and away from him. "This was a bad idea."

He chuckled. "No, it wasn't."

Leah gathered her clothes, said nothing. Ethan sat in his boxers, his erection poking through the fly of his boxers. He chuckled at that, too. It looked so idiotic, like an eel he had seen in some underwater documentary program once, poking its head out of a hole on the floor of the ocean. He noticed that Leah was half dressed and realized that whatever might have happened was off.

"I thought we were going to…," he said, and his voice trailed off, because at that point it was just a rhetorical observation. They weren't going to do anything. He reached for his own clothes and started getting dressed.

.nine.

Ethan's other friend at school was Isaac. Ethan called him after he left Leah's, and they met at the entrance to McKoy Park. "You look like somebody died," he told Ethan as he joined him on the bench.

Ethan gave a grunt. Isaac lit a cigarette and offered him one. "The last thing I need to do is go home smelling like cigarettes," Ethan said. "Mom's in my business enough as it is." He took the cigarette anyway, and dragged on it.

"So, how did it go with Leah?"

Ethan heaved a sigh and told him. "I was just too nervous, I guess," Ethan explained. "I really didn't expect her to come on so strong."

Isaac smoked his cigarette and listened. They'd discussed Leah and Ethan's attraction to her at great length, and Isaac always did his best to be supportive and encouraging, while at the same time being clear that he knew Leah better than Ethan did and that he'd heard other guys talking about how easy it was to get with her. Ethan shrugged it off; he was not deterred.

"You don't think she'll… you know…" Ethan hated to say it.

"Talk shit about you to everybody at school?"

Another grunt from Ethan.

"I wouldn't worry about it," Isaac said. "People like you, so she can say whatever she wants and it's not like people are going to point at you and laugh in the hallways." He dropped the butt of his cigarette and ground it out under his shoe. "People talk about me all the time." He shrugged. "It's not so bad, and at least they're not talking about anyone else." Then he stood. "I'm hungry."

They took the bus back up McDonough Street to Decatur Square, to Victory Sandwich Bar. Ethan's phone rang and he silenced it when he saw it was Amy.

"Your mom?" Isaac asked.

"Yeah. I told her I wasn't coming home tonight after she got into my business about Leah and told my dad."

Isaac chuckled. "Wanna hide out at my place?"

He'd hoped Isaac would offer. They were roughly the same size, so he could stay overnight and not have to report to school in the morning wearing the same clothes. Isaac's parents were pushovers, too, and always so eager to impress their son's friends from school with how cool and in touch they were with the youth of today. All he would have to do is tell them his mom was out of town—they would never suspect otherwise—and that was it.

"Your parents won't mind?" He already knew the answer, but asking was part of the protocol.

"Do they ever?" Isaac asked around a mouthful of food.

Ethan envied him. His parents had adopted him from Eastern Europe—Hungary, if Ethan recalled correctly—so coupled with their laissez-faire style of parenting was their adoration of him as the child they thought they would never have, so they gave him everything he asked for, as long as he said please and asked with a smile. "Dude, we really need to trade parents," he said. Ethan's phone rang again and he groaned at it.

"You really should call her."

"Let her worry," Ethan growled.

The next time it rang, it was his dad, so Ethan turned the phone off and crammed it into his pocket. They'd probably meet about it again and present a united front (their term, which Ethan hated), but he didn't care. They needed to learn how to parent him and respect him as an individual who had interests apart from being their son.

"Well, you can stay at my place, but you need to let your mom know. I don't want her mad at me, and I *really* don't need her showing up at my house because she's pissed at you for lying."

That irritated Ethan and he was ready to tell Isaac to just forget it, he'd just go home and lock himself in his room and ignore his mom, when he glanced past Isaac to the door and saw Adam walk in. "What the—?"

Adam noticed him, too. "What are you doing here?"

"Eating," Ethan said, simply.

"No shit, Sherlock." Adam's phone buzzed in his hand. He held it up and glanced from it to Ethan, then answered it. "Hey." A pause. Even with the activity in the restaurant, both Ethan and Isaac could hear Amy, shrill and strident. "Well, as a matter of fact, he's right in front of me."

"Jesus…" Ethan said, and rolled his eyes.

Adam ended his call and said to Ethan, "She wants me to bring you home."

"I'm eating." And Ethan sat back in his chair and crossed his arms, the way a child might refuse to eat his broccoli.

"That's cool. I'm gonna get something and join you guys." Adam walked to the counter to order.

Isaac asked Ethan, "Is that your dad?" His tone suggested that he doubted it.

"That's my uncle. He and my mom are a tag team on pretty much anything." He was furious, but he didn't know who to be furious at—himself for not going directly to Isaac's, Adam for being at the right place at the right time when Amy called him, or at Amy for being so determined to track him down, or, even at Isaac for the way he was checking Adam out right then.

"I think I'll head out," Isaac told him. "Call me later. Or text. Whichever." He shrugged his jacket on and left Ethan fuming over his predicament.

Adam took the seat left vacant by Isaac. "Your friend leave?" Ethan just glared at him. "Have I met him before? I can't remember." He unwrapped his sandwich, lifted a corner of the bread to check the contents, took a bite. "You kids all look the same to me anymore." He chuckled at what he'd said. "I sound like Uncle Stanley, don't I?"

"I'm not going home," Ethan told him. "And what are the fucking odds you'd be in Decatur today?"

"I had an errand," Adam said, then: "And what… you're gonna get a hotel room? Where do you think you're gonna go?"

Ethan shrugged. "Wherever. Dad's."

"Well, your Dad is over at your house right now, and they're both pretty fucking pissed at you, so…" He let his voice trail off. Ethan lapsed into silence.

Amy was waiting for him when they pulled into the driveway. "What the fuck, Ethan? Where have you been? Why didn't you call me or something?" And to Adam: "Has he been with you the entire time?" And she held up her phone, showed them both the time on it, proof that Ethan was over three hours late getting home. Mike appeared behind her in the doorway, his brow knit with concern.

"I was out," Ethan said, and walked past them both into the house.

She opened her mouth to yell at him, to say something to his back that would make him stop and turn and explain himself, but she could think of nothing and Mike gave her a tight shake of his head. She turned to Adam as his proxy. "What the fuck?"

Adam just shrugged. "You guys need to talk," he said and walked around to the driver's side of his car.

"That's it?" Amy fairly shrieked it. Her voice tended to rise in both pitch and volume when she was irritated.

"Pretty much," Adam said.

She laughed. "Well, how about a hint? I mean, obviously, you know what's wrong, since you guys have been hanging out all day."

"It wasn't all day," Adam pointed out. "I found him at a place on the Square. He was with a friend. The friend left, I sat down and ate, then I brought him here. But you guys need to talk." He glanced to where Mike still lurked in the doorway. "All three of you."

Amy held her hands in front of her face like she was praying, the tips of her fingers over her lips. "I'm going to lose my mind," she said, more to herself than to Adam. He had started the car anyway, and was starting to back down the driveway.

"I'll text you tomorrow," he called to her through the open window.

She just waved a hand and went into the house, walked past Mike as if he weren't even there. "Ethan!" she called, didn't get an answer, so she marched upstairs and knocked on his door.

He didn't open the door. "What?" he asked, his voice small but still clearly upset.

"Let's talk," she said, and tried the door knob. It was locked.

"No," he said, simply.

"Fine," she told him. "Then your dad and I will just talk about you *without you.*"

This time, though, he just said "Okay," and then music came blaring through the door at her. She rolled her eyes and went back downstairs.

"Wow," Mike said. "Were we this bad when we were fifteen?" He remembered being really into music and sports and always trying to find a way to buy beer without his parents finding out. Girls, too, but there was minimal trouble with them, and what there was never affected him like this.

"He's being a jackass," she said. "And now he's locked himself in his bedroom and he won't talk to me. Can you see if he'll talk to you?"

Mike shrugged. "I can try," he said. Amy stayed in the kitchen, poured herself a glass of wine while Mike went upstairs and knocked on Ethan's door. He returned in less than five minutes, so she knew he was no more successful than she'd been.

"This is so not like him," she said.

Mike had to agree. "Both his parents who rarely speak to one another suddenly together against him because he didn't come directly home after school like a good little boy?" He grunted. "I'd probably respond the same way."

"That's not what I meant," Amy said.

"Well, that's what it looks like when you're a teenager."

Amy thought about it. He could be right, but she would never say that out loud. Also, what if she was overreacting? Ethan was a teenager, and teenagers did things out of spite—God knows, she had done plenty herself to spite her own mother. And maybe she shouldn't have said anything about Ethan's interest in the girl in his biology lab to Mike. She should have known he would mention it to Ethan, nudge him with an elbow and want to bond over something like that. Mike would have pointers to give, and what better way to bond with his son than to compare notes on the opposite sex?

"Are you hungry?" Mike asked, out of the blue.

"Huh?" She wasn't sure she'd heard him correctly.

"I asked if you were hungry. We could have dinner."

Amy laughed. "I'm not going to dinner with you, Mike."

"Not like a *date,*" he said, and she hated how patronizing he sounded when he said it that way. "Just food. It's time for dinner and we could figure out what to do about Ethan."

She hadn't eaten anything but a doughnut all day, and that was first thing in the morning. She was starved and when she got home and found Ethan wasn't there, she forgot how hungry she was, but now it came roaring back, and having dinner with her ex-husband didn't sound *that* bad, after all.

"Fine," she said.

They went to a Thai place on the square in Decatur, since that was convenient and Amy knew it would be crowded, so neither would be tempted to cause a scene. They invited Ethan, but he didn't answer them through the door, so they left him with his music blaring. "I'm famished," she confessed, and studied the menu. She knew she would order basic pad thai because that was all she ever ate at Thai restaurants, but she studied the menu anyway so she wouldn't have to make small talk with her ex-husband.

Mike asked, "You want a glass of chardonnay?"

"I don't really like chardonnay anymore," Amy lied. When their server came, she ordered the pad thai and a glass of sauvignon blanc just to show him that she had changed since the divorce and that she was capable of ordering for herself, even if it was something she didn't really like.

"So what's up with E?" he asked, and Amy had to bite back the urge to correct him. Ethan had never complained when his father called him E, so why did it bother her so much? Guys did that; they addressed one another as letters instead of their full names. Or "Bro." Or "Buddy."

"No clue," she said. "Everything was fine, and when I got home from work, he wasn't home and I called his phone and it kept going straight to voice mail, which means he turned it off, and then I called Adam—why not, right?—and Ethan was with him." She paused. "Or they were, coincidentally, at the same place. That's about the time you came over. and then we left him in his bedroom with the door locked, listening to acid rock." She wondered if Ethan had dropped acid. Do kids still do acid? She abandoned the idea, though. Adam would have noticed the signs and been laughing about it when he dropped Ethan off.

"Is it school, maybe?"

Amy shrugged. Her wine came. She took a huge sip of it and wished it was chardonnay, but she willed herself not to grimace and choked it down.

"Or maybe girl trouble?"

She shrugged again.

Mike's eyes widened as a thought occurred to him, and he opened his mouth to voice it, then just as quickly clamped his lips shut again.

"What?" Amy asked him.

He shook his head. "Nothing. Just thinking."

"About Ethan?"

"It's nothing…"

She made a face at him. "Look, you were the one who suggested we come here and talk about whatever's bothering our son, so you can't do that shit." She made a gesture toward his face. "You can't have an idea and then not share it with me. There are things he talks about with you that he doesn't share with me... Guy things, I assume." She considered that, then realized Ethan didn't really share much of anything with her, and it made her sad. "Has he talked about her? That girl at school? Her name is Leah." She paused, then added: "I wonder if she's Jewish."

Mike sipped his beer. "He's mentioned her a couple times, but nothing major. They have a class together, and he's considering asking her on a date, but he doesn't talk about her non-stop."

"Does he talk about any other girls?"

Mike shook his head.

Amy laughed as she recalled thinking, when he was younger, that Ethan might be gay. She'd read an article somewhere that argued homosexuality was genetic, and being so, it was prevalent in some families and not others. She figured since Adam was gay and several cousins on the Schecter side of the family in Florida, there was a high probability Ethan might be, too. Then he'd started mentioning girls, dropping their names into casual conversations about school, and she'd felt something like relief—although she would never admit it if asked—that he might be straight.

"What's so funny?"

She waved a hand to dismiss it. She certainly didn't want to discuss it with Mike.

"Nothing. Just a thought I had."

"About E?"

Amy shook her head.

"You know, I used to think he might be gay," Mike said, and laughed. It sounded almost exactly the way Amy's laugh had sounded. He quickly added: "Not that it would matter. You know I don't have a problem with it." Amy had to give him that. Mike Cohen was definitely not homophobic or close-minded, but it did surprise her that he, too, had wondered if their son was gay.

"Why in the world would you think that?" she asked, determined to keep up her charade.

He shrugged, scraped at the label on his beer with a fingernail. "He just never really seemed into sports, you know. I wanted to teach him tennis, and golf, and I'd buy tickets to Braves games and Falcons games, and he'd go. He never complained about it, either. I guess he didn't want me to feel bad. Or something." He shrugged again. "But he just never talked about girls the way I did when I was growing up. I mean… I hit puberty and if I wasn't thinking about tennis, I was thinking about girls."

And nothing has changed, Amy thought. *Well… except maybe he doesn't think about tennis as much anymore…* She just smiled, and listened, and nodded.

"He's a good kid, though," he said, and raised his empty beer bottle so their server could bring him another.

"He is," Amy agreed.

"We did a good job."

"Yeah."

And then Mike was staring at her, and she was certain that there was something she was supposed to be reading in his eyes, but she kept telling herself that what she was seeing was impossible, so she sat there and continued to nod in agreement. He nodded, too, and he wouldn't look away, not even when the server brought his beer, and it seemed to Amy they sat there forever, nodding, and it might never have ended if she hadn't stood suddenly and said, "I really need to go to the restroom." A lie, but so what? She grabbed her purse and fled.

In the ladies room, she texted Adam.

Mike is hitting on me, she texted. Then added, *I think*.

It seemed forever before Adam's reply came through. *So, hit on him back.*

She was typing out her response, explaining that this wasn't just any Mike, when another text came through.

Wait. Mike WHO?

Cohen, she typed back, and waited for Adam's response.

Instead of a text, he called. She answered it halfway through the first ring.

"What the actual fuck, Amy? Tell him to leave."

Of course, Adam thought Mike was at her house. The last

thing he knew, he'd dropped Ethan off and they were both at her house. "He's not at my house," she said, and squeezed her eyes shut against Adam's reaction. There was only silence from his end, though. "*We're* not at my house, I mean."

Adam found his voice at last. "I'm confused," he said.

Amy laughed. "Yeah, so am I." Adam didn't laugh with her, so she jumped right into the explanation of how she had ended up on the phone with him, in the ladies' room of a Thai restaurant after her ex-husband had flirted with her. Hearing herself explain it made it sound questionable and she wished she hadn't bothered him. "It's probably nothing," she said. "And I should be getting back before he gets suspicious."

"But... why are you even there?" Adam wanted to know. "You guys couldn't have talked about Ethan at home? Or over the phone?"

Amy heaved a sigh and rolled her eyes. "Look, never mind. Forget I called. Bye." And she ended the call before Adam could press her for a better explanation. She didn't know why she hadn't told Mike no; she also hadn't expected him to look at her that way. Maybe she should have just said no to the dinner invitation, but it seemed so genuinely harmless.

A toilet flushed and Amy busied herself looking like she'd been inspecting her makeup when the woman stepped out of the stall and up to the mirror to wash her hands. She smiled, and Amy felt judged.

"I thought you fell in," Mike said when she returned to the table.

She didn't have a witty enough comeback, so she just gave him a half smile and sipped her wine.

"So, what's been up with you?" he asked, and leaned in more than he should have. "Like... how's life? You know... all that."

Amy stared at him in disbelief. Was he seriously asking about her life? And where should she start? Before the divorce when she found out her husband was fucking his hygienist, or after that when she found out he had been fucking other women the entire time they were married? What did Mike really want to hear, though? Surely neither of those. He probably wanted her to say how she was just coping as best as she could, getting along day by day, keeping her chin up. She'd heard that so many times she'd lost count, from women on talk show couches, soggy tissues squeezed tight in white knuckled fists as they sobbed their way through accounts of their perfect courtships, followed by their fairytale weddings to their very own knights in shining armor, the births of their perfect, pink-cheeked children, then the horror of a phone call from a friend or a letter from an anonymous tipster left in the mailbox: Prince Charming was seeing someone else! These declarations always elicited a gasp of surprise from the audience, like no one but Amy ever tuned in.

"Oh, for the love of God," Amy would cry at the television. She did not work then and sat through as many of them as she could every day. She hated them all, but she never missed an episode. "Of course, he's cheating! They're always cheating! There wouldn't be a show if they didn't cheat!" And she'd throw some article of clothing at the screen from the piles she was folding.

It never occurred to her that she might be one of those women herself, no. Because real husbands didn't cheat on their dutiful wives, who they'd met in college and who they loved with all their hearts. Only the wives on talk shows got cheated on, and weren't these things fake, anyway? Some of the other topics, when they discussed something other than cheating husbands, seemed so off the wall to Amy that they could only be fiction.

So, when she realized that Mike *was* cheating on her—and she didn't need an anonymous phone call or a note left under her windshield wiper in the grocery store parking lot—she could almost hear the gasp of surprise from the studio audience that wasn't there, could feel the look of pity from an invisible talk show host who shook her head in utter dismay to know such a thing: Amy had been cheated on. Poor Amy. Look at her there in her laundry room with her husband's cell phone in her hand, it buzzing to alert her that there were more messages coming in, and her staring in disbelief at them as they piled up on the screen.

"*All* guys cheat," Adam told her once. This was before she found out that her husband was one of those men, and she had felt the need to argue. Because she watched those daytime talk shows and she had to believe that somewhere in the world, there was a man who actually loved his wife and only wanted to be with her and never so much as thought about being unfaithful, and clung to the belief that it was Mike Cohen.

They were both younger then. Adam had just broken up with his third boyfriend in a year, and he wasn't as hopeful as Amy. She was newly married and planning the rest of her life, amending it on a daily basis: two kids, both boys… or maybe one boy and one girl? And they could get a beach house on Cape Cod. Or Nag's Head. Or anywhere, really.

"That's pretty depressing, don't you think?" she asked him.

He shrugged.

"Well, I don't believe it," she said, and wondered even then whether she was trying to convince herself or Adam.

"You'll find out," he said, and Amy was furious at him because she felt he was basically telling her to prepare herself for the day she learned Mike was seeing someone else, and that didn't seem fair to her. She wanted to yell something at him, but she wasn't sure what that should be. In the end she let it go. Adam was just in his feelings about guys because he was having trouble finding and keeping one.

What she didn't know about Adam's love life was that Adam wasn't always the one being cheated on, that sometimes he was the one going outside of his relationship and being found out and ordered out of the apartment. Or that even when Adam told her that his boyfriend had cheated, it was only half true. They were having sex with other people. And there were even times when Adam met someone and got serious and the two of them just realized that neither of them was ready to settle down with just one person, and that was fine, and they could both go their own way, no harm done. Those particular instances, few and far between as they were, always seemed so grown up to him, and he felt so accomplished afterward. But Amy wouldn't understand, so he never shared those with her. Only the ones that got messy, because she always took his side and he liked hearing her talk her way through the range of emotions that he himself was feeling.

When she learned Mike was cheating, Adam didn't respond the way she wanted. "I told you," he said, and didn't even raise his voice. "Remember that time we were talking and I told you that all men cheat? And you said you didn't believe it? And I said you'd find out?"

Amy wanted to slap him and choke him, but she just laughed and drank her wine. They were sitting on the floor of Adam's apartment with the television muted and Adam's next door neighbor, who did drag on the weekend, playing the same Adele song over and over. "I just thought you were being an asshole."

Adam gulped his wine. "I'm not a fortune-teller," he said, and shook his head. "I'm a historian."

They touched glasses.

While she was married to Mike—before she found out he was cheating and moved back in with her parents—she had a circle of women friends she had very little in common with. They were young like herself, newly married, and in varying stages of motherhood: expecting, nursing, with toddlers, or day drinking because they'd just dropped their twins off at pre-K. The oldest of them was a particularly officious woman named Liz Beth and she advised the rest of them like some hoary veteran of a war only she had fought. "I was the same," she told the mother of the twins, whose name was Julie. "I couldn't wait to get rid of them for the day so I could have some time to myself for a change." Then she got a faraway look in her eyes that Amy was certain she had spent days perfecting in front of a mirror. "And now I wish I could just spend a little more time with them at that age…"

The other women rushed to assure Liz Beth that she was an amazing mother, that there was no way she could have possibly done any more for her children. Amy suspected this was the whole purpose of most of the memories Liz Beth shared with the group and always found a reason to excuse herself when the fawning began.

"When are *you* going to start?" Liz Beth asked Amy. She meant when was Amy planning to get pregnant. The other women turned to her, their eyes wide with expectation and accusation.

She didn't like Liz Beth and was already scheming ways she might get away from the entire group once she did find out she was expecting. But she just smiled sweetly and said, "We're working on it!" The other women laughed like a pack of macaques at what that suggested.

But she was stuck with these women because Mike worked with their husbands in one capacity or another, and it was important that she build relationships with them the way he was building relationships with the men. Amy had only a vague understanding of the logic behind that, and it sounded outdated to her, like something from an episode of *Bewitched* or some other show from the sixties.

"It is important, though," Susan told her when she mentioned it. "Your part is just as important as his in the grand scheme of things. Like your father and me. I drank a lot of coffee with a lot of women I wouldn't have given the time of day to otherwise, but it was part of the big picture."

Amy resented her for that response, but she decided not to argue over it. Susan was old-fashioned and Amy knew that. She'd never considered a career of her own, and instead had thrown herself into supporting Joel getting tenure. Amy should have expected nothing else. The next week she found out she was pregnant.

After dinner, Mike wanted to sit and talk, but she'd had enough of playing the amicable divorcée, and she just wanted to go home. "I *really* need to get back," she said. "Maybe Ethan has stopped hating me by now." She checked the time on her cell phone and it was almost ten o'clock.

"Just one more drink," Mike said. "One more glass of wine. C'mon..."

"It's tempting, but no." They'd already argued over the check. Mike wanted to pay and Amy would have none of it. Whatever his motive—and she hoped it didn't mean what the women who sat in her chair every day said it meant: that when a man pays, it means he expected sex—she did not play along and gave her credit card to the server with the instructions to split the bill. "Don't you have to get home, too? Don't you have work in the morning like the rest of us?"

Mike stood, too. "It's whatever," he said, which didn't really answer the question.

"Well, I have to go. It was nice seeing you." They hadn't really discussed Ethan enough to come to a conclusion or find a solution to what might be bothering him. They agreed it was probably adolescent in nature and might or might not involve the girl named Leah.

"I'll walk you out," he said.

"I'm good."

He ignored her and walked her out anyway. She was parked a couple blocks away, in a community parking deck. They didn't speak. She didn't really have anything to say, but it seemed that Mike might be about to say something several times, then he fell silent again and they kept walking.

"This is my car," she said when they reached it.

Mike looked at it and nodded. Then he kept nodding, but he wouldn't say anything, and Amy felt a curious mixture of annoyance and dread. Couldn't he just let her go home? Or if he was going to say something, just fucking say it, or ask it, so she could respond and go? But he just kept nodding.

"What?" she asked, finally. Barked it, really. "What do you want to say to me, Mike? I know this wasn't really to talk about Ethan since we barely mentioned his name, and now you won't let me get away, so *what?*"

He took a deep breath and he stood there staring hard at her car in the sickly yellow light of the parking deck. Then he looked up at her and said, "I'm sorry."

Amy was so irritated, it didn't even make sense that he was apologizing to her, or why. "For what?" she asked.

Mike gave a small chuckle. "What do you mean for what? For everything, Amy. For being such a dick and cheating on you the way I did. I'm sorry. You never deserved it."

She actually staggered back a step or two in the wake of that apology. From the force of it, she guessed. And she had to reach out and steady herself against the trunk of her car. Mike stepped toward her, smiling. Amy laughed. She wasn't sure what else to do.

"I'm serious, though," he said, even though his smile didn't fade.

"And I believe you." She wondered if she did, though. Because if he had said he was sorry even a month ago, or a year ago, she would have called him a liar and told him he was incapable of actually feeling remorse. But fuck it, she guessed. He'd apologized and she was going to accept it. It didn't mean she forgave him, and she would never forget it, but she could be grown up about it and accept his apology. What was the worst that could happen?

"Thank you," Mike said. "I'm glad."

The next thing she knew, he had stepped even closer and his hands were on her—one at her waist and the other on her arm—and his face had moved in close. It all happened so fast that Amy didn't even register it was happening until it was too late and his lips were on hers.

She pulled away like she'd been scalded. "What the fuck are you doing?" she asked. Her voice was shrill and it echoed in the cavernous parking garage.

He grinned. "Kissing you."

She put her fingers to her lips and pulled them away again, inspected them like she might find blood. "I know *what* you're doing... but *why* are you doing it? God!" She realized then that she couldn't even escape from him because he was standing between her and her car.

Mike seemed to seriously think about it. He even rubbed the stubble on his chin. "I... I don't know," he said with a shrug and a small, nervous chuckle. "It just seemed like the right thing to do at the time."

She gave him a scathing look and pushed him out of the way. "God, Mike... You said you were sorry for being such a dick to me for all those years and I was actually accepting your fucking apology and then you pull that shit. Fuck!" She pulled the car door open and threw herself into the driver seat. "Like, did you think the apology itself wouldn't be enough, so you'd *show* me how sorry you were by acting like a fucking dick all over again? You think a kiss makes it all better...?"

"I... don't know what I thought," he confessed, and stared at the ground with a sheepish look on his face.

"God," she said again. She said it the way she might say it if she used a public toilet and realized there was no toilet paper—with a mixture of disbelief and disgust.

"I'm sorry," he said again.

Amy started the car, backed out, and left him standing there with his hands stuffed into his pockets.

When Amy got home, she went to Ethan's room to see if he was ready to talk, but he wasn't there. His door was open and the silence in the house had an empty quality. She called out to him and her voice echoed back to her. When she called his phone, it rang and went to voice mail.

She was dialing Ethan again when a call from Mike came through. She declined it and called Ethan's number. It went to voice mail again. "Ethan, goddammit!" she screamed, as another call from Mike came through. She answered it and practically screamed "Stop calling. I'm trying to find Ethan. He's not here."

"What—?" She heard Mike ask it as she ended the call and hit redial on Ethan's number.

If he didn't answer her this time, she was going to—what? What could she do? She didn't even know where he was, so it wasn't like she could shake some sense into him, or slap the shit out of him like she wanted. And as she stood there and listened to it ring into nothingness, it occurred to her that he might have just taken a walk around the block and was ignoring her calls as he strolled along, enjoying the knowledge that she was going out of her mind wondering where the hell he was and what the hell might have happened to him.

Right about the time it should have clicked over to Ethan's recorded voice mail message, someone answered, but it wasn't Ethan. "Hello."

"*Dad?*" Amy actually held the phone away from her face and stared at it, like she might see through it.

"Yes, honey, it's me," Joel said, and the way he sounded—so calm, like nothing in the world was wrong with him answering her son's phone—almost pushed Amy over the edge.

"What the *fuck?*"

"Now, calm down…"

Amy laughed. "*Calm down?* Where's Ethan?"

"He's here with me and he's fine," Joel said, in that same annoying tone that Amy was certain would be the death of her.

"I want to talk to him," she said.

"I don't know if—"

She didn't let him finish before she ended the call and grabbed her keys. She was out the door and in her car, backing down the driveway before she realized she was doing it. She was so furious she was close to tears, but she was relieved, too. A pair of headlights swung into the driveway behind her and she slammed on the brakes.

It was Mike and he was out of his car, marching up the driveway toward the house. Amy wondered, inanely, if she had locked the door behind herself. Mike didn't stop to acknowledge her, so she slammed the car into park and jumped out. "What are you doing here?" she asked him.

"Did you find him?" he asked.

"He's at Dad's," she said. "I need you to move your car."

Mike, visibly relieved, fished his keys out of his pocket. "I'll drive you over there."

"I'm okay to go on my own," she said.

"He's my son, too, Amy."

All the fight just left her then. "Fine," she said, and killed the engine to her own car.

Joel was surprised to see Mike and said so. "This is unexpected." He looked at Amy when he said it, his eyebrows raised.

"It's a long story," she said.

But Mike said, "We had dinner."

She felt like kicking him, but she kept her cool. "Where's Ethan?"

"He's downstairs," Joel told her, and to his former son-in-law: "It's good to see you, Mike. It's been a while. You look good. Will you be at the unveiling?"

Amy went in search of Ethan. The basement still faintly smelled of Adam and the years he had spent there; or maybe that was just the basement's smell and Adam had soaked it up—the smile of the wood paneling and years. "Ethan!" she called out.

He was on the old sectional there, completely engrossed in a game of *Mario Kart* on Adam's forgotten Nintendo system. "What are you doing here?" he asked. He didn't turn to her when he asked it, and she didn't like the sound of his voice.

"Well, when I got home and found that my son wasn't there, I called him, but he wouldn't answer," she said, and hoped she sounded as condescending as possible because she wanted him to feel patronized and talked down to. Amy wanted him to leap off the sofa and tell her to stop talking to him like he was a child, because she wanted to tell him that when he acted like a child, she had the right, as his mother, to treat him like one. It was a textbook Susan Schechter Benjamin line and Amy had heard it herself so many times she'd lost count.

Ethan continued to ignore her.

"So imagine my surprise," Amy continued, "when my dad

answered *your* cell phone and told me that you were over here. So, to answer your question, *son*, I am here because you're here."

Mike stepped up behind her, followed by Joel. "What's going on, E?" he asked.

"I'm not talking to you, either," Ethan said, focused on his game.

Mike grunted and walked past Amy, around the sofa, to stand in front of the television. Ethan threw his hands up and slumped back onto the sofa. "Jesus," he muttered. "I'm not going home," he informed them, and folded his arms across his chest. "Grandpa and I already talked about it and he said I can stay as long as I need to."

Amy threw Joel a look. He shrugged, like someone else had made the decision and it was out of his hands. Mike crouched down in front of Ethan. "Well, let's put that on hold for a minute, where you're gonna spend the night," he said, and Amy had to give it to him, he sounded exponentially calmer than she felt. She would be in Ethan's face, screaming. She wasn't certain what was holding her back. "Why don't you tell us what the problem is?"

Ethan turned away and stared into the corner. "You guys wouldn't listen if I did," he mumbled, and sank deeper into the cushions of the sectional.

"I think we both do a pretty good job of listening, E," Mike said. "What makes you think we won't listen to you this time?"

Ethan heaved a sigh. "Because you won't."

"Try us," Mike said.

Amy was mesmerized. She'd never seen Mike parent Ethan like this, though she guessed there had to be moments when they were together where this was the dynamic.

Ethan opened his mouth and his lips moved, but in the end, he shook his head. "No," he said.

"Let's go home, then," Amy said, and gave her car keys a shake so they rattled and punctuated her edict. She was tired and they could yell at each other some other time. Hell, she'd even be open to a therapy session with the three of them to hash it all out, but right then, she'd been going long enough and she just wanted to be at home knowing where everyone was and that everyone was safe. The rest would work itself out.

"I'm not going home, and I wish you'd stop talking to me like I'm five years old," Ethan said, and he glanced from Mike to Amy and back again. "Both of you."

They stared at one another, astonished. They had no idea who this person was. Surely it was not the child they had created between them, who would always need them and look to them for guidance. This was someone else's child, asserting himself in ways he'd never done before, making decisions for himself.

"Maybe we should go upstairs," Joel suggested. Amy had honestly forgotten he was there. "Let Ethan think for a bit and decide what he wants to do. I'll make coffee."

Amy opened her mouth to tell her father that he might not know what Ethan was going to do, but she knew: he was going to stand up and march upstairs and he was going to leave with her. But Ethan cut her off. "I already know what I'm going to do," he said. "I'm going to stay here until I'm ready to go back home." He shrugged. "Or not."

Mike's eyes darted to Amy. She threw him a look that said *Do something*. It was almost like they were still married, but she couldn't recall them ever working so well together.

"Okay…," he said to Ethan. He drew it out, gave himself time to think. "But can you at least give us some idea why you're so pissed off at us both? And why you had to scare the hell out of your mom to get your point across?"

Ethan sighed. "I didn't mean to scare her."

"But you did," Mike reminded him.

"Well…," Ethan said, and shrugged again.

Mike stood. "Fine. Stay here and be a little prick."

Amy could not hide her surprise. She'd never heard Mike talk to Ethan that way, either, and while she had to agree it was probably warranted, she wasn't too sure it would help. If anything, it would probably make things worse.

Ethan stood and turned to him, and Amy had her answer. "Okay, fine. You guys want to know what's wrong with me? *You're* what's wrong with me." He pointed both his forefingers at them across the sectional. "Mom's telling you she's worried that I might be interested in a girl at school, and you're worried that I might be gay because Grandpa is gay and so is Adam."

They stared at him, mouths agape. This was most certainly a side of Ethan none of them had ever seen. Amy and Mike both opened their mouths to speak at the same time, but Ethan held up two fingers to silence them.

"I'm not finished."

They looked at each other, then at Ethan, then back at one another.

"You guys have been so focused on being divorced, it's like you both forgot you had a kid, then I'd pop up with something I need from one or both of you, and it's like a major hassle. Everything anymore is a major hassle for you guys. So you just pass me back and forth. 'Ask your Mom' or 'Did you ask your dad?'"

Amy felt like her insides were dissolving. She felt she needed to cry out, to argue with Ethan, to make him understand that she had never done that; she'd never forgotten she had a son, no way. But as her mind raced, giving her glimpses to illustrate what he was saying, she knew he was telling the truth and she felt herself redden. She glanced at Mike to see if he was feeling the same sense of shame she was. His cheeks were crimson and he was staring hard at a spot on the floor, the muscles in his jaw clenching. This was not about her telling Mike that he was interested in that girl. Well, maybe it was a little, but that was apparently just the spark that lit the fuse and now he was ticking off everything the two of them had ever done—or not done.

"I'm tired of it," Ethan said, picking up his monologue. "So, right now, I'm not going home. I'm not going anywhere with either of you." He looked past them both to where Joel stood. "Is that okay, Grandpa?"

"You can stay here," Amy said, mumbled it.

"You can stay here," Joel said, too.

Ethan nodded, and looked at Amy. "And Mom, I did have a thing for the girl in my biology lab, but she's not interested in me anymore, so you can stop worrying about it so much." He wasn't about to go into all the details of *why* Leah was no longer interested in him, so he just left it there and turned to Mike. "So, that means I'm not gay, Dad. You can stop worrying."

"I wasn't worried," Mike said, and it was apparent from the over exaggerated look of innocence on his face that he had, in fact, been worried about it.

"I still don't want to play golf with you, or go to Braves games... but I'm not gay. I just don't understand the attraction you have to basically every sport there is. I like other things."

"Okay...," Mike said, but everyone in the room knew he was crushed.

"So, you guys can go now."

Upstairs, Joel poured them both wine and they leaned against the counter and said nothing as they sipped it. Amy spoke first. "I guess our little boy isn't so little anymore." She sounded like the mom in a mediocre sitcom that would probably get canceled after three episodes.

"How did he get over here?" Amy asked him. She knew he hadn't walked.

Joel shrugged. "He called me and said he was on his way, and five minutes later, he showed up. Uber, I guess...? Or a cab? Anyway, I was watching television, then Ethan called me and there he was, and he asked if he could stay here. Of course, I told him he could."

"You should have told him to call me," Amy said, and anger flared hot in her chest.

"I did," Joel said. "He said he didn't want to talk to you, and when I asked him why, he said it was a long story."

"I'll say it is," she said. She was still reeling from the accusations he'd made.

When she was thirteen, she "ran away" from home because she decided she couldn't stand the indignity of Susan knowing about her period and sharing it with the ladies in her bridge club, and making comments all the time—to Amy and to anyone else in earshot—about her growing breasts. So she walked to the nearest pay phone and called Aunt Rhoda and Uncle Stanley and asked if she could stay with them. Stanley came shortly after and picked her up in his Buick, which was spacious and air conditioned and smelled like Grey Flannel. He lectured her about the dangers a young, pretty girl like herself might face, alone and unprotected in the world, like he was some kind of authority on the subject. "Your parents are probably worried sick," he said, and Amy remembered how bored he sounded when he said it, like he wasn't sure at all whether or not Joel and Susan were worried sick. Like he was reading from a script.

Rhoda sat her down and demanded to know exactly what the problem was, and when Amy tried to tell her it was a long story and leave it at that, Rhoda would have none of it. "No, ma'am," she said, and leaned in close. They were sitting at the kitchen table and Rhoda had made her a turkey sandwich. "If it's bad enough for you to run away from home, it's bad enough for you to tell me, so spill it. Or else I'll have your Uncle Stanley load you right back up and drive you right back home."

So Amy told her and Rhoda hugged her and said, "Oh, honey, all mothers are like that. It's a wonder Sheila hasn't run away a million times already." Amy made a face at the mention of Sheila, who she didn't like. "Your mother isn't doing it to embarrass you. She's doing it because she loves you and she wants you to be okay with it all, because it all happens so fast and it can be overwhelming."

"But... why does she have to *embarrass* me like she does?" Amy asked in return, and Rhoda laughed.

"That's another thing mothers do, honey. We embarrass our kids." She waved her arms in a circle, encompassing the world and every mother and child in it. "Kids embarrass their parents, and parents embarrass their kids. This goes back to The Flood."

When Susan arrived—because Stanley had gone into the other room and called her—she frowned at Amy and said, simply, "You scared me to death."

Amy burst into tears and they didn't even discuss it as Susan drove them back across town in her Ford Taurus, which was nowhere near as spacious as Stanley's Buick. The air conditioner didn't work, and it smelled slightly of mildew because Susan left the windows down once and it rained.

Now, Amy was reminded of that episode and she felt acute shame, because one thing she had vowed to herself—and to Susan, when they argued—was that her own children would never have the same problems with her that she'd had with her mother. Susan had laughed. "Yeah, keep telling yourself that," she said, which further enraged Amy.

But here she was with a son who was so mad at her he didn't even want to be around her, and she had done the unspeakable—she had embarrassed him, and she knew how: by assuming his relationship status and sharing it with Mike. "I guess I'd be pissed, too," she said, thinking out loud. Mike was driving her home.

"I was thinking the same thing," he said.

They were both silent for a long moment, then Mike said, "We did well."

Amy stared at him, unsure of his meaning. He needed to shave and she noticed the gray spreading through his beard and into his temples. He would look good with a beard, but she knew he would never allow himself to grow one. Guys like Mike Cohen settled into who and what they were early in life, there was no deviation from that, and she pitied him suddenly because he would never allow himself the freedom to be anything other than what he had always been. And she promised herself—like she had sworn to her mother all those years ago—that Ethan would know that he could evolve as necessary.

"I mean with Ethan," Mike explained when he realized she was staring at him and waiting for clarification.

"Oh," she said, but she still wasn't sure where he was going.

"He's a good kid."

She smiled. "He is." That didn't mean she didn't still want to wring his neck, though.

When Mike dropped her off, she felt she needed to say something, but she couldn't decide exactly what. Should she thank him for the way he'd dealt with this new, unexpected Ethan who had his own opinions and wasn't a little boy anymore? She wasn't sure she'd be able to do it without sounding condescending, though, because it was Mike's responsibility to act like a father to their son, and she was sure that would come through in her tone. Or should she just give him a quick "Thanks," and a "Talk to you later?"

"Well," she said at last, and got out of the car. "Thanks."

"Yeah," he said, and gave her a small, lopsided smile. She'd thought it was the cutest thing in the world the first time she'd seen it, all those years ago and all those miles away. It struck her as cute for years, and then came the infidelity and it wasn't cute any longer. Or maybe he just hadn't smiled much while they were going through the divorce. Or maybe Amy had forgotten what it looked like, or stopped noticing. But now she noticed, and for the briefest of moments, it was cute again. Then an alarm sounded in her brain and she snapped back to her senses.

"Talk to you later," she said, shut the door and very nearly ran up the driveway to the door. Mike stayed in his car, watched her as she hurried up the sidewalk and fumbled with her keys. It was irritating, then she realized he was probably waiting to see that she got inside. She waved to him and smiled, then she was safe inside and he backed down the driveway and was gone.

Amy breathed a sigh of relief and slumped against the door. Then she realized how silent and empty the house was and her relief turned to sadness immediately. She'd been at home without Ethan before—sleepovers and summer camp—but never like this. It was different this time. Those other times were fun, planned for weeks and months, so she'd been able to prepare herself mentally and emotionally to come home to an empty house. And this silence was a different kind of silence. It mocked her.

She called Joel.

"Everything is fine," he said with a chuckle when he answered.

4"I just wanted to be sure," she said.

"He's downstairs on the... game thing... whatever it's called."

"Nintendo," Amy said, more to herself than to him. "Is he mad at me?"

"No!" Joel said. Then, "I mean... you heard him. He's upset, but he's not mad at *you* in particular." He paused. "Or Mike, even, for that matter." Another pause. "I think he's going through some stuff and he needed to get some things off his chest, and he did that. He'll be fine. We'll go for breakfast in the morning and he'll probably want to come straight home afterwards. You'll see."

"Maybe," Amy said, and realized she was crying.

"Are you crying?"

"No," she lied. "I've gotta go." And she ended the call before he could say anymore or ask her why she was crying, or tell her again that everything was going to be just fine. She didn't want to hear anything other than the voice in her head that was telling her she had failed as a daughter, as a wife, and as a mother. She would have called Adam—because she was pretty sure she hadn't failed as a sister, at least not yet—but she knew he turned his phone off when he was asleep.

She got up and went into the kitchen, blew her nose on a paper towel, and poured herself a glass of wine. If she was going to be miserable, the least she could do is add alcohol and be the best miserable she could be.

.ten.

Adam needed an excuse to skip the unveiling, but couldn't think of one.

He tried for the better part of an hour and nothing believable would come. He rolled over and checked the time on his phone where it rested on the bedside table. He had two more hours. *Think*, he commanded himself, but when he lay back and closed his eyes, all he could see was everyone's disappointed faces, gathered around his mother's grave as Rabbi Mendel recited the psalms. He wished it was raining, but it was a perfectly beautiful fall day.

"You want me to go with you?" Orson asked several times, and Adam always said it wasn't necessary, mainly because he didn't want Orson to feel awkward not knowing what was going on. "I don't mind," he assured Adam, and Adam believed him. Orson was like that.

In fact, Orson was unlike any guy he'd ever dated, and Adam wondered if that wasn't the reason he told Orson that attending the unveiling wasn't necessary—because he didn't want to expose Orson to his family and have them pick him apart the way they picked everything apart all the fucking time. He liked having Orson to himself, so much so that he hadn't even told Amy that he was dating someone.

Now Orson slept beside him, hot as a furnace under a pile of blankets, snoring just slightly, the way children did when they pretended to snore. Adam moved to spoon him and he stirred. "Hey, baby," he said, and was asleep again the next second.

Adam fell in love with Orson at least twenty times a day, and that both thrilled and shamed him. Because he wasn't supposed to feel that way about a guy, right? Hadn't he lived his entire life by that edict? That's what other guys said, slumped over their cocktails and beers in gay bars from coast to coast—"Honey, I don't need *no* man!" And maybe Adam didn't technically *need* a man. He had a job and a place of his own; his bills were paid and he could take a vacation when he wanted. But it was different with Orson, and he was fine with that. He actually *wanted* Orson.

They'd met at the bakery where Adam worked. Orson walked his dog—a white behemoth of indeterminate breed named Puck—every morning and stopped in for coffee and a pastry and a dog biscuit. Puck stood at the door and gazed inside with longing. Adam noticed the dog first. It took a few more times before he became aware of its owner.

"Hi," Orson said to him as Adam refilled the croissants in the pastry case.

Adam glanced up and smiled. "Hi. That your dog?" He nodded to where Puck sat waiting for Orson to emerge with his biscuit.

"That's my buddy," Orson said, and laughed nervously.

"He's enormous."

Orson laughed. "Yeah," he said. "He thinks he's a lap dog, though."

The mental picture of the dog sitting in Orson's lap made Adam laugh, too. "What's his name?" he asked.

"Puck."

"Awww. What mix is he?" Adam had walked around the counter and was on his way to where Puck waited, tail now thumping against the sidewalk, pink tongue lolling.

"What *isn't* he would probably be a better question," Orson said.

On the sidewalk, Adam crouched to pet the dog and Puck licked his face.

"He likes you," Orson said.

"He's sweet," Adam said, and scratched Puck's ears.

Orson crouched down, too, and if anyone had walked by they would have looked like any other gay couple out with their dog, stopping at the bakery to get coffee and doughnuts. "My name's Orson," he said, and extended his hand.

Adam gave his hand a cursory shake. "I'm Adam," he said, then turned his attention back to Puck. "He's a good boy. Yes, he is." He said it singsong, like he was talking to a baby. "That's an interesting name," he said as he bent down and presented his puckered lips for Puck to lick.

"Puck?" Orson asked. "It's from Shakespeare."

Adam chuckled. "No. *Orson.*"

"Oh." And Orson blushed. "It was my grandmother's maiden name."

They stood and Adam sized him up, took in the frayed shorts and the holes in his t-shirt, his big feet in flip flops. There seemed to be a solid foot of height difference between them, and they were total opposites in every regard: Orson was large, blond, so fair he was practically pink around the edges; Adam was smaller, darker, hairier. "You look like an Orson," he said, and turned to go back inside. He was aware that he was flirting, but he couldn't say why.

"Is that good or bad?" Orson asked, and followed Adam back to the counter where Adam washed his hands and dried them and slipped on a latex glove.

"Depends on your perspective, I guess," Adam said, and leaned against the counter. "Now… what can I get you this morning, Orson?"

Orson stood, caught off his guard. His cheeks turned an even brighter shade of pink. "I'll have a bear claw," he said, finally.

"That's it?" Adam asked, and Orson only nodded.

It took him several days and another visit to the bakery—without Puck this time—to work up the nerve to ask for Adam's number, but it worked. He wore a polo shirt with no holes and pants that time, with Chucks instead of flip flops. He combed his hair and trimmed his beard, and he walked right in and marched right up to the counter, only Adam wasn't at the register, so he got a cinnamon roll and a coffee and loitered until Adam came out of the back bearing a tray of doughnuts.

"Hi," he said through a mouthful of cinnamon roll, and waved the way a child might.

"Hi," Adam said and smiled.

Orson stepped up to the counter as Adam filled the case.

Adam turned and stared past him out to the street. "No puppy today?" he asked, and made a face like it broke his heart.

"No," Orson said, turning and looking for Puck himself. "He's at home."

"That's too bad…"

"Yeah…"

Then they were facing each other and Adam was smiling and the look on his face told Orson he was waiting for something.

Orson laughed, the nervous laugh of a fourth grader about to deliver his first oral book report, or sing the national anthem at an assembly. "Yeah, so I wrote down what I wanted to say and practiced it in the bathroom mirror until I had it memorized," he said, "but I left the paper at home and standing here like this right now, I can't remember a single word of it." Two tiny blooms of pink had blossomed in both his cheeks and Adam felt his heart melt. Adam knew all along that this was where Orson's frequent visits to the bakery were leading, and he knew he could have done or said something to nudge it along, but he couldn't remember the last time a guy acted like this toward him, so he decided to see how long it would take Orson to get to the point. And now he stood there with Orson addressing the case of pastries behind him, listening to this guy pour his heart out, and he thought it was the most adorable thing he'd ever seen. "Look, I've never been good at this. I see a cute guy and I just fall apart—I forget how to speak, and my palms get all sweaty, and I feel like I'm gonna throw up… and then they walk away and I never see them again." He paused to take a breath, then continued. "And when I saw you that first time, I was like, 'He'll never talk to me,' but then you did. I mean… I know it was only because of Puck, but you talked to me. And I'm sure I sounded like an idiot—I can't even remember what we talked about, only that you were talking to me and cute guys never talk to me. And I keep coming here to see you and talk to you and I keep not saying what I want to say because I guess I already know the answer—because it's always the same answer, only the guys are different." He shrugged. "Anyway, I wrote out this whole thing, but now I forget it all. I was going to ask if I could get your number and see if you want to have dinner sometime." A pause. "Or lunch." Another pause. "Or even just coffee." He stopped, glanced around, then rushed to add, "Unless you're completely sick of coffee because you work in a bakery and smell it all the time. It doesn't have to be coffee. It could be tea or something. Anything." He stopped finally, looked down at his feet, at the counter between them, but not at Adam.

"Okay," Adam said.

Orson reacted as if he'd been slapped. "Okay?"

"Yeah." Adam gave him his number. "You're not gonna write it down?" he asked.

Orson fumbled his cell phone out of his pocket and entered Adam's number. His cheeks were pink and he was grinning and he kept saying "Great!" Over and over, more to himself than Adam. "Great."

Adam said, "Great," too.

Orson called him the next day and they went for tacos and beers, then to play pool. Adam wasn't very good, but Orson was patient with him, put his big, soft hands over Adam's and showed him how to hold the cue, to line up his shot. He was sure everyone in the place was staring at him and whispering behind their hands, but he wanted Orson to like him, so he stuck with it. Later, Orson drove him home and walked him to his door and thanked him. Adam was dumbstruck. "You don't wanna come in?" he asked.

"Not this time," Orson said and smiled. Adam saw a dimple for the first time, peeking through his beard.

"Oh." Adam wasn't sure what the next move was. He was used to going on a date then going to either his place or the guy's and having sex, even if it was just a blow job. This was something altogether new—a nice night out with a nice guy (who had a dimple, nonetheless) who didn't want to fuck on the first date. And he didn't even have to get dressed up.

"I'll call you tomorrow, then?" Orson asked.

"Yeah, sure…"

"Great." Orson said that a lot. And he gave Adam a thumbs up, then he was gone and Adam was left wondering what he'd done wrong.

He called Amy. "What are you doing up?" she asked, genuinely surprised.

"I had a date," he said.

She heard the tone in his voice immediately. "That bad, huh?"

"He just thanked me and left," Adam said. "Oh, and he gave me a thumbs up. Like… who the hell does that?"

Amy thought it sounded like something her ex-husband would do on a date, and she wondered if he'd given Bethany a thumbs up after their first date. She laughed, though. For Adam's sake and so she didn't dwell on thoughts of Mike and Bethany.

"I don't think he likes me," Adam said.

"Because he gave you a thumbs up?"

"No, because he didn't want to have sex."

"Oh." She was silent a moment, to give him the time and the opportunity to respond or to elaborate, and when he didn't, she said, "Maybe he did, but he didn't want to insult you by expecting it on the first date."

"Maybe…," Adam said, but he wasn't convinced. After he hung up, he opened the Grindr app on his phone and felt so guilty about it, he closed it and uninstalled it, then texted Orson instead.

Hi. You still up?

Yea, came back immediately and Adam cringed at the sight of it. He knew Orson meant "yeah," and probably didn't know the proper pronunciation of "yea." Lots of people made the same mistake, and he needed to just let it slide, because for some reason he couldn't articulate, he wanted Orson to like him and he wanted that to be clear. He guessed because he liked Orson, and that both unsettled him and thrilled him at the same time.

I had a great time tonight, he texted back, *and I'm not sure if I thanked you. So, thank you.* Adam proofread all his text messages before he sent them for punctuation and spelling. He hoped that didn't annoy Orson.

He received a smiley emoji, then Orson texted *I can't wait to see you again,* and that made Adam feel better. He still couldn't explain the sudden attraction to a guy like Orson, when he'd only ever preferred much smaller, much thinner guys who might have been underwear models or porn stars, and who might or might not have worn makeup.

Now, months later, Orson was offering to go with him to the unveiling of his mother's headstone, creating two potential problems: first, Adam was convinced that Orson would find the entire ceremony tedious since he'd never known Susan, and who in their right mind would want to listen to memories shared about a person he'd never met; and secondly—Adam still hadn't introduced Orson to Joel or Amy.

"When do I get to meet your family?" Orson asked it at regular intervals, and Adam always had a response prepared: Amy's schedule was crazy, his dad was out of town for the weekend, whatever. Anything, really. But if Orson had asked him to explain *why* he'd never introduced them to one another, Adam would not know what to say, because he didn't actually have a reason. He just hadn't. Or maybe he knew why and as long as he didn't admit the reason to himself, he could claim that there wasn't any particular reason, and pretend that it was the half-baked excuses he kept giving. He didn't want his family to meet Orson because he didn't want them to pick him apart. Amy would nag him until she had squeezed every tiny detail about his life and his family's history out of Orson, the way their mother did with every other boyfriend he'd ever introduced them to. Joel, he knew, would pretend to be interested, but would quietly condescend the whole time. Orson was smart, so he would pick up on it and decide if dealing with the Benjamin family was the price he had to pay to date Adam, he would just check out as early as possible. And Adam wanted Orson to stick around.

"Maybe we could have them over one night," Orson suggested. He owned his own home, instead of renting, which was another thing that set him apart from any other guy Adam had ever dated. "I'll do lasagna."

In his defense, Adam still hadn't met Orson's family either. Granted, they were all in Wisconsin, but if he needed to, he could fall back on that argument, though Orson never really pressed him other than to mention it every other week or so. Adam suspected he was more worried about it than Orson was— yet another thing different about Orson: nothing much got to him. He hadn't met Adam's family? Oh, well. He'd never spent the night at Adam's apartment? No big deal, they could just stay at his place.

Orson woke and rolled onto his back. He yawned, scratched his head, stretched. "You're going to be late, baby."

"Yeah. I should probably go." Adam said it into Orson's shoulder, but he made no move to do so.

Orson sat up. "I really don't mind going," he said again, and Adam knew what he was really saying was *Take me with you to this thing and it will take care of two things at once: I'll meet your family and I'll be there for you.*

Adam hadn't explained the situation between him and Joel to Orson, either, and the last thing he wanted to happen was for Orson to see a flare up of the hostilities the first time he got to meet the Benjamins. "You'd just be bored," he said, and kissed Orson's ear, then his jaw, then his dimple.

A look of disappointment flashed across Orson's face, then he smiled. "You're probably right." He swung his legs out of bed. "I'll just go to the comic book store or something."

Adam wished he could do that instead. He wished he could do *anything* instead. He called Amy.

"Are you going?" she asked when she accepted the call.

"I don't want to. Are you?"

"Of course I'm going!" she cried, and her voice was just a bit too strident for him to believe that she hadn't considered not going, too. He knew her better than that. "I don't want to go, but I'm going."

Adam sighed. "Can I call in sick?"

"No. If I'm going, you're going."

Joel left early because he didn't know what else to do with himself. Ethan sat silent on the trip from Dunwoody to the cemetery. "Have you talked to your mother?" Joel asked. He suspected—or worried, rather—that neither Amy nor Adam would attend the unveiling.

"No," Ethan said. "Why?"

"I was just wondering if she remembered today," Joel lied. "Maybe give her a call and make sure she's on her way."

Ethan turned away and stared out the window. "I'd rather not."

"Well... that's fine. I'll call her when we get to the cemetery."

"I talked to Dad and he's coming." The boy didn't sound any more enthused when he spoke of Mike than when he spoke of Amy, Joel noted, but he would leave it alone. He had his own problems with Adam.

He wondered how they had all reached this point—where he and Adam were on the outs, and Ethan wasn't speaking to Amy—and what Susan would think or say about it. She never shied away from conflict, but she refused to endure petty squabbles, and Joel was certain she would label both these as such. She would give them all their space and time to deal with how they were thinking and how they felt about the situation, its causes and its possible solutions, and when she decided—usually without having consulted either party in the disagreement—she would step in and call for an end to it. "This has gone too far!" she would declare, and preside over the negotiations until a solution was reached.

She had done just that when Adam decided to give Joel the silent treatment over acting lessons and ballet when he was younger. Thinking of it now was like a hot knife plunged into his chest; he actually felt the physical pain of a shame that was almost thirty years old. And he was sure Adam had held onto his resentment all that time, too, and that was part of why he reacted the way he did when he found Joel with Kent that morning, because here was a man who had not allowed him to do things because of the stigma attached to them—"gay things," he told Adam the other kids would say—yet here was that same man coming out as gay and engaging in gay things himself. Never mind that it was three decades ago, no. Adam held that grudge and added his fury at Joel's infidelity to it.

And what if Adam did surprise him and show up to the unveiling? "Just smile and thank him and don't start a scene," Susan would say. "You can cause a scene when we get home, but not here. It's tacky." It was one of her greatest fears, to have other people think they were tacky, the measurement of which seemed very low or very high, depending on the behavior. An argument in a cemetery, at an unveiling, he was sure would have reached a new level of tackiness in Susan Schechter Benjamin's book.

"Are *you* okay?" he asked Ethan.

"Yeah," the boy said. "I'm fine." He smiled and it seemed genuine. Then again, he wasn't upset with Joel.

Rhoda and Stanley were waiting for them when they reached the cemetery. Rhoda sat in the car while Stanley took photographs of the Holocaust memorial as if it had changed since the last time he'd seen it. "We got here early," he called to Joel, and shrugged as if to say, *What can you do? We tried to be late, but here we are.*

Rhoda rolled her window down. "How are you, Joely? You good?" She fanned herself with what appeared to be a mailer for pest control, despite the air conditioner blowing in her face.

"I'm fine, Rho. Thanks for asking."

"Good, good," she said with a frown. "Oh, there's Ethan." She waved. "Where's Amy? Is she not going to make it?"

"She's on her way," Joel said with a tight smile. "Adam, too.

They're on the way." And he moved away to join Stanley at the memorial. Ethan took his phone out and leaned against the trunk of Joel's car, texting furiously. Joel hoped he was texting his mother, but Amy pulled into the parking lot a second later. He craned his neck to see if Adam was with her, but the passenger seat was empty.

She parked and took a few minutes to touch up her makeup in the rearview mirror. Rhoda was out of the car now. "There's Amy," she declared, as if no one else could see. Stanley pointed his camera at the clouds and snapped.

Amy got out of her car and went to where Ethan leaned. "So, how's it going?" she asked, and tried to make her voice sound light.

"Fine," he said, without looking up.

"Good," she said, and glanced around. Joel and Rhoda waved to her and she waved back. "I'll be over in a minute!" she called to them. To Ethan, her voice lower, she asked, "How's it at your grandpa's?"

He shrugged. "It's okay, I guess."

Amy nodded. "Do you need anything?"

He shook his head, continued texting, did not look at her.

"Okay…" She had more questions, an entire scene she had played out in her mind as she drove from Decatur: she would ask Ethan, sweetly the way a concerned mother should, how he was doing at Joel's, how he was feeling about things now that he'd had time to think them over, and was he ready to come back home now? And he would say no, she knew that. Or he'd just say nothing, just shake his head, and she would lean in, whisper close to his ear, that after the unveiling, he would climb his happy ass into her car and they would drive to Joel's, where Ethan would retrieve everything he had moved from their house to Joel's, and he would load it into the car and they would drive home because this shit had gone on long enough and the only point he was making was what a fucking dick he was.

That was what she'd planned, but the real Ethan was even more unbothered than the imaginary one, and she wasn't sure now how to proceed. Then there was a car horn, and everyone turned to see Mike parking his Maserati. Amy cut just enough of a look at Ethan to see his face light up, and that took even more wind out of her sails. From behind her, Amy heard Stanley grumble, "At a cemetery, this *nudnik*, he blows his horn."

"Oh, so what, Stanley?" Rhoda asked. She, like Susan, always swooned and fawned over Mike.

Joel asked Amy, "How're things with Ethan? I saw you talking."

Amy shrugged and hooked a thumb back over her shoulder to where Mike and Ethan were huddled together like they were plotting an assassination. It made her blood boil and she had to turn away and occupy herself with something, so she dug her phone out of her purse and called Adam.

"What?" he asked.

"Where are you?" she asked. "And don't fucking tell me you're not coming."

"I'm on the way," he said, and the way he said it made her think he was lying.

Off to her side, Rhoda asked, "Where's the rabbi?" Then she glanced around like he might be hiding from them all.

"Better yet," Stanley asked, "where's Adam?"

"We can have an unveiling without Adam, but not without the rabbi," Rhoda pointed out.

Amy told Adam, "Everyone's waiting on you."

"I'm on the way, but I need to hang up so I don't kill someone," he said. And to punctuate his statement, a car horn sounded on his end. "Bye," he said, then was gone.

Mike had his arm around Ethan's shoulders and Amy was wondering when the hell that started. Behind them, a minivan pulled into a space and Rabbi Mendel got out, grabbed his kippah as the wind lifted it. "Shalom," he called out. "Sorry I'm late." This he said to Joel as they shook hands.

"You're fine," Joel said. "We're still waiting on Adam."

"How are you, Rabbi?" Rhoda asked, a bit too loudly. "It's so good to see you again. I was just talking about you to my daughter. You remember Sheila?"

Amy pulled Mike a few steps away. "What the hell is this?" she hissed, because she was trying to look like she was smiling so Rhoda wouldn't get suspicious.

"What the hell is *what?*" he asked. He really had no idea. Ethan was being interrogated by the rabbi—about school, about sports, about joining a teen task force at *shul*. Ethan was being as polite as he could, but even Amy could tell he didn't want to be having that talk.

"Putting your fucking arm around Ethan like you guys are buddies now," she snapped. "He won't even speak to me, and you guys are pals? What the fuck, Mike?"

"Relax," he said, then immediately realized his mistake. Telling Amy—hell, telling *anyone*—to relax was as good as telling someone to shut up completely. Her eyes widened and her smile vanished. "I mean—"

"I'll relax when you don't undermine me where Ethan is concerned," she said, and she didn't bother to whisper it. Everyone glanced in their direction.

"Underm—" He lowered his voice. "I am not undermining you, Amy."

"Then what the hell do you call that shit?" she asked, pointing to the spot where he had walked moments before with his arm around Ethan. "A week ago, he didn't want to speak to either of us. Remember? We were *both* his problem, and he wanted space to deal with... whatever it was he needed to deal with, and we agreed to give it to him. Now, you guys are all chummy and he won't even look up from his fucking phone to talk to me."

Joel stepped over. "Is everything okay?" he asked, and it was clear he asked it so they would lie and say it was and stop arguing in front of everyone.

Amy said "No," and Mike said "Yes," and they said it in unison.

"Well, whatever it is, fix it or shut up about it," Joel said, and fixed them both with firm glares of disapprobation. "You can fight somewhere else later, where the rabbi can't see you, and where I don't have to explain to Rhoda what's going on. Unless you want your problems all over Atlanta by tomorrow morning."

Amy threw Mike a dark look and stepped away. "What are you doing?" Ethan asked her.

Amy stalked off without responding.

Ethan reacted as if she'd slapped him. "It's nothing," Mike lied, and threw his arm around his son's shoulders, steered him toward the entrance to the cemetery.

Amy dug her phone out of her purse. "I'm calling Adam," she said in answer to the disapproving look Joel gave her, just as Adam's car appeared over Joel's shoulder, pulling into the parking lot. Amy met him as he climbed out of the driver's seat. "Jesus, Adam!" she hissed.

"What?" he asked, though he already knew.

"It's Mom's fucking *unveiling*."

Adam rolled his eyes, but he was wearing sunglasses, so she didn't see it. "I'm here, aren't I?" he said, and left it there. It wasn't like he was late to the funeral, or the *shivah*. Amy was just being dramatic, like she always was because she worked closely with gay men every day.

Joel joined them. "I'm glad you made it," he said, and gave Adam a small smile.

"I'm here for Mom," Adam said, and stepped away. Rhoda hugged him like she hadn't seen him in years, and Stanley clapped him on the back like he'd won a trophy.

Let's just get through this, Joel told himself. *Let's just get through this, then everyone can go back to hating each other, and no one will have to speak to anyone else until Rosh Hashanah, and it'll be okay...*

"Are you ready, Joely?" Rhoda called to him.

"I'm coming," he told her.

Rabbi Mendel waited patiently while everyone assembled around Susan's headstone, which had been erected a year before and was now covered for the symbolic "unveiling." Adam and Amy stood together and shared a look that seemed to question the entire enterprise. Mike stood with his arm around Ethan, and Joel stood with Stanley and Rhoda.

"It's a nice day out," Rhoda remarked.

The rabbi gave her a smile, then turned to Joel. "I thought we might start with a few psalms," he said, and addressed everyone else in turn. "And since we don't have a *minyan*, we can recite the prayer for the soul of the departed—the *Kel Maleh Rachamim*." They all exchanged worried glances, like students who had been surprised with a test for which no one had studied.

"You think I memorize this stuff?" Stanley could be heard asking Rhoda.

"Shh!" she said, and slapped his arm.

Rabbi Mendel smiled and produced papers from the inside pocket of his blazer. "It's okay. I took the liberty of printing the prayers out." He handed them to Joel, who then distributed them to everyone.

"Thank God," Adam muttered, and Amy elbowed him in the ribs.

"Shall we begin, then?" the rabbi asked, and Joel answered him with a nod.

The rabbi's voice was clear and strong as he started in on the psalms. Joel joined in first, then Rhoda and Stanley, then Mike. Amy only half-heartedly participated, and Adam crammed his hands into his pockets and stared at the cloth covering Susan's headstone. Ethan glanced at Amy off and on, then pretended to look elsewhere when she tried to meet his gaze and give him a look that made it clear she was displeased with him.

Adam wished he'd stayed at home, then felt like he was dishonoring Susan's memory somehow, and tried to pay better attention.

"Would anyone like to share their memories of Susan?" Rabbi Mendel asked, and smiled around the circle.

They all looked at one another with polite deference, no one really wanting to be the one to share a memory but wanting to seem like they did. The rabbi was patient as the looks were traded around. Rhoda and Stanley whispered to one another, their heads bent close, like they had so many memories of Susan they couldn't decide which one to share, but they wanted it to be a good one, a memory that no one else would share.

Finally, Joel spoke up. "I'll go first," he said, and the relief that swept the small circle was visible. He stepped forward, cleared his throat, and stood like he might deliver his memory in a song rather than speak it. "I miss her," he said, and his shoulders slumped the slightest bit once he had said it. Then, as if someone had challenged his confession, he added, "I do. She was in my life longer than anyone but you, Rhoda." And there he turned and gave his sister a tiny smile.

"She was," Rhoda confirmed, and Stanley gave her a quick nudge and threw her a look that told her not to interrupt.

Joel turned back around, addressed the cloth that covered Susan's headstone as it fluttered in the wind. "And what a presence she was," he continued. "She could have done anything, really—she could have been an actress, or a writer, something like that. Something big and important, you know…? On the world stage. I always wondered why, of all the things she could have done and been, she decided to marry me and be a mother." He shook his head. "She loved you kids," he said, flicking his eyes from the covered stone to where Amy and Adam stood, wary looks on their faces. "More than she loved me," he added, and laughed. Everyone else laughed, too, but it was the laughter of discomfort. "That's a good thing, too. That's how it should be. Mothers love their kids more than anything in the world. More than they love themselves, even."

"Where is this going?" Adam asked Amy, lowering his head when he did it, so only she could hear him.

"I don't know, but I am incredibly uncomfortable," she said.

"She was just such a character," Joel continued. "Larger than life, really. What did you kids call the way she dressed? *So Boca?*" He chuckled. "She was *So Boca*." Then he was crying, and it happened so quickly that no one was entirely sure of what they were seeing for a few seconds. Even Rabbi Mendel continued to smile and nod at Joel as if he were sharing more memories of Susan. It wasn't until Rhoda stepped forth and pulled Joel into a sideways embrace that he realized what had happened.

Amy and Adam both looked away, across the cemetery, at the clouds, at the trees, but not at Joel and not at one another.

Joel said, "I'm sorry…"

"It's okay," Rhoda assured him, and gave him a squeeze. "You're fine. She was definitely a character."

"Would anyone else like to share a memory of Susan?" the rabbi asked.

It was Mike who responded, and Amy was both surprised and glad that he had so she wouldn't have to. "She was a great lady," Mike said, and did not elaborate.

Amy wracked her brain for a suitable memory to share, but all she managed to come up with were arguments or disagreements with Susan over everything from prom dresses to the appropriate shoes to wear to a *yizkor* service, to how to best trick Ethan into eating foods other than macaroni and cheese when he was a toddler. Everything, it seemed to her then as she stood and stared hard at the cloth that covered her mother's grave stone, had been a fight about something.

"Get mad at me, I don't mind," Susan always said to her toward the ends of these arguments. "You'll realize I'm right, though. I've been there and I've done it and I was the same way to my mother, but she knew best and it almost killed me to admit it." Amy always just rolled her eyes. "But when you do realize that I was right—because I am—don't worry about it. Don't call me to thank me or anything because it isn't necessary, believe me. I already know."

"God, will you shut up already?" was Amy's usual response.

Susan answered it with an exaggerated shrug, flung her arms wide in a gesture of complete surrender. "I'm shutting up," she said, and she smiled because, like she had already stated, she knew she was right.

And Amy did realize she was right, and it so infuriated—and, secretly, relieved—her that to admit it aloud to anyone would have shamed her, so she sat and stewed. She followed the advice Susan gave her, but she hated it. And so Susan was right again: Amy never called her to thank her.

Now she wished they could have had a fight about how Amy was supposed to act after her mother died. Grandma Schechter passed away when Amy was a sophomore in college, and Amy had watched as Susan went through the prescribed stages of mourning—she was well aware of them and knew what was expected of her during each stage, so that wasn't the issue. What she needed to know was what to do with herself once there was no longer a script to follow. And what was she supposed to do to stop feeling the way she felt—that she had been so focused for so long on being the typical rebellious daughter, who grew into the typical rebellious young woman who went as far away as she could for college and married a man she met there, who grew into the typical rebellious young mother who would raise her child the way she wanted and not rely on the outdated ways of her hopelessly out of touch mother, who grew into the typically rebellious divorced single mother, whose mother could have no idea what she was going through and could therefore give no advice… that she had forgotten the *daughter* part and had only ever succeeded as rebellious.

She sighed.

Adam asked her, "You okay?" He'd just watched the emotions play across her face.

"Yes," she said, right before she burst into tears the way Joel had.

Adam took a step back. Joel was still sobbing quietly, and now Amy was practically wailing. Ethan started, too, and he even saw Mike make a quick swipe at his eyes. Adam felt like a tourist surrounded by people who spoke a language he didn't. He exchanged a quick look with Rabbi Mendel. They were in this together, that look said, only neither of them knew what to do to get themselves out of it.

"Let's say the prayer, Rabbi," Rhoda said. "The prayer for the departed."

"Yes… yes…"

Everyone fumbled with their papers as the rabbi began, his voice clear and strong as he chanted the *Kel Maleh Rachamim*. Joel and Amy tried, their voices faltering; Rhoda's voice challenged the rabbi's, with Stanley's deep baritone a vague counterpoint, as he managed to stay just slightly off from everyone else.

Adam stared at the ground, puzzled that the grass had grown so thick over Susan's grave in just a year. He'd expected it to be sparse, sickly, in need of the same attention her abandoned garden at home needed. And when Joel removed the cloth from the headstone, he read and reread what was inscribed there, though he already knew it because he had helped with the decision:

SUSAN LOUISE SCHECHTER BENJAMIN
Beloved Wife and Mother
1960-2017

She would have hated that, he thought again, just like he'd told Joel and Amy when they were discussing what it needed to say. "It's unnecessarily sentimental, and you both know she hates shit like that," he argued then. "It should just have her name, maybe her Hebrew name, and the day she was born and the day she died. That's it."

Susan herself often wondered about it aloud. "Why do people put poetry on their gravestones?" This was even before her diagnosis, before she herself needed to start seriously considering what would be put on hers. "Just the stupidest shit, sometimes. I had an uncle who put *'Veni, vidi, vici'* on his, and I've always wondered about that. He never conquered anything! He was a goddamned kosher butcher in Jersey!"

Joel suggested poetry and oft-repeated quotes from the likes of Emily Dickinson and Sylvia Plath. "No," Susan said to each in turn. "No, no, no! God!" Then one day she was alone with Adam in the den and she leaned in and whispered, frantically, "Do *not* let your father put some sentimental bullshit on my headstone, Adam."

He only half glanced up from the magazine he was reading. "Okay...?"

"I mean it. Promise me!" She hissed it at him, like a curse, so he promised.

"Okay."

Then Joel insisted they put the word "beloved" on the stone, and when Adam pointed out, politely, that it wasn't really Susan's style, Joel scoffed and said something to the effect that he had known his wife longer than Adam had, and he would make a better choice of what did or did not go on the stone. Adam shrugged and said, "Whatever," but now, seeing it infuriated him because now he knew things about Joel, and about the relationship between his parents, that he hadn't known then, and that word—*beloved*—just looked and felt like the biggest lie ever told. It felt like Joel's guilt at having lied to Susan and everyone else, and it felt like a Band-Aid over the cancer that was all the lies he'd told for the thirty-eight years they were married.

Adam knew he needed to do something before he did or said something there in front of everyone—Rhoda and Stanley and the rabbi—that he wouldn't be able to take back, so he turned and stalked away. "Where are you going?" Amy called after him.

"Over here," he said, which sounded dumb, but it was better than nothing.

"I have a little spread at the house," Rhoda announced. "Everyone's invited. It'll be nice."

Everyone tried to think up a sufficient enough lie that would excuse them from going, but Rhoda was persistent. And Stanley joined in, too. "That's very nice of you, Rho," Joel said, and blew his nose. "Very thoughtful. Of course we'll all come."

Amy threw Adam a beseeching look. He called past her to Rhoda: "Sorry, Aunt Rho. I've gotta get back to work."

"But I thought you said you took the whole day off," Amy said, her tone mock-innocent. She even batted her eyes at Adam.

"You can come by for a bit, surely," Joel said, and Adam gave up quicker than he'd expected to.

He just shrugged.

At Rhoda's there was enough food to feed them all for a week. "Just a little something I threw together," she said as she removed casseroles from the oven and unwrapped salads from the refrigerator. "It's so rare that we're all together like this. It'd be a shame if we didn't take advantage of it. Stanley, can you get the salad tongs out of the drawer there? No, the other ones. Yes, those."

Amy pretended she had to make a phone call and stepped out onto the back terrace. Adam followed her, despite Rhoda's insistence that he eat.

"It'll get cold," she said, though most of it was already cold.

"Just a minute," he said, and closed the door as his aunt started complaining about her husband's choice of wine. He asked Amy, "What's the matter with you?"

"Nothing."

He knew it was a lie. "Yeah, right. You won't even look at your kid."

That was all he had to say and she wheeled on him. "Did you see that shit?" she asked, and waved an arm in the general direction of everyone sitting inside.

"What shit?"

"Ethan! And Mike! What the hell is all that?"

"Calm down," he said, because they were on full display there through the French doors leading from the dining room where everyone sat, passing kugel and whitefish salad. He saw her eyes widen and knew he shouldn't have said it, so he took her by the arm and led her away, out of sight of everyone, toward the back of the yard where Stanley's gardening shed threatened to collapse into the weeds that surrounded it.

"Don't tell me to calm down," she said, and jerked her arm free.

"Fine, then don't calm down, but don't freak out where everyone can see you."

She glared at him, then she glared back at the house. Then her shoulders slumped and she seemed on the verge of tears again.

He laughed, but not because he thought what she'd said was funny. "Look... I'm no expert, but this seems suspiciously like a nervous breakdown, so I'm asking: are you okay? Because you don't seem okay, and I don't know what to do."

"I'm okay," she said, but neither of them was convinced. "I just don't know what to do."

Adam fished his cigarettes out of his pocket, then he remembered where he was and put them back. Rhoda would have a fit, and with the state of the lawn and shrubbery, it would probably start a fire. "Well, I hope you don't think I can help. I'm still trying to get around the fact that our dad is gay and fucked around on Mom." It still surprised him that he wasn't over his initial fury. He would think he was fine and go about his business, then something would remind him of it, and he'd be furious all over again.

"I'm so pissed at Ethan right now, I could wring his neck," she said. "And I know I should feel really bad about that, but I don't." And she laughed. "God, I'm a horrible mother..."

"You're no worse than all the other mothers in the world," he said, and reached again for his cigarettes.

"I cut these women's hair and they just go on and on about the things they do for their kids and how they feel about their kids, and what great kids they have, and I just want to beat them all bloody with my brush because I know it's all fucking bullshit." She swiped at the remains of Stanley's cannas. "But then I wish that I could say all those things about Ethan, and I can't, and I feel like a shitty mother. Then I start to think that I only feel like a shitty mother because Mike cheated on me and turned me into a shitty mother."

Adam couldn't follow her logic and it showed on his face. "What...?"

Amy heaved a sigh. "Nothing," she said, then corrected herself. "Because if my husband hadn't cheated on me, I wouldn't feel like a failure. I would have been able to focus all my energy on raising my kid and I just don't think we would be here right now, with him acting out the way he is, and me wanting to strangle him."

"He's a teenager," Adam reminded her. "He'd be acting like this even if you and Mike had stayed together, because he's a ball of raging hormones right now and he doesn't know his ass from a hole in the ground."

"Maybe…"

"What are you kids doing out here?"

They turned to see Joel approaching across the dry lawn. "Nothing," Adam said. It came out snippier than he'd anticipated.

"We're just talking," Amy said.

"Well, Rhoda's starting to get worried, and you know how she gets, so maybe you guys should come on inside before she comes looking for you."

"I'll probably just go on home," Adam said, and made like he would do just that, fished his keys out of his pocket and started away from them toward what remained of the side gate out of the backyard to the driveway.

"How long is this going to go on, Adam?" Joel asked, his tone a mix of annoyance and exasperation.

Adam froze where he stood, but didn't turn. "How long is *what* going to go on?" he asked, and it sounded to Amy like he was speaking through a clenched jaw.

"This…," Joel said. "Whatever this is that you're doing… not talking to me, walking away whenever I come near you…"

Amy knew she should say something, step between them and diffuse the situation before it actually became a situation, but it escalated quicker than she could move. Adam turned and stepped toward Joel and when he spoke, his voice was only barely more than a whisper. "I don't know, Dad. How long did you fuck around on Mom? Thirty-eight years? Let's start there."

And Joel's reaction came just as fast, only louder. "So, you're going to hold that over my head for the rest of my life?" And he laughed, a short, sharp bark of derision. "Your mother's been gone a year now, Adam. Staying pissed at me forever isn't going to change that. My having sex with men didn't give her the cancer, you know."

Joel couldn't believe he'd said it out loud, and the look on his face made that clear.

Amy had to admit he had a point. "Let's not fight," she heard herself say, and it sounded like it came from over the fence, in the neighbor's yard. "We should be remembering Mom today…" But hadn't she told her own son not to speak to her? Could she be any less convincing?

"I hate you," Adam said to Joel, his voice louder now. He pointed a finger at Joel and continued: "And I've always hated you. I tried not to, because I thought if I did, it would make me a bad person. Even when you wouldn't let me do a *single thing* I wanted to do when I was a kid, because you always said you wanted to spare me the indignity of being called names by the other kids… but now we know it was just because you didn't want your son to be gay where anyone could see… because it might alert people to the fact that you were a raging fag yourself. You remember all that, right, Dad? All your bullshit excuses? I hated you then and I felt bad about it, but right now… I hate you and it feels good."

Joel stared hard at a spot on the ground between himself and Adam. He guessed he might have said he was sorry, but he'd said it enough. And saying it had changed nothing. Adam was still pissed, Amy was still walking on eggshells around him, Kent had practically disappeared, and after today, he was pretty sure the entire family was falling apart, and there was nothing he could do about any of it.

"You don't mean that," Amy said to Adam, then to Joel: "He doesn't mean that."

"Yes, I do," Adam said.

"You're just upset." And Amy tried to fix her brother with one of those looks of Susan's from their childhood that told him to behave and not make a scene, but it was an ill fit and Adam wasn't falling for it anyway.

Then Rhoda materialized out of nowhere. "What's going on out here?" she asked. The look on her face was grim and it was clear—at least to Joel—that she knew very well what was going on.

"We were just talking," he told her, and tried to smile, but it fell flat.

Rhoda grunted. "Yes," she said. "I heard."

"Adam's just in his feelings," Amy said, trying to make light of it and defend her brother at the same time.

"It's nothing," Joel said. "Let's all go back in and eat." And he stepped past Rhoda and Adam to do just that.

No one else moved, and Rhoda said, "It's easy to be mad at your father." She said it to Adam, even though his back was to her.

"Rhoda..." Joel said, his tone a warning, but what could he really do? She would say what she was going to say and he wouldn't have any way to punish her for it. She wasn't a child, and neither were Amy and Adam, and maybe it was time they heard the entire story.

"You don't know anything about this," Adam said, but his voice was barely above a whisper.

Amy said, "I'm not sure what's about to be said here, but I don't like it already." It was like she was talking to herself.

"Rhoda, really," Joel said. "It doesn't matter."

"It does," Rhoda barked. Then she pointed her finger at Adam. "And you, young man, can hate him all you want, but if you're going to do that, then you're going to have all the information, and I hope you're ready for it."

Adam turned to her then, his eyes squinted slightly with confusion, like peering at his aunt might help him see better where she was going with all this.

"Rhoda, please..." That from Joel, but his tone was one of defeat. He knew there was nothing to be done at this point. The subject had come up several times since Joel told her he was gay and how Adam found out. She was also well aware that Adam wished Joel was dead. "This isn't necessary."

Amy's suspicions were adequately aroused now. "Apparently Aunt Rhoda feels it is," she said, and there was a slightly scathing tone to her voice. She glanced past her aunt to where Adam stood, inspecting his fingernails, like he couldn't have cared less whether Rhoda divulged anything or not.

Rhoda threw them both a look, first Amy and then Joel, but

when she spoke, it was to Adam. "You think what he did was so unforgivable?" she asked, and Adam continued to check his fingernails. "Answer me. You came here and ruined a perfectly nice afternoon because you think what your father did to your mother was so horrible you'll never be able to forgive him? That's what you're saying?" Rhoda turned to Amy. "You feel the same way?"

"I—" What? She didn't think she did. Had she said something that made Joel think she couldn't forgive him for being gay, for going outside his marriage for fulfillment? "No," she said after a moment, and she was certain of it.

"Good," Rhoda said. "Because your mother wasn't a victim." She glanced back at Adam, then again at Amy. "She wasn't a fool and she wasn't a victim."

Adam heaved an enormous, overly dramatic sigh and rolled his eyes. "Look, whatever," he said. "I don't know what this is about, or what it's supposed to be about, or where the hell it's even going, but I'm done. I'm going. It was great seeing you, Aunt Rho, and I'm sorry I can't stay longer, but I am really, *really* not in the mood for a lecture on… whatever it is this lecture is about." And he turned to go back inside.

"Fine," Rhoda said, and Amy noticed the color rise into her cheeks. "You can go, but before you do, hear this: your father wasn't the only one who went outside the marriage. Your mother did, too."

Adam paused, glanced back over his shoulder at Joel but not at Rhoda. It seemed he might say something, but he reconsidered, and then he was gone, leaving the door open in his wake.

"What the hell's going on out there?" Stanley called from inside, but no one answered him.

"It just came out," Rhoda said to Joel later as they wrapped all the uneaten food with Saran wrap and returned it to the refrigerator. "I heard the yelling and I came to see what was going on and there the three of you were, and I realized what was going on and… it just came out."

"It's okay," Joel said, although it wasn't. It was said and it couldn't be taken back, so they were all going to have to deal with it somehow, but that didn't make it okay. He just didn't know what else to say.

Over his thirty-eight years of marriage to Susan—and the accompanying years of infidelity—little about the men he'd been with stuck with him. He vaguely recalled a few faces, and a name here and there, but everything about them had faded over time until the only clear recollection he had of any of it was the guilt he felt after each infidelity. And how he had, to alleviate his own guilt, hoped that Susan herself was not sitting around waiting for a miracle to give her the husband she thought she'd married. Especially after the kids were born and she had seen them through infancy and toddlerhood and into school, Joel had hoped that she, like himself, was finding fulfillment somewhere.

He hoped, and then started looking for the signs that would assure him she was. Susan was crafty, though, and it took him some time before he realized that the most mundane things, the things she had been doing all along, were the signs he was looking for: lunches that took longer than they should, meeting "the girls" for dinner on the other side of town although none of the other faculty wives lived outside the Perimeter, the sudden appearances and subsequent disappearances of bottles of perfumes. "Turns out I didn't like it as much as I thought," she told him with a shrug when he asked, which was rarely. "I returned it and got the money back."

Joel wondered if she had seen any of the men he worked with, and if so which ones. Those would be the easiest, he supposed. She knew them all and she knew their schedules and the schedules of the wives who were all her friends. It would also be the most awkward should anyone—a wife more likely than Joel—learn of it, so perhaps she went outside that particular social circle. The eighties did not present the same types of opportunities that the internet age would a decade later, but people found ways around it, Joel knew.

Rhoda succeeded where Joel failed and found proof, albeit accidentally. Joel found out much later, from Susan. "She isn't talking to me, apparently," she told him with a shrug. He'd suggested they collaborate on the Seder for Passover

"What?" Joel asked. He'd heard her, but it didn't register. Rhoda and Susan always got along great.

"She's not talking to me. I saw her at *shul* last weekend and she avoided me like the plague. I kept trying to talk to her, but she kept walking away or she'd see me coming and start talking to someone else. Then she was gone. Didn't speak to me the entire time." And there Susan gave one of her dramatic shrugs.

"That's ridiculous."

"Yeah, I know." She flipped the pages of her magazine. Joel suspected she wasn't really paying attention to it.

The next day, he called Rhoda from his office.

"She said that?" Rhoda asked, and laughed. Even through the phone, it sounded fake to Joel. "I was busy was all. Then as I was driving home, it hit me that I'd seen Susan there and never got to talk to her."

That sounded plausible to Joel. "Well, call her and apologize. She thinks you're mad at her."

"I'm not," Rhoda said.

"I know that, but she thinks you're mad, so call her. And the two of you need to plan the Seder."

There was silence from Rhoda's end.

"Hello?"

"Yeah, Joely, about that. About the Seder…" And she told him that they'd been invited to another one already, with the Friedmans, and Joel knew something was wrong because they always did First Night Seder together.

He asked her, "Okay, Rho, what's the matter?"

And she said, "Nothing. I told you."

"Bullshit."

Rhoda heaved an audible sigh on her end. "She says she has no idea?" she asked, relenting. "Fine. She has no idea what the problem is, but Joely... what's going on with the two of you?"

Joel's blood turned to ice. He lived daily with the fear someone would find out he had sex with other men; that one of the men he did it with would be found out and it would ripple outward, sweep him up. Or that he would be seen entering a hotel, no matter how far outside the Atlanta metro area he went to do it. And now, he was certain that Rhoda had found out. Someone she knew saw him and asked her about it and the reason she wasn't able to speak to Susan that day—and the reason she has made other plans for the Seder—is that someone asked her about it and she didn't know what to say. Then she saw Susan and instead of saying the wrong thing, she said nothing. And now, with Joel, she is still unsure. "What do you mean by that...?" he asked.

"I mean just that—what's going on with the two of you?"

"Nothing," he lied. "Nothing's going on with us."

"Then why is Susan having lunch with strange men, Joely?"

He was so relieved to hear her ask that, he had to clamp a hand over his mouth to keep from laughing. Then he was so relieved, he felt like crying. Then he said, "Rhoda, that's—you sound ridiculous. What are you even talking about?"

She told him about being at Colony Square one afternoon last week with Marge Fisch and how they'd dipped into the food court there for a quick nosh and there was Susan sitting and laughing with a man Rhoda had never seen before. "In broad daylight," Rhoda declared.

Joel did laugh then. "Well, what else?" he asked, his relief at not being found out like a drug spreading through his body. He didn't even mind that Susan might be having an affair of her own.

"What do you mean *what else?*" Rhoda was appalled. "What more do you need?"

And Joel explained that there was probably a reasonable explanation—even though he couldn't think of one right then—and that Rhoda shouldn't jump to conclusions. Susan was on the board at the JCC, so it might have been someone from there, or it could have been an old friend from college in town. Honestly, there were any number of explanations. "But whatever it is, there's no reason to cancel the Seder and give Susan the silent treatment."

"Okay, fine," Rhoda said. She didn't sound fine, but Joel was not going to press it.

"Just call her and talk to her and work this out."

"Fine."

"And stop saying that," Joel said.

"Okay, fi—" She sighed. "Okay. I'll talk to you later, Joely."

Now she brought it up to Amy and Adam and Joel felt unmoored, even more so than when forced into coming out because he'd slipped up and let himself be caught. This seemed more disrespectful to Susan's memory than anything he might have done.

"I'm sorry, Joely," Rhoda said again.

"It's fine, Rho," he said, and tried to think how he might make it that way.

.eleven.

"Now what?" Amy asked when she and Adam got together a week after the unveiling. They were on her back patio and the cicadas and tree frogs were deafening. Soon the sun would set and she had already turned on the lights and lit citronella torches to keep the mosquitoes away.

"What's that even mean?" Adam asked. He hadn't wanted to come but Amy insisted, so he brought beer and a fresh pack of cigarettes. She told him he couldn't smoke, so he told her he'd go back home. She relented.

Now they sat with their feet on the railing overlooking the dense overgrowth that constituted the back half of Amy's property. At one time there were plans to clear it all and put in a pool, but Mike cheated and she filed for divorce and now it was an urban jungle. It was nice to sit at night in the summer and watch the fireflies in and among the leaves, but it scared Amy a bit, too. She'd seen raccoons and possums and suspected there might be even worse. Like, what if there was a homeless camp in there somewhere? Forget that she could see through it to the back of the house on the other side; she would not be convinced her fear was irrational.

"I mean," Amy said, "what now? You and Dad aren't speaking. Ethan and I aren't speaking." She grabbed his pack and shook a cigarette out. "And apparently, Mom was fucking around on Dad, too."

He cut her a suspicious look. "You don't smoke. And good for Mom."

"Maybe I'll start." She lit the cigarette and took a drag,

coughed, but was undaunted. "And how is it good that Mom was cheating, but it isn't okay that Dad did?"

Adam gaped at her. "Is that a serious question?"

"Of course it's a serious question." Her voice rose in pitch and volume from one end of the remark to the other. "They both had needs and they both deserved to live a fulfilled life, so they did what they needed to make that happen."

He rolled his eyes. "That's about the weakest argument in defense of marital infidelity I've ever heard." He lit his own cigarette, then continued: "It isn't like they sat down and had a discussion about it and agreed to an open marriage. Dad was dishonest."

Amy laughed. "And you think Mom wasn't? Come *on*, Adam…"

He was tired of this conversation all of a sudden. "Okay, fine. Subject change: you should make Ethan come back home," he said, and sipped his beer. "You let him get away with too much and now he's running the show."

It was Amy's turn to gape.

"And don't give me that look." Adam aimed his beer bottle at her. "You know what I'm talking about and you know I'm right, so don't bother clutching your pearls. You've always spoiled him, then when you guys got divorced, that just made it worse because neither of you wanted to tell him no, so he's turned into a thirty-year-old teenager." He paused and nodded to where her mobile phone sat on the table between them. "You get on the phone and you tell him to get his ass home."

Amy looked for a second like she might do just that, but instead she grabbed the bottle of wine and poured herself another glass.

"Not to mention there's no telling what kind of example Dad is setting for him." He grunted. "And I'm sure he'd rather have Ethan out of there, too."

"Now you're just being an asshole, Adam."

He shrugged. "Whatever."

Amy had wondered it, though. Like, Joel said Ethan could stay as long as he wanted, but did he *really* feel that way, or was he just trying to keep the peace? Joel was that way: he said and did things to avoid conflict; and there was already enough conflict—between him and Adam, between Amy and Mike—so giving Ethan a place to stay away from all of it seemed like a good idea, but was it really? And what must it be like for Joel, so new to his own lifestyle and eager to enjoy it but unable to because he had to consider his teenaged grandson at home. What kind of buzzkill was that, when he told men he had to get home to his grandson? Amy could only imagine.

"He's let Mom's garden go to shit."

Amy wasn't sure what Ethan had done to Susan's garden, then she understood he meant Joel. "I'm sure it wasn't intentional."

Adam shrugged. "Maybe."

He drank his beer and Amy sipped her wine. An owl hooted from the trees. "You can't avoid him forever," she said, finally.

"I could move away."

That won him a laugh. "To where?"

"I don't know. Seattle. San Francisco. Somewhere."

"You're not going to move, Adam."

She was probably right. Moving to a new apartment three blocks away was enough stress; he couldn't conceive of what moving across the country would entail, and just thinking about it made him itch. And what would he tell Orson? "Hey, I'm moving to the other side of the country because I hate my dad *that much*. You wanna come, too?"

He wanted to be with Orson, instead of there rehashing everything he felt and thought about Joel. It dominated every conversation these days and he was tired of always having to discuss it, especially since he felt he'd made himself quite clear. With Orson, they watched cheesy old sci-fi films and ate junk food and had sex. Or not. Sometimes, Adam just slept, curled into a ball with his back against Orson's hip while Orson read (usually some massive history or fantasy). Later they would go in search of tacos or pizza and they wouldn't talk about Joel at all.

Amy, on the other hand, brought it up any chance she got. She would call him on her lunch break just to ask if Adam had relented and called Joel. Or she texted him throughout the day.

Have U called Dad?

Have U talked 2 Dad yet?

U and dad should really sit down and talk this out. I hate 2 C U both like this. Call me.

Adam wished she would use actual words. And he stopped responding to them. Amy was well aware that he had not and he would not, no matter how much she harangued him about it.

As soon as the idea to go be with Orson came to him, he sat up and stuffed his feet into his shoes. "I'm heading out," he said, and shoved his phone into one pocket, his cigarettes and lighter into the other.

"Already?"

He checked the time on his phone. "I got here over an hour ago," he said.

Amy looked panicked. "I thought we were having a good time."

"We were. But I've got to go now." And he headed into the darkened house toward the front door.

Amy followed him. "Wait, what happened?"

So, he told her. "I'm just tired of talking about Dad all the time and it seems like that's all you ever want to discuss, and you try to make me feel bad because I don't want to talk to him. It's like when you used to tell me Mom would just stay after you and stay after you about something, even after you'd told her whatever you needed to tell her, but she'd keep on, and you always said how it drove you crazy, but now *you're* the one doing it, and you're doing it to me, and I'm tired of talking about Dad all the time. I mean it, Amy. I'm done."

She could only stare at him, and when she found her voice, all she could say was, "Okay."

"So, I'm going."

"Well, we don't have to talk about Dad…"

Adam laughed, fished in his pocket for his keys. "Yeah, Amy, I know that. But it's all you want to talk about."

"Well, we can talk about anything."

They were at the front door now and she didn't want him to leave because she didn't want to be alone. She just didn't say it out loud; she wanted him to infer her meaning from what she was telling him and the way she was following him all the way out.

"Nah," he said. "I'm gonna go. I'm tired."

"But you said you're off tomorrow," she reminded him.

"Yeah, but it was a long day."

She sighed. "Okay."

They hugged and he walked out to his car, where he texted Orson. *Hey, can I come over?*

The response was instant, as if Orson was sitting and staring at his phone and waiting for Adam's text to come through. *Of course,* accompanied by a string of hearts, each one a different color. Corny, but Adam loved it.

Amy returned to the patio and tried to convince herself she was fine, that she was alone but she wasn't lonely, that lots of people she knew would kill for the solitude she had: a day off work, an entire house to herself, and wine. Women sat in her chair daily and shared with her how they longed for just an hour each day to themselves where there were no children or husbands or coworkers to demand anything from them. "It doesn't even have to be anything fancy," they cried. "Just a whole hour every day that belongs to no one but me. I don't even know what I'd do." And they laughed at the realization. "I'd probably spend the entire hour trying to figure out what I wanted to do with it!"

She needed less than a minute to decide what she would do with the time given her. "Fuck this," she said, and stuffed the cork back into the bottle of cabernet. She rushed upstairs, ran a brush through her hair, swiped on some mascara and lip gloss, and put on a clean t-shirt. She was on her way back downstairs when it struck her to put on a clean pair of jeans, so she went to do that and decided she might want to wear clean panties. "Just in case," she told herself, and grinned at her reflection in the mirror. Who was she trying to fool? She knew what she was doing: she wanted to be around people, she wanted something stiffer than wine, and she wanted to bring a guy home.

She went to the nearest sports bar and quickly made up her mind to flirt with the bartender. He was probably ten years younger than she was, and he probably had a girlfriend (because they all did, it seemed), but he was cute and she saw tattoos and muscles, and she would not be discouraged. "Hey, handsome!" *God, I sound like every miserable housewife in the world,* she thought.

"Hey there!" he replied, and she knew immediately that he was gay. "What can I get you?"

"Bourbon," she said.

"Neat?"

"On the rocks."

She slammed it back and motioned for another, which she nursed while she scanned the crowd. Two guys at the opposite end of the bar were engrossed in some game or other on a television above their heads. To their left, two girls hunkered in conversation. Behind them were pool tables and small groups of people throwing darts, and Amy appeared to be the only single in the entire place.

"You meeting friends?" asked the bartender. Small talk.

Amy chuckled. "No. I actually came here hoping I'd find a guy to go home with." She didn't care telling this guy; he was gay and he was a stranger, so what did he even care beyond what kind of tip she left him. And then she shrugged. "Guess I came on the wrong night."

He laughed. "You never know."

"Maybe."

She wondered how Susan managed it. With Joel, she was pretty sure she knew how: he'd gone to gay bars, or he probably didn't have to look much farther than the campus where he worked. But how did married women like Susan, who didn't work and who had to be at home in the afternoons when the kids arrived from school, go about seeing to their needs in a sexless marriage. (She could think of no better term for it, though she knew—

or, rather, she *hoped*—she was right in thinking that though they may not have been attracted to each other physically, Joel and Susan had, at least, cared for one another very deeply.)

On television and in the movies, there were the unsatisfied wife tropes who hired gardeners that looked and sounded like Antonio Banderas, or who, checking the ripeness of melons in the produce section, attracted the attentions of younger, virile college students. Or they took tennis lessons from hirsute and swarthy Frenchmen or cooking lessons from wildly gesticulating Italians. Amy could not picture Susan Benjamin, always so pragmatic and never one for anything too adventurous ("My nerves," she would claim as an excuse) falling for any of that, especially in public where she might be seen. Well, apparently, Rhoda had seen. Or was it all conjecture? She could call Joel and ask, but she wasn't sure he would tell her. He, more than anyone, seemed committed to preserving Susan's legacy unblemished.

"Another one?" the bartender asked when he saw that her glass was empty.

"Why not?"

He poured her a double and gave her a wink that told her it was either on him or he would only charge her for a single.

It was always so much easier for men to cheat, she decided. It was for Mike; he just started fucking one of his hygienists. Joel worked in academia, so surely there were music teachers and drama teachers, easy pickings with the right word or gesture or glance. Susan would have had to sail the uncharted waters of marital infidelity on her own, with no one to give her pointers or to even confide in about it. That made Amy sad, though she couldn't say why. She pictured her mother always desperate, always longing to be touched just so by a man, but always unfulfilled in the end because she always had to return to a husband who would never desire her and children who would never understand.

A voice cut through her musings: "I'll have a beer. You have Michelob? Great. And one of whatever the lady is having."

She turned and there was Mike Cohen, grinning at her from under the tattered bill of an Atlanta Braves hat. "What are you doing here?" she asked, as if he'd shown up in her living room.

"Buying you a drink," he said.

"No," Amy said. "No, no. Don't buy me a drink. Don't," she said to the bartender, "I'll get my own drink. Put it on my tab." Then to Mike: "No." Again. "Don't buy me a drink."

The bartender glanced from one to the other, seeking guidance.

"I've got it," Mike said and presented his card.

"Gah!" Amy turned away. "Why are you here? Aren't you supposed to be with our son?"

"It's your weekend," he answered. She looked stricken and he quickly added: "But he's at Joel's. He's fine. Everything's fine. I talked to him earlier."

It did little to calm Amy. It upset her when she turned and found him there and now she was upset that he was rubbing her nose in the fact that it was supposed to be her weekend with their kid, but Ethan still wanted nothing to do with her. "Great," she muttered. The bartender set her bourbon in front of her and she slammed it back in one gulp. "Can I settle up?" she asked him. She just wanted to leave now. Her mood was ruined.

"Whoa," Mike said. "I just got here."

Amy threw him a look as she scrawled her name and a tip on the credit card receipt. "Stop being such an ass," she snapped.

"I thought I was being nice."

"You were being smug."

Mike sighed. "I don't wanna fight, Amy. Sit down. You don't have to leave."

"I was leaving anyway," she told him, and that earned her an arched brow.

"You were always a shitty liar."

She barked a short laugh of disdain. "Yeah, you're one to talk about shitty liars, but it takes one to know one, I suppose."

He grabbed his chest as if she'd just stabbed him. "You wound me."

Amy rolled her eyes. "I'm leaving," she said again, but was no closer to actually doing it than she had been before.

Mike patted the barstool. "Sit. Let's talk. We'll have a drink and we'll talk."

"About what?" she asked, and climbed onto the stool.

"Ethan," he suggested, and shrugged. "Or your dad. Anything. What do you want to talk about, Amy?"

She had three bourbons in her and she was feeling invincible, so she said, "Fine. Let's talk about why your girlfriend left you."

Mike gave a small laugh, then he nodded, but he didn't look at Amy. "Okay," he said, though, which surprised her. "She wanted to date someone closer to her own age, so..." And he shrugged. "Here I am. At a bar. Hanging out with my ex-wife."

Amy felt a quick stab of sympathy for him. She imagined being told he was too old felt the same for him as it had for her when she'd learned he was having a full-blown affair with someone fifteen years younger than she was. Then she felt avenged. Someone had given him a taste of his own medicine (as much as she hated that platitude) so she felt she could finally stop being mad about it. She even let out her breath, not that she'd been holding it, but she exhaled with a kind of relief she hadn't been expecting.

"So much for talking about Ethan, huh?" It was all she could think to say.

Mike laughed. "Yeah, he's been a real asshole lately, hasn't he?"

They talked about Ethan, then Joel, then Adam. Mike told her about his younger sister, a doctor, who was in Syria working with Doctors Without Borders. Amy felt small hearing about such self-sacrifice. There she was, drunk on bourbon and contemplating switching to tequila, wondering how she would react if Mike unexpectedly kissed her the way he had in the parking deck that last time. She laughed when she caught herself.

"What?" Mike asked. He had brought up maybe ordering some wings and was perusing the menu.

"Nothing," she said, and waved a hand of dismissal.

"No way," he said, and when he smiled she noticed the way the corners of his eyes crinkled and recalled how she'd always liked that. "You had me tell you why Stephanie broke up with me, so you can't burst out laughing about something and then say it's nothing. Especially if it's that funny."

"It's *really* nothing," she insisted, and motioned for the bartender. She would be damned before she told him what she'd been thinking. "A shot of Patrón. A double." Then: "Actually, make it two!"

"Hang on." Mike held up a hand. "Tequila?" he asked Amy.

"Just one shot," she said. "Come on. It'll be fun. It'll be like we're in college again. Just pretend we're back in Wisconsin and there's three feet of snow on the ground and it's fifteen degrees below zero outside and we're only doing them to stay warm because we have to walk back to the dorm."

Mike relented, but one shot led to two and then to three, and when they both decided they'd had enough and were walking back to their cars, it was Amy who reached for him and turned him to face her and planted a crooked, sloppy kiss on his lips. "What are you doing?" he asked through it.

She pulled away and asked "What does it look like I'm doing?"

"Honestly? Doing something we'll probably both regret later," he said.

Amy rolled her eyes. "Fine." And she walked away in search of her car.

"Well, that doesn't mean I don't want to do it," he called to her. "Just that I accept that I'll probably regret it later."

She spun back around to face him and they regarded one another in the harsh light of a street lamp.

"My place is closer," she said.

"I know," he said. "I used to live there."

.twelve.

ADAM WAS RIGHT ABOUT one thing: Joel was ready for Ethan to move back home. He felt bad about it, too; after all, he'd said that the boy could stay with him for as long as he needed, but that was the old Joel talking. Grandparents said things like that because they were magnanimous and wanted to find solutions that would make everyone happy. Susan would have done the same, he was sure of it. And it had seemed like the best idea at the time, when everyone was standing in his basement yelling at one another.

"I'm not sure what to do," Joel confessed to Kent. They were having coffee at Ansley Starbucks because they could ogle men going into and out of L.A. Fitness while getting their caffeine fix and catching up with one another. Kent had just broken up with a guy named Rick who Joel had not even met, that's how brief the relationship was. They'd met, Joel told Kent he couldn't wait to meet him, then Rich had flown Kent to Hawaii, and two days after they returned, Kent told him it was over. Joel was flabbergasted, but he kept it to himself.

"Is that rhetorical, or do you really not know what to do?"

Joel scowled at him. "I'm being serious."

"Call your daughter and tell her it's time for her to come get her son."

Joel nodded, but he imagined the worst, as was his habit. Amy would yell at him for allowing it in the first place, and want to know why, suddenly, it was time. And would Joel tell her the truth? Would he even have to? "It sounds so easy."

Kent frowned at him. "Is there something I'm missing?"

Joel shook his head. "No. I just... Well, what if she wants to know why?"

That made Kent laugh. "Then you tell her the truth or you make up a lie, same as anyone else would do in the situation."

He called Amy.

"Dad? What's wrong?"

He longed for the day he could call one of his children and they would not assume the worst. "Nothing's wrong," he said, with what he hoped sounded like a reassuring laugh.

"Okay, then? What?" And Joel heard her whisper on her end, "It's just Dad."

"I think it's time for Ethan to go home," he said. He hated it the instant it was out of his mouth, but he couldn't take it back, and it hung between them for a long moment. He felt he needed to explain, so he did. "I'd really like to be able to go out when I want to and have people over… and a teenager kind of throws a wrench into anything like that."

Amy listened on her end and when it was clear Joel had said all he needed to say, she said, "Um… yeah, okay." She knew all about wanting to do things and not being able to because there was a kid in the house. She wanted to laugh at her father for presenting it as if he were the first person in the history of the world whose social life had suffered due to the presence of an adolescent.

"So… maybe come talk to him and tell him he's gotta come home? You and Mike both?"

Amy turned to where Mike lay in bed, his brow furrowed. She felt caught, like Joel could see through the phone and knew that Mike was with her. "Yeah…," she said.

"Today?"

"Yes," she said, irritated. "I get it. You want Ethan out of the house. We'll come get him."

Then Joel tried to dial his desperation back. "Well, you make it sound like I can't wait to get rid of him. I didn't mean that at all."

Amy scowled. "I said we'd come, Dad."

When she'd hung up with Joel, Mike fired a round of questions at her. What was wrong? Was Ethan okay? Was there a problem between him and Joel? He liked to think if there were one, Joel would have informed them both, but still. He stood and started getting dressed. "Like, did Ethan do something?"

She dressed, too. "No." Then, "I don't know." She considered it, thought about what Joel had just told her and recalled what Adam had said. "I think he just wants to enjoy himself, and having Ethan there makes that hard." She looked everywhere but at Mike. It was good to have this—Joel's call—to talk about, because otherwise there would have been that awkward kind of silence that always hung thick in the air after a night of drinking had led otherwise rational adults to behave irresponsibly.

"Well, he could have said that at the beginning," Mike pointed out.

"Yeah… but he didn't, so now we have to go get our kid." She stuffed her feet into running shoes and stood, still not looking at him.

"I can drive," he offered.

"No. We'll go separately."

Joel met them at the door. "Well, I didn't mean *right now*," he said, but Amy suspected he was glad they'd come and would never admit it. Ethan was in the kitchen eating cereal and reading the back of the box when they walked in.

"Is this what it looks like?" he asked them, though he directed it at Joel.

"That depends on what you think it looks like," Mike said with a laugh and reached out like he might tousle Ethan's hair, but the boy ducked.

Amy cut to the chase. "It's time to come home, Ethan," she told him. "Your grandpa wants his life back, and this has gone on long enough. We get the message: we're both horrible parents and you know better than we do what you want and what's best for you."

Ethan glared at each one of them in turn. He settled on Joel and said, "You said I could stay as long as I needed to."

"I did say that, yes," Joel said, nodding, "and I meant it when I said it, but… well, like your mother says, it's time to go home. You've made your point, but I think we're all ready for things to go back to the way they should be." He never stopped nodding as he spoke.

"So, finish eating and go get your things," Amy said. She decided to make coffee and went to do so. If she didn't do something, she would get mad at someone—maybe Joel, maybe Ethan—and this entire enterprise might result in a shouting match, and she was hungover. She needed coffee.

Ethan abandoned his bowl of cereal and stalked out of the kitchen. "You all suck," he grumbled as he went. No one argued.

"Well, that went pretty easy, wouldn't you say?" Joel said once Ethan was gone.

Mike gave a silent nod. Amy scooped coffee.

"I really expected him to fight it. You know, especially after last time." Joel glanced from one to the other. Mike cut a look at Amy as she turned away from making coffee and opened the refrigerator.

"Do you have cream? Creamer?"

"In the door," Joel told her. Then: "You seem upset."

"I'm fine." Amy checked the date on the cream, popped the carton open, sniffed. She opened cabinets, located mugs and sugar.

"You don't seem fine," Joel said. "What's the matter?"

She laughed. "*This* is the matter, Dad," she said, and spread her arms to mean everything happening in the kitchen at that moment, or everything that had ever happened in the history of the world. "You should have stayed out of it back then. Now I'm gonna have to deal with a kid who just got kicked out by his *grandfather* because you want to bring guys home." And she punctuated that declaration with another of those laughs. "I mean, if you'd told me fifteen years ago I was going to have to explain to my kid that he can't stay here because his grandfather wants to bring men home and have sex, I would have punched you in the throat... and yet here we are. Because you're gay, Dad, and you're like Adam was when he first started going to the bars and meeting guys, and I get it. I really do. But *you* don't get it. You don't see all this from our perspective because you've been living inside it your entire life, but it isn't simple." She raked her fingers through her hair and looked from Joel to Mike and back again. "I wanted it to be simple. You're gay and Mom is gone and I wanted it to be as simple as you just living your life the way you always wanted, but you can't be this new person and the same man you were before. You can't. Because that guy is the one who stepped in and told Ethan he could stay here as long as he needed... but it's the new Joel Benjamin who's decided that's a pain in his ass now. And we all have way too much shit of our own going on to add that to our plate."

Joel stared at her, speechless, his mouth hanging open.

Mike broke the silence. "I'm gonna... use the bathroom. Excuse me..." And he left.

Amy selected a cup, poured the coffee, added cream, tasted it. Set it down.

From behind her, Joel said, "I didn't know I was causing so many problems for everyone..." It was mostly a lie—of course he knew; he just tried not to be a problem and assumed he wasn't one because no one told him otherwise. Now this.

"But how could you not know?" Amy guessed she would ask all the questions she hadn't asked the first time now, since she'd already started and there was no turning back. "Dad, seriously... this isn't easy for you. I get that. But you act like it should be easier for the rest of us."

"I don't act that way," he said, and heard the peevish note in his voice.

"You do, though. I don't think you mean to, but you do it."

"Well, it's all new to me..."

"Only it isn't!" Amy's voice had risen in both pitch and volume. "You've *been* gay, Dad. It's new to *us*. The only thing that's new for you is being able to do it and not get caught." She heard the words coming out of her mouth and couldn't believe she was the one saying them. She sounded like Adam. Maybe she was channeling him, all his emotions about it, processing it for herself and for her brother.

Joel looked stricken. "I don't think that's fair," he said.

"Maybe it's not," she said. She felt the fight drain from her at the same time. She didn't want to fight, but that's exactly what she was doing, and she knew she sounded unreasonable and shrill, and she couldn't stop herself. "But it isn't fair that your coming out has become the focus of the entire family, and now it's affecting us all one way or another." She folded her arms across her chest and stared hard at her own feet. Hadn't Adam said basically the same thing to her only last night?

Joel opened his mouth to speak, to argue, to insist she was wrong. Only she wasn't and they both knew it. "Well," he said, and crossed his own arms. "I never planned it that way." Hadn't he put off telling them because he hadn't wanted to be a burden? "I put it off for over a year, Amy, and even when I was sure it was time to tell you kids, I still couldn't do it. Because I didn't want this—" And it was his turn to wave his arms in sweeping arcs."—To happen. Now everything is falling apart."

They faced one another but stared anywhere else—Amy at the floor, Joel at the butcher block counter between them. Ethan found them that way. "What's going on?" he asked, and looked from one to the other.

"Nothing," they said in unison.

He nodded to the bag slung over one shoulder. "I'm ready." And he left them where they stood.

Amy heaved a sigh and went after him. "I'm sorry," she said over her shoulder to Joel.

He didn't think she was, but he said, "It's fine."

At home, Ethan locked himself in his room. Amy stood with Mike in the driveway and talked about Joel because that was the safest thing for the two of them to discuss. "Sorry about that," she said.

He shrugged. "There's a lot going on. Everyone's feeling it."

He felt confused for the most part (he still wasn't one hundred percent sure what was going on with Ethan), but now there was the newly minted guilt from getting drunk and sleeping with his ex-wife.

"Yeah, and we don't need to make it any worse," she said.

Mike nodded again. They both knew what she was talking about. "Yeah, that... Look—"

Amy held up a hand to silence him. "No, no. We don't have to discuss it. I'm embarrassed enough. All we need to do is agree not to do it again." She still couldn't even say why she'd done it, and she did not want to fall back on the excuse that she'd had too much to drink. And she'd been telling herself— screaming it inside her head—not to do it the entire time she was actually engaged in doing it. There had to be a name for something like that. Dissociation? A psychotic break? If she hadn't stopped going to her therapist, she could talk to her about it. Then again, therapy had never helped much anyway. She went in, she talked about the divorce and how she felt about it, and how she thought Ethan might feel about it, and how she thought she felt about the way Ethan felt about it, and one day she realized she spent an hour twice a week talking in circles to a woman she wasn't even sure was listening. And if Amy asked her what she thought it meant, the response was always "Well, what do *you* think it means, Amy?" So she stopped going. Now, she wondered if perhaps those one-sided, circular conversations wouldn't lead her to some explanation for why, after all this time, she'd decided to do shots of tequila and have sex with her ex-husband.

"Fine with me," Mike said, and got into his car.

Amy stopped him just as he was backing out. "Wait. Is it my weekend with Ethan, or yours?" She'd honestly forgotten.

"It's yours."

"Okay, yeah. Right."

It wouldn't be much of a weekend, though, she decided as she slouched back into the house. Ethan would stay in his room with his headphones on, gaming or blaring music, and pretend she didn't exist. She would drink wine and watch insipid cooking competition shows where everything was a war—cupcakes, wedding cakes, barbecue—and all the contestants looked like they hadn't bathed in a year, or movies where impossibly beautiful women with perfect breasts and noses ended up happy, on a beach in Hawaii or strolling beside the Seine with men who would be mistaken for gay in the real world.

.thirteen.

JOEL NEVER HAD TROUBLE focusing at work, not through all the years of infidelity or Susan's battle with cancer, but he was finding it difficult to stay on task with his lectures and the grading of papers. If he weren't the department head, he would have worried about a reprimand. Instead he found himself contemplating stepping down or retiring early. And as usual, there was no one he could discuss it with. Adam still wasn't speaking to him and now Amy was pissed at him. There was Rhoda, but he wasn't so sure she would be able to give him advice on something of this magnitude. She would listen, and she would try to give advice, but he was pretty sure Rhoda wasn't the right source.

That left Kent, who seemed irritated when he called. "It's been a while," he told Joel, and his tone was short. It was a month since they'd had coffee, when Joel asked him how he should handle getting Amy and Mike to come get Ethan. In that time, Joel had done exactly what he'd wanted to do: he'd gone out, met men, and brought them home. Kent had called and texted a few times, to see if he wanted to get dinner, or go to drag queen bingo, but Joel had been otherwise occupied and had to beg off, if he replied at all.

"Well, I need someone to talk to." Then he went ahead and said what he was certain Kent was thinking: "You know I only ever call when I need something." He laughed to fill the silence.

They met at Kent's store and walked down the street to a sandwich shop. Joel took an inordinate amount of time deciding what he wanted because he wasn't really hungry, but eating would give him something to do in case there were awkward stretches of silence, which he fully anticipated.

"So, how have you been?" Kent asked him when they were seated.

"I've been doing well," Joel said. Then, "Well, maybe not *that* well, but I guess I can't complain." Then because he'd called Kent for help with his life, he said, "I mean... everything just seems to be getting worse by the day, and now I can't even concentrate at work."

Kent's brow furrowed. "Bad how?"

"I think I've pissed everyone off." He paused, studied the sandwich in front of him, sighed. "Amy really let me have it that day, too. Basically told me my coming out was selfish."

"She actually told you that?"

Joel shook his head. "No, but she didn't have to." He paused. "And I thought getting Ethan out of the house so I could get my life back would help. And at first, it did. I went out, I met guys, I had sex." He could tell these things to Kent because he knew Kent was doing the same things and Kent wouldn't talk like it was no big deal while thinking, as Amy had been doing all along, that he was being selfish and not thinking of anyone else. "Does it *ever* get easy?"

Kent was confused. "Does what get easy?"

"Coming out," Joel replied. "People settling into it."

"God, Joel...I don't know. I guess...?" He would not admit that there were still members of his own family—cousins he was close to growing up, especially—who had not spoken to him since he came out, and even more immediate family still only barely tolerated it, and then just to avoid conflict. "There's no general issue coming out experience. It's different for everyone and for every family."

"Amy made a pretty good point the other day," Joel told him. "She said I'd been living inside it—*it* I took to mean *being gay*—my entire life, and that I couldn't see it from their perspective... and they'd only had a couple months to deal with it. And me."

"It's a good point."

"And she said I was like Adam when he first came out, and I wish I knew what that meant, but I really distanced myself from

Adam back then. Because I was afraid it would show in me, too, and it scared me to death." He wanted to laugh. It sounded so asinine, but it was exactly what he'd felt: that daily dread he might be standing with his son or talking with him and someone would notice a gesture or hear the inflection in his speech, the accent he put on a particular syllable or the way his voice rose at the end of certain words and know somehow, and everything would be over—his marriage, his career, his life. It amazed him that he'd made it out of his thirties at all.

"She's probably referring to the, you know… the wanting to bring guys home." And Kent waved his hand in a circle, wiggled his fingers.

"Oh."

"We all went through it at first. You're just doing it later than most of us did."

"Oh." Joel wasn't sure whether he should be insulted or not. He was more promiscuous before he came out. Well, before Susan's diagnosis, at least. So, he guessed he was insulted that everyone was assuming he was a raging sex fiend, and he wondered if maybe he shouldn't go ahead with it since everyone had made up their mind about it already.

They walked back to the store.

"It's Wednesday, so why don't you come out with the guys. We'll be at Blakes and probably end up at The Heretic, like always."

Joel pretended to think about it. "Maybe…"

Kent rolled his eyes. He knew Joel would be there.

Kent had introduced Joel to his circle of friends months ago, not long after Adam caught them together and Joel seemed on the verge of falling apart before he'd even really experienced what it was like to be out and live openly. The idea was to give Joel a support system because there would be more falling apart and Kent would not always be there. Drinks for the most part, because that was what gay men in their age group seemed to do: they met for what they called dinner (which was really just an assemblage of appetizers shared among the group) then adjourned to any bar that served stiff drinks.

Joel was thrilled to be a part of it all.

It was a small group: Kent, of course, then Dave and Dan, a longtime couple often referred to as "Double D" when they weren't around, the flamboyant Gregory, who'd met someone and made only occasional appearances, then Pete and Russell, both single and imperious. They reminded Joel of the grouchy, old Muppets who sat in the balcony on *The Muppet Show,* Statler and Waldorf, observing everything around them and always ready with criticism. He suffered their barbs just to be able to say he had, at last, a circle of gay friends. "Don't mind those two," Kent told him. "They treat everyone like shit at first, but when they finally decide they like you, they'll accept you and then you couldn't buy more devoted friends."

Joel certainly hoped so. They harangued him about everything: his haircut, his clothes, how pale he was, his choice of wine (pinot gris) and liquor (bourbon), the songs he liked, the men he found attractive. There wasn't much of anything he said or did that they were not able to find fault with. "They never let up," he complained to Kent. "They just peck and peck and peck. Like two old hens."

Kent laughed. "Well, they *are* like a couple of old biddies."

"I don't think they like me," Joel concluded.

"Don't let it bother you."

It did bother him, even though he tried to ignore it. He showed up for drinks once in shorts and they were relentless. "Girl, the last time I saw legs like that, there was a message tied to them," said Pete.

Russell cackled like a hyena. "And when was the last time they saw the sun?"

Joel was mortified, but even though he started tanning, that wasn't enough because they found something new to pick at him about. "What do you call that shade of green, sweetie?" Russell asked when Joel showed up in a blazer he'd paid too much for and was never really sure about.

"Bile?" asked Pete, and the two of them tittered like birds.

They took their drinks to a table by the window that looked out over Tenth Street. It was prime real estate in Midtown, the best place to see and be seen. Kent checked his phone. "Double D says they're on their way," he said.

Joel grunted an acknowledgment. He'd locked eyes with a guy across the room at the bar, waiting for his drink. "Don't make it obvious," he whispered to Kent, and tried not to move his lips too much, "but do we know that guy at the end of the bar? The one with the beard, in the Seattle sweatshirt?"

Kent pretended to twist so as to stretch the muscles in his back. He'd seen guys at the gym do it. He gave the guy a once over and turned back around. "I think I had sex with him once." He paused for thought, then added: "Maybe twice."

"You're joking, right?" Joel's face was deadpan.

Kent was, but didn't admit it. The guy looked familiar, but a lot of gay guys looked the same, especially now that everyone seemed to have a beard and the same haircut with a hard part. He may have had sex with the guy once or he may have dated him for six months. "Go talk to him."

Joel hunkered in his seat, like he might make himself smaller and not be seen. "No," he gasped. Then: "I don't know..." But he knew, because he'd done it before; he just felt that this was part of the ritual of gay dating: if you acted too eager, it was seen as desperation and that wasn't cute. Even if the other guy was just as desperate, there was a whole performance that had to take place. Joel had played it hundreds of times with varying degrees of success and he always longed for the day when he wouldn't be a straight, married man in a strange hotel in a city on the other side of the country who could walk into a local gay bar, see a man he was attracted to, and just walk up and start talking. That fantasy reached a fever pitch as Susan's cancer progressed and he allowed himself—albeit secretly—to imagine coming out after Susan passed and doing just that.

Now here he was, and there was a good-looking man across the room who had made eye contact with him, and Joel was acting like it was his first time in a gay bar and he had no idea what the protocol was. "Well, maybe if you sit here and stare at him long enough, he'll feel drawn to you and come say hello," Kent said.

Joel threw him a look. "You're not helping."

Kent laughed. "Here." He pushed a somewhat soggy napkin toward Joel. "Write him a note and I'll take it to him. Put 'Do you like me?' and a box for *yes, no,* and *maybe*. It'll be just like third grade, only gay this time."

When Pete and Russell arrived, they joined Kent in laughing at Joel's expense. To escape them all, Joel grabbed his drink and fled to the other side of the room where the guy stood alone, staring intently up at Kylie Minogue's "Stop Me From Falling" video playing on a monitor above their heads. He was older than Joel had assumed, and that put him at some measure of ease. He saw gray in the guy's beard and tiny lines at the corners of his eyes. "Hi," Joel said, and smiled. He felt like he might say the wrong thing, so he took a sip of his drink.

"Hi," the guy said.

Then silence. They watched the video.

Joel said, "I didn't think people still made videos anymore." And he chuckled. "Not like they did in the eighties and nineties. Guess I was wrong."

The guy shrugged. "I don't even like this song," he confessed. "I just didn't have anything else to do but stand here and watch it."

Joel loved the song, had to fight the urge to argue its merits. Instead he said, "Yeah, I noticed you standing here."

"I saw you, too."

That made Joel blush.

His name was Jeff and he was from out of town. Joel saw no ring and admonished himself for leaping to conclusions; then he tried to see if there was any sign that Jeff usually wore one, but it was too dim in the bar. From across the room, Kent seemed to glare at them, but Pete and Russell threw him a thumbs up.

"In town for business?" Joel asked. He hated small talk more than anything else in the world, but could think of no other way to pass the time until he could start signaling this stranger that he'd really like to go someplace else.

"Pleasure," Jeff said, and Joel understood immediately.

"Ah," was all he could manage.

Jeff threw him a wink and sipped his beer. Joel was never good at this part, where he was supposed to make his intentions known after picking up on all the obvious clues. Jeff had left the door wide open for him, all Joel needed to do was step in and say the right thing and they could get out of this place and go to Jeff's hotel room, or to Joel's house—although it was probably farther than Jeff had planned to go for sex.

"I live in Dunwoody," Joel said. It sounded like someone else's voice, coming through a wall.

"I'm staying at the W," Jeff said.

Joel nodded. "Let me go tell my friends."

"I'll wait outside."

It felt like it had thirty years ago, when he would enter an unfamiliar gay bar in a strange city with the sole purpose of meeting someone and going back to his hotel room for sex, and for probably the first time in his life, Joel was astonished at himself. He was older now, wiser, and he should conduct himself accordingly. But this was what he'd wanted for years—to not have to creep around and meet men, to be able to walk up to a man, in plain sight, in front of people he knew even, and let his intentions be known. And it did feel nice not having any guilt attached to what he was doing, but there was still that voice in the back of his head telling him he should know better. Then there was Amy's voice, telling him he was like Adam was when he'd been fresh out of the closet, and that was what he kept in mind as he told Kent and the others he would catch up with them later (though they all knew he wouldn't) and catch up with Jeff on the sidewalk outside.

Jeff's hotel room looked unoccupied aside from the small duffel bag sitting on a chair in the corner before the window. Joel stood, uncertain, while Jeff closed the blinds. He was still making up his mind whether or not he wanted to do anything, when Jeff swept him into a clumsy embrace and kissed him. The rest happened so fast it was all over before Joel had processed what they did: they were kissing, then their clothes were off, then Joel was bent over the bed getting fucked.

Later, while he dressed, Jeff said, "So, I'll see you around, I guess."

"Yeah, sure. Can I get your number?"

There was the briefest of pauses, then Jeff said, "Yeah... I'm married, so..."

"I understand completely," Joel said. "You want to get a drink or something?"

Jeff shook his head. "I'm actually getting ready to head over to The Eagle."

Joel waited for an invitation to accompany him, and when it didn't come, he said, "Oh."

He walked back to Blake's in a fog, certain that everyone he passed could tell that he'd just been fucked by a stranger in a hotel room, but confused why now, after all these years, he was feeling such a sense of shame. At Blake's, he searched for Kent and the others, but they were gone, probably to Mary's by now. He considered joining them there, but just took a seat at the bar and ordered a vodka on the rocks. He was halfway through his second drink when it occurred to him that Jeff had not used a condom.

.fourteen.

Adam wasn't so sure about himself and Orson anymore, and he hated himself for it.

Orson was a great guy and he was the first guy who'd ever treated Adam like something more than a source for blow jobs and loans to make it until payday, but Adam had reached that same point in this relationship that he reached in all the others, be they long- or short-term: he was bored.

At night, he would trek to Orson's and they would watch old sci-fi films from the fifties and sixties on the couch under a blanket that smelled so much like Orson that it made Adam lightheaded. But he thought of other guys as Orson's toes playfully gripped his own; of the guy who'd just started coming into the bakery. His name was Max and he'd just moved from Portland. He liked cream cheese Danishes and dark roast coffee. He had blue eyes and the beginnings of a beard and Adam found it impossible not to flirt with him, and he always felt terrible after he had. No one seemed to notice it, though, because everyone at the bakery flirted with the customers; it was expected in retail. Flirt with them, bat your eyes, and they'd buy anything you suggested. *Didn't you want to get a scone to go with your chai? That's what I thought.*

But he also thought of his exes, and guys he'd had sex with but not dated, and guys he'd met online and had the kind of sex that seemed only to exist in porn until you found that *one* guy online who was in the same situation—fresh out of a relationship and eager to do all the things committed people are always too shy to suggest—and the stars just seemed to align.

He still loved Orson, though.

"What's wrong?" Orson asked often.

And Adam said, "Nothing." Sometimes he added, "Stop asking that. You're going to give me a complex."

"But you just keep zoning out."

Adam felt himself blush. "I'm not zoning out." Only he was, and he knew it. "I'm just not into this movie as much as you are." He would lie and Orson would believe him and they'd search for something, usually settling on reruns of *The Mary Tyler Moore Show* or a show where unbelievably wealthy couples in their early twenties searched for beachfront property in the Caribbean. Orson almost always ended up falling asleep.

He finally brought it up to Amy. "So, I've been seeing this guy…?"

Amy responded as if he'd told her he'd grown a third testicle overnight. "*What?* Since when? Oh my God, Adam, why didn't you say something?"

"Because I knew this was how you'd react," he muttered.

"Well, tell me about him!" She didn't give him time to respond before she started firing questions at him. "What's his name? Where did you meet? How long have you been dating him? Why didn't you tell me? Is he Jewish?"

Adam rolled his eyes. "You sound like Mom right now."

That shut her up long enough for him to pick up his narrative. "Anyway. I've been seeing this guy—Orson—and it's pretty serious and you know how when you're in your twenties and you're filled with the hope of finding that one person to spend the rest of your life with, only you never do because you're in your twenties and people—gay people, especially—in their twenties are about as interested in settling down with one person as they are in contracting the plague?"

"I guess…," she said, and tried to follow him. "His name is Orson?"

Adam nodded.

"Like Orson Welles?"

"Yeah…?"

"Who names a baby Orson?"

"Just let me finish," he said. "Anyway. We've been seeing each other and I really like him... like, *a lot*. More than I ever thought I could, because he isn't exactly the type of guy I imagined myself wanting to settle down with, and I wasn't even looking for a relationship, but there he was. He came into the bakery, and he has this dog. A Great Pyrenees mix, or something. He's huge. His name is Puck." Adam realized he was rambling. "And he asked me out and we went out and now it's been a while—almost five months—and I'm in love with him but all I ever think about is having sex with other guys. Or the sex I used to have with guys when I was single. Or the guys I had sex with before I met Orson. It's like, literally, all I ever think about."

Amy frowned as she listened. "And you guys don't have sex?" It was a familiar concept to her: she and Mike stopped having sex after Ethan was born.

"We do," Adam said. "That's just it. It's not like I don't want to have sex with Orson. We have sex all the time. But when we do, I'm thinking of other people. And I feel like a turd because of it."

Amy waved a hand, dismissed his guilt and the reason for it. "Everyone thinks about other people when they have sex," she said. "I did it with Mike and I've done it with every guy I've had sex with since. It's nothing."

"I'm no expert," he said, "but I think you may be wrong."

"I'm not. Don't you ever read those idiotic articles in *Cosmopolitan* when you're sitting in the doctor's office, where they talk about how everything you've been told your entire life is wrong and you should feel bad about it—like masturbation and foot fetishes—is really just healthy human sexuality?"

"No."

"You should. And thinking about having sex with someone else other than the person you're actually having sex with is the *least* freakish thing in those articles."

"I didn't know you had a foot fetish, though," he said.

"I don't." The look on her face suggested she was insulted. "I was just using that to make the point. Some people have fetishes, other people imagine someone other than their partner when they're having sex." She shrugged. "Now, about this Orson guy…"

She wanted to know everything, so Adam told her, and no matter how much he told her, it never seemed to be enough.

"He's in marketing? What kind of marketing?"

Adam had no idea. "Just… marketing, Amy. Shit… how do I know?"

"Well, don't you talk about it? Doesn't he come home from work and complain about how much he hates his job and wishes he could throw a hand grenade into the whole operation and run away to a yurt in Patagonia?"

He scowled at her. "No one acts like that about their job."

Amy raised a hand. "Um… I do. Every fucking day of my life."

"Then quit."

She rolled her eyes.

"It's not like you have to work with the alimony and the child support and the money Mom left you. Quit. Go live in a yurt." He had only the vaguest of ideas what a yurt actually was, but he didn't care enough to research.

That got a laugh out of her. "And do what? Stay at home and knit? Bake cookies?"

"Do whatever you want," he said. "Meet a man and remarry and make more babies. You're still young enough."

Amy laughed. "Yeah, right. And maybe I am doing what I want." She'd loved it at first, she was certain of that. And actually, she did love the creative aspect of being a stylist, but listening to people bitch and moan about their problems while having to deal with coworkers and their problems—which no one seemed capable of not bringing to work with them—took its toll and there were days when she considered quitting and going back to school to learn something, anything else. The problem with that was she had no idea what she might go back to school for.

It was his turn to roll his eyes. "And you love it so much, you fantasize about throwing a grenade into the salon every day. Right."

"Stop that. We aren't even talking about me, we're talking about you."

Adam corrected her. "Actually, we were talking about Orson. And I still don't know what kind of marketing he does. We don't talk about that."

"Well, what do you talk about?"

Adam shrugged. "Things. Like, he'll come over to my place or I'll go over to his, and we'll sit and ask each other what we want to do for thirty minutes... and once we settle on going out to get something to eat, we then proceed to spend another thirty minutes trying to agree on a place. He doesn't like Ethiopian and I'm basically sick of Chinese, so we usually end up calling for pizza or wings." Another shrug.

"Why haven't you let us meet him?" Amy wanted to know.

He didn't have an answer for that.

She grunted. "Well, cat's out of the bag now, so you have to introduce him to us." Her face lit up as a thought occurred to her. "Hey, I can have us all over for dinner!"

He barked a laugh at her. "Yeah, and Orson will have to do all the talking because Dad and I aren't speaking, you and Ethan can't talk to each other without arguing, and by then I'll be so pissed at you, *I* won't be speaking to you. Sounds like fun, Amy."

"Fine," she snapped. "You can have it at your place and have us all over." She paused, then added: "And Ethan and I are on speaking terms again, thank you very much." It just happened one morning—fueled by his need for lunch money—and it was an uneasy truce, but it was progress and she would take it. He never mentioned Leah and she did not dare ask. According to Mike, Ethan didn't mention Leah to him, either.

"I don't know if I want to introduce him to you guys," Adam said, and at the look Amy gave him, he threw his hands up. "I'm just being honest."

She narrowed her eyes at him. "*All* of us or just Dad?"

Adam said nothing.

"That's what I thought," she said. Then: "Look, you literally just told me that you think of fucking other guys when you're having sex with your boyfriend, so how can you still be mad at Dad? And—" She aimed a finger at him. "—You've even cheated on other boyfriends, so I'm not understanding any of this anymore. You're just being a drama queen."

"It's not the same thing," he said. "It's not the same thing, and you know it, and I've got to go."

"Oh, for fuck's sake, Adam." And she followed him out to his car. "Stop running from this and just admit that you want to hold Dad to a different standard than you hold yourself. Than you hold everyone else in the world to, actually."

"What do you even know about any of this?" he shot back. "You think you know all the reasons people cheat because your ex-husband cheated on you? Ha! Yeah, Amy, you're an expert."

"No one has to be an expert to see your double standard, Adam."

"I fucked around on guys who were fucking around on me, Amy," he said, and waved his hands more than he needed to. "That's what all gay guys in their twenties do to each other. It's like an unspoken rule. We pretend we aren't doing it, but we are. And we act like we can't believe it happened to us when we find out about it, but it's all part of the act." He hooked a thumb over his shoulder, in the general direction of wherever Joel might be at that moment. "Dad cheated on his wife, not his first boyfriend in college. Mom wasn't in on it."

It was Amy's turn to gesticulate. "But Mom was fucking around on Dad, too, Adam, so how can you even be sure she wasn't in on it? God!" She put a hand on her forehead. "For the life of me, I don't remember you ever being this fucking stubborn before."

"You actually believe Aunt Rhoda?" he asked, and gave her the most theatrically derisive laugh he could. The truth was, he had believed Rhoda at first, too. Then he went to a bar and really thought about it while drinking several beers and chasing them with several shots of Jack Daniels. He decided that there was no way Susan would have been sleeping around, too, because Susan Schechter Benjamin just didn't do shit like that. She sat at home and clipped coupons and transcribed recipes from *Family Circle* and *Woman's Day* onto recipe cards, and she played bridge and Yahtzee with other mothers from *shul*; she shopped and she met friends for lunch and she did aerobics and Jazzercise until she decided she looked like a fool flailing about, so she quit and took up power walking around the mall. How in the world would she ever have been able to orchestrate clandestine encounters with men when she was packing lunches and folding laundry in the morning, meeting Bev Harman for lunch, shopping, and getting back home in time to see the kids home from school and get dinner started? There was no way, he reasoned. Then he called Orson to come pick him up because he was too drunk to drive.

"I'm just saying… Mom didn't deserve to just sit around being the dutiful wife while Dad ran around looking for dick." Amy said it with a shrug. "We can argue until we're both blue in the face, but you know I'm right." She dug in her purse for her keys. "I would stay and do just that, but I'm going to try to surprise my kid with a trip to Gamestop and pizza, so wish me luck."

They hugged and touched cheeks and Amy held him at arm's length for a long moment after they'd pulled apart. "What?" he asked, still grouchy.

"Look at us."

"What about us?"

"We never argued like this before. I just realized that. Now here we are and it seems every time we talk it ends up an argument." She sighed, hugged him again, then started away. "I'll call you when I decide on a night for us all to have dinner."

Adam wanted to call after her, tell her no, it was a horrible idea; he and Joel would only end up arguing, or not speaking at all and ruining the whole evening for everyone else. Instead he sighed and realized she was right: they'd never argued until Joel came out.

Orson was concerned. "What's wrong?" He'd made matzoh ball soup—his first attempt—and they were sitting cross-legged on the floor of Orson's apartment watching M*A*S*H.

"Why do you keep asking me that?" Adam asked, and tried to sound perturbed.

Orson chuckled and touched the tip of his forefinger to the tiny wrinkle between Adam's eyebrows. "Because when you're upset about something, you get this. It's kinda cute, but it's stuck around longer than usual this time and I'm starting to get worried."

"It's nothing."

Orson sighed. "Okay…"

"Seriously." He tried to sound as sincere as he could, because he didn't want to drag Orson into it. He liked keeping all the Benjamin family drama compartmentalized, so that Orson could be his escape from it. So far, it worked, but with Orson asking more and more questions every time they were together, Adam knew it was only a matter of time before he wouldn't be able to shrug it off anymore. Especially with Amy texting and calling him daily to pressure him about getting everyone together so they could meet Orson.

Have U picked a day 4 dinner 2 meet Orson? she texted, and Adam ignored it.

Then: *Stop ignoring me.*

She called and left a message because he didn't answer. "Dude, seriously, stop avoiding me and stop avoiding this. You can't be *that* ashamed of us… unless it's him you're ashamed of, which I doubt, otherwise you wouldn't be dating him…" Amy had a tendency to ramble in her voice mail messages sometimes. "Anyway, you need to call me. Stop being an asshole. Call me. I love you. Bye."

For the first time in his life, Adam considered moving away from his family. "What's Wisconsin like?" he asked Orson, who chuckled, but looked at him askance.

"Why?"

Adam shrugged. "Just curious."

Orson chuckled again. "No one is curious about Wisconsin," he said.

"It has to be better than Georgia."

"Well, let's see," Orson said. He set aside the book he was reading and sat cross legged on the bed, faced Adam, started counting facts about Wisconsin on his fingers. "It's probably the whitest state in the entire country, there are no Jewish people there, we have more cows than we have people, and the winters are hellish." He paused. "Why do you think I moved here?"

There was also Florida, where Susan's family lived. His uncle Sammy, his mother's brother, told him at the *shivah* there was always a place for him in Boca. Adam hugged him and thanked him and thought *What the hell would I do in Boca, of all fucking places?* But that was before Joel turned out to be gay and a shitty husband, and suddenly Boca Raton didn't sound so bad. He could work in a bakery there just as easily as in Atlanta. He probably wouldn't make as much money, but he could get a second job waiting tables or something.

He didn't mention Boca to Orson, but he did finally slip and mention all of Amy's tweets and calls about dinner. Orson was thrilled with the idea. "I could make lasagna!"

"Yeah, well... we'll see," Adam said. "Everyone's schedules are so out of whack, it's hard to get everyone together at the same time, in the same place." He was lying, and he hated himself for it, because he was lying to Orson, not because he was lying about his family.

"I wish you'd mentioned this before." Orson stood and surveyed his apartment, like everyone was on their way over that minute and he needed to redecorate, paint, and resurface the hardwoods and he only had five minutes to complete everything. Puck stood with him, wagged his tail, uncertain but eager as always.

"We can talk about it later," Adam told him.

"I know, but we need to plan." Orson was a planner. Everything was a list or a spreadsheet or a reminder sent to his phone or his inbox.

"We can plan later."

Orson was not so sure, but he returned to his seat on the sofa and tried to focus on the movie they were watching. Adam cuddled in close to him and continued to agonize over how he was going to keep his family away from his boyfriend. And how he was going to keep himself from cheating on Orson.

.fifteen.

THE FIRST FEW TIMES Joel was tested for STDs and HIV, in the eighties and nineties, the results took longer, and he would spend two agonizing weeks, convinced that a mild case of hay fever was the herald of a diagnosis he would not be able to explain to Susan. And she always seemed to notice his anxiety, too.

"What's wrong with you?" she would ask him across the table at dinner.

"Nothing," he replied, perhaps a bit quicker than he should have. "Why?"

"You're jumpy."

Joel tried to laugh, but his throat was dry. "I'm fine," he lied.

"Okay…" But Susan was far from convinced and Joel knew it.

The results always came back negative. He knew they would, but that didn't stop him from imagining the worst. He was careful to the point of being annoying, and he could tell it from some of the reactions he got from the guys he had sex with, but he had too much to lose. They did, too, but they seemed not to care as much about that as Joel did, and he was both perplexed by their nonchalance and envious of it, too. He wanted to let go and just have sex for a change, without the specter of disease always hanging over the experience, but he just couldn't.

"I'm clean," those guys would tell him, and that usually meant they wanted to have sex without the condom, but Joel trusted no one. He read stories in *The Advocate* of men who contracted HIV because they trusted their partners when they shouldn't have, and he was sickened and terrified the same would happen to him, so he would go a month or two without sex, convinced that he would be able to go without it until they found a cure. That was foolish, of course. Life didn't work that way, and masturbation was never enough for very long, and as soon as he was able to get out of town for a conference or if Susan flew to Boca to spend a week with her family, Joel located the nearest bath house or gay bar and picked right up where he'd left off.

The test was quicker now, so it was only an agonizing twenty minutes or so that he spent in his doctor's office, his legs and back exposed by the thin examination gown. "Your results are negative for everything," his doctor informed him. Joel's relief was so visible, and his sigh so audible, that the doctor asked, "You are being safe, aren't you?"

"Of course," Joel answered, and then decided to be completely up front, since this was his doctor. "Well, I had an experience recently, and it happened so fast, well... I mean... it was over before I realized he hadn't used protection."

The doctor nodded. He was younger, probably about Adam's age. Joel had no doubt he heard similar—or worse—stories daily, since the practice served much of the gay population of Atlanta. "Have you ever considered PrEP? It's pre-exposure prophylaxis. I have a lot of my patients on it."

"I've heard of it," Joel said, "but, really... I'm always safe." He paused, considered that, then corrected himself: "Well, usually."

Later, Joel told Kent. It led to an argument.

"It isn't a free pass to fuck everything that moves," Kent told him, and Joel thought he was more upset than he was allowed to be. "You still have to use your head. There are guys who have been using PrEP for years who are testing positive." He'd read it in the news and been aghast.

"I'll be careful," Joel said, and was amazed at how like a surly teenager he sounded.

"Like you were with that guy?"

Joel threw him a look. "That was... an unusual situation." He'd told Kent all about it, and he didn't feel like telling it again.

It was over, his test came back negative, and he would probably never see Jeff again, anyway. "And I don't need you to lecture me about safe sex."

Kent laughed. "Well, someone needs to." He mumbled it around the neck of his beer bottle, as if that would muffle it so Joel wouldn't hear it.

"And what the hell is that supposed to mean?" Joel snapped it.

"Exactly what I said," Kent snapped back. "You don't mind being lectured when you ask for advice, but when it's unsolicited—and valuable—you get pissy. So, do whatever you want to do, Joel, but stop asking for all this guidance if you're just going to get your ass on your shoulders when it's something you don't want to hear."

Joel gave a bark of derisive laughter. "I don't have my ass on my shoulders," he said. "And anyone would react the same way if someone basically called them a whore."

"I didn't call you a whore."

"You said not to fuck everything that moves."

Kent held up a finger. "I did say that, but you got pissed about me calling you out for not being careful with that trick."

Joel folded his arms across his chest and sulked. Kent drank his beer. They were joined by Dan and Dave, who sensed the tension immediately. "Lovers' quarrel?" Dan asked, and Joel wanted to slap the stupid grin off his face.

When Adam finally told Orson everything, he felt such an overwhelming sense of peace that he thought he finally knew what all those New Age devotees were always in search of with their crystals and meditation and yoga retreats to Tibet.

He'd hauled out the box of memorabilia Susan had packed for him and was going through the photo albums she had dedicated to him. There were six in all, and he was amazed that he'd forgotten the contents of them existed until that dinner when Joel had presented them to him. Why had none of these albums and these boxes of Polaroids and Instamatic shots been taken out at Rosh

Hashanah or Hanukkah and laughed over? Wasn't that what mothers did? Wasn't that what *families* did? "I don't think we were normal," he declared, only half aloud.

Orson aimed the remote at the episode of *Deep Space Nine* he was watching and turned. "What's that?"

Adam repeated himself. "Growing up, I always thought everyone else in the world was more exciting and outrageous than we were. Like *The Brady Bunch* or another one of those totally unreal TV families. Like the Huxtables."

"I'm pretty sure every kid thinks they have the most boring family in the world," Orson said. He set the remote aside and joined Adam on the floor, sat cross-legged and studied the collection of photos without touching them.

"Maybe," Adam said.

"I know I did," Orson told him. "You grow up on a farm in Wisconsin and it's easy to believe everyone is cooler than you are. Then, you make it out and you meet people who lived on Central Park West who thought the same thing, so it's all a bunch of bunk." He selected a photograph and held it up to Adam. "Is that you as a baby?"

Adam peered at it. "Yeah. I was fat," he grumbled.

"You were perfect. Is that your mom?"

"No, that's Aunt Rhoda. Dad's sister."

Orson replaced it among the spread. Adam took a deep breath and said, "I guess I was wrong. All the dysfunction keeps it interesting for us."

Orson gave Adam an expectant look.

Adam picked photos up at random, studied them, then set them back down into an order that was only apparent to himself. "Mom was fucking around on Dad, too, evidently," he said without preamble and without looking up. But he wasn't really saying it to Orson; he was just saying it, and Orson just happened to be there to hear it. "Aunt Rhoda told us. After the unveiling."

Orson listened. Surely Adam would eventually give him some clue as to what he should say.

"So, there's that," Adam said after a long silence, and continued picking up the photographs one by one, examining them, and placing them into piles according to his own system.

Adam held up the photos and Orson studied them. Adam at various stages of his life—he hadn't changed a whole lot since he was a baby, which Orson commented on. "I looked like W.C. Fields when I was a baby," Orson said. "I still haven't grown out of it."

Adam looked the same now as he had when he graduated college, and high school, and when he'd bar mitzvahed and when he was in kindergarten. The clothes changed, but the dark mop of unruly hair, the eyes, the mouth all stayed the same. "I guess I've looked thirty-five years old my entire life," he said. "I'm gonna look like hell when I'm in my sixties." He was silent as he shuffled the photos around on the floor between himself and Orson, and it seemed he might say nothing further on the subject of his mother's infidelity. Orson was fine with that. Then Adam spoke. "And I guess I should be pissed at Aunt Rhoda for telling us, and I suppose I was at first—especially since she chose the day of the unveiling to bring it up—but I realize now that I'm not. Because it wouldn't change anything."

Orson listened.

Adam went on. "The truth is that Dad lied from the get-go, and Mom probably figured it out at some point along the way and figured what the hell… if he was gonna fuck around, so could she." And he chuckled. "God, I can't believe I'm even saying these things. Like, who'd ever think of saying it's okay for their mom to fuck around?" He saw the look on Orson's face and frowned. "You must think I'm a real shit, huh?"

"No," Orson said.

"I shouldn't have even bothered you with all this." Adam moved his hands to indicate the photos, the memories, his family, his torment. "Sorry." He started gathering them up, stuffing them back into their envelopes and boxes.

"Baby," Orson said, "I'm not bothered by this, but you are… and that bothers me." He nodded to the box as Adam crammed things into it. "And I have no idea what to tell you, and *that* bothers me, too. Because I can see it's eating you alive and I can't make it stop."

"Sorry," Adam said again.

"No. You don't have to be sorry. There's nothing to be sorry about."

"It's not fair to you, though. *That's* what I'm sorry about."

Orson sighed. Adam echoed it.

Later, in bed, Adam muted the *Friends* rerun he was watching and said to Orson, "I think I'm going to have to talk to my dad."

Orson used a finger to hold his place in the book he was reading and nodded. "Okay…"

"Only what if it's to tell him there is no way I will ever be able to forgive him and basically tell him I never want to have anything to do with him ever again?" Even though he'd been thinking it for a while, hearing the words actually come out of his mouth surprised him. It also surprised him that he was telling Orson, who continued to nod. "Am I crazy?"

"No, baby. You're not crazy." He said it with a reassuring chuckle.

"Does it make me a bad person?"

Orson stopped nodding and shook his head. "No, baby. The world is filled with people who don't speak to their parents for a million different reasons. It doesn't make you a bad person, as long as you're sure it's what you want to do."

"Would you even want to be with someone like that?" He couldn't look Orson in the eye when he asked it, so he stared at the patch of hair in the center of his chest.

Orson reached out and played with one of Adam's curls. "Do you even have to ask that?"

And Adam had his answer, which relieved him immensely. Because he would have no problem breaking ties with Joel if that's what it came to, and if that meant Amy never wanted to have anything to do with him for the rest of their lives, he could probably deal with that, too; but he didn't want to lose Orson, and knowing that he wouldn't was such a relief, he thought he might cry. "Good," he said simply, and turned back to *Friends*. Orson stretched over and kissed his ear.

In the long run, knowing that he and Orson would be fine helped to clear his mind enough that he was able to map out what he would say to Joel, and how and also when. The best place, he decided, would be at home—well, Joel's home. And he would have to make it clear that they were not having dinner or a drink or anything. He would let Joel know that he was coming over to talk and that was it. After he delivered his decision and his reasoning, he would leave, and that would be much easier than doing it in a restaurant or at his own apartment.

We still need to have dinner, Amy texted him. *I want 2 meet your BF.*

I'm trying to avoid that, actually, was Adam's reply. He'd made a commitment to himself to be honest with everyone going forward.

That's a DICK move Adam, she texted back.

Then she just showed up at his apartment two days later with three bottles of wine and bags filled with junk food. Orson answered the door because Adam told him to see who it was. They stood for a long moment, blinking at one another in the glare of the bare bulb above Adam's front door.

"Um... hi," he said.

"Oh my God, hi! Are you Orson?"

Adam appeared behind him, his face a caricature of horror. "Amy, what the *fuck?*"

She invited herself in. "I brought wine. And Cool Ranch Doritos." To Orson: "Do you drink, Orson? If not, I suggest you start, because the Benjamins love their booze." She displayed the bottles of wine on the bar between Adam's tiny kitchen and the living room. "I brought red, white, and rosé."

Adam grabbed her elbow and steered her away from Orson, toward his bedroom. "Can I talk to you, Amy?" They left Orson standing, mouth agape, and Adam slammed the bedroom door behind them. "I can't believe you just showed up here like this. Have you lost your fucking mind?"

"No, but apparently you have." She pointed through the wall, in the general direction of Orson. "Are you ashamed of him or us, Adam?"

He had no answer for that. Well, he did, but it was longer and more involved than he had time for right then, so he rolled his eyes and said, "Neither, and you know that. And you know why I've kept him apart from you all."

Amy crossed her arms. "Well, you can't keep using Dad as an excuse to be a shit, Adam. Introduce me to your boyfriend." She shifted her weight from foot to foot. "*God.* I hate this person you've become."

He opened his mouth to speak, to argue, to demand that she explain to him just what kind of person she thought he had become, but the door opened behind him and Orson's head appeared.

"Yeah," he said to them when he saw the looks on their faces—like he'd caught them at something illicit or illegal. He hooked a thumb back over his shoulder. "I can hear every word you guys are saying, so why don't you come in there and talk about me?"

Amy laughed. "I like this guy," she said to Adam.

So they moved their discussion to the living room. Orson introduced himself and Amy started in with all the questions Adam had hoped to avoid. She sounded more and more like Susan the older she got, but he did not dare point that out to her.

"Wisconsin, huh?" she asked. "That's… a long way from here."

Orson laughed. "Yes, it is, and that's just the way I like it."

That led them to compare Wisconsin winters to Michigan winters. "So, you were, like, an honest to God dairy farmer?" Amy turned to Adam, wide-eyed, impressed with this information. "I can honestly say I have never met one of those before."

"Well, my dad was," Orson said. "And his dad before him and his dad before him… all the way back to whenever the first Hoffman climbed down out of the Alps and marched to the nearest port and got on a boat that would bring him here." He paused. "I'm just an IT guy. I hate cows. And snow. And subzero temperatures."

Amy laughed again. "I was just the opposite! I escaped the searing Georgia heat for all that snow and ice."

"But you came back," Orson reminded her.

She waved a hand. "Yeah... marriage will make you do shit like that." She took a huge gulp of her wine.

They lapsed into silence and Adam said, "Okay, so you guys have met and you've hit it off. Great!"

Amy cut him off and turned to Orson. "Adam's doing that thing again, where he acts like a dick because he's afraid of what we'll say to each other if we're left alone together for too long."

Orson glanced from her to Adam and back again, unsure.

"Ignore her," Adam told Orson. "She's assumed the role of matriarch and feels it's her job to embarrass everyone else in the family." He fixed his sister with a look that challenged her to continue or to argue.

Amy addressed Orson. "Don't mind any of this, Orson. This is not how we are. Like, I really don't just show up at people's houses uninvited, but I've been calling and texting my brother for months—" And she turned a pointed glare at Adam. "—Trying to get him to commit to a day and time where we can all get together for dinner so you can meet the Benjamins, but he keeps blowing me off and making excuses." Another stern glare at Adam. "So, here I am." She threw her arms out. Like there had been no other recourse.

"Sounds good to me," Orson said. He grinned and his dimple showed. "Why didn't you tell me? I've been *dying* to meet your family." He said it like he had, in fact, been dying.

"Because it's not that important," Adam said, "and there's been a lot going on. You know that. Both of you know that, and you both are acting like it's no big deal, but I don't want to introduce my boyfriend to Dad because Dad doesn't deserve to meet him." His voice was rising, becoming shriller as he talked. "There.

I said it. So can we please fucking stop this, Amy? Please?"

Amy's mouth opened and closed as she sought the words, but it was Orson who spoke first. "It's really been bothering him." He said it to Amy.

"So you really hate Dad so much that you don't even want to let him meet Orson?"

"Yes." Adam's voice was small but clear. He said it to the floor between Amy and Orson.

"Well, that's ridiculous, Adam." And she laughed to show the ridiculousness of it. It was so nonsensical to her that the only response she could give him was to laugh, and if she laughed loud and hard and long enough, it would become clear to him and he would realize that he was being absurd.

But Adam wasn't laughing. Orson wasn't laughing, either. He said, "I'm going to step out for a minute and let you guys talk." He jingled his keys in his pocket to underscore it.

"You don't have to leave," Adam said.

Orson kissed the top of his head, "You guys talk this out," he said, almost a whisper. "I love you. I'll be back in a bit."

Envy and longing battled it out within Amy. It was such a simple thing, Orson kissing the top of Adam's head like that, and saying he loved him, but it led her to the realization that she longed for gestures and words like those, yet the best she could manage was drunken sex with her ex-husband. She felt like a failure all over again and suddenly didn't want to have whatever conversation this needed to be with Adam.

He seemed reluctant, too, as he leaned against the counter with his hands crammed into the pockets of his shorts, staring down at his toes, wiggling them like he was checking to see if they still worked.

"Seriously, dude. What the fuck?"

"What?"

"I thought you were just being difficult," she said. "I didn't think you *really* didn't want us to meet him. God, Adam, that is messed up."

"I kept telling you no," he said, then corrected himself: "Well, no... I just kept giving you excuses why we shouldn't. You just didn't get the hint."

Amy wanted to tell him he was wrong, that he wasn't going to lay all this on her, but she knew he was right: he *had* told her, repeatedly, that getting everyone together for dinner wasn't a good idea, and that he wasn't really sure he wanted Orson to meet everyone. And now here he was, telling her he never wanted Orson to meet Joel.

"He seems like such a great guy," she said, and nodded in the direction Orson had gone.

"He's awesome," Adam said, and meant it. "I'm sure I'll do something soon and fuck it all up."

Like not introduce him to your family? she thought, but instead said, "I doubt that. He's got it pretty bad for you." And again that ache of longing pierced her in the space between her chest and her gut. She wanted a guy like Orson, who would kiss the top of her head and tell her he loved her and mean it. She would bet money that Orson wasn't cheating on Adam, that he wouldn't even consider it.

"He's not the one I'm worried about," Adam said.

Amy could have pursued that, but she let it go. Then she went ahead and let everything else go, too. "Okay, then," she said. "I'll leave you alone, and I promise not to pester you about Dad anymore." She collected her wine, popped corks back into bottles, stuffed them back into the bag. "If you guys wanna work it out, great. If you don't, great."

Adam peered at her, suspicious, his eyes narrowed.

"I'm serious," she said. "Cross my heart and hope to die." Then she went ahead and crossed her heart to prove it to him. "I'll talk to you later, I guess." *Or maybe not,* she thought, and for the first time in their adult lives, she started to leave without giving him a hug or asking for one from him. She did turn and look back at him, framed in the kitchen doorway, leaned against the counter in the same position: head down, hands stuffed into his pockets.

It was the strangest feeling, but for the first time, the wondered if maybe she weren't looking at him for the last time. It was not rational, and part of her mind knew that, but the other part was finally starting to put together all the pieces of their conversations since Joel came out and she saw a pattern of words and behavior that seemed to add up to Adam cutting ties—not just with their father, but with all of them.

He glanced up and caught her staring. "What?"

Amy shook her head. "Nothing. G'bye." Then she left, saw Orson downstairs, leaning against the trunk of his car and staring at his phone. She waved to him as she drove away and he smiled and waved back.

.sixteen.

Ethan relented and went to see a therapist, but he insisted that it not be Amy's or anyone his father might suggest. "I don't know," Amy told Mike. They'd had sex again and were getting dressed. Evidently, whatever it was between them—attraction or simple boredom—was their new normal. "It seems like he's up to something."

Mike laughed. "Like what?" He had one sock on and was looking for the other.

"I don't know. Like he might want to talk about us and what incredibly shitty parents we are."

He laughed again. "Of course he wants to talk about us. Isn't that what therapy's for?" He still hadn't found his sock. "You go and you sit and you blame someone else for everything that's wrong with you for an hour to someone who won't interrupt you or tell you that you're wrong. Have you seen my sock?"

Amy considered what he said. She'd started going to her own therapist again, and maybe she was doing it all wrong, because she went and sat for an hour and complained about everything she imagined was wrong with *her* to someone who wouldn't interrupt or correct her. Maybe she needed to go to Mike's therapist so she could start blaming someone else for all her shortcomings. "I just don't want his attitude toward me—toward *us*—to get worse because he sits in a therapist's office twice a week and magnifies everything that's wrong with us." She found his sock with her pants and tossed it to him.

"Maybe he doesn't even mention us," he proposed.

Amy scoffed. "Yeah, right."

Ethan did discuss them, but he talked about everything else, too.

"It just feels like my entire family fell apart after my grandma died," he confessed to his therapist upon his first visit. "Like, everyone was totally there for each other after her diagnosis and everyone was all tight, right up to the funeral and the shivah, and then... it just crumbled and nobody noticed it except for me."

"Is it possible they noticed and just responded to it differently than you did?" His therapist was a young man who reminded Ethan a lot of his uncle Adam. He'd asked Isaac's parents for the recommendation because the last thing in the world he wanted was to have to go to his mom's therapist and talk about her. For all he knew, anything he shared would go directly to Amy, doctor-patient confidentiality be damned. He didn't trust it, and he didn't ask his dad for a recommendation either. He imagined Mike confiding in someone who was a psychoanalytical dude bro, pictured them tossing a baseball back and forth and reaching conclusions by using sports analogies. He didn't want any of that, either. Isaac's parents had no dog in the fight, so their referral would be unbiased.

"I suppose that's possible," Ethan confessed, "but they sure didn't act like they noticed it."

"For instance, how did your grandfather respond?"

Ethan liked his therapist. He was young enough for Ethan to relate to, but old enough to introduce himself as Dr. Levin—not Dr. Daniel or Daniel, like his mom's therapist used her first name with her patients. Like she and Amy were sisters and not doctor and patient, and their sessions were girl talk and didn't cost thousands of dollars a year. Ethan suspected he was in his early to mid-thirties, single, and probably gay—though he couldn't be sure anymore. Dr. Levin was of the generation that had fought against the stereotypical gender tropes and won, and now the only way to know things about a person was to wait until they told you.

"He came out of the closet," Ethan said, matter-of-factly. They had covered all the highlights in their initial session, so this would be no surprise to the doctor.

"And what was that like?"

Ethan had to chuckle. "Surprising."

"How so?"

"Well, that's not really something you expect to happen." He heard himself and grimaced at how closed-minded he sounded, so he rushed to explain. "I mean, it isn't a problem that he's gay. I have friends at school who are gay. My best friend Isaac is gay. It's just—you know, it's your grandfather, and he's married to your grandmother, and they had kids. I mean... I know it was way different back then, and people really had to hide who they were, and that's the case with my grandpa. He couldn't really be himself, so he got married." He shrugged.

"How did your parents respond?"

Ethan had to laugh again. "Well... they got a divorce not too long after my grandmother got her cancer diagnosis, so we've all been dealing with that, too. Then Grandma died and that sucked... then Grandpa came out of the closet." He paused as he realized Susan's death was not what sent everything into a tailspin.

Dr. Levin saw the look on his face and said, "You look like you just thought of something important."

"Maybe..."

"What is it?"

Ethan told him. "I think everything was going to hell before Grandma died. Like, I think—for me, at least—it started when my parents split up."

"Do you want to talk about that?" Dr. Levin asked.

Ethan didn't, actually, but he knew that was why he was there—to talk. And there was this quality to Dr. Levin's voice that made him not mind so much if he did talk about it. "My dad was cheating on my mom." He heard himself say it, but it sounded like he was overhearing someone else's conversation. "My mom found text messages and voice mails. It was..." His voice trailed off.

"What?" Dr. Levin's voice was just barely encouraging. He sounded more like someone who was just being a good friend and listening to him spill his guts.

"Bad," Ethan said. "Like, the whole thing…? I was at a friend's house when it happened and my uncle came and got me and told me that when I got home, my mom was going to be in a really bad mood and I needed to be nice and supportive of her. It was confusing. I honestly thought she'd overdosed or something, but I couldn't really wrap my brain around what he was telling me because everything had been fine earlier and all of a sudden he was telling me that. It didn't make sense."

"Have you talked to your father about that?"

Ethan shook his head. "No way. I don't even know how I'd bring it up."

"And your mom?"

"Not since it happened." He gave Dr. Levin an abbreviated timeline of his parents' divorce: the initial period of spontaneous arguments followed by an uneasy truce leading up to the legal proceedings, then Mike moving all his things out of the house (Ethan came home from summer camp and found very obvious gaps where Mike's things had been; he and Amy never discussed it), then a more managed armistice as Mike and Amy had to get along for the sake of their son as he made his way through puberty. "And now, they're speaking again. It's weird. I really don't understand adults sometimes."

Dr. Levin actually cracked a smile at that one. "Well, all human beings are very complex. It isn't just the grown-ups."

At another session, Dr. Levin only asked him questions about himself. "How is school going?"

Ethan shrugged. "It's high school. It pretty much sucks."

"You're a sophomore?"

"Yeah."

"Would you consider yourself popular?"

The question caught Ethan off guard. He laughed. "God, no. I don't want to be popular."

Dr. Levin's brow furrowed. "Why is that?"

"No one likes the popular kids." Ethan paused, considered that, then clarified: "Well, they all like each other. And themselves, of course. But no one else likes the popular kids."

"Do you have many friends?"

Ethan shrugged again. "There's my friend Isaac. We've been friends since elementary school. And a few more." He pictured Leah and felt himself frown, but Dr. Levin didn't see it and that made Ethan glad, because the last thing he wanted to do was explain what happened with Leah.

"So, you have a group you hang with regularly?"

"Not really. Mostly it's just me and Isaac hanging out, but I speak to a lot of people. You know, like, in the halls and in class. Like that."

Dr. Levin smiled as he made notes. "Sounds pretty popular to me," he remarked.

Ethan scowled.

"No offense," the doctor said. "But if people are speaking to you, and you're speaking to them, I'd say you were pretty popular."

"Not like that, though." Ethan was still scowling. "My dad's not a millionaire and I don't get dropped off in a Bentley so everyone will see and be jealous. I try to be nice to everyone, not just the rich kids." He crossed his arms and sat back on the couch. "And I don't see what me being popular or not has anything to do with anything. School isn't what's bothering me."

Dr. Levin looked up, nodded. "Okay then, Ethan. Let's talk about what's bothering you."

"Nothing's bothering me."

"You seemed very upset when I suggested you might be popular."

Ethan heaved an enormous sigh, threw his head back, and stared at the ceiling. "I'm not upset. I—I just don't want people to think I'm like those kids. They're mean. I try not to be mean."

And of course Amy tried to get him to tell her what he discussed in his sessions with Dr. Levin. She imagined she was being slick, but Ethan knew immediately what she was up to. "So, how do you like your therapist?" She was driving him to school and they were stuck behind a bus on Ponce. "What's his name? Dr. Levine?"

Ethan corrected her. "Levin. And he's okay, I guess."

"So you don't like him…?"

"That isn't what I said, Mom."

"Well, you can always go see Kate. I'm sure she would be glad to make room for you in her schedule."

Ethan was turned away from her so he could roll his eyes and she wouldn't see it. He had a feeling "Kate" never said anything of the sort, and it grated on his nerves the way his mother talked about her therapist like they were best girlfriends, like the woman wasn't making thousands of dollars off her. Hell, maybe she did tell Amy she would work Ethan into her weekly schedule of sessions; the more appointments, the more money.

"I'm fine with Dr. Levin," he muttered.

"Well, that's good," Amy said, then repeated herself. "That's good." When she did that, Ethan knew it almost always meant that what she was thinking or feeling did not match what she was saying.

They rode in silence. The traffic crept along.

Amy asked, "So, you think it's helping?"

Ethan wanted to throw her a look of disbelief, but he shrugged instead. "I guess."

"Well, again—if you want to start seeing Kate instead, just let me know."

"I will," he said, to end the conversation.

Dr. Levin seemed especially interested in having Ethan talk about his relationship with his mother. It made no sense to Ethan, but he went along with it.

"We get along okay, I guess," he said. "She can get a little nosy sometimes, and we usually get into a fight about that, but we always iron things out."

"How is she nosy?" the doctor asked him.

"Just sticking her nose into things that aren't any of her business," Ethan said, and laughed, because he thought the definition of *nosy* was pretty universal and unlikely to change from person to person, or to fit situations. Nosy was just that—nosy.

"Like going through your things? Your cell phone?" Dr. Levin asked, and Ethan was so relieved that he would not have to bring up the subject of Leah and his miserable failure that afternoon that he decided to go with those examples.

"Yes," he said. And to make himself feel a little better about lying, he added: "But it isn't all the time."

The doctor nodded, scribbled notes. It infuriated Ethan when that was his only response. Like Ethan had answered incorrectly or something. "And you're an only child?"

"Yes," Ethan said, further irritated because now he couldn't understand what being an only child had to do with anything. He checked the clock on the wall above where Dr. Levin sat. He had forty more minutes. Or maybe he could end the session early.

"Did your mother work outside the home when you were growing up?"

"Not until after the divorce," Ethan said. His irritation worsened and he snapped, "What does that have to do with anything?"

Dr. Levin glanced up, smiled. "It helps me understand the relationship you have with your mother."

Ethan was only slightly mollified. "Oh. Okay…"

"And when was the divorce?"

"Like, four years ago."

"And you live with your mother?"

Ethan nodded. "Yeah. I alternate weekends with her and Dad."

"Do you enjoy your time with one more than the other?"

He shrugged. "It's about the same, really. They live about three miles apart. I get two weeks with Dad in the summer, and that's when we go on vacations and stuff. Like, last year we went to Hawaii. I think we're planning to go to Mexico this year." As he said it he realized he couldn't recall the last time he and Amy had taken a lengthy vacation to somewhere like Hawaii or Mexico, and it sounded like he was saying that time with his father was no better than the time he spent with his mother, then telling the doctor that his dad took him on trips to exotic locations. It sounded bad, unfair to Amy, and he wanted to correct it. "Mom and I do cool things, too, though."

Dr. Levin did not glance up, nodded as he wrote, and it exacerbated Ethan's frustration.

"Like, she's not a very good cook and she admits it, so we go for Ethiopian food a lot. That's cool. And she's not very strict overall, not like some kids' parents, so I pretty much get to do whatever I want as long as I don't hurt myself or anyone else." He felt the blood rush to his face as he rambled on, intent on not painting Amy as some wicked ogress who kept him at home and never let him experience the world the way his father did. "But, like—I mean—she doesn't just let me run wild. There are rules and all, but it's not like a prison." He made himself stop, but before he did, he said again, "We do cool things, too."

What he realized about therapy—and this happened when he wasn't sitting in Dr. Levin's office talking—was that he reached his own conclusions. That's what the process was. He sat down and Dr. Levin asked him the first question and he answered it and that led to more questions and answers which made Ethan think long after the session had ended (and usually when he lay awake at night), and the combination of the sessions with Dr. Levin and the stream of consciousness at night as he put himself to sleep generally led him to the understanding that was the entire point of seeing a therapist in the first place.

He realized he didn't hate his mother, but he realized that she thought he did, because of the things his father did for him that she couldn't, either for financial reasons or because of time constraints. Mike owned his own practice; he could close the place for an entire year and sail around the world if he wanted to. Amy worked for someone else and did not have that kind of autonomy. She could quit her job, he supposed, but he knew how much having that job meant to her, so he knew she would always complain about it—her boss, her clients, the bitches she worked with—but she would never give it up because it was the most outwardly apparent proof that she was more than just the ex-wife of a dentist and the mother of that dentist's child. She was a strong, independent, intelligent single mother who had taken the worst possible situation and turned it into a personal success.

And Ethan hated how he'd made her feel less than. He just didn't know how to make it up to her.

"His doctor won't tell me anything," Amy told Mike. "I asked, and he said no." She seemed truly perturbed by this. "Like, he's a kid and I'm his fucking mother, and this asshole won't talk to me about what my kid tells him."

"You really asked E's therapist for a progress report?" Mike asked, and laughed.

They were in bed—Amy's bed, which used to be their bed—basking in the afterglow, Amy supposed, though she hadn't enjoyed it. Maybe because she was so preoccupied with Ethan and what he may or may not be divulging about them all to his therapist, but also because sex with Mike had become perfunctory. Just like when they were married and he was having sex with all those other women, only now it was reversed and he was the enthusiastic one while Amy wished she was anywhere but where she was the entire time.

"Of course I did," she said, and threw the covers back, swung her legs out of bed. "I'm sure he's blaming us for everything." She knew because she had done the same when Susan put her into therapy in high school, and she also knew that Susan had asked her therapist what Amy was sharing because her therapist—a militant feminist named Roberta with a buzz cut that Amy, as a teen, found completely fascinating—told her and asked Amy if she consented to her mother having access to her record. Amy, aghast and feeling empowered for the first time in her life, had refused and therefore got to delight in watching Susan sulk.

Mike went to the bathroom. He left the door open and that irritated Amy. "We already know what he's talking about," he called in to her.

"No, we don't," she called back, and if he told her then that he had spoken to Dr. Levin, that Ethan had granted him access, she would probably stab him. She opened the drawer in the nightstand to see if there was something sharp inside, like a nail file.

He appeared in the doorway, leaned against the frame in a pose best reserved for men modeling Jockey briefs in the Sears catalog from when they were kids, only he was naked and it only increased her irritation. "Of course we do. He talks about us and he talks about your dad and he talks about his grandma dying. What the hell else is he supposed to be talking about? He doesn't *have* anything else to talk about. He's fifteen years old!"

Mike had lost his athletic physique and now looked like any other fortysomething dad. The muscles were all still there, but they were hidden under a layer of fat that Amy hadn't really noticed before. Or she usually turned away from him afterward while he dressed, and that reminded her that what they were doing was nothing to be proud of, and she wondered if Ethan knew, if Mike had told him or let something slip, and if *that* was what Mike meant when he told her that Ethan was clearly discussing them when she went to his therapist.

"I guess I'll just ask him myself," she said, and stood to get dressed.

When she did ask Ethan, though, he gave her a look of disdain and said, "You know you aren't supposed to ask me that, right?"

Amy rolled her eyes. "I tell you what I discuss with Kate," she pointed out.

"That's because you can't keep anything to yourself," he reminded her. "And I don't ask you to tell me. You just do it. I don't even want to hear it."

"Okay, fine. I won't bother you with all my boring problems anymore."

She wanted to call Adam, but made herself not do it. They would just end up arguing, and she didn't have the energy for it. Adam could be miserable without her involvement. So she called Joel.

"Is something wrong?" he asked, by way of a greeting.

Amy laughed. "No, Dad. Nothing's wrong." *Except that it feels like everything is wrong,* she thought. "I just called to see how you were doing."

"I'm fine, I guess," he said. "Getting ready for the summer break."

They talked about his plans for vacation—he was going to Provincetown with "the girls," which she knew to mean his group of friends—and she found herself sounding more like a parent when she told him to be careful. She meant it in just the context he would take it, and Joel understood immediately.

"I'm always careful," he assured her, and chose not to divulge his scare after the hookup with that Jeff guy. "And I've got a prescription for PrEP now, but even so, I still use condoms."

Amy had to interrupt him. "Wait... what?"

"Condoms," he repeated. "I know they're kind of old-fashioned, but I guess I'm old-fashioned that way. I guess I'm a prude." And he chuckled.

"*Dad!*" Amy fairly shrieked it.

"What?" Joel asked. On his end, he was on his knees in the remains of Susan's garden, attacking the weeds that had promulgated since her death and choked the life out of everything else. He was focused on the task before him and his conversation with Amy and was afraid he'd missed something.

"I don't need the *details* of your sex life, my God!" Amy was truly surprised and though they weren't face to face, the color had crept into her face and she was embarrassed, though whether for Joel or for herself, she couldn't say. Then she laughed.

Joel laughed, too. "Well, you said be careful, so I explained how I was going to be."

"I'll just take your word for it," she said.

There was a slight pause, then he asked, "Have you talked to your brother?"

"No," Amy said. She could have left it there, but she didn't. "We aren't really speaking right now."

"Oh, God," he groaned, and it sounded like he was in genuine physical pain.

"What? What's wrong?"

"Everything, I guess," he said, "and it's all my fault. I guess I was fine with Adam being mad at me and not speaking to me, because I knew he had you, but you two need to stay on speaking terms, Amy. You have to. Adam doesn't have anyone else. You know he's always been something of a loner. And your mother knew this would happen, I guess."

Amy had been following him until he mentioned Susan. "How could Mom have seen this coming? And anyway, Adam has someone. He's dating this guy named Orson. I met him. He's nice."

"Oh," Joel said, like he was surprised Adam was able to find someone. "That's good to hear." Then he sighed. "I've been thinking a lot," he said. "And no matter how I thought about it, I always concluded that your mother must have known." A pause. "About me," he said, in case Amy might think he meant something else. "And I know you're mad at your aunt Rhoda for what she said about your mother, but I think that was true, too, and I think she deserved it. She deserved to be found attractive." Another pause. "I loved her very much, but—well, I didn't think of your mother in those terms. I don't think we had sex at all after she got pregnant with Adam."

That made perfect sense to Amy, and yet she still had to fight the need to argue, to defend some point that clearly no longer mattered. "Probably," she said, softly.

"But I mean your mother knew that Adam would have a hard time after she passed," he said. "And I think she told me that because she knew… about me."

"She said this to you?"

"She told me Adam would have a hard time."

"But not that she knew about you?"

"No."

Amy wondered, though. Susan was no fool, and any woman in a sexless marriage did not need anyone to help her reach the conclusion that if her husband was not having sex with her, he was more than likely having it with other people. But would she have determined it was with other men? Amy had never suspected Joel was gay. He wasn't the most rugged, masculine specimen of manhood she'd ever encountered, but she'd never suspected her father might be gay. And apparently, Adam hadn't either. So the chances of Susan being able to see something no one else could seemed slim.

"There's no way she could have known." She said it more to herself than to Joel.

"Maybe," Joel said.

He knew he never left any physical evidence lying around that she might find, like unexplained strips of condoms in his jacket pocket, or the receipts from adult bookstores crammed into the back pockets of his corduroys. He never brought the porn home; instead, he devoured it in his hotel room, committed each page of every magazine to memory. This was before the internet, and he shuddered to think how many thousands of dollars he had spent on those glossy, overpriced magazines that he studied the way medical students studied diagrams of the central nervous system, only to toss them into a trash can at the airport before boarding his flight back home.

So if Susan had known, she never let on that she did. Joel never caught her staring hard at him across the dinner table and he never awoke in the middle of the night to find her looming over him, studying him for some sign. He was always so terrified of being found out that it made him careful. It sucked any real pleasure out of the experiences themselves, of course, but it kept him from being discovered.

The fear of contagion made him more cautious, too. It made him more selective. In bars, he politely refused the advances of any man he thought looked unhealthy—cheeks too sunken, skin too sallow. He actually believed that more weight on a man equated to health and therefore gravitated toward the more portly men. "Dad bods" they were called now.

And Joel always had a fantasy wherein he met one man—another married man, like himself—to settle into a semi-regular semblance of a relationship. They would be faithful to one another if not their wives, and if anyone chanced to see them in public together, there was nothing to be alarmed or concerned about—it was just two guys out for a drink. Perhaps they would even socialize with their wives, and if that led to their wives becoming friends, then it would be considered a win all around: the wives would have one another for friendship, and the husbands would have one another for their needs. Joel thought it was the perfect arrangement, but somehow that guy never materialized.

Joel couldn't stand the silence on the line any longer, so he changed the subject. "I ran into Mike the other day," he said. "He mentioned you and—"

Amy's vision faltered. Her heart stopped and the blood pounded in her ears. It all happened in less than a second and she screamed into the phone, "He did *what?*" Of course she imagined the worst case scenario: they'd run into one another in the produce section at Publix and Mike had let something slip—that he'd been over at Amy's yesterday, or he would ask Amy when he saw her, or something careless like that. She would punch him in his stupid face next time she saw him. Only she had already decided she wasn't going to see him again. This idiotic escapade of theirs was over, effective immediately.

"Um... He just mentioned talking to you...?" Joel said, slowly. "About Ethan...? Amy, I had no idea the boy was in therapy and I certainly hope it isn't because of me."

Amy returned to herself just as quickly as she'd fallen apart. Her breathing and heart rate returned to normal, she could see again, her hearing was back. "Oh, that. Yeah, but... it's not you." That wasn't entirely true, so she clarified. "Well, it's all of us, I guess. I don't know because he won't talk to me about what he discusses with his therapist."

"Well, I feel bad," he told her.

"Don't," she said. "Really. He's only doing it as a favor to me and his dad because we both got tired of his moping around like the weight of the entire world was on his shoulders. I'm sure he'll declare himself cured before much longer."

"Well, don't let him miss a session. It's expensive."

"He can't skip out because I drive him."

Ethan didn't want her sitting in Dr. Levin's waiting room, either. "No," he insisted. "I'm not a child. I don't need my mommy waiting for me. Go do something." He imagined her creeping closer and closer to the door of Dr. Levin's office, positioning her ear as close to the door as she could in the hope that she might catch a word or a phrase here and there. Ethan would have none of it.

So Amy had coffee in the Starbucks on the ground floor of the building, or she sat on a bench in the building's miniature park and texted with Finn, who was seeing two guys at the same time and didn't want to break up with either of them. He always initiated the conversations; Amy participated half-heartedly. Finn was exhausting. She wasn't sure how she'd missed that about him at the beginning. Or maybe she was just too old for fabricated drama.

"Hello again," one barista said to her every time she was there, like she came several times daily instead of twice a week.

"Hi." She perused the menu board, like she didn't know exactly what she was going to order.

"Amy, right?" he asked.

It always caught her off guard when someone remembered her or her name. "Yeah." And of course, she didn't remember his name.

"Grande non-fat latte with caramel drizzle, right?"

Suddenly Amy was ashamed of herself and the way she ordered her coffee. It sounded particularly vapid being repeated back to her by this grinning kid. His name tag read JULIAN. He looked like a Julian, with a few stray curls escaping his beanie and his scruff and the wooden plugs in his ear lobes. She would show him. "Usually, but I think I'm going to shake it up a bit."

Julian's grin widened. "A woman after my own heart," he said.

Amy gave a nervous laugh when she realized he was flirting, but she chose to ignore it. "I'll have a tall iced vanilla latte with soy milk." She tried to make it as obnoxious as she could.

"Coming right up."

She chose a seat in the window to wait, and he brought it to her instead of calling her name. "Thanks," she said, uncertain.

"No problem at all," he said, and started wiping the narrow bar where she sat. Amy guessed he needed to look like he was supposed to be there so she wouldn't think he was creeping on her. "So, I see you here a lot."

Amy nodded. What was she supposed to say? She wasn't about to give this kid—and he *was* a kid—her life story.

"Work in the area?" Julian was persistent.

"Something like that," she lied.

"Cool, cool." He continued to wipe. Amy noticed that the cloth he used was dry. She thought she might remark on that, decided not to. There were twin blossoms of color on both his cheeks, so he was embarrassed enough. She felt like laughing at how ridiculous it was to have this kid flirting with her. She could honestly have been his mother, or at least his older sister.

"I guess you're a student at Tech, then?" she asked.

He nodded. "Biomedical Science."

"Interesting. Like cloning?"

"Something like that."

They kept the small talk going until he had to take care of the occasional guest, then he returned to pretend he was wiping the bar. Amy considered telling him it wasn't necessary, but seriously wanted to see how long he would keep the charade up. Turned out he was a graduate student, which meant he wasn't as young as she'd thought. He just looked like a hipster twentysomething because of the way he dressed and the ear plugs, but he was thirty. Amy relaxed a little.

"So, since you work in the area, maybe we could get lunch one day," he said, at last. Then he caught himself and his blush deepened and he said, "Unless you're married, which would make me a real creepster for just assuming you weren't."

Amy laughed. "I'm not married."

Julian was visibly relieved. "Okay… whew." He even gave a theatrical wipe across his brow.

"And I don't really work in the area," she confessed. They'd been talking for close to an hour and she got the feeling he was being totally up front with her, so she owed him the same in return. "My son is seeing Dr. Levin upstairs." And she pointed upward. "That's why I'm here twice a week."

Julian nodded and Amy was sure the mention of Ethan and Dr. Levin was a deal breaker for him. But instead he just grinned and said, "Cool, cool." He said that a lot, actually. When it was time for her to leave, he waved to her from where he was helping a lady find Ethiopian roast coffee beans and said he would see her next time.

Usually, she would call or text Adam and give him the rundown on what had happened. He always told her to pursue it and she always decided not to. In this case, she would conclude that she was imagining Julian's interest in her and that they wouldn't have much in common anyway, since he was going for a PhD in biomedical science and she cut hair for a living. He was just being nice. That's what baristas did. They flirted with people and those people left them bigger tips. *But he remembered your name,* said the little green man in her head.

Amy isn't hard to remember, she countered.

And your regular order.

It's his job to remember what people drink.

And he invited you to lunch.

She could argue in silence with herself for hours, but she wished she wasn't still upset with Adam because she really needed someone to talk to about it.

"Just fuck him already!" Finn screamed at her across his salad when she told him.

Amy rolled her eyes. "Never mind," she said. He made it sound like she'd been going on about it for days, hours at a time. She checked the time on her phone and saw that it had been less than five minutes since they'd sat down. She really needed someone else to hang out with besides Finn.

In the end, she gave up and called Adam. "I thought you were mad at me," he grumbled when he answered.

"I am," she said, "but I need someone to talk to, and I'm on my way to your place. Are you at home?"

He was. "I'm babysitting Puck," he explained as he opened the door, and the dog bounded toward Amy.

"Is Orson okay?" Amy asked it and instantly wished she hadn't. It really was a Benjamin family trait to leap to the worst conclusion about everything.

"He went home for a wedding," Adam explained. He poured food and water into Puck's bowls, scratched the dog between his ears, and grabbed his keys off the counter. "Let's walk down to Willy's. I'm starved."

He ate while Amy related the encounter with Julian. "I mean, he remembered my name *and* he remembered what kind of fucking coffee I order. It was, like… cute, but maybe slightly weird…? I don't know."

"He's a barista," Adam pointed out.

"See, that's what I keep telling myself. That's what baristas do."

"And he's also a PhD candidate, so he probably has a memory like Sheldon Cooper."

Amy hadn't considered that. It made it seem less strange. "Maybe…" She grabbed a tortilla chip off Adam's tray and chewed it while she thought. "Anyway, it's all probably nothing."

Adam shrugged. "Could be." He really didn't care either way, but he was glad Amy had come over. He didn't really like it when they weren't speaking to one another, even if he was justified in his reasoning.

"He probably doesn't have a lot of time for dating and stuff anyway," she remarked.

"Probably not."

Julian remembered her every time she went in for her coffee, though, and she caught herself on the verge of asking for his number more than once, but she always decided against it. So it was a relief when he asked for hers.

"Do you ever come to this part of town when you aren't bringing your son to his therapist?" he asked with a grin and an arched brow.

"Well...," she said, and sipped her coffee. "I work at 10th and Piedmont. Is that considered this part of town?"

Julian's reaction was one of incredulity. "No way!"

"Way." Amy wasn't sure he was being genuine; it seemed very theatrical.

"I live there," he said. "Right by the park. We should hang out sometime."

Amy nodded. She wondered if saying "Small world" would apply in this situation. She didn't want to come across as one of those people who used words and phrases incorrectly. He didn't seem like one of those guys who would say "Well, actually..." and then correct her with the actual usage and the history and origin of the phrase.

When she didn't immediately respond in the affirmative, Julian said, "So... this is where you say 'Yeah, we should *totally* hang out, Julian,' and then I ask for your number."

Amy laughed. It burst from her like a bubble and it left her relieved, the way a good scream at nothing or a cry in the dark did. Julian frowned, and she rushed to explain. "No, no, no. I'm not laughing at you. I'm just laughing." She paused. "At myself, I suppose." And she laughed some more.

Julian gave a small chuckle, too. "Okay..." He didn't seem sure, though.

"No, seriously." And she told him about her talk with Adam, all the doubts she'd had about him being even remotely interested in her or, if he were interested, having the time. "And I'm divorced," she said, then turned scarlet, like she'd confessed to being a murderess.

It was Julian's turn to laugh. "I certainly hope so," he said. "I think if you were still married and giving me your number, we're already headed in the wrong direction."

"And I have a kid," Amy went on. "And he's fifteen now and he's mouthy and I want to slap the shit out of him, and I guess that's why he's in therapy upstairs right now. But I need you to understand what you're getting into." That sounded ominous, and she caught herself. "I mean, I know you didn't ask me to marry you, but just dating... that's a lot. I mean, it sounds simple, like... hey, it's just a date, right? But I haven't actually been on a date in... well, a long time." She did not count her rolls in the hay with her ex-husband as dates.

Julian listened. He nodded when it seemed she had said all she wanted to say. "Okay..."

"Like, over a year."

"Okay..."

"And my mother died. And my dad is gay. And my brother hates him because of it."

Julian reached out, put a hand on her shoulder, gave it a gentle squeeze. "Okay," he said, simply. "Really. We'll go out and have fun."

"I don't want you to think I'm a basket case," she said, and could not look him in the eye.

He laughed again. "I don't think that at all."

"Okay, good. Great."

.seventeen.

JOEL HAD NEVER SEEN anything like Provincetown in his life. "Stop staring like that," Kent told him, and laughed. "People will think there's something wrong with you."

They'd landed in Boston and taken the ferry over and Joel was agog from the moment they left the ferry terminal. He'd heard stories and he'd seen photographs, but none of it was enough to prepare him for the reality of Gay Pride week in Provincetown. Ken and the others were veterans; Joel, as usual, was the odd man out.

"She's going into shock!" shrieked Dave.

Dan joined in immediately. "Quick! Someone call an ambulance!"

The crowd surrounding them ignored it. Cattiness was part and parcel of Provincetown at the height of its Pride festivities, so unless someone actually hit the ground, or there was blood visible, everyone just went on about the business of dancing, sipping cocktails, and ogling one another.

"Atlanta Pride is nothing like this," Joel remarked as they all crowded into a shuttle for the ride to the beach house they had rented for the week. Actually, there were many similarities, but no one bothered to point them out to Joel. They let him gape at the bare-chested men, the men in jock straps and combat boots, the drag queens in Vegas showgirl regalia. Atlanta held its Pride festival in October to coincide with national Coming Out Day, while Provincetown's festival was in June, the traditional month that commemorated the Stonewall Riots and the original marches across the country. That meant more scantily-clad men of all ages, shapes, and sizes.

Really, though, this would be Joel's first official celebration of Pride. He had attended Atlanta's a of couple times when he could, with Susan always leading the charge to show their support for Adam. "We should march with the PFLAG moms and dads, Joel," she said to him as they watched the parade meander down Peachtree Street toward Piedmont Park.

"I don't know," he said.

"It'll be fun! Look at how much fun they're having!" And she pointed to the mothers and fathers passing them, signs held aloft, arms around their gay sons and daughters, their faces alight with joy.

Joel was both fascinated by and jealous of those men and women carrying banners that declared their love and support of their gay children, and later when the faculty and students from the university passed—some of them men he'd had sex with—he wanted to hide, but they pointed at him and waved. "Professor Benjamin! Happy Pride!"

Joel turned crimson, but he waved to them all, shook their hands as they offered them, accepted gifts of beads and flyers. "Yes," he said. "Happy Pride to you, too. Happy Pride to you all."

Another time, they spent the entire parade waiting for Adam to pass by. He was on a float with his then-boyfriend, a man named Randy who was close to Joel's age and who Susan never fully trusted. "There he is," Susan cried when she spotted him at last. "Adam!" She pointed him out to Joel. "Do you see him? Adam!"

Joel waved.

"Adam! Happy Pride, sweetie!" Susan called, and waved.

Adam turned at the sound of his name, shielded his eyes against the sun, gave a half wave, then pretended he didn't know either of them. Afterward, Susan wanted to follow the crowd to the park and stroll through the festival. Joel begged off. He didn't trust himself in the open like that, vulnerable to being seen by men he'd been with. Standing on the sidewalk in front of The Vortex with his wife, watching the parade for his son was one thing, and there was a built-in excuse should someone see him there. There was less control in the park, he felt, so they did not go.

Now, in Provincetown Joel was overwhelmed. At the rental house, they broke off and chose their rooms. Joel and Kent would share a small room on the ground floor with its own bathroom and a door that opened onto the beach. Joel sat on the bed that would be his for the week and stared out at men on the beach. "This is unreal," he said.

Kent chuckled. "You act like you've never seen a good-looking man in a swimsuit before."

"I've never seen so many in one place before," Joel said. "It's like—" He couldn't think of the proper words or phrase to convey what he was feeling, which was a peculiar feeling of elation and leftover guilt. This is what he'd always wanted, what he'd played at on all those trips out of town, and now that he had it, this complete freedom to do exactly as he pleased with whomever he pleased, sitting on that bed in Provincetown, staring out the French doors at those men throwing a Frisbee and walking their dogs on the beach, he realized that he would have none of it were it not for Susan's death.

"Like what?" Kent asked him.

Joel shook his head. "I don't know." That wasn't exactly correct, though, so he said, "I mean… this is what I've always wanted. Being out. Like, completely out, in public." He paused. "Where people can see and no one will think there's anything wrong, and I should feel relief." He hadn't intended to deliver a soliloquy, but he couldn't stop himself. "And I do, I guess." A pause. "No, I mean, I *know* I do, but… there's this nagging little voice in the back of my head that's telling me I wouldn't even be here if Susan hadn't had cancer and died." Another pause. "I guess I'd still be creeping around the gay bars and the sex clubs back home, and cruising the internet and meeting up with other married guys in hotels outside the Perimeter and pretending." Another pause. "When Susan was first diagnosed, I thought I'd stop it," he said, and glanced over his shoulder at Kent. "Fucking around, you know? I mean, I seriously thought that I would stop meeting men over the internet and hooking up with them because my wife—who I'd cheated on the entire time we were married—suddenly had cancer, and that I would respect her and not do those things." He gave a small chuckle. "I guess we see how that worked out."

A disruption in the hallway broke the silence then and the others appeared. "What's going on in here?" Dave demanded to know. "You girls are taking forever and we need cocktails!"

"Well, they still have their clothes on, so it's not what we thought," Dan observed, and everyone else cackled like a brood of hens.

Joel stood up, smiling. "We were just talking," he said. "Nothing important."

"Good, because I am *parched*," Pete said.

They went to the closest bar. A drag queen dressed as Edna Turnblad presided over a wet underwear contest. Kent asked Joel, "Are you okay?"

"I'm fine," Joel said. He sipped his cosmopolitan.

"Okay, but you didn't seem fine earlier."

Joel dismissed it with a wave of his hand. "I was just thinking out loud," he said. "You know how it is. You know how I can get sometimes." He was already embarrassed by the episode. Thankfully, Kent spoke in a low enough tone that no one else at the table heard their discussion over the drag queen and the roars of the crowd as they cheered for the contestant of their choice. From what Joel could tell, a guy built like a defensive lineman with a red beard and a shaved head seemed to be winning, although if Joel were judging, he would have chosen the guy on the end, who was younger and more muscled and had a much larger package.

"Well, you need to enjoy yourself this week," Kent said, as if he were issuing an edict. "You're on vacation. You don't sit around and brood on vacation, Joel. You could have stayed home and done that."

"I'm fine," Joel said again.

"Good," Kent said, and they left it at that.

There was always gentle disagreement about what they would do after dinner each night. Joel suggested dancing. He'd never been able to really go dancing, and he craved that feeling of abandon now that he didn't have to slink about in the shadows. Dan and Dave voted for drag shows, and Pete and Kent argued that if you'd seen one drag queen lip syncing Liza Minnelli, you'd seen them all.

"Maybe a drag show and *then* dancing," Joel suggested, wanting to be magnanimous and get the discussion over with before it got too late. Then again, it never seemed to get too late in Provincetown. There was always something to do.

"If you've danced to one Madonna remix, you've danced to them all," Dan said with a smirk and a roll of his eyes.

"Whatever, bitch," Kent said, but they all laughed and decided on a drag show after dinner, then dancing.

Of course there were men to meet, too, and it was understood that no one was obligated to stay with the group if a better opportunity came along. "I mean, I love you ladies, but if any dick swings my way, I don't know a single one of you." That from Pete.

"We know you better than you know yourself, Liz Taylor," said Dave.

"Well, if I'm Elizabeth Taylor, that must make you Zsa Zsa Gabor."

Dan silenced them both. "Ladies, ladies, please. It isn't like either of you are the marrying type, so Dave, dear, you can't be Liz. And Pete, honey, you are hardly Zsa Zsa." He paused, sipped his mai tai dramatically, then said, "It's clear one of you is Madonna and the other Jennifer Lopez."

Both men feigned offense, then the table erupted in laughter. "I guess that makes me Mary Pickford, huh?" Joel whispered to Kent.

"Mary Pickford?" Kent considered it. "If by that you mean someone who *acts* innocent but really isn't, then absolutely."

More laughter. Joel was chagrined, but joined in the laughter himself. He was starting to warm to the cattiness that prevailed among these men, the name calling and the double entendres that seemed inherent in every utterance. This, too, he reminded himself, had been lacking all those years he spent in the gay bars of distant cities. This, and dancing, and drag shows, and not having to skulk around when Susan traveled to see her family. And if he thought about it too much, he would end up depressed again, and he didn't want that, so he pushed it all to the back of his mind and joined in his own roasting.

"Yes. Mary Pickford. That's me."

"Coquette," Dan declared and aimed a finger at him. "Oooh! That would be a killer drag name!"

"Coquette St. Jacques!" Pete crowed.

"Isn't that a clam dish or something?" Joel asked no one in particular.

"Mussels, I think," Kent said, though he seemed unsure, too.

He tried to imagine himself in drag and could only picture himself in Susan's old get-ups: the enormous sunglasses with the melamine bangles and matching necklaces, the lurid floral and geometric patterns. His imaginary drag self looked nothing like these accomplished artists in sequins and feathered headdresses, their waists cinched and their breasts rivaling any woman's. Susan would have gotten a kick out of these drag queens, he thought. But thinking too much about Susan would lead him back down that rabbit hole of inadequacy and survivor guilt he'd started down earlier, and he didn't want to go there. It had settled in his chest, all that remorse, and felt like an elephant sitting there. He took great gulps of air.

"You okay?" Kent asked, genuinely concerned.

"I'm fine," Joel said. "Probably just too much fried food."

"You need another drink!" Pete announced and motioned for their waiter.

"No, no," Joel said, and stood. "I'll just go out on the deck for a minute, get some fresh air." He tried to laugh, to put everyone at ease, but their smiles were starting to fade and worry was spreading across their faces. "Really, guys. I'm fine. I'll be right back."

He felt a bit better just standing, and the breeze blowing in from the bay helped. The dock adjacent to the bay afforded him a partial view of the drag show and there was still good cruising—which was the entire point of coming to Provincetown during Gay Pride Week. He was both ashamed of himself and amused by it. After all, he still felt like he was forty years behind every other gay man in the world and needed to move as quickly as he could to make up for all that lost time. He walked to the end of the pier and sat on a bench there. It was not long before someone sat next to him.

Joel gave the guy a nod and a smile. "Hi."

"Hi."

He was younger than Joel, but still not too young. Joel guessed him to be in something corporate or banking. He was freshly shaved and his hair was parted and swept back from his face.

"It was getting a little loud back there," the guy said, and hooked a thumb back over his shoulder in the direction of the drag show. "Dim All The Lights" could be heard and Joel felt the bass reverberating in the bench and the boards of the pier.

"Yeah," Joel agreed. "I needed some air."

"Well, this is a great place for it." Then silence as they both gazed out at the colors the world turned as the sun set. After a time, the guy held out his hand. "I'm Dean."

Joel shook it. He always felt awkward shaking hands outside of work. "Joel. Are you in for the week, or are you one those lucky people who get to live here year-round?"

Dean chuckled. "I'm up from Florida with friends. I don't know if I could live here year-round," he said. "Too much of a good thing and all."

"True, true," Joel said, then they lapsed back into silence.

Dean broke it by asking, "Would you like to go for a walk? That's what I was doing when I came out here and saw you, and... well, I must confess, you looked nice and I thought I'd introduce myself." He nodded back toward the club and the drag show and the music—now it was "Prove Your Love" by Taylor Dayne—that continued to blare. "And that's not really my idea of the best time, if I'm being honest."

Joel chuckled. "Me, too. I guess I have officially turned into my father. But to answer your question: yes, I would like to go for a walk." He was starting to feel that same discomfiting pressure he'd felt earlier and thought standing and walking might relieve it.

They stood together. "Great," Dean said. "Just let me text my friends so they don't get worried and think I fell off the pier or something."

Joel did the same. *Going for a walk,* he texted Kent.

Whore was the reply a few seconds later. Then, *Have fun. Be careful.*

They walked. Dean was, it turned out, in corporate banking. He was impressed when Joel said he was an English lit professor. "It sounds a lot more romantic than it really is," he said.

And Dean laughed. "Because corporate banking is?"

Joel shrugged. "It's a lot of reading poorly written essays arguing points that have been settled for centuries, and arguing with aspiring poets who refuse to learn where to place a comma or accept that everything doesn't have to rhyme."

"Sounds better than dealing with the bloated egos of CEOs all day."

"Maybe."

Dean noticed Joel rubbing his chest now and then. "Are you okay?" he asked. "You keep doing that."

"Indigestion, I think," Joel said. "I've eaten a steady diet of fried seafood since we got off the ferry." Saying that made him realize it didn't start with vacation. Since Susan's death—and before, really—he'd always gone for whatever was easiest and quickest, and that usually meant fast food. A salad was never complete without fried chicken tenders, not to mention the flood of ranch dressing he would drown it in.

He rubbed his chest and searched for a drug store as he and Dean walked along. "Acid reflux, maybe?" Dean asked. "I have to take pills for that."

"Could be," Joel said. "It feels better when I stand."

"Well, I have my prescription in my room here." They had stopped in front of one of the many inns in Provincetown, this one painted a robin's egg blue and flying a rainbow flag. Joel grinned and Dean returned it. This, they both knew, was the purpose of Dean's invitation to go for a walk. They were not young; men their age did not collide, shirtless, on a dance floor and fall into a lusty kiss, then adjourn to a stall in the men's room for foreplay. Men their ages met on a bench at the end of a pier as the sun set and did not say outright, "Let's go have sex at my place." A walk was suggested, there was conversation—small talk, really; nothing too deep—then suddenly, there they were standing in front of one or the other's house or apartment or, in this case, hotel, and a possible case of acid reflux with the promise of relief was just the excuse needed.

Dean was attractive, though not exactly Joel's type. He was soft without being effeminate—not like Gregory—and so pale it only increased the impression of softness. In a span of mere seconds, Joel flipped through his internal Rolodex of every possible excuse he could think of not to accompany Dean into the inn and up to his room. Dean noticed the hesitation and said, "We wouldn't be bothered. I'm not sharing a room with anyone."

And Joel heard himself say, "Sure."

This was what he and Kent had planned for when they were planning the trip to Provincetown: meeting guys and having casual—albeit safe—sex with guys with zero strings attached. This was ideal, Kent pointed out, because at the end of the week, those men would ride the ferry back across the bay to Boston and board a plane to wherever it was they came from, and they would never have to see or speak to them again. Joel and Kent would return to Atlanta with no other baggage than the suitcases filled with their dirty laundry and sand, and there would be no fear of running into those men on the ice cream aisle at Kroger or at the beer bust at The Eagle. "And it's at the beach," Kent said, "which makes it all even better. Not to mention that every man in Provincetown will be there for the exact same thing, so no one will get his feelings hurt when you don't want to exchange numbers or friend each other on Facebook."

In Dean's room, which was as neat and nondescript as Dean was, he swallowed a Nexium and they met in an awkward embrace. It was immediately clear to Joel that Dean was more interested in him then he was in Dean, and he willed himself to just pretend. It would be over soon and he could go meet back up with Kent and the guys at the drag show.

His chest felt tighter as Dean tugged at his shirt, pulled him closer to the bed. Joel moved to follow him and felt a strange sensation in his left leg. "Wait...," he said, against Dean's mouth. "Something's wrong..."

Dean pulled away, a perturbed look on his face.

"My leg is numb," Joel said, to himself more than Dean. "And my chest..." Then he felt the pain in his left arm and fear gripped him as he realized he was having a heart attack. He'd never had one before, but men his age knew the symptoms because of the ever-present risk. These were all the classic symptoms: the numbness in his leg, the pain in his arm, and the tightness in his chest. He was having a heart attack. Dean seemed to realize it at the same moment and neither of them moved for what seemed an inordinately long time.

"I'll call an ambulance," Dean said and went to do that just as Joel clutched hard at his chest and began to gasp for breath.

Added to the pain was fear that nothing either of them did would be enough and he would die in a strange man's room at an inn he didn't even know the name of, in Provincetown during Gay Pride. There was a joke in there somewhere, Joel felt, but he was too busy willing himself to stay alive to piece it together.

.eighteen.

ADAM'S RESPONSE WAS SILENCE when Amy delivered the news of Joel's heart attack.

"Adam?"

"I'm here," he said.

"Well, fucking say something."

"Okay. I'll get the tickets and you can give me cash," he said. His voice was small, like he was in a barrel.

Amy swallowed her anger and gave him the flight information.

"All right. I'll see you in a couple hours."

She had two glasses of wine while she threw clothes and shoes into an overnight bag and fought the urge to call Adam and tell him what she'd wanted to tell him earlier: that his father had a heart attack and was in the hospital and the least he could do is get his ass off his shoulders long enough to be concerned. Mike texted and she ignored it, but he was more concerned than Adam was. And it reminded her that she needed to break it off with him when she got back now that she was seeing Julian.

"Fuck." She'd forgotten she was supposed to meet Julian for dinner and drinks later. She called his number and threw up a silent prayer as she waited for him to answer.

"I have a bad feeling about this," he said when he accepted the call. He said it with a laugh, so Amy was hopeful.

"What I'm going to say to you is going to sound like the most clichéd bullshit excuse in the world, but I swear to God, every word of it is true, and I feel like shit enough as it is, and I've been drinking, and I'm really on edge right now, and my brother is being a dick, and I really want you to listen to me with an open mind, okay?"

Julian laughed harder. "Okay."

Amy squeezed her eyes tight and just said it: "My dad had a heart attack and he's in a hospital in Boston and I have to fly there right now with my brother and that means I'm not going to be able to have dinner with you and I know it took forever for us to finally sync our schedules and I know that it sounds like I'm just making up an excuse to get out of going out with you, but I'm not, and I know what you're thinking because I'd probably be thinking it, too, but like I said, I swear I'm telling the truth, so please believe me, because I *do* want to go out with you, but my dad had a heart attack." She stopped, finally, because she was out of breath.

"Well," Julian said on his end, and followed it with a silence. Amy pictured him scratching his head or rubbing his chin as he considered how he would say what he wanted to say, which she was sure wasn't nice. "Is he going to be okay?"

Amy exhaled then and it sounded like the air being let out of a tire. She hadn't expected concern from him and was caught off guard. "Yeah. Well, he's stable, so..."

"That's good," he said. "So, go take care of your dad, and give me a call when you get back in town. I'm not going anywhere."

Adam was sullen when she picked him up at his apartment. He didn't want to go, but he wasn't going to tell her that and start an argument, so he stayed silent and let her think he was processing everything.

At the airport, they got their tickets and boarded the airport train to their gate. "I need a drink," Adam said when he finally spoke.

"Me, too," Amy admitted. "You think it's bad?"

He shrugged.

"I know he's in stable condition, but that doesn't always mean things are good." She was, as always, imagining the worst; Kent hadn't shared everything with her when he called and she felt certain of that somehow. She wished she had a prescription for something, but all she had was alcohol. "I need that drink," she said again.

They were able to get three drinks in before they boarded their flight. Mike called as they found their seats, and she sent it to voice mail, then texted him. *Plane's taking off so can't talk.*

Just calling to see how U R, he texted back.

I'm fine. Talk 2 U when I get back.

What she meant was she would break it—whatever *it* was—off with him when she got back from Boston. She never should have done anything in the first place and she felt like a fool and needed another drink, but she had to wait until the plane was in the air.

"You wouldn't happen to have a Valium, would you?" she whispered to Adam.

He laughed. "No. I have Klonopin."

"Can I get one?"

He threw her a look, but dug the bottle out of the backpack he had crammed under his seat. "You need to get your own prescription at some point, Amy. I can't always keep supplying you."

"Whatever. You make it sound like you're my dealer or something, Adam."

"No. Dealers get paid, you just hit me up for free shit."

Amy rolled her eyes. "You make it sound like I'm hitting you up every day. Shit, forget it." She held the pill back out to him. "If you're going to be such a dick about it, just keep it. Fuck."

Adam refused to take it back.

"Here, Adam. Take your fucking Klonopin back. I'll just be a basket case the entire flight and the whole time we're in Boston." She whispered it as loudly and forcefully as she could without drawing the attention of everyone else on the plane.

He turned to her and his eyes flashed. "Take the fucking Klonopin, Amy. And don't turn this trip into another goddamn meltdown about Dad."

She opened her mouth to argue further, but that stopped her before the words were out of her mouth. She just blinked at him, her eyes wide.

"And don't stare at me like you can't believe what I'm saying," he hissed.

"Well, I actually *can't* believe you're saying this, so I can stare all I want." She dug her bottle of water out of her bag and threw the pill back. She couldn't wait for it to start working. "Why did you even come if this is how you feel?"

"I don't want to talk about this," he said, and since he couldn't exit the plane at that point, or move seats (it was a full flight), he found his sunglasses in his backpack and slid those on, followed them with his ear buds.

Amy grabbed a passing flight attendant. "I will give you all the cash I have in my purse right now if you will bring me a vodka on the rocks with a lime." He laughed and hurried away to fill her order.

Adam did not speak until they were off the plane at Logan International and headed for baggage claim. "I can't believe you brought luggage," he grumbled. "How long do you think we're gonna be here?"

"Long enough," she said, "and I hate doing laundry in those hotel machines." To prove her dislike of it, she made a face. "You never know what people have washed in it before you. Like, what if someone killed someone and then washed the blood out of their clothes and it gets into all my stuff and I become a suspect in a murder investigation because they test my clothing and find traces of the victim's DNA?" Apparently, she realized, the Klonopin had done little for her anxiety.

Adam laughed. "There is pretty much zero precedence for something like that."

"You never know."

"Yes, you do, because it has literally never happened before."

They collected her suitcase and got the first available cab.

"Welcome to Boston," the driver greeted them with the epitome of the stereotypical Boston accent. "Where are we headed?"

"Mass General," Amy told him.

Adam realized he didn't even know what hospital Joel was in and that gave him a slight twinge of guilt.

"Nothing too serious, I hope, miss," said the driver as he navigated their way out of the pick-up and drop-off lanes.

"Our dad had a heart attack," Amy explained.

"Oh, man. Sorry to hear that. Had one of those myself eight years back. Scared the hell outta me, I'm telling you. Very scary. I don't wish that on nobody." And so they were treated to the entire story of the man's poor eating habits and exercise routine preceding the heart attack, and the way it had opened his eyes to the things that were important in life: his wife, Joyce (there was a photo of her stuck to his dash); their three children; their twelve grandchildren.

"That's a lot of grandkids," Adam said.

"Thanks! They're the love of my life, every single one of them, you know?"

Adam just nodded. He hadn't been paying the man a compliment, he'd just been pointing out how surprising it was that, in the twenty-first century, people were still having so many children.

At the hospital, Amy persuaded the nurses stationed outside Joel's room to allow them to see him, though visiting hours had ended long ago and Joel was probably asleep. "Just stick your head in, see if he's awake," she told the woman, who was named Mindy (according to her badge), but looked more like a Doris, Adam thought. "If he's asleep, we'll just leave him a note and he'll see it first thing when he wakes up in the morning and know we were here." She had never sounded more like her mother in her life.

Mindy looked uncertain. Her eyes darted back and forth between Amy and Adam. Behind her, phones quietly rang and lights blinked, silent, on a switchboard. The other nurses spoke in hushed tones to one another and to the people on the phones.

Adam remembered then that he hated hospitals. Even to see Amy after Ethan was born, he'd felt like a traveler in a country where he didn't speak the language. Now he wished Mindy would just make up her fucking mind and either say yes or no.

"Let me see," she said, and they both understood immediately that Mindy hated her job. She hated being asked to do things she didn't care to do, she hated being the one to make the decision whether or not to allow someone to see their loved ones after visiting hours. She was probably nicer during the day, on first shift, when her comings and goings ran parallel to the rest of the world, but it was clear that Mindy wanted to be anywhere in the world at five minutes to ten at night than where she was.

She shuffled down the hallway, the soles of her shoes squeaking on the polished floor, and knocked so gently on one of the doors that it barely made a sound. She opened the door, stuck her head in. In another minute, she was motioning Amy and Adam down the corridor. "He's awake," she whispered to them.

"Great," Amy whispered back.

"I can give you five minutes, then you can come back in the morning."

"Perfect," Amy said.

Mindy let them into the room and closed the door behind them. Joel waved to them from the bed. He seemed small—even smaller than usual—in the enormous hospital bed, surrounded by all the equipment monitoring his vitals. "Hi, kids," he said, and smiled weakly.

Amy nodded back over her shoulder to indicate Mindy. "She's a barrel of monkeys, huh?"

Joel gave a weak laugh. "She's not so bad once you get to know her."

Amy threw her purse into a chair and leaned across the bed to hug him. She burst into tears. "You scared us to death," she told Joel.

"Well, I scared myself," he said, and looked past her to where Adam leaned against the wall just inside the doorway. "Adam…"

There was a note of hope in his voice, the way he said it, and his eyes seemed to light up at the sight of his son.

"Hi, Dad."

Joel gestured to the chairs to either side of the bed. "You kids have a seat. That's one of the good things about a private room: they give you more than one chair for visitors."

"The nurse said we only had five minutes," Amy told him.

He dismissed that with a wave of his hand. "Oh, her. She's all bark. I think they require her to say all that so no one sues the hospital." Amy sat in the chair closest to the bed. Adam stayed where he was, hands crammed into the pockets of his shorts.

"Well, I don't want to get thrown out," Amy said.

"It'll be fine." To Adam: "You can come closer. I'm not contagious."

Adam did not reply. He and Amy exchanged a glance as he slid into the other chair.

"So, what happened?"

Joel told her everything from packing in a rush the morning he was flying out ("You know how I am about waiting until the last minute."), to the flight ("We had *the* cutest little flight attendant!"), to the first couple days in Provincetown ("If you've never been here, you should come. You'll love it."), giving asides about the restaurants and the nightlife, which drag queens were his favorites, like he was a seasoned veteran of Pride Week in Provincetown. "And the next thing I know, I'm having a heart attack," he said, and threw his hands up. He left out the part about Dean so they wouldn't assume he was in the middle of something lurid when it happened. "I thought it was indigestion," he confessed. "I mean, fried food has never really agreed with me."

"Well, did the doctor say why it happened?"

"I'm old," Joel said.

Adam actually laughed. "Your doctor said that?"

Joel shrugged. "He didn't come right out and say it, but that was the gist of it. And you know, heart problems run in the family, so I guess it was just a matter of time." He paused, then added, with a laugh: "Time and too much dancing with cute boys, I guess, but he didn't mention that last part."

Amy tried not to, but she couldn't help imagining Joel huffing poppers and dancing shirtless, surrounded by a bevy of beglittered twinks (Did people still call them that? She'd have to ask Finn), as Lady Gaga thumped in the background. She knew that wasn't what he meant, but now she couldn't get the picture out of her mind. "Well, you need to take it easy," she said. "I guess he's putting you on medication? Exercise?" She had a feeling Joel Benjamin had never exercised a day in his life outside of the required physical education classes in elementary, middle, and high school. That, she suspected, would take more work than anything else.

"I've got to change everything about my life if I want to live to see retirement," Joel said, and scowled, like the very idea of wanting to live longer was an affront.

There were so many questions Amy wanted to ask, and all of them reached the tip of her tongue at that exact moment: where had he been when he had the heart attack? was he using drugs, even poppers? or had he over-exerted himself (and yes, she meant sexually)? But she wasn't sure how to broach such topics with most people, so she certainly couldn't just nonchalantly start lobbing such questions like hand grenades at her father. And she felt horrible for even thinking them. They sounded like the questions bigots asked when they engaged with gay men when they didn't actually want to, when they called lifelong partners "friends" and could never speak the word "gay," so they said "like that" or "that way." *"Did the heart attack have anything to do with your being, you know… that way, Dad? Were you huffing poppers on the dance floor, or sucking dick at a glory hole when it happened? Because we all know that's all you people do: dance, do drugs, and have sex!"* She gave her head an actual shake to clear it.

"I'll have to haul out all your mother's old cookbooks," he said, and smiled, wistful. "Remember how she'd always be the first on the latest nutrition kick?"

"That chicken and sweet potato thing she used to make was the worst," Adam said.

"The one that was just chicken breasts, sweet potatoes, and onions?" Amy remembered it, but just barely.

"Yeah."

She shrugged. "I kind of liked it."

"It was so bland," Adam reminded her. "I called it Nursing Home Chicken and it pissed her off."

Joel chuckled. "I think it was supposed to be good for our digestion," he said, "or something like that. Circulation? Memory function?" He shrugged. "Anyway, God... she had a library of diet cookbooks and I still have every single one of them. The healthy heart diet, the Scarsdale Diet, the Sonoma Diet, the Atkins diet. Did any of us ever lose a pound eating all that *dreck?*"

"I did," Amy said. Her weight, like all teenaged girls, had rollercoastered and yo-yoed throughout her teens and into her married life. She'd been—or, rather, felt—the size of an elephant while she carried Ethan, but then lost her pregnancy weight and settled into a size she was comfortable with, as if by some spell she'd accidentally conjured and couldn't remember the steps to. She drank wine, she ate what she wanted, and she stayed within five pounds of the same weight without working out or running, and for that she was glad. She also worried that she would wake up one day and be the size of Aunt Rhoda.

Adam shook his head.

Joel said, "I'll need to start going to the gym, too."

"I thought you already worked out," Amy said.

He shrugged. "I play at it," he confessed, "but now I'll need to actually do it." He hated anything physical like that and really only paid for a gym membership so he could go there, climb onto an elliptical and pretend to be interested in fitness while he cruised the other men who were there to do the same thing.

Mindy stuck her head in then. "Okay, folks. Time to wrap it up. You can come back in the morning."

Joel made the kind of face a child would make when adults

declared it was time for bed. Amy hugged him and kissed the top of his head. "We'll be back first thing tomorrow," she promised. "Do you need me to bring you anything?"

"I can't think of anything."

"Well, call me if you do." She hugged him again.

"Bye, Dad," Adam said from the doorway, and gave a hasty wave.

In the elevator, Amy realized she hadn't found out what time visiting hours started. "Or if we'll be able to meet with his doctor and find out when he'll be discharged." She was thinking aloud. "Let's go ask Mindy." She pressed the button to return to the floor Joel was on.

"You can," Adam said. "I'll just go on to the hotel." When the elevator stopped on the first floor, he stepped off, oblivious to the look of disbelief Amy gave him.

"Are you serious?" she called to him from the elevator. Other people squeezed past her, selected their floors, waited. Amy held the door open with one arm.

Adam was confused. "Um... yeah...?"

"Dad had a heart attack, Adam, and he's up there alone and we're the only people he has, so the least you can do is go back upstairs to ask these questions with me."

He laughed. "Amy, for fuck's sake, it doesn't take two people to ask what time visiting hours start. Or what time Dad's doctor will be able to speak with us."

The people behind her were started to get annoyed. Amy ignored them. "God, I can't believe you're doing this," she said.

"And I can't believe you're doing *this*." He gestured to the elevator and the people glaring at her. "You're holding up an entire elevator filled with people because you want to tell me—again— how much better a person you are than me. Don't you ever get tired of trying to convince me that you're the good Benjamin kid? Hell, I'd be exhausted by now."

Amy turned and saw to the disapproving looks. "Sorry," she said, and stepped off the elevator. "I'm so sorry," she said again as the doors slid shut, then she wheeled on Adam. "And I do not try to convince you that I'm the good kid." She said it through her teeth. "Do you never get tired of being an insufferable dick all the time?"

He rolled his eyes and turned away from her. "I'm going to check in," he said. "You can stay here and ask questions all night if you want to."

She followed him, and when he was out of the hospital and on the street, she swung her purse at him, connected with the back of his neck and one shoulder. "Asshole!" She screamed it and people turned to find the source of this epithet.

Adam lifted his arms to block any further blows. "What the fuck, Amy?"

She dropped her purse and went at him with her hands, swinging wildly, landing a slap on this arm, that shoulder, a glancing blow to the top of his head. She aimed for his face, but his arms kept getting in the way. She wanted to hurt him, or slap some sense into him, whichever she was able to accomplish first. She kicked at him, too, but he dodged her. Then he fought back, his swings just as clumsy and ineffectual as hers. "Fuck you, Adam!" She screamed it over and over. "I fucking hate you!"

"What the hell is wrong with you?" He asked it and swung at the same time, each word punctuated with a swing.

People stared and some moved closer, because people loved to witness other people making fools of themselves. It was always comforting to know there were people with worse problems, and clearly anyone who fought on the street outside a hospital had it worse than the majority of people in the world. Amy heard those people discussing the display she and Adam were putting on, and though it shamed her, she kept swinging because she felt if she could just land one good, solid blow, it would somehow wake Adam up to the reality of how he was acting toward Joel. If she could just get him to realize that, she felt that all their lives could return to some semblance of normalcy and they could move on.

"Stop," Adam said. He had grabbed one of her arms and they circled one another in a hug the way professional wrestlers hugged. It was an awkward dance and neither of them was very good at it.

"No," she said. "Stop being an asshole."

"Stop being a bitch."

"I hate you so much right now."

"I hate you even more." It was the fight they never had as children, and Amy was determined to win it. Adam was just determined to get her to stop before the cops showed up. "Stop it," he said, and tried to grab her arms as she swung at him. "Seriously, Amy, fucking *stop it*. Someone's going to call the cops." He avoided acknowledging the crowd of spectators that had assembled and finally managed to grab one of her arms and hold it fast. "Stop."

She swung with the other one, landed several blows across his shoulders. A couple actually hurt, but he bit down on the pain and managed to grab her other arm, got both his arms around her from behind and held tight. "Let me go," she said through her teeth, and spittle flew.

"No. Calm down."

"Fuck you."

"Fuck *you*," he shot back. "Calm down. We can do this all night. I don't have anywhere else to be."

She struggled against him, but it was pointless, and she was surprised how strong he was. He'd never struck her as having that much strength. "People are staring," she said, surprised at the size of the crowd that had gathered and was slowly drifting away now that the show was over. Some of them had their phones out and she felt physically ill to think a video of herself and Adam fighting on the sidewalk outside Massachusetts General would end up going viral on the internet. "Let me go."

"Are you over your bullshit?" Adam wanted to know.

"Just let me go."

He loosened his hold on her ever so slightly and when he was satisfied she wasn't going to start swinging again, he let her go and stepped back. "Okay," he said. "Now…" And before he could continue, Amy turned on him, her arm extended, and slapped him hard across the face.

"There," she said, calmly. "Now I'm over my bullshit."

Adam grabbed his cheek where she'd struck him, then pulled his hand away, checked it for blood or something, he wasn't sure. "What the fuck was that, Amy?" He screamed it. The people who were walking away now turned back, not wanting to miss a second of this drama.

"That was me slapping the shit out of you," she said. She picked up her purse where it had dropped in their struggle, checked the contents, scanned the area around them in case anything had fallen out. "I need a drink." And with that, she left him standing in front of the hospital and walked across the street to their hotel.

"Oh, stop," she told Adam later. "I didn't hit you that hard."

"It hurt like a motherfucker," he said.

Amy rolled her eyes. "Pussy."

They were checked into their rooms and having drinks in the lounge. Amy kept checking her phone, either for a change in Joel's condition or a call or text from Ethan. She knew she should just relax, it was late, anything that happened could be dealt with in the morning, but she just couldn't let it go. Joel had looked fine and he seemed to be in good spirits when they'd seen him earlier, but that didn't mean his condition couldn't worsen in seconds. She watched *Grey's Anatomy* and felt she had more than a basic understanding of the way life worked out, especially if there was a hospital involved.

Adam texted with Orson and Amy was jealous. Then she was angry, because why wasn't Julian texting her? Then she realized it was almost midnight and felt bad for how ready she was to write him off as just another guy who probably didn't want anything else from her but sex. As if on cue, a text came through from Mike Cohen.

How's Joel?

She grunted her disgust and turned her phone over so she wouldn't see if any more texts came through.

"Now what?" Adam asked.

"Nothing," she said. Then: "Everything." She grabbed fistfuls of her hair and made like she might tear it out by the roots. It felt surprisingly good.

Adam drank his beer. "That doesn't make any sense."

Amy heaved a huge sigh. "We had a knock-down, drag-out fight on the sidewalk outside a fucking hospital, Adam. The day after Dad had a heart attack. Look at us." She swept her arms in giant circles. "We're like an episode of *The Jerry Springer Show*, only we didn't get compensated for acting like idiots where people could see us doing it."

He held up a finger. "To be fair, I was merely defending myself. You were the one whaling on me."

"Never mind," she said, and drained her vodka on the rocks.

"Seriously, though. Where the hell did that shit come from, Amy? Like… what in the actual hell are you dealing with in your life right now that would set you off like that? And don't tell me it's Dad's heart attack, because that just happened, and there's no way in hell that much crazy built up since we left Atlanta."

Amy opened her mouth to respond, then closed it again. "It's like," she started, and then stopped again, because she knew exactly where it had all come from, she just wasn't sure how to put it all into words, nor was she entirely sure she wanted Adam knowing it. "Ever since Mom died," she said at last. "It's like we buried normalcy with her."

"We were never normal," Adam reminded her.

"That's bullshit and you know it," she snapped. The bartender set her drink down.

Adam scoffed. "So, a closet case father and a mother fucking other men because she's so miserable is normal?" He laughed, drank his beer, and laughed some more.

"How do you know she was miserable?" Amy pivoted on her stool to face him. "Did she tell you or are you just guessing?" Adam said nothing. "I'm gonna go out on a limb and say that Mom knew Dad was gay the moment she set eyes on him, and I'll go even further and say that she didn't marry for love in the first place." She wanted badly to slam her drink back, but she forced herself to sip it. "I'll bet she saw Dad and saw financial security and stability and never really cared if he wasn't attracted to her."

"You're out of your mind."

She shrugged. "Maybe so, but it wasn't like they got married in the Dark Ages. It was 1979, Adam. Gay men were everywhere and women were marrying them. This isn't exclusive to us." She paused, sat straighter on her stool as a thought occurred to her.

"What?" he asked, though he wasn't sure he wanted to know.

"What if we aren't even Dad's kids?"

Adam knew she was being totally serious, but the look on her face—not unlike the overwrought expression of a silent film actress—made him actually cackle.

"I'm serious," she said.

"I know." And he laughed until he couldn't breathe. When he could finally speak, he said very slowly, because he knew she was tipsy, "Amy, you look exactly like Dad if he did drag. Of course we're Dad's kids." He heard himself and stopped, surprised that these words were coming out of his mouth after such a long period of wanting to disown Joel and have nothing to do with him. Now he was defending his honor?

"I look like Mom," Amy said.

"You look like Dad. Trust me."

Amy huffed. She'd never thought so and she wasn't going to start just because Adam said so. She finished her drink and knew she needed to call it quits, though she wanted more. She also had the most insane urge to smoke. "Do you have your cigarettes?"

Adam gave her a sidelong glance. "Why...?"

"Because I want to smoke one. Let's go outside."

She settled their bill and they sat outside the main entrance to the hotel, the ashtray between them. "Look at us," she said, picking up the thread of their earlier conversation. "Dad's in the hospital across the street, they're monitoring him in case he dies, Mom's already dead..." She gestured at nothing in particular, at the world, or at the injustice of everything. "My kid hates me. I'm fucking my ex-husband. Your life is pretty great right now. You have a great guy, but you hate Dad. And here we are, sitting on the ground, smoking like a couple of high school kids." She punctuated her statement with a drag on the cigarette. Drinking, she had decided, made smoking much easier; she wasn't coughing and it actually tasted and made her feel good. "We're kind of a fucking mess."

"Wait," Adam said. "What did you say?" He had only half been paying attention while he replied to a text from Orson.

"I said we're kind of a fucking mess."

"No, before that."

Amy tried to remember but couldn't. "Hell, Adam. I don't know what I said. I'm drunk, I've got diarrhea of the mouth right now, and I'm premenstrual. What did I say?"

"You said you were fucking your ex-husband."

"Oh. That." And Amy giggled. "Yeah, but it's over with now. I mean, I guess it's over..." She paused for thought, gave a firm nod. "Yes. It's over. It was kind of lame, to be honest."

Adam laughed, too. "So what was the point of getting a divorce?"

"Well, I'm not getting *back* with him. God..."

Adam shook his head. "Straight people are so messed up."

Amy laughed. "Like you are some paragon of virtue, right? Please, Adam. I fucked my ex-husband. You've had sex with your exes before, and don't even try to tell me you haven't, because you used to call and tell me about it."

He would have argued, but she was right.

"Anyway," she said with a sigh. "That's what I meant when I said look at us." Again with the gesturing at nothing. "We haven't been the same since Mom died and it sucks."

Adam could have argued, but there was no point. She was right. Susan's death had all the effects they'd anticipated, but what they hadn't seen coming was how untethered to one another they ended up. It saddened him and he wished Orson was with him. "I'm going to bed," he said, and stood. "You coming?"

"Not yet," she said, and stared away at something that wasn't there.

He wondered if he should be concerned. "You sure?"

Amy nodded. "I'm just going to sit here for a few minutes and think about some shit."

"Okay." He handed her his cigarettes and lighter and went into the hotel.

.nineteen.

In the morning, Amy and Adam were able to speak with Joel's doctor. He was young and attractive and he ignored Joel's obvious flirting. "The good news," he told them, "is that he got to the emergency room when he did."

"I should have come sooner," Joel lamented.

The doctor addressed Amy and Adam. "He'll need to take it easy. Nothing strenuous, no sudden surprises. His heart still has to recover." To Joel: "Lots of rest. Read, watch TV. Nothing above a walk around the block."

"And the pills." Joel made a face when he said it. They marked him as old, he felt; old and broken down, and he had to blink back tears.

"Get in to see your doctor as soon as you can, too."

"So, are you discharging him?" Amy asked.

He gave a practiced smile to reassure them all. "I don't see why he can't go home. I'll have the nurse bring the papers."

He left and Amy started making plans for them all. "He didn't say anything about flying," she said, thinking out loud. "Are you okay to fly, dad?"

"I'm fine," he said. "And that's a few days away, anyway. I'll be rested up by then."

Amy stopped, her mouth agape. She looked at Adam, then at Joel, then back again. "We'll be flying home tomorrow," she said, and held up her phone where she had been booking their flights. "The earliest flight I could get us on with three seats together is at 9:45."

Joel scoffed. "I'm on vacation, sweetie," he said. "I have four more days."

"You just had a heart attack," she reminded him.

Adam spoke up at last. "Hey, the doctor said to take it easy, and I'm pretty sure arguing is not taking it easy."

Amy ignored him. "You almost died, Dad. I get that you're on vacation and all, but it's not like you sprained your ankle. You need to be where someone can check in on you and help you out." In her mind, she had already mapped the next couple weeks out: she and Adam would alternate checking on him, and once school was out for the summer, Ethan could help him with all the things he didn't need to be doing around the house.

"I'm here with friends," Joel told her. "There's a house full of them. I'm not going running, I promise not to dance, I'll lay off the booze. But I'm finishing my vacation, and I'm not going to argue about it. Like Adam said, that isn't taking it easy." He shifted to a higher sitting position on the bed, crossed his arms, lifted his chin in defiance.

As if on cue, there was a light rap on the door and Kent stuck his head in. "Oh," he said when he saw Adam and Amy. "I didn't know you had guests already. I can come back later."

"No," Joel called out. "It's fine. Come on in." He even waved Kent into the room, used both his arms, like a grandmother summoning her grandchildren in for a hug.

Kent entered slowly, sheepishly. He was aware he was interrupting something—he guessed a discussion about what Joel should and shouldn't do following his heart attack. "I'll just sit here," he said, and took the chair farthest from them all, in a corner. Whatever this talk was, he did not want to be a part of it.

Joel then proceeded to pull him into the discussion anyway. "I was just telling Amy and Adam—by the way, have you guys met? I can't remember."

"Hi," Amy said, her voice terse.

Adam waved from across the room. "We met that once. Kind of. You know…"

Kent nodded. To Amy: "Hi." To Joel: "I'll just sit here." He paused, then: "Or maybe I'll go get some coffee…"

"No, no, no," Joel said. "Stay. Really. We were just discussing how I'm going to stay and finish my vacation because I've already paid for the damned thing. Weren't we, kids?"

Adam threw his hands up in a gesture of defeat. "I don't really have a dog in this fight," he said.

"I would just feel better if you were back home," Amy said.

"I'll be fine," Joel said again. He turned to Kent. "Tell her I'll be fine."

Kent didn't really know what to say.

Thankfully, Amy responded first. "You make it sound like I'm being a shrew, Dad. I'm just worried about you."

"I'll be fine." Again to Kent: "Tell her."

So Kent said, "I'll look after him."

Amy glared at them both, then turned and glared at her brother. "You're just gonna sit there?"

"What?" Adam wanted to know. "What am I supposed to say, Amy? He can do what he wants. He's not a kid. Shut up about it and let's go home." He was tired. Tired of being in Boston, tired of the way Amy was trying to handle everything the way she thought Susan would have handled it and failing miserably, and he was tired in general. He hated flying, then the beers he drank last night made it difficult to sleep, and now he just wanted to be done with all of this and go home to Orson and Puck. Nothing was ever required of him when he was with Orson.

Amy stifled the urge to scream. Then she laughed, like someone had told a joke and the joke was on her, so to make herself look less like a fool, she laughed so everyone else in the room would think her less a fool. "Fine," she said. "I give up."

"It's not about giving up," Joel said. "Really, Amy, honey…"

"No, really, Dad. It's fine. Whatever. Stay and finish out your vacation. Call me when you get home." She picked up her purse, gave Joel a quick kiss on the top of his head, and started for the door.

Adam sprang from his chair. "Are we going?" he asked.

"I am," Amy said. She gave Kent a clipped, "It was nice to meet you." He nodded in response, and then she was gone.

Adam gestured with his chin toward the door, said, "She'll be okay."

"I really will be fine," Joel said. "I'm not going to do anything that might kill me. It will probably be the most boring vacation I've ever taken, but at least I'll be alive."

They all nodded. No one said anything until Kent said, "And I'll make sure he takes it easy."

Several things that he might say flashed through Adam's mind, but he decided against them all, said instead, "That's good." To Joel, "I'll call when we're back home. Amy will be fine by then."

"Thanks for coming," Joel said.

"Yeah."

"No, Adam, I mean it. We haven't been on very good terms since—well, since I came out." He realized then that everyone in the room at that moment was the same people who'd been in the room then, and he felt like laughing but he started to cry instead. "It means a lot," he said, choked on the words and blinked away the tears.

Adam stared down at the floor, then at the wall. "Yeah, well…"

"I mean it," Joel said again, dabbing at his eyes with the corner of his blanket. "Everything sort of fell apart after your mother died, and I guess that's my fault, mostly. I should have done more to keep us all together. Or something. Maybe if not *more*, then something *different*, at least." He paused, considered that, shrugged. "I don't really know what else I could've done, though…" His voice trailed off.

"It's okay, Dad. I don't hate you."

Joel gasped audibly, almost theatrically.

Kent tried to make himself even smaller in his chair.

"I did for a while, I guess," Adam confessed, still not able to look at Joel. "I mean, I thought I did." He had, and he knew he had, but he was tired of all that, too. It took a lot of energy to stay that mad at someone for any length of time, and he was just too old to keep it up. His father could have died. And Adam suspected had that happened, he would have ended up in therapy about it. He'd avoided therapy so far in his life, and would rather not start in the wake of having Joel die without them ironing things out.

"It's okay if you did," Joel said.

Adam nodded. "Maybe."

"I may have deserved it," Joel said as fresh tears flowed. "And I'm sorry, son. I should have said it already."

"You did," Adam reminded him.

"I did?" Joel couldn't recall when he'd said it, or what he'd said.

"Yeah. A few times." And Adam was kind enough to remind of the times when he'd said it.

"Oh. Well… I'm saying it again, and I still mean it. I'm sorry. The last thing I ever wanted was to hurt you kids and it seems like that's the only thing I ever really managed to do."

"It's not so bad," Adam said. He heard himself saying it, and while he couldn't believe the words were coming from his own mouth, he was fine with them being said. He was tired of holding that grudge against Joel, and of Amy always pointing out that he was holding Joel to a double standard. He was, he supposed, tired of the person he had always been. He just wanted to go home and be with Orson and become the person he knew he would be if he just made the best of that.

"Well, it feels bad." Joel wiped his eyes again, grabbed a tissue from the box on the table by the bed and blew his nose.

There was a commotion outside the door, voices, then it opened and Amy's head appeared. "You're still here?" she asked Adam. "Come on. I checked us out. The cab's waiting."

"I'm coming," Adam told her.

She glanced from him to Joel to Kent, then back to Adam. "Am I missing something?" she wanted to know.

"No." Joel and Adam said it in unison.

Amy was unconvinced. "Whatever. Come on, Adam." And to Joel: "Bye, Dad. Love you. I'll call you when we land in Atlanta."

They had drinks while they waited to board their flight back to Atlanta. Adam texted back and forth with Orson. Amy sat silent, alternated between rage and confusion. She was on her third gin and tonic when Adam set his phone aside and asked, "Okay, *now* what's wrong?"

"Nothing," she lied.

"Bullshit."

Silence. Adam motioned for a beer. "So, we have about forty-five minutes before we start to board. You want to take this out into the parking lot?" He hooked a thumb in the general direction of outside.

Amy threw him a look. She wanted to stay mad, but she laughed instead. "I've already kicked your ass once. That'll have to do."

"What*ever*," he said, but he laughed, too.

"Seriously, though," Amy said after a moment. "What were you and Dad talking about? And when did this whole change take place?" She made a motion with her hand like she was performing a spell. "Like, when are you guys on speaking terms again, and why wasn't I involved?"

Adam nodded. So that was it: she felt left out. He guessed it made sense, but convincing her it was no big deal was going to be difficult. "I just got to thinking," he said, and shrugged. "I mean, I'm still pissed, but it's manageable now. I guess I got it out of my system?" Another shrug. "Plus, Orson said I was being a major fucking dick, and that I came very close to losing Dad—and let me just pause for a minute to add that at *no point* was Dad's condition *that* dire, and I need both of you to stop being such drama queens—and how would I feel knowing, if Dad had died from this heart attack, that holding a grudge was more important to me than speaking to him, and that I would live the rest of my life feeling guilty about all that. So he told me that I needed to come up here and get over it."

Amy waited a beat, and when he didn't continue, she asked, "He said all that?"

"More or less."

"Wow. He's good." She was impressed. Orson sounded like he might have given Susan Benjamin a run for her money.

What he didn't tell her was how Orson had basically threatened to break up with him if he didn't settle things with Joel once and for all. He didn't use those words, but if Adam had learned nothing being the son of Susan Schechter Benjamin, he had learned to read between the lines.

Adam had been half-heartedly packing while Orson read comics. "Maybe I'll just stay here," he said, thinking aloud really. "Amy can handle it." He stared into the duffel bag he was packing at the extra underwear, the change of jeans. He'd just rolled them up and stuffed them in. His mother would be appalled if she could see it.

Orson regarded him over the comic book, the latest *Justice League*. There was a small stack to his left. He tended to binge read them, then would pack them away in plastic bags with stiff cardboard so that they held their shape and did not wrinkle. Adam found the practice both perplexing and endearing, like most of Orson's habits.

"Are you being serious?" he asked.

"Yes," Adam said.

So Orson set the comic he was reading aside and sat up straight on the bed, crossed his legs, and fixed Adam with a firm stare. "Okay," he said, and placed his elbows on his knees, steepled his fingers in front of his chin. "I've kept my mouth shut about this and I've kept my opinion to myself, but I'm going to say this—and I promise it will be the first, last, and only thing I say to you about it, because ultimately, your relationship with your father is really none of my business." At that point, Adam had still not introduced Joel to Orson. Everything he knew about the man was what Adam had told him, and all of that was colored by Adam's opinion. "I really, really like you, Adam. Like, a lot. I've never had a relationship last this long, and that tells me that you *probably* feel the same way about me."

"Well, yeah…," Adam said, and felt his brow furrow. He suddenly dreaded where Orson was going with this.

"And I hope," Orson continued, "that I get to feel like this for a really, *really* long time. With you." And he aimed his steepled fingers across the bed at Adam. "But I don't think I will, and not because I don't want to and not because you don't want to, but because of this... this... whatever it is you have for your dad."

"But he doesn't have anything to do with us, Orson," Adam pointed out.

Orson sat for a long moment with his mouth open, prepared to say one thing but now stymied by what Adam had said. "That's *kinda* right... but not really, see, because the way you are about it—the things you say, the way you feel—see, you bring all of that into what we have, and so it may not have anything to do with us, but it's affecting us."

He paused there for effect. Adam frowned at him.

"And my concern," Orson said when he spoke again, "is that you are going to keep allowing this to eat at you and mess with you, and you're not going to make any kind of effort to resolve it with your dad, and it's going to make you miserable for the rest of your life. And if I'm still with you, it's going to make me miserable." Another pause. "And there we'll be, two miserable people, and by then, neither one of us will be able to remember what made us miserable in the first place, we'll just know that we were always miserable and we had to keep it that way. Or—" And there, he held up a finger. "—We won't even get that far... and, like I said, I'd really like for this to last."

Adam stood there, staring into the duffel bag.

"And one last thing," Orson said, and sat forward again. "Your dad just had a *heart attack*, Adam. He could've *died*. You've already lost your mom, and I know how that's affected you; you almost lost your dad, too. So stop being such a fucking dick and go up there and settle shit between you once and for all."

He left it there, sat back on his pile of pillows and reached for his comic book. Adam stared at the pair of boxers he was holding in his hand, like they'd just appeared there.

Amy laughed when Adam related the story to her.

"It's not funny," he said, then laughed, too.

"What did you say?" she asked. "What did you do?"

"I came up here and… I guess I settled things with Dad?" He shrugged, sipped his beer.

She perked up immediately. "So, you apologized? That's good."

"Well… yeah," he said, fully prepared to let her think he had.

"Wait. You didn't apologize?" She glowered at him. "So, you didn't settle things with Dad."

"No, we did settle everything, but I didn't actually say the words 'I'm sorry.' Dad did, and I told him I didn't hate him and he said it was okay if I did, but I told him I didn't, not anymore, and he said he understood if I had. *That's* what I meant when I said we settled things." He sipped his beer, checked the time on his phone, stared across the concourse at the passengers milling at another gate, anywhere but at Amy, because she knew he was giving him one of her looks.

"Well, I guess that's a start," she said. Then she asked, "Should I have another drink, d'you think?"

Adam started to say no, but boarding for their flight was announced. "You can get one on the plane," he said, and finished his beer in a single gulp.

.twenty.

ONCE HE GOT BACK to Atlanta, the remainder of Joel's summer was spent repainting and updating the house, with Kent's help. "This is, seriously, like the coolest house," Kent kept declaring as they went from the bold colors of the 1960s, when the house was built, to the more subdued colors of the twenty-first century with accents of bamboo green and ochre and pumpkin. Not merely green or yellow or orange, and Joel found the names for the paints ostentatious.

"Oh, this is nice," Amy said when she saw the results. She checked on Joel regularly now, always with a reason for stopping by. She was at the mall, and since it was so close, she thought she'd drop by. Or she was updating her license and registration, and it was quicker at the location on Roswell Road, so she was on her way back home and figured she would check in and see how he was doing.

"You know you can just come by," Joel pointed out. "You don't have to have a reason." He suspected the majority of her reasons were fake anyway.

"I know," she said.

"I mean, just call and say you want to come over. Or that you're on your way, or whatever."

"I know, Dad."

It was Adam who needed to be coaxed into visiting, and the visit needed to be planned well in advance. Even then, it was ten or fifteen minutes maximum, then he was checking the time and announcing his departure. Like Amy, Joel felt his reasons were made up, for the most part: doctor's appointments, teeth cleanings, he was going to pick up Orson's dog up from the vet.

"But I hardly ever see you," Joel said. He really thought they'd made significant progress in that hospital room in Boston. "I see your sister all the time. I can't keep her away. You, I have to schedule a visit with, then you're half out the door before it even starts."

"I've got a lot going on," Adam said, and shrugged.

Joel mentioned it to Amy and she showed up at Adam's place in a rage. He had barely opened the door before she was screaming at him. "I can't fucking believe you're still doing this shit, Adam."

"What?" He really had no idea.

"With Dad. I thought you guys ironed everything out when he was in the hospital. Now he tells me you rarely visit, and when you do, you're there five minutes before you have to leave." She had slammed the door behind her and backed him into his apartment, down the hallway from the front door and into the tiny kitchen, where she cornered him.

"What do you want me to do?" he yelled back. "You stayed after me for months to talk to him, then I talk to him. You wanted me to fix whatever was wrong between us, and I did. Now, I don't visit him enough. God, Amy, is anything ever enough for you?"

"Not when it's this shit you keep pulling with Dad," she said.

"You're fucking your ex-husband, Amy. I don't think you are in a position to advise anyone on how to work out their problems."

They stood there in a silence so compete, Adam could hear the electricity buzzing through the walls. Amy gaped at him and he waited for her to lash out at him, scream and call him names and ask just who the hell he thought he was. He considered apologizing. He hadn't meant to bring that up; he didn't really care who she had sex with.

But then she turned and stalked out of the kitchen, down the hallway, and out of the apartment, slamming the door behind her. Adam thought he might go after her, apologize, say he was just kidding or something. He really was tired of all the arguing. But in the end, he let her go. They could hash it out another time.

Amy sat in her car with the engine running and called Mike. "Hey there," he said, and when he chuckled it made her want to scream. "Are we getting together tonight? I forget…"

"No," she said.

"Oh."

"We're not getting together tonight," she continued. "Or ever again, really."

A beat of silence, then:

"Wait. What?"

She rolled her eyes. It was always the smartest ones who acted like they never understood any fucking thing when it wasn't in their favor. "I don't want to see you anymore," she said, and was amazed at how steady her voice sounded when she said it. Because she wanted to scream it at him. She wanted to tell him in person so she could scream it into his face and watch him recoil.

"I don't understand," he said.

Amy laughed. She'd figured he would say that, but she still had nothing prepared to say in return. "What's not to understand?" she asked. "I don't want to see you anymore."

"Well, can we talk about it?"

"We *are* talking about it, Mike."

He sighed, and through the phone it sounded like a gust of wind. "I meant in person."

"Yeah, no," she said. "I don't want to do that."

"Well, what happened? I thought everything was going great. I mean…" His voice trailed off and he never really said what he meant.

"It just happened," she told him. "I guess I was lonely…? Or something…? I don't know. It was like… I was there and you were there and it just happened."

"But it happened more than once," he pointed out, and Amy realized the whining tone he was using was putting her on edge. She wanted a drink or a cigarette. Or both.

"Yeah… that was dumb of me," she said, and it felt good to say. She doubted she would be so honest if they were face to face, even if she wanted to be able to scream in his face. "It was dumb of both of us. We're smarter than that and we never should have done it the first time."

Another sigh into the phone.

"And don't act like you're so fucking disappointed, Mike," she barked. "We got divorced for a reason."

"But I thought we were working things out…"

She laughed, a loud, derisive guffaw. "Oh, please, Mike. We got drunk and fucked. Then we fucked a few more times. We never even talked, so we weren't working anything out." She paused, then added, "And anyway, I've met someone."

That silenced him.

Amy knew how it must sound—like she was only saying it to hurt him or humiliate him—so she rushed to explain, then caught herself. She didn't owe him an explanation, and he wasn't asking for one, anyway. And she *had* met someone, and it was perfectly reasonable to not want to focus on whatever she had with her ex-husband and instead turn her attention to what might be with someone new.

"Well," he said.

"Yeah," she said, and felt bad for him. Then she reminded herself that he'd cheated on her for years, then he was a real asshole during the divorce and had his twentysomething girlfriend with the cheerleader name not decided he was too old for her and left him, Mike Cohen never would have started being nice to her and they never would have been in a situation that might lead to them having sex. So, why the hell she felt bad for him was beyond her, and she wanted to end the call so she could go get a drink.

Mike said nothing.

"Anyway, that's why I called," she said, finally. "To let you know. It's nothing personal." (Though it was, really; break-ups were always personal, and she hated when people said shit like that and now she was the one saying it.)

"Yeah," he said.

"So, Ethan's with you this weekend. I'll bring him by the office on Friday after school."

She ended the call, sat for a long moment arguing with herself over whether she'd been too abrupt and abrasive, then killed the engine and walked back upstairs to Adam's apartment.

He was surprised to see her back. "What is this about?" he asked, convinced that it could only be something unpleasant.

"I just broke it off with Mike," she explained as she stepped in and past him. "What have you got to drink?"

"Beer," he said. "And vodka that's been in the freezer forever."

They sat on Adam's screened-in balcony and drank, and Amy chastised herself. "I honestly don't know what the hell I was thinking," she said, several times. "Do you have any cigarettes?"

"Nah, I quit. Orson kept telling me I smelled like an ashtray."

"Hmph."

"But it's good you broke it off," he said, and gulped his beer. "He treated you like shit while you were married, then he was a gigantic dick hole while you guys were going through the divorce, and then you tell me you're having sex with him, and I thought I was having a stroke or something."

"I know, I know," she said, and leaned forward so that her hair shrouded her face and the look of shame on it. "I was out of my mind. Like, seriously, that's the only reason I can think of. I must have had a psychotic break or something." Then she laughed, sat up and asked him, "A dick hole? That's a thing now? Calling someone a dick hole?"

"Yeah, I guess," he said, and shrugged. "I mean, it's a real thing, you know."

Then they both laughed.

"See," Amy said presently, "this is the way I like us—laughing at stupid shit and getting drunk on your balcony. I didn't like what we turned into. I hated us."

Adam regarded her with a sidelong glance.

She aimed the neck of her beer bottle at him. "And don't act like you don't know what I'm talking about. You know exactly what I mean."

"Yeah," Adam said. "I know. Maybe." He paused. "I guess we all had a psychotic break."

"Any excuse is better than none, I guess," Amy said, and they laughed again, because the beer was starting to take effect.

When they'd updated all the paint and refinished the hardwoods and rigorously stripped and revarnished the knotty pine paneling, Joel sat and stared at it and expressed his doubts to Kent. "I don't know," he said, though he liked it.

Kent scowled at him. "I thought you said you liked it. Actually, you said it repeatedly."

"I do like it," Joel said, although he was frowning. "It's fresh and updated and it doesn't look like forty years ago anymore." He chuckled. "And forty years ago, it was already twenty years out of date, but we got such a great deal on it, and we were young and stupid and didn't really know any better. So we left it the way it was." He laughed again. Then he was crying.

Kent was never good when people started crying in front of him, and this was no exception. He found a box of tissues and offered them to Joel, sat across from him until the tears subsided and he blew his nose.

"Thanks," Joel said. Then, "Sorry."

"It's fine."

"I just feel like I've desecrated her memory. Again."

Kent grunted. "By painting the walls and updating the counters?"

"She loved this house," Joel explained. "She fell in love with it the second she laid eyes on it. Called it her 'Brady Bunch House,' though honestly, I don't think it looks anything like the Brady Bunch house."

Kent didn't see it either, though he loved the house, too, and remembered back to the night he and Joel first met, online, and tried to hook up. He could see why Susan would love it, too, though he would never understand why anyone would live in a house for almost forty years without updating things. "Change is good," he said, and hated himself the moment the words were out of his mouth.

"I know," Joel said. "We were just never very good at change, Susan and me. Maybe having kids did that to us." He shrugged. "We got so busy raising kids that we never noticed how stuck we were." He stared hard across the den at the cold, empty fireplace. "Or, rather, she did. I was—well, we all know what I was..."

Kent sighed. "You're still feeling guilty about that?" he asked.

"I guess..."

"Well, you need to stop. Seriously. It isn't going to change anything and you'll just be miserable, and honestly, Joel, I'm tired of your mood swings." Kent stood, tossed the box of tissues aside. "Come on. Let's go."

Joel was uncertain. "Where?"

"Out. Anywhere. Hell, to McDonald's. Anywhere you won't sit and feel bad about being gay again."

Joel dismissed both the thought and Kent with a wave of his hand. "I don't need to go out," he said. "You can go. I need to straighten things up around here."

Kent wanted to argue with him, insist that he get out of the house and go be around people and have fun, but he also figured that Joel was probably tired of him always suggesting that, which Kent did any time Joel displayed any measure of melancholy. "Well, call your kids and invite them over. Or your sister."

"I think Rhoda's still hurt I didn't call her first when I had the heart attack," Joel mused. "And anyway, I want everything to be nice when I reveal all the changes." Joel stood and started rearranging things, picking things up and setting them in different spots, fluffing cushions and straightening lampshades that weren't crooked.

"I worry about you," Kent said, which surprised him. He'd thought it, told himself not to say it, then said it anyway.

Joel turned to him, perplexed. "What in the world for?" he asked, and chuckled.

"Because you're always sad," Kent explained. "The first time I met you, I could tell you were just miserable, and you haven't changed since. And it worries me. I've seen this before in people—in guys I was dating, in friends, in family. Sadness that never goes away never ends well."

"I'm not miserable," Joel said, and pretended shock. If anything, he was shocked that Kent was finally calling him out on it. Everyone else seemed to know about it, acknowledge it, but none of them ever mentioned it. Well, except maybe Amy. She'd expressed concern that one time, too.

"You don't have to pretend you aren't, either, Joel. It's okay to be sad." Kent stopped, cocked his head to one side, then continued. "Well, I mean—yeah, it's okay to be sad, just not all the time, and you've been sad as long as I've known you, and I don't know what to do."

Joel sighed. "You don't have to do anything," he said. "It's my problem. I'll fix it."

Kent nodded. "Okay. Fair enough." He wanted to ask how, and when, but it wasn't his place and Joel would just tell him that again, and they'd be back where they started, acknowledging the problem but not having a solution. He fished his keys out of his pocket. "I guess I'll get out of here."

Joel nodded.

"You're sure you don't want to go? I was going to Blake's, and maybe get something to eat at Willy's."

"I'm good. I've got a lot to do around here." He took it all in—the dusting, the sweeping, the polishing of the floors—with a sweeping gesture.

"Okay." And Kent stepped forward, swept Joel into a hug. "I'll call you."

"I'll be here."

It was a lot to think about, and of course he thought maybe he should bring up all his concerns to Joel, but he knew that Joel would just wave it away, laugh at him for being too concerned, and assure him that everything was fine. That's how Joel was, and Kent was the only one of them who understood that to be part of the problem.

.twenty-one.

RHODA CROWED WITH DELIGHT when she saw the updates Joel and Kent had done to the house. "It looks like a TV show!" she declared, as she stroked the knotty pine paneling, the freshly painted walls, the newly upholstered Barcelona chairs in the den. "Is this *real* suede?" Joel assured her it was.

"And you did all this yourself?" Stanley asked him.

"Kent was a big help."

They both glanced around him to where Kent stood in the kitchen, uncorking a bottle of wine. They passed a knowing glance between them, but said nothing.

"It's not what you're thinking," Joel told them, and laughed.

"I'm not thinking anything," Rhoda said, and threw her arms up. "It's good that you have someone." She paused, then added: "To help. You know, with stuff like this. It's not easy doing renovations like this alone." She continued on through the house, Stanley at her heels, admiring all the changes.

"It was time for a change," he heard Stanley say. "This place looked like a time capsule for forty years."

"Not so loud, Stanley!" Rhoda whispered it, but it carried through the silence of the house like a gunshot. "He'll hear you."

They'd come from the *Neilah* service at the synagogue, all of them still solemn but glad the Yom Kippur services were over so they could break their fasts. Amy and Ethan were arranging food on the buffet in the dining room.

"My sister thinks we're dating," Joel told Kent.

"Everyone thinks we're dating."

They laughed, but it was the truth. Even their friends teased them mercilessly about it and were certain they were just denying it, though no one could really see a reason for them to do so. Even Amy had asked Joel about it once. "Why *don't* you date Kent?" she wanted to know.

"Because having a friend is more important to me at this point in my life than having a boyfriend," he said. "I'm not looking to settle down with anyone right now." He caught himself saying things like that and a sense of dread settled over him, albeit briefly. He wasn't exactly young; he didn't have all the time in the world to meet someone, take the appropriate time to get to know him, then decide if it was worth the trouble to pursue a relationship or not. Staying single was also an option, he reminded himself often. There was nothing wrong with that, no matter how people seemed to think otherwise.

"I just want to see you happy," she said.

"Sweetie, I *am* happy." He kept having to remind people of that, because they were measuring happiness by some standard that Joel couldn't comprehend.

Amy remained unconvinced. She was happy, though, and it made her stop in the middle of whatever she was doing—cutting hair at work, doing laundry at home, driving to Midtown to see Julian—when she realized it, like a sharp pain.

"What is it?" Julian asked her when it happened.

"Nothing," she said, although she was smiling.

"Doesn't look like nothing," he would grumble, and that made her smile more, because it reminded her of all of them—the entire Benjamin family—the way they were always anticipating the worst-case scenario.

"Seriously," she said. "It's nothing. Don't worry."

They'd been dating since the day after she broke things off with Mike. Ethan had an appointment, so she'd ended up at the Starbucks downstairs, apologizing for missing their date and insisting that they reschedule immediately. "Like, tonight even." That made Julian laugh, but he relented, and they agreed to meet her for pizza and beer. That was five months ago.

Now, Joel called in to her, "Is Julian not coming, Amy?"

"He's on his way," she called back.

Rhoda glanced around like she'd just become aware of where she was. "And where's Adam? He was right behind us as we were driving down Briarcliff."

"He and Orson ran home for just a bit to walk the dog," Joel explained.

"We should get a dog," Ethan said to Amy as they arranged bagels and different cream cheeses on the buffet. It came up more often now than it had before, because of Puck and also because the girl he was seeing—her name was Katie, and Isaac had introduced them—also had a dog. "I've been looking online at rescues."

They'd never had a dog growing up, mainly because Susan didn't trust them to properly care for a dog, and she didn't want to be the one stuck doing it for them. "Dogs are easy," Joel had argued for the kids. "You give them food, you give them water, and you take them out.

Susan grunted. "It'll be like everything else around here—cooking, dishes, laundry. I'll end up doing it all." She flipped the pages in her magazine. "They can get dogs of their own when they have their own places."

Then they'd both moved out and neither had ever gotten a dog. Amy considered that. Maybe Ethan was right and it was time for them to get a dog. "Okay," she said. "We can look at them together later."

His face lit up. "Really?"

"I said so, didn't I?"

He laughed. "Yeah, but..." He shrugged. "Never mind. Yeah. We'll look at them together."

In the kitchen, Rhoda admired the new counters. "Is this quartz, Joely?" She stroked it, peered at it, made a fist and knocked on it.

"Jerusalem stone, Rho," he called back.

She and Stanley traded a look. "What the hell is Jerusalem stone?" she whispered.

"Sounds like something somebody gave a fancy name to so they could charge more for it," he whispered back.

"It's nice, though," she said, and admired it, ran her hand along it.

Joel found them like that, inspecting the countertop and examining the backsplash, sharing their observations under their breath. "Kent suggested it," he said, and nodded back over his shoulder and out of the room, in the general direction of where Kent might be. "He knows a lot more about all that stuff than I do."

Rhoda and Stanley nodded, said nothing.

Joel felt he needed to say more. "I was almost ready to sell the house," he said, and made a sweeping gesture. "After almost forty years, it was time for a change, and I wasn't sure I had the energy to go through renovating it, finding a designer and choosing all new everything. I mean, I've thought a lot about renovating since Susan passed. She loved this house." And he reached out, patted the bar area that separated the kitchen from the dining room the way you might pet a dog or a small child to reassure it that you still loved it, that you would never abandon it. "Anyway, Kent started convincing me to just update a few things. And he knows a lot of people in the business, so that part was pretty easy. Then he helped me do all the simple stuff—the painting, redoing the paneling, and the new furniture, and *voilà*... it's like a brand new house."

"He's a very nice man, Joely," Rhoda said.

Her real meaning was clear, and Joel laughed. "It's not like that," he said.

Stanley was confused. "Like what?"

Rhoda patted his arm the way Joel had patted the countertop. She said to Joel, "It's okay, Joely."

He laughed harder, louder. "I know it's okay, Rho. But it isn't like that."

She gave an exaggerated shrug of defeat.

"I'm confused," Stanley said. "What did I miss?"

"I'll explain later," Rhoda whispered to him, but Joel heard it anyway. "Let's go see what they did with the bathroom."

"It's nothing, Rho," Joel called after them. "Seriously."

Kent appeared, his arms filled with bottles of wine, a six pack of beer in each hand. "What's nothing?" he asked, winded. He'd just climbed the stairs from the basement.

Joel waved a hand. "Nothing," he said, then added: "I'll tell you later." He hoped Kent would forget.

The doorbell rang and Joel heard Amy shout, "It's about time!" Adam appeared in the kitchen, rolling his eyes, casseroles in his hands. Orson smiled at her from behind him.

"We were getting worried," Joel said. Not really, but it was more polite than asking what the hell took them so long. "Your Aunt Rhoda was ready to send out a search party."

"We had to go back for the kugel," Orson explained, and Adam held it up as proof.

It was Adam who relented in the end, and asked Orson if they could host Joel for dinner. Orson was stunned. He had given up on ever meeting Joel, and he'd decided long ago not to press Adam to introduce them. "Of course we can have your dad over, Adam."

By this time, they were living together. Orson had insisted. "Look," he said to Adam. They were in bed and he turned onto his side, propped himself on one elbow. "I'm about to suggest something, and I don't want you to freak out about it."

Adam peered at him, already suspicious. "Okay…" In the time they'd been seeing one another, Orson had come to begin everything important he wanted to say to Adam—whether to ask or to tell— with that preamble. Apparently, Adam guessed, he had a tendency to react negatively, which he didn't agree with, but there it was.

"I'm going to suggest it, and I want you to think about it."

"Okay…"

"I mean, *really* think about it."

Adam scowled. "Are you about to suggest that we open up our relationship or something?"

Orson laughed. "No! God, no! What the hell, Adam? I just want you to think about moving in with me." He laughed again.

Adam was relieved. "That's it?"

"Well, yeah… I mean… isn't it enough?"

"You made it sound a lot worse."

They lay in bed, Orson reading a *Batman* comic and Adam scrolling through Facebook and Twitter on his phone. By the time he reached out to turn off the light, Adam had made up his mind. "Okay," he said. He was already spending more time at Orson's than his own place, and Orson's place was much bigger, to accommodate Puck. They'd been dating for close to a year and it didn't make sense to keep paying rent on two apartments.

"Okay?" Orson asked.

"Yes. Let's live together."

It was that easy. The second major decision they had to make as a couple was inviting Joel to dinner so that Orson could finally meet him. "I'll make lasagna," Orson said. Then: "Can your dad eat lasagna? Is that kosher?"

"Dad doesn't keep kosher," Adam explained.

"Okay, good."

Joel came with Kent, and it was a nice, uneventful dinner. He wanted to know everything about how they'd met, how long it took them to realize this relationship was the one, what were their plans together as a couple. Adam sat, perplexed into silence; this was not the Joel Benjamin he was used to. Orson answered all the questions with aplomb, and Adam was grateful for that.

"So, how long have the two of you been together?" Orson asked them.

Joel and Kent traded a look, then they both laughed. "Oh, we're not dating," Joel said. "We're just really good friends."

"Oh," Orson said, and from the tone of his voice, Adam knew he was not convinced in the least. "Then I apologize."

"Everyone makes that mistake," Kent said, and waved a hand.

"We're used to it by now," Joel explained.

"Yeah?"

Later, after Joel and Kent had left and the kitchen was clean, Orson said to Adam, "I could have *sworn* they were dating. Your dad probably hates me now."

"He doesn't hate you." Then Adam told Orson that Kent was the man he'd found Joel with. "So, they've had sex, but they're not dating." He shrugged.

"And you're sure of that?"

"Pretty sure. They just do everything together. Like, Kent was there in Boston when Dad was in the hospital, and he's helping Dad redo the house." Adam stopped there. It did seem like they were dating and now he was suspicious. Maybe they were just saying they weren't dating. Maybe Kent was married or had a partner; maybe he had kids and they wouldn't understand if their father introduced them to his boyfriend. Maybe they were too young to really understand what "...and this is Daddy's special friend Joel" meant. Or hell, maybe they were just friends and didn't want to date. Perhaps they'd tried dating and realized they were better off as friends.

Really, though, it didn't matter to him whether they were friends or more. That was their business. And he realized, as they sat at dinner, that though he'd decided to stop being angry with Joel, he still had a lot of processing to do before he was completely comfortable with the knowledge that his father was now an openly gay man who liked to—as gay men will do—talk about the men he found attractive (apparently, Joel had a thing for Stanley Tucci) and which gay bars he preferred (Woofs made stronger drinks; The Eagle was just a little "too much" most of the time).

"My dad hangs out at The Eagle," he grumbled to Orson, who chuckled. "What? It's not funny."

"Sorry, baby," Orson said, and moved a hand over his mouth like he might literally wipe the smile off his face. "But, like, who else do you know can actually say that their dad hangs out at The Eagle?"

Adam turned away from him in the bed. He couldn't even turn the conversation around on Orson in this case, because Orson's father was a staunchly Lutheran dairy farmer from the Wisconsin hinterlands and would probably accept any form of punishment short of death rather than step inside The Eagle, all this according to Orson himself.

"I just hope he doesn't hold that against me," Orson said.

"He won't," Adam told him, and he was right.

Now, Joel was thrilled that Adam and Orson had arrived at last. "You've never been here, Orson," he declared. "Let me show you around." And he took Orson by the arm, showed him back to the front door so that he could give the complete tour and history of the Benjamin home, through the first time he and Susan had seen it, through the births of Amy and Adam, through every coat of paint and every inch of wallpaper and contact paper applied throughout the years he'd lived there. "I was ready to just put it on the market, but Kent talked me into renovating."

"It's an awesome house," Orson said.

"Susan called it her Brady Bunch house."

That got a laugh. "I can see that."

They ran into Rhoda and Stanley in the guest room. Rhoda was remembering the wallpaper from before, when Joel and Susan had first moved in. "Remember it, Stanley? It was *horrid*. Avocado green chandelier pattern, and *textured*." She described it the way she might have described an incurable and highly contagious skin condition. "Oh, here's Joel. Remember that wallpaper, Joely? It was just *horrible*."

"I remember it, Rho," he said.

"I forget what you changed it to, though…"

"Susan feather painted it, remember?" Joel recalled the entire ordeal: Susan had steamed away the wallpaper and sanded the walls smooth, applied the base coat of white and then, as was the trend in those days, dipped a feather duster in the accent paint—in this case, a medium shade of federal blue—and brought the room into the seventies.

"If I ever get a bright idea like that again, Joel, slap me," she said when it was complete and they leaned in the doorway, admiring her handiwork.

"It looks good, though," he said.

"It fucking sucked. Seriously, slap me."

It eventually became Amy's room, and she plastered the walls with posters of New Kids On The Block and Jason Priestly and Ian Ziering, so Susan could have just left the offending wallpaper for all it mattered in the end.

"I remember that," Rhoda said. "It was nice, but I like this better." And she stroked the nearest wall. Joel had painted it a pale shade of taupe. Then she became aware of Orson. "You must be the boyfriend."

Orson laughed.

Joel said, "This is Orson, Rhoda. Adam's boyfriend." It suddenly occurred to him to ask what term Orson preferred. "Boyfriend" seemed trite, out of fashion, but "partner" sounded both pretentious and inappropriate. He guessed he should have asked beforehand, like with the non-binary people he kept meeting who had preferred pronouns.

"Oh," Rhoda said. She turned to her husband and said, "This is Orson, Stanley." Like he hadn't heard the entire exchange, or like she was translating it into another language. "He's Adam's boyfriend."

Stanley offered his hand and they shook the way two businessmen sealing a deal might shake hands over an overpriced lunch and drinks. "A pleasure," he said. "You're not Jewish, are you?"

Rhoda was aghast. *"Stanley Shor!"*

"What? It was just a question…"

Orson was laughing. "I'm not," he said, and considered apologizing for it. "I hope that's okay."

Joel patted his arm. "Of course it's okay."

Adam warned him in advance that he would be put on the spot about it. "Just laugh," he said. "It'll be funny, so you'll laugh anyway, but just know that they don't mean anything by it. They only ask because they don't really have anything else to talk to you about." He explained that Rhoda had always been a housewife and that Stanley was in the printing business until he retired and sold his company for more money than it was worth. "And if they invite you to Shabbat services, don't accept. Make up an excuse. Lie."

Orson had expected to accompany Adam to Yom Kippur services, but Adam talked him out of it. "I love you, but you need to trust me on this. Jews only go because they have to. No one goes voluntarily." So it was decided Orson would join them for breaking the fast after the *neilah* service. "Amy's new boyfriend is going to be there, too."

Julian arrived then as if on cue. "Am I late?" he asked of no one in particular.

"You're fine," Amy told him.

"Everyone's got a new boyfriend," Rhoda declared, like she was saying everyone had grown wings or sprouted tails. "I should have invited mine!" Then she cackled at herself while Stanley groaned and rolled his eyes.

"She's here all week, folks," he grumbled.

In the dining room, Amy introduced Julian around. "And this is Orson," she said. "He's Adam's boyfriend and he's not Jewish, either."

Julian shook Orson's hand with exaggerated relief. "We've got to stick together, bro," he said, and Orson was unsure whether or not to laugh.

"He's joking," Amy explained.

"Anyway, you're both still way outnumbered," Adam said. "The only thing you have going for you is that we're all out of shape."

"When are we going to eat?" Stanley wanted to know. "I thought the requirement was twenty-five hours. I'm dying here."

So they ate. Adam pointed to anything he thought Orson might be unfamiliar with, explained each thing: whitefish salad, lokshen kugel, pickled herring. "We only have that because Uncle Stanley asks for it every year," he whispered, bent close to Orson's ear. "Don't eat it. It's disgusting."

Amy did the same with Julian at her end of the table. Julian was intrigued. "Like, pickled fish?" He prodded it with a fork, lifted it to his nose, sniffed it.

"Yeah," Amy said with a grimace.

Julian and Orson both tried it and liked it, to everyone's disbelief and Stanley's amusement. "They know good food when they taste it," he said with a shrug.

"Dad eats it, too," Ethan remarked, and for the first time in a long time, Amy did not flinch at the mention of Mike Cohen.

Rhoda asked Joel about work. He'd stepped down as department head and was, again, actually enjoying what he did, which was teaching English literature to people who chose to major in it. "I feel thirty-years-old again," he told them all, and laughed.

"Everyone deserves to be happy in their work," Rhoda said. She'd never worked a day in her life that wasn't volunteering at the synagogue or the JCC.

"And in their retirement," Stanley added, and raised his glass of Manischewitz.

Afterward, Kent and Orson cleaned up and washed dishes, talking in low tones, but about what no one could be certain. Julian and Ethan disappeared downstairs to play on Adam's old Nintendo 64. "It'll be like my angsty teenage years all over again," Julian declared as he went down the stairs to the basement.

"He's nice," Adam remarked. "But you know he isn't your type."

Amy rolled her eyes. "I'm too old to have a type anymore," she said. "And like Orson is your type. You even told me he wasn't."

Adam turned and looked past her to where Orson and Kent laughed at something one or the other of them had said. "Yeah... I think he changed my type, though."

They sat in newly purchased midcentury-style chairs that faced Susan's garden. Everyone still called it that, though she was gone and it was Adam who had made it was it was then: lush and verdant and well-lit with solar landscaping lights deftly hidden among the foliage. He'd spent days and hours uprooting all the old, sickly remains of Susan's work. He'd spent thousands of dollars on trees and shrubs and flowering perennials, glazed stoneware planters and a fountain. The only thing that remained was the Japanese maple Susan had planted the first year she and Joel had lived in the house, just before Amy was born.

"It's beautiful even in the dark," Joel said, stepping up behind them. He had a bottle of wine and refilled their glasses, pulled over a chair and sat with them, admiring Adam's handiwork.

"Yeah, like, since when are you a landscaper?" Amy wanted to know.

Adam shrugged. "The internet," was his answer, and it was the truth. He'd consulted gardening websites and online horticulturists, so all he could really take credit for was the manpower. And the finances. Joel tried to reimburse him, but Adam wouldn't have it.

Joel lowered himself onto the flagstone step they were seated on. "Your mother would love it," he said. "I think this is what she always envisioned, but she didn't really have the know-how to make it happen. Or the patience, as you know."

They chuckled.

"If something didn't grow fast enough, or bloom the way she wanted, she'd tear it up and plant something else," Joel went on. "Seeds were the worst for her."

"She should have done vegetables," Adam remarked. He sipped his wine, wished it was beer.

Amy laughed. "Mom growing vegetables? You might as well suggest she grow a second head."

"That sounded like something she would say, you know," Joel told her, softly.

"Ha!" Adam said, and nudged her with his elbow. "You're turning into Mom." And he cackled like a hyena, his head thrown back, the wine in his glass sloshing.

Amy elbowed him back, opened her mouth to argue, but couldn't find the right words. Or maybe it wasn't such a bad thing, after all, becoming more like Susan as she got older. And she wondered if, in the end, Susan knew—without Amy needing to tell her—despite all the arguing they'd done, all the names Amy had called her, all the curses she'd flung at her, that her daughter loved her and that now, only now, did Amy realize it. "I just miss her," she said, as tears clouded her vision.

Joel slipped his arm around her. "We all do, sweetie."

"She told me I would," Amy went on. "When we would argue? I'd scream at her and call her names and tell her I hated her…" She said it like they didn't know, like they hadn't witnessed it themselves. "And she'd point at me and tell me that she wouldn't be around forever, and one of these days I'd realize how much I missed her." She wiped at her eyes, but fresh tears flowed.

Adam was crying, too.

Not long before she passed, he'd been sitting with her in the den. She was bundled up in a thick robe and wrapped in blankets though it was still, technically, summer. Adam was flipping through the channels on the television, waiting for her to tell him to stop should something catch her eye.

"You need to watch out for your sister," she told him, her voice a croak.

"What for?" Adam asked. He did not turn. He thought she meant Amy was upset with him about something and Susan was warning him that next time he saw her she would have something to say to him.

"She's going to need help," Susan said. "She's always needed help, you know… but she's really going to need you after I go." She made it sound like she was leaving a party, or going on vacation. *After I go.* "She's always tried to act like she's stronger than she really is, like to hell with everybody else, she can take care of herself. And your father's going to have his own stuff to worry about, so you'll need to make sure Amy's okay." She paused again, winced at some pain. "I guess that's mostly my fault, too. She had to show *me* she didn't need me or my nagging or my nosiness, so she's convinced herself she doesn't need anyone, and she doesn't even realize it anymore. So make sure she's okay."

Adam turned then. His mother's face was only barely visible in the mound of pillows and robe and blanket, like a wizened oracle from ancient times. "I will," he said, even though most of what she was saying made no sense to him.

"Good," Susan said. "And I think *Judge Judy* is on now. Is it four o'clock?"

"I was a shitty daughter," Amy said, and made another swipe at her eyes.

Joel hugged her tighter. "Nonsense," he said. "Your mother loved you."

"I know that," she said. "*Now*. But it's too late, and she was right, and I was fucking horrible to her." Her shame made her sick, and she wondered what she was expected to do with the weight of it, now that it was too late and there was no longer anything she could do about it. She couldn't apologize to Susan, she couldn't take back every mean thing she ever said to her or about her, but at the same time, she thought it appropriate, this late-blooming sense of shame, the hopelessness. What better punishment for her than to live with the knowledge that she'd waited too long to do or say the right things to Susan, and that her mother had died with it all still hanging over them both.

"All kids are horrible to their parents," Joel said, and tried to remember if he had been respectful, especially to his mother. His father was less of a concern; Joel was always deferential and polite, though he'd seethed in silence, and he wondered if his father had felt it, Joel's hatred of him. He doubted it. With his mother, though, he'd made it a point to be there, especially in her widowhood and toward the end of her life. "Your mother loved you," he said again, "and she knew you loved her, even if you didn't always show it."

Adam spoke at last. "She knew," he said, and swirled his wine in his glass. "She told me."

Amy turned to him, glowered at him. "What's that supposed to mean?"

"It means what I said," he explained. "I was sitting with her one day, it wasn't long before she passed, and she told me you would take it hard. Her death. And she told me to make sure you were okay." He looked at her. "So she knew. You don't have to beat yourself up over it."

She sobbed, her forehead on Adam's shoulder and Joel's hand on her back, patting and then rubbing. He and Adam exchanged a look over her head. Neither was ever much use in situations like this and they were both well aware of it. They let her cry. From inside the house came the sounds of laughter. Julian and Kent trading stories.

Joel said, "She told me the same thing about you." He said it to Adam.

"Me? What about me?"

"That you'd take her death hard."

Adam opened his mouth to comment on that, then shut it again. He'd taken Susan's death rather well, he thought. Certainly much better than other people he knew had taken the deaths of their mothers. He considered it, and while he was considering it, Joel spoke again.

"But, really, I don't think that's what she meant. I think she meant me."

Amy sat up straight, wiped at her eyes, and she and Adam stared hard at him in the dim light coming from the garden.

"I've thought about it a lot, and I think she knew," he said. He took a deep breath and let it out slowly. "I think she always knew." There he paused, cocked his head to one side, and corrected himself. "Well, maybe not *always*, but I think she figured it out at some point early on, and there at the end, she told me you'd take it hard." He nodded to Adam. "And that's what I think she meant."

They sat in silence and watched moths flutter around the lights in the garden. At last, Amy heaved a sigh and said, "When does it get easier?" She didn't ask it of anyone in particular, and she didn't expect an answer, she just needed to put it out there.

"I don't think it does," Joel said.

Adam said, "I go days, weeks even, thinking I'm good, and then I'll think 'Hey, I should call and tell Mom about that.' Then I remember I can't, and that kind of sets everything else in motion, and I'm depressed for the rest of the day, and everything reminds me of her." He paused, then added: "I don't think it's supposed to get easier, I just think we get better at dealing with it."

That silenced them all again. Inside, Julian and Orson laughed, and Ethan could be heard asking, "Anybody seen my mom?"

Later, alone, Joel took down his own box from Susan. Like the ones she'd made for Amy and Adam and Ethan, Susan had carefully curated this one for him, then hidden it where he would find it, but not too soon. When he did—he was overhauling his wardrobe, emptying drawers and closets—his blood turned to ice and he felt found out though he'd done nothing. Susan was gone, had been, by that time, for close to six months, yet here she was and here was this box that she had left for him and it seemed to point a finger at him. He did not dare open it, and so he left it where it was.

Now it was covered by a fine layer of dust, but he'd had enough to drink and felt that he could, at last, face whatever he found inside. It wasn't heavy and the contents shifted as he took it down from the shelf. Photographs, he knew. He set it on the bed and stared hard at it for a long moment, his resolve gone. He left it, went and poured himself another glass of wine, came back and stared at it some more. Like it might reveal its contents to him on its own.

He considered putting it away, not just back into the closet where she'd left it for him to find, but in the attic, where he would forget about it. Years from now, after he was gone and the kids were cleaning everything out of the house to put it on the market, they could find it and think what they would of it, of him, of Susan for assembling such an exhibit. Then again, there was little else to reveal to them: he'd come out, they'd put two and two together and realized he was unfaithful throughout his marriage.

And hadn't he come to terms with himself about that? He felt he'd done nothing but come to terms with himself over the past year and a half.

And so he sat down, lifted the lid on the box, and beheld the story of his and Susan's life together, from its beginnings at Emory, through the births of Amy and Adam, the archaeology of their lives together. There were, as with the boxes she'd made for the kids, photo albums and boxes of Instamatic prints and Polaroids: he and Susan on the sofa at his mother's house (his father had passed by that time) in the late Seventies judging from their clothes and hairstyles. Joel laughed to see his own hair so thick and wavy; his memory of it, as it thinned and became grayer with age, seemed to fade with the hair itself, but there he was in a Members Only jacket and a turtleneck, enormous glasses perched on his nose, he and Susan laughing at something he would never be able to recall.

Another shot of them at a wedding, not their own—perhaps Susan's sister, Cynthia's? He wore a light gray suit with a vest and he had a mustache that he'd forgotten; Susan wore a pale yellow dress and a white hat with a wide, floppy brim. They looked as if they were caught off guard, like someone had called their names and when they turned, had snapped the photo.

They were so young, surprisingly so. He'd forgotten being so young, yet there was the proof. He was twenty-two when they married in 1979; twenty-three when Amy was born. Susan had gathered these photographs and presented them in chronological order so that he could see himself mature and change through them: their wedding, the chuppah slightly lopsided for a reason he had forgotten. Susan chose spring colors and so there was a photo of Joel smashing a glass with his pale blue yarmulke slightly askew atop his head, held in place by bobby pins. Next came a series of photos from their honeymoon in Israel: together on the beach in Tel Aviv, Joel at the Western Wall in Jerusalem, both of them at the Dead Sea, Masada, at a marketplace in Haifa. Then a photo of him holding Amy, glancing up into the camera as he fed her a bottle, his expression that of a deer caught in headlights. *Amy does look like me*, he thought. People always mentioned it, but he'd never seen it, insisting instead that she favored Susan more. Then he moved on to the photos of himself with Adam as an infant.

Other than the photos, there were other mementos: concert tickets (they'd seen Carole King and James Taylor at different times when they were dating), movie tickets to *Yentl* and *Raging Bull*. He marveled that she had kept all of it, wondered where she'd kept it all those years and why hadn't he come upon it, grumbled about it, insisted that she throw it out? Susan Schechter Benjamin, it seemed, had thrown nothing away. Instead, she had squirreled everything away, their entire history, all about the Benjamins. There was nothing in the box implicating him in anything other than being a husband, a father, a grandfather. He was ashamed he ever assumed otherwise, and so he stood, dumped the entire contents out onto the bed and resolved to arrange it all in order from start to finish, from that first photo of them on his mother's couch to the last, a digital photo of them all at a dim sum restaurant the Christmas before Susan was diagnosed.

That was when he found the envelope, sealed like it was meant to be mailed, but with only his name written on it in Susan's tiny, precise script. *Well, here it is,* was his first thought, and his hand shook as he lifted it, peered at it like he might see through it to the letter it contained. He stood with it, like he might fit it into the timeline he had spread across the bed—maybe sometime shortly after Adam was born? Or later, when Susan was diagnosed?

Instead, he took it with him into the kitchen, poured more wine, then took it outside onto the patio, sat where he had sat earlier with Amy and Adam, stared at the garden and sipped his wine, rested the letter across his knees. It occurred to him that he might call the kids back over, present the letter to them, have them read it aloud to him. But would that somehow lessen the impact of what it might say? Joel chuckled. Because he had no idea what it even said and he was already trying to mitigate its content.

Just open the goddamned thing, he told himself, but made no move to do so.

You're acting like an idiot. What could be so bad?

He emptied his glass and went inside to refill it, set the letter on the counter and stared at it.

"Oh, what the hell?" he said out loud, grabbed it, and tore it open.

He'd expected a many-paged missive, but there was only a single page, written in blue ink on Susan's personal stationery. He took a deep breath, leaned against the counter, and read.

> *My Dearest Joel,*
>
> *I don't know how long it will take you to discover this where I've placed it at the bottom of your box, but I trust that I am long gone and I trust that you were considerate enough not to put any sentimental shit on my headstone. (Just kidding... kind of...)*
>
> *I hope that you enjoyed reliving all our moments together via all the photographs and mementos I collected over the years and I hope, more than anything, that it helps you to understand—to KNOW—how very little it mattered to me that you were gay.*
>
> *Yes, Joel, that means I knew, and it means that I always knew. It also means I didn't care. I found what I needed elsewhere, same as you, and while that certainly isn't the ideal, textbook example of a marriage, it worked for us. I mean, look at what we built together: two beautiful, intelligent, successful children, a functional home for them and for ourselves, and a legacy that will stand after I—and eventually you—are gone.*
>
> *I couldn't have asked for anything more, not as a wife or as a mother, and I thank you for that. And I don't want*

you to beat yourself up over anything. I want you to find love and be happy, and I want you to live the rest of your life that way, and know that I didn't hate you then and I don't hate you now. (I know how you are, you worry about those things. Don't.)

I could ramble on and on (you know how I am), but I won't.

Go live your life, Joel. Be happy. I love you. Miss me every now and then, will you? I'll certainly miss you.

S.

Joel folded the letter, slid it back into the envelope, wiped his eyes with a paper towel as he walked back through the house to the bedroom, where he put the letter at the end of the timeline, next to the last photo taken of him and Susan together at Ethan's fourteenth birthday dinner, when she still looked good and would allow her picture to be taken. In it, they are laughing and that was how he would remember them.

.acknowledgments.

Thanks, as always, to Debra Ginsberg and Rebecca Weisberg for being the voices of reason and wisdom throughout the process.

This time, thanks also to Jessica Lucci, who has been my biggest cheerleader since she picked up my first book.

But also thanks to everyone who bought a copy of that book, or grabbed a free copy for Kindle when I ran a promo on Amazon, who read it and gave me feedback, or who posted a review on either Amazon or Goodreads. Y'all the real MVPs, yo.